T0058012

Also by Heather O'Neill

Lullabies for Little Criminals

The Girl
Who Was
Saturday
Night

The Girl Who Was Saturday Night

HEATHER O'NEILL

Farrar, Straus and Giroux   New York

Farrar, Straus and Giroux
18 West 18th Street, New York 10011

Originally published in 2014 by HarperCollins Publishers, Canada
Published in the United States by Farrar, Straus and Giroux
First American edition, 2014

Library of Congress Cataloging-in-Publication Data
O'Neill, Heather.
The girl who was Saturday night : a novel / Heather O'Neill.
    pages   cm
    ISBN 978-0-374-16266-5 (hardback) — ISBN 978-0-374-70933-4 (ebook)
    1. Sisters—Fiction.   2. Twins—Fiction.   I. Title.

PR9199.4.O64 G57 2014
813'.6—dc23

2013038863

ISBN 978-0-374-53610-7

Farrar, Straus and Giroux books may be purchased for educational,
business, or promotional use. For information on bulk purchases, please
contact the Macmillan Corporate and Premium Sales Department at
1-800-221-7945, extension 5442, or write to
specialmarkets@macmillan.com.

www.fsgbooks.com
www.twitter.com/fsgbooks • www.facebook.com/fsgbooks

The author wishes to acknowledge the generous support
of the Canada Council for the Arts.

The Girl
Who Was
Saturday
Night

CHAPTER I

Girls! Girls! Girls!

I WAS HEADING ALONG RUE SAINTE-CATHERINE TO sign up for night school. There was a cat outside a strip joint going in a circle. I guessed it had learned that behaviour from a stripper. I picked it up in my arms. "What's new, pussycat," I said.

All the buildings on that block were strip clubs. What on earth was their heating bill like in the winter? They were beautiful, skinny stone buildings with gargoyles above the windows. They were the same colour as the rain. There were lights blinking around the doors. You followed the lightbulbs up the stairs. They were long-life lightbulbs, not the name-brand kind. The music got louder and louder as you approached the entrance of the club, like the music in horror films.

Cars filled with American boys would come up to see the girls, girls, girls on the day the boys turned eighteen. The boys from Ontario came in on the train and slept nine to a hotel room downtown. Because you could do anything you wanted with the Québécois girls. You could stroke their asses. You could lick their privates with everyone watching. You could take them behind a little curtain and fuck them while wearing bright blue condoms that the girls could keep their eyes on.

The girls were backstage, getting ready. Their big toes were getting stuck in their fishnets. Their yellow ponytails were being put up lopsided. They were putting on too much makeup. Their bangs were in their eyes. Their tummies folded over the elastic bands of their underwear. One was wearing big glasses because she'd lost her contact lenses. One drank a glass of water that made her feel cold inside, and she wondered if she was going to have a bladder infection. And one of the girls yawned, and everything is so catching in these clubs that everyone started yawning and yawning.

The ones who had been dancing awhile looked like Barbie dolls with their muscles and knee-high boots and their no-nonsense attitude. They were like superheroes. The new girls showed up onstage with inappropriate underwear and bikini bottoms and high-heeled shoes a size too big. One eighteen-year-old girl was wearing a sailor hat from her grandfather's closet in Saint-Jérôme. She'd been raised for this life, whether anyone wanted to admit it or not.

We were all descended from orphans in Québec. Before I'd dropped out of high school, I remembered reading about how ships full of girls were sent from Paris to New France to marry the inhabitants. They stepped off the boat with puke on their dresses and stood on the docks, waiting to be chosen.

They were pregnant before they even had a chance to unpack their bags. They didn't want this. They didn't want to populate this horrible land that was snow and rocks and skinny wolves. They spoke to their children through gritted teeth. That's where the Québec accent came from. The nation crawled out from between their legs.

CHAPTER 2

The Pageant

I ENDED UP BEING A BEAUTY QUEEN THAT DAY IN 1994. I was nineteen years old. There wasn't much of a pageant. There weren't many contestants even.

I always thought my twin brother, Nicolas, was the better-looking one of us. He used to get scouted by modelling agents when we were taking the metro. He was tall and skinny. He had a really long aristocratic nose and blue eyes. He would raise his eyes to indicate he was bored and had about a hundred other facial expressions that clearly conveyed disdain. This made him very handsome and otherworldly. He crossed his legs and slouched in his chairs and shook his head as if disgusted by the world, even when we were in church. He was always in a hurry, another quirk of handsome men. They were always on their way someplace else. They never allowed you time to just sit and look at them.

I guess I looked like Nicolas. Except for the nose, and everyone said that I smiled more. Maybe it was because I was more cheery that I didn't have the same je ne sais quoi.

Somewhere along the line, Nicolas had decided that laughing at anyone's jokes but our own was beneath him. Which was strange, because he would smoke cigarette butts off the side of the road, look through a garbage can for a bottle to redeem, and yell obscenities at passing schoolgirls. None of those things were beneath him.

We both had black hair that wasn't curly or straight, and always looked a bit dirty. Our hair ruined all photographs of us as children. No matter what the setting, even if it was our own birthday party, we looked like Gypsies at some internment camp in Eastern Europe. We looked like we'd escaped terrible persecution in our own country. We looked like the type of people that had driven our car five thousand miles with a refrigerator strapped on top of it. But really we had spent our whole lives in the same apartment on Boulevard Saint-Laurent in Montréal.

My grandfather Loulou was encouraging me to sign up for high school because he said that I would meet a better class of men. He said that I could meet an English lawyer if my English was better. I wanted to go because I'd always felt lousy about having dropped out with Nicolas.

I was going to the Ukrainian Centre, where registration for night school was happening that day. The Ukrainian Centre was on the same block as a church. A wedding that was taking place at the church had toppled out into the street. I remember that men in tuxedos were everywhere. They were sitting on the hoods of the cars. They were at the corner store buying cigarettes and lottery tickets. Some of them ducked into the peepshow booth at the local movie theatre. They were sitting on a bench outside the laundromat. There was a man in a tuxedo with a flower behind his ear, and one at the back of the store playing Donkey Kong. It was funny because it was rare to see anybody dressed up at all in this neighbourhood. It was the bottom of the barrel, so to speak.

I was standing on the street, looking up and down for Nicolas. I felt like murdering him all of a sudden. Nicolas had sworn black and blue that he was going to meet me and come with me to sign up for night school. But he hadn't shown up.

I went into the Centre. There was a white cat named Alphonse who lived there. The cat was skinny like a nineteen-year-old boy wearing a wife-beater undershirt. It was walking tentatively, as if the floor was hot. Everybody had a cat. The neighbourhood was lousy with mice.

I leaned into a little room with a desk, where a lady was stamping some papers. The night classes didn't start until the following Tuesday and there was nothing for me to do after filling out the forms except go on back home.

I was going to leave but I heard the sound of trumpets and people coming from the ballroom down the hall of the Centre. Of course I had to go see what it was. We could never say no to a party. The sound of fun drew us to it like the sound of a tuna can opening summoned a cat.

The ballroom was so big that everyone you loved could fit into it at once. There were red stars in the tiles on the floor. They were holding a rehearsal for the Saint-Jean-Baptiste parade that was happening in a few weeks.

There was a group of trumpet players standing together. One kept blowing into the trumpet, trying to get the right sound out of it. It was like he was poking an elephant in the butt. There was a man sitting on one of the chairs, wearing a tiger costume. The head of the tiger was sitting on the chair next to him. Both he and the tiger head were looking straight ahead, as if they had had an argument and weren't speaking.

There was a flamenco dancer wearing dark pants that went up to his nipples and a white shirt and vest. I'd never seen anyone exhale so deeply from a cigarette. I spoke to him for a short while. He said that the only reason he was alive was because he smoked eighteen cigarettes a day. He had a briefcase filled with Bounty bars, a carton of milk, and a paperback copy of *Le Matou*. He must have been homeless when he wasn't flamenco dancing, I figured, since he was carrying that junk around.

I saw Adam playing the piano. There was a sign-up sheet for the piano and often kids took their lessons on it. Adam would play for two hours at a time. He was wearing the same suit he always wore and a red scarf. He was cute enough. He had blond hair and blue eyes and a small mouth that always looked as if it was puckered up for a kiss. He composed his own tunes, some of the worst I'd ever heard. I happened to sort of like the one he was playing at the moment. It was all high notes, like someone stirring the tea in a teacup with a silver spoon. I went and leaned against the piano. He grinned like crazy when he saw me because he was madly in love with me.

"What do you call that?" I asked.

"*Le minou est un minou et pourquoi pas.*"

He was English and he deliberately spoke in nonsensical French sometimes. He winked at me. We'd dated a little bit here and there, but I never really wanted to have anything more to do with him. Perhaps because it was my brother who had introduced us.

I picked up a paper flower that was lying on the ground. I stuck it behind my ear and began dancing around the piano seductively. Adam was just about to get up and come and grab me when someone else took hold of my arm. I turned to see that it was the priest. I thought he was going to scold me for behaving like a *salope* around an agent of the Lord.

Instead, he asked me if I wanted to try out for the pageant. I wasn't even dressed up. I was wearing a black sweater with stars on it and red shorts and some cowboy boots that I'd stolen from Nicolas. I had a barrette with a plastic daisy in my hair.

I told the priest I had no intention whatsoever of participating in their beauty pageant, which was insulting to women. I was a feminist and was here to sign up for night school. I was about to walk away, but this old man in a suit put his arms out to block me from going any farther. He was one of those men who are absurdly short. They were children during the Depression and had to eat boiled stone soup. They didn't like to talk either; they were just always gesturing for you to do things. Now he put his arms around me and then started pushing me up onto the stage.

"Mais, t'es complètement malade!" I cried.

The priest seemed to be perfectly okay with all of this. The absurdity of the situation struck me and I just started to laugh and laugh. I yelled for Adam to come and save me. But he called out that it served me right. That's what I got for trying to be such a big shot.

Here I was up onstage again. It came back to me how your feet made an echo on the stage as if you were a giant. There were six other girls standing there. One seemed to have a head cold and kept sneezing violently.

The priest and three other men sat in a row of chairs in front of the stage and looked at us. The priest liked to be involved in anything that was happening. If there was a pickup game of basketball in the park, he would want to be part of it. He liked to procrastinate from saving souls, I guess. One of the men had a mop leaning against his chair, so he was probably the janitor. They asked us to strike different poses. We had to close our eyes and pretend that we were flowers. We waved our arms up in the air as if they were petals. One of the men, in a yellow sweater that was five sizes too big, asked us if we could blow a kiss at him. A girl who thought that this was beneath her climbed down off the stage. The janitor said that we should hold our hair up over our heads.

The priest asked us whether or not we had any particular talents. One girl could say the alphabet backward. I thought this was lovely. The janitor shrugged his shoulders and said that it wasn't a very sexy talent. Another girl made her lips look like those of a fish. She apologized for having a zit on her forehead, then started giggling.

There was a girl with blond hair. She was so pale, it gave the impression that she'd been scrubbed clean. I thought she was prettier than me. She was able to do the splits. The men looked impressed.

I didn't have any talents. But when it was my turn, for some idiotic reason, I recited the lyrics from one of my dad's songs as if they were a poem.

I chased a black cat down the street
It led me to your door
You were wearing your grandfather's hat
At first I thought you were the ugliest girl
That I had ever seen.

"Marie-Jo! Marie-Jo! Marie-Jo!" they all started singing together.

"Aren't you Étienne Tremblay's kid? Little Nouschka Tremblay!"

"Little Nouschka!" Everyone started chiming in.

The men put their heads together, then looked at us and announced that I had won. They did a quick photo shoot of me holding a sceptre and standing in front of a large piece of black paper covered in stars. They said it was to go in the hallway. Plainly, I just got the title because of who I once had been. I was trying my best to straighten out my life, but I always ended up in the middle of some festive waste of time.

CHAPTER 3

My Father Is Étienne Tremblay

I SUPPOSE I SHOULD TELL YOU RIGHT NOW WHO our father is. Everybody else knows. Étienne Tremblay had been a pretty famous Québécois folk singer in the early seventies. A chansonnier. He recorded two albums that were everywhere. Back in the day, he could come home from a show with a paper bag filled with women's underwear. Outside of Québec nobody had even heard of him, naturally. Québec needed stars badly. The more they had, the better argument they had for having their own culture and separating from Canada.

There was a signed black-and-white photograph of him over the counter at the hot dog place. Mostly he wore a black suit and a top hat. The top hat was his trademark. He bought it at a costume shop in Vieux-Montréal and fell in love with it. He had blue eyes and a giant nose and was ridiculously tall. He had been really handsome, as handsome as an American. A lot of people had said that he could have been a huge star if he had learned to sing in English. But he hated the English. Hating them was the true passion of his life.

Étienne Tremblay had a terrible singing voice. I had heard him trying to sing a Pepsi tune while washing out a coffee cup and it sounded awful. He couldn't even carry "Frère Jacques." Once a newspaper article had called him the Tone Deaf Troubadour. People would ask Nicolas and me if we had inherited his musical abilities. It was safe to say that we had, seeing as we didn't have any at all.

His real talent, what people went crazy for, was his knack for writing song lyrics. There was a song about a mechanic who builds a snowmobile that can go faster than the speed of light. There was one about a grandpapa who has gas. There was a song about a tiger that escapes from le Zoo de Granby to go eat poutine. He had a song about a man who finds a magical cigarette that doesn't end, and he never has to come back from his cigarette break. He made the ridiculous squalor that was everyday life sublime. There was no subject that was beneath Étienne Tremblay.

And he was a bon vivant. Everyone loved him for it. He inhaled helium and sang a Gilles Vigneault song on a variety show. There was an interview with him where he claimed to have slept with three hundred women by the time he was twenty-one. He was arrested at a raid at a dirty movie theatre, but this only made people like him more because he had a song about Édouard who finishes work and goes to the dirty movie theatre and always has to make up crazy excuses to his wife about where he has been.

He got caught with prescription pills that weren't his and was arrested again. He did well in jail. All the other prisoners liked him. He talked to the other prisoners about what some old washed-up *vedettes* from the seventies were like in bed. He claimed to have gone down on Petula Clark. He came out of prison each time like a war hero. Until he finally ended up being sentenced for eight whole months.

To say that Étienne's fame had gone to his head would be an understatement. He really believed that he had a higher calling. I think he ranked himself up there with Jesus, and I'm not even exaggerating.

Oh and, how could I forget, in the middle of all this he had two kids who became famous too because Étienne always brought them onstage and on talk shows with him. He would make us come out and wave wildly at the audience and blow kisses and say adorable things that he'd written for us to the hosts. We were known by everyone as Petite Nouschka and Petit Nicolas.

CHAPTER 4

The Old Man and the Spaghetti Jar

I HURRIED HOME. I WANTED TO SEE NICOLAS SO that I could tell him about the janitors singing Étienne's song. I was feeling lousy about it, but he would laugh it off.

It was only about a twenty-minute walk back to our building, across the street from an old theatre that now sold electronics. The building was falling apart but the wooden doors were still painted gold every year. Sticking out above the door was a neon sign that wasn't ever lit up and said CHOW MEIN. There used to be a Chinese restaurant in one of the apartments. Pigeons sat on the sign, crammed together like a group of teenagers making trouble on a bench. The noise they made sounded like a marble rolling across the floor all day, every day.

A girl with messy blond hair was standing in the lobby. She had on a white raincoat and sneakers. She gave me a sad look. I knew she was hoping to run into my twin brother. She reminded me of the Little Mermaid, right before she was going to have to throw herself back in the water because the prince had rejected her. Lonely, crazy girls always thought that Nicolas was going to save their lives. He gave off that impression. Lord knows why. He had probably already slept with this girl, but I knew he wouldn't have any interest in her now. I smiled and ran past her up the one step and down the hall.

Our apartment was on the ground floor and it was small. There was yellow wallpaper with canaries in the hallways. There were old-fashioned lamps on every surface. There were secondhand paintings all over the walls. There were a lot of sailboats. There was a painting of Jesus rolling his eyes up at the sky in every room.

Nicolas and I had been raised by our grandparents since we were babies. Our mother had left us on their doorstep, so to speak. Our grandmother had died when we were five, so actually we'd more or less been raised by our grandfather. His mother regretted naming him Léonard only five minutes after she did so, and no one had ever called him by his real name. Everyone just called him Loulou.

Loulou was in the kitchen wearing an old suit jacket over an undershirt. He had fixed a hole in the sleeve of the jacket with a staple gun. He wasn't wearing any pants. His undershirt was tucked into his boxer shorts, which were covered with little golden paisleys. They looked like goldfish that were all dressed up for church. He was always crapping his pants, so he stopped wearing them at home. It just made life easier. He crapped his pants every time he smoked a cigarette.

Loulou's nose was big, a family trait, but then what old man didn't have a huge nose. His ears were enormous too. He had blue eyes and his eyebrows were wild. It was impossible to know anymore what he had looked like when he was young.

He had a pair of dentures, but they were too big for him and made him have to grin ludicrously when he was wearing them. Loulou once told me that it was perfectly acceptable to slap a man in the face for being forward when he was young. That's why men of his generation lost all their teeth, because the roots were weak from having been slapped all the time.

"Bonjour, Loulou!" I said.

"Where have you been?"

"Out slaying dragons."

"There were still dragons when I was little. They were a sickly bunch. They would hang around garbage cans in the alleys behind Chinese restaurants. They would smoke cigars so that they could have smoke coming out of their mouths."

"I know, you told me."

"I'm glad they went extinct. Fucking ruined the Middle Ages for everybody. Oh, they didn't like it when the shoe was on the other foot."

"I'm starving."

Loulou started making dinner. He never let anyone else cook. He had a dishrag tossed over his shoulder with roses on it. He had an oven mitt that was shaped like Babar the elephant. The spaghetti fell onto the floor like a burst of applause when a famous person makes a surprise cameo on a television show.

"Oh my fucking God. What the fuck just happened here? Am I losing my mind or is there spaghetti over the floor? I've gone senile. I can't fucking stand it."

As I brought a broom, Loulou put on a new record that he had found in the garbage. He played it at full volume and it was hard to make conversation. I had to scream bloody murder for him to pass me the salt. Loulou was drinking milk out of a plastic measuring cup. He always thought that Nicolas and I and everyone else our age had AIDS. He wouldn't let us use the same cups as him.

"Did you know that you can get into the zoo for free if you're on welfare? Why aren't I on welfare? Sign me up."

"You are on welfare."

For a long time, Loulou had collected scrap metal for a living. He still stopped to lift up a refrigerator with his bare hands every now and then to show people that he could. He carried around a briefcase filled with spark plugs and telephone wires and a wrench that weighed five or ten pounds.

But he was getting old and was always having tiny heart attacks while lifting things into the back of his truck. He would get faint after pushing a stove up onto the flatbed of his truck and fall over. People would call 911 because they would find him lying in their garbage heap staring up in the air. He had the look of a bewildered little kid on his face when he came to. His rescuers were always moved by the expression of absolute innocence that he had on his face at those moments. When he would tell Nicolas and me about these episodes, we would laugh so hard, we couldn't speak. We would even burst out laughing in bed in the dark when we thought about it. A few days ago, he'd found a fridge in the garbage. He put it on a little red wagon and pulled it down the street. He had to stop in order to have a heart attack. Nicolas lay on the kitchen floor screaming with laughter when I told him. Mortality didn't mean anything to us because we were so young. We just thought of old age as some sort of clown routine.

A cat crawled in the window. There was a catnip tree in a yard in the alley behind the building. Every time I looked out my window, there were cats in the tree. They often jumped onto the balcony and into my room. It was hard to have a memory without at least one cat in it.

*****

Later that night Loulou got drunk and went into the living room to watch television. There were stains on the gold cushions of the couch. I spent about five minutes trying to get a channel. Loulou had made an antenna out of five coat hangers that sometimes picked up a channel from New York.

"Sit down already. That's as good as you're going to get it."

I threw myself down next to him on the couch. He put his arms out in front of him, as if we were in a small boat that might capsize. I guess I figured it was my duty as a granddaughter to sit next to Loulou and listen to his nonsense. In Québec, people took care of their parents and not the other way round.

The news was on and they were talking about how there was going to be another referendum within the year. Québec would again vote on whether or not to separate from Canada.

"Oh my goodness," said Loulou. "All this again. Your father was nuts about separating. Oh my goodness. He was at all the marches. Do you remember that?"

"How could I forget, he dragged Nicolas and me to all the rallies."

"That's right. You guys used to wave those flags around. Nicolas would really get into it. Man, what a little guy. He was yelling for a free Québec, wasn't he?"

"You voted *oui* too."

"What do I know? When Jean Lesage came into power he took all the electricity companies away from the Anglos and the Americans. Then my heat bill came down. I'll always remember that the Anglos made me freeze to death. Oh, and everyone in this building was voting *oui*. I just wanted to make everyone happy. Who did you vote for?"

"I was seven years old."

"Of course. Did you sign up to finish school?"

"I signed up without Nicolas."

"You were better in school than he was. He was always antagonizing the teachers. It's good to do something by yourself. I used to beat you to stop you from sleeping together in the same bed, but you still did. You ate out of the same plates. You wore the same clothes. You said the same things at the same time. You took baths together. It was disgusting."

I slammed my glass on the table.

"Laisse-moi tranquille avec ça."

Loulou was right about Nicolas never fitting in at school, though. He was diagnosed by the teachers as having every learning disability they could think of. They assigned a different one to him each year. He broke his leg playing musical chairs in Grade Three. He acted like it was the only chance he was ever going to get to win anything.

Nicolas used to say that he dropped out because the teacher had made him use the word *incandescent* in a sentence. He said that it was emotional abuse. But we just stopped going when he was sixteen because he hated it so much and was failing every class.

I was able to sit still in class and did okay on my report cards, but I left with him anyways. After that, we were educated by secondhand paperback books and madmen on Boulevard Saint-Laurent. Anyways, even though we were high school dropouts, people still treated us like precocious geniuses just because we'd been on television.

We had so much fun together during those years. We stayed out all night. We were always drinking. Even when we were teenagers, we would sit in our bedroom and drink until we cried. We would hug our stuffed animals like lovers and pass out in our clothes, with one leg out of our pants and the other leg in.

CHAPTER 5

The Teddy Bears Are Drunk

I WALKED TO THE BEDROOM THAT I HAD SHARED with Nicolas since I was a baby. On top of the bureau, there was a pile of VHS tapes on how to teach yourself karate. Nicolas had been watching them for years. He was actually really good at a lot of the moves. He looked like he was good at them anyways.

We never threw anything away. We had Valentine's Day cards from elementary school. There were storybooks on the shelf next to some of Nicolas's dirty magazines. There was a *Peter and the Wolf* record. There were action figures on the windowsill.

There were postcards that Étienne sent us from when he was in prison. We stuck them religiously to the wall, and now the Scotch tape was all yellow and peeling. There was a postcard of a man on a unicycle. There was a postcard of a strongman pulling a bus. There was a postcard of a naked woman completely covered in tattoos. That was particularly horrifying for us as children. We would spend hours looking at it.

The room had been our dad's long before we were born. The closet was still filled with his clothes. Grandmother and

Loulou never bought us new toys because they figured we could just play with Étienne's. Our stuffed animals were wretched. They had wanted to retire after Étienne. They had wanted to just chill out at the bottom of a toy box. They could barely hold their heads up and were missing eyes.

Still, we wheeled them down the street in an old doll carriage. We tied bibs around their necks and stuck empty spoons up to their mouths, begging them to eat. We changed their clothes and straightened their hair. We told them we loved them. They just said, "Yeah, yeah, yeah."

Nicolas and I slept in the same double bed. There was a single mattress by the window, but we just used that as a couch. We slept in our boots some nights under the giant old quilt that was covered in green roses.

I closed the window and the blind and lay on the bed. I started reading where I'd left off in *Les Misérables*. With the exception of Lucky Luke comic books, Nicolas did not share my fondness for reading. It was hard to concentrate on anything once Nicolas came home with his latest plight and crazy antics.

I was excited that I had signed up for school. I didn't know why. I felt as if I had had an unusually productive day. He would be very sorry indeed when he found out what kind of day I had had. Wouldn't he be amazed to find out that I had been nominated queen of the entire city? I couldn't wait to make him regret having stood me up.

But it got later and later and Nicolas still didn't show up.

I figured that he was probably at the Polish Social Club. There was a big dance floor there and he really liked to show off with his terrible moves. For some reason girls couldn't resist him when he was dancing. The visions of what he was doing kept building and building in my head, until I was imagining a whole bar filled with people raising their glasses in the air, toasting him.

I decided that I might as well go out and look for Nicolas.

I put on a pretty dress. It was navy blue and had white buttons in the shape of flowers going down the front and little puffed sleeves. I rummaged through the drawer, pushing Nicolas's boxers and gym socks out of the way until I found a pair of grey corded tights. I pulled them on. There was only a hole in the left foot where my big toe stuck out and another one behind my right knee. They were practically brand-new as far as my tights went.

A cat slipped in the window, lay on the bed, and rolled onto her back happily. She had just been impregnated. She lay there on her back with her paws on her chest, reliving the evening nervously in her mind.

I stuck a barrette with a silver star into my black hair. If I was going to be popping my head in and out of bars like a wife who was looking for her husband who had just got paid and was squandering all the money, at least I was going to look unbelievably fantastic while I was doing it. And if I didn't find Nicolas, I might find someone else to distract me.

CHAPTER 6

Romeo Is in the House

O H, WE HAD A LOT OF SEX BACK THEN IN Montréal; it wasn't just me. Blame it on the cold. The roses in everyone's cheeks made them seem way more appealing than they actually were. We confused the indoors with intimacy and electric heating with connection. Every night seemed like the last night on earth because we would all freeze to death shortly. Every night was a sad farewell party, a retirement party, the last few hours of a wedding. We were always bidding one another adieu. The line between having sex and not having sex was a lot finer than at any other time or place in history.

I had to admit that I had a strong tendency to date jokers. I couldn't say no to them. I would sit across from someone I was dating and try and imagine who in the entire world would date this nimrod other than me. But I always had to have a boyfriend. They distracted me from being sad. They baffled me with their stupidity. I refused to believe that finding love was difficult.

When we were very little, I don't even think that Nicolas and I were aware that we were different people. It was only when we started dating that we were able to spend any time away from each other. In these heightened experiences we were distracted from missing each other.

And a one-night stand made you feel as if you had just been invented. You were with someone who couldn't quite believe in your existence. They marvelled over you the way that people marvelled over a brand-new baby, where they couldn't get over you having ten toes and fingers.

It was exciting and scary like the first day of elementary school. There was something so innocent about it. In longer relationships you end up having to think up all sorts of fantastic fantasies to be excited by the person. But now, this first night you are enough. Who really wanted to know themselves? Instead I could exist happily in this world of first impressions.

It was raining outside and the whole street smelled of pee. I started peeking into a couple of bars but Nicolas was nowhere to be seen. I decided to give up and go to the social centre where I could go dancing myself. There were coloured lightbulbs all around the door. They sold beer for a dollar at happy hour. If you'd had enough to drink, coming out, the different-coloured lights looked like the aurora borealis.

Inside there was still the backdrop to a play that the children from the elementary school next door had put on. There were clouds cut out of cardboard hanging from strings. There was a little brick house that the big bad wolf couldn't blow down. The edges of the curtain were tattered, like pants that had been dragging on the ground.

A man was playing this huge, out-of-tune piano. The melodies from it filled up the hall. Some of them floated out the door and through the neighbourhood. This piano had been brought over on a ship from the old country. Nobody was used to tunes that were that sorrowful. The pigeons would fall right out of the sky.

There were streamers on the ceiling. And all the balloons were lying on the floor. They moved from our shoes to make room for us.

I walked up to the bar. Everyone yelled out and clapped, happy to see me. I had a black purse with tiny mother-of-pearl beads that were always falling off that I flopped onto the bar. I decided to try gin. I was always looking for a drink that wouldn't make me feel completely plastered after one glass, but I never succeeded. Patrick, the bartender, poured me a shot. The stools on either side of me were immediately filled up.

They laughed at everything that I said. Nicolas and I were always trying to make every single person we met fall in love with us. What a job. It was a bad habit that we had picked up as child stars. But maybe it's the same for everybody.

I drank my gin as I listened to the ridiculous guys trying to charm me.

A man named Gaston had a box of Turkish delight. He opened the box and offered me one. Another guy whose date had stood him up pinned a corsage on my dress. A boy named Luc gave me a lucky rabbit's foot that was dyed bright green. I didn't know that people still believed in lucky rabbit's feet.

I noticed a man my age, who was wearing a black toque over a mop of blond hair, staring at me. He was missing a front tooth. He still managed to be the sexiest guy in the bar. He was so young and handsome that the missing tooth seemed like a charming novelty. He came over and sat on my lap. He pulled a gold necklace with a rose pendant hanging from it out of his pocket. He'd probably stolen it from his mother.

"Would you like to have dinner with me? I know a little place where they set the cheese on fire."

I pushed him off my lap while laughing. I was considering his offer. I was so bored and I wanted to be with someone.

I looked up at the ballroom ceiling and it seemed as if the whole lot of us had been swallowed by a whale. As if we were all in here as a punishment for running from our calling.

Misha came in at that moment, carrying a paper bag filled with groceries. He was wearing a long navy blue trench coat over his suit. His hair was long and grey and went to his shoulders. His face was wet from the rain. His lips were jutting out in concentration as he looked around the hall.

Misha was so fat, he made a lot of noise just breathing. He had something wrong with his tear ducts, so they wept all the time. He always had handkerchiefs in his pockets. He took one out that was made of polyester and had tiny cowboys and horses on it. I had worn a very similar one on my head when I was a baby.

The tears made his eyes seem sparkly. His eyelashes were dark and glistening—like the kind that kids draw on their dolls with ballpoint pen.

I could tell Misha had just come from work. He worked as a salesman selling toilet paper. He mostly sat behind a desk doing inventory all the time. He never really even got close to the toilet paper. According to Marxism, this was very damaging for his psyche. He should have been allowed to drive the toilet paper in the trunk of his car up to people's houses and sell it to them and watch them wipe their asses with it.

The guy in the stool next to me spotted a pretty redhead and bounced off. Misha sat down. He swirled around a glass of brandy that had a fever in it. I'd slept with him before. He was the oldest person I'd ever dated, but I liked that about him. It made him seem unique.

"My father was a ventriloquist," Misha began. He didn't want to waste any time. He knew that he was in competition with all the other guys at the bar and he knew that I could never resist his stories. "His puppet was so mean. One night the puppet killed him during a performance. The police didn't know whether to call it a suicide or a homicide."

I laughed. All of a sudden I felt like the prettiest person in the world. Then I blushed because I wasn't sure whether or not he knew I was feeling that way.

I liked that he was Russian. My favourite book at the time was *Crime and Punishment*. Étienne had left it behind after a visit. I never actually finished it, but I got the gist of it. I thought Raskolnikov was sexy.

"Tell me about Vladimir," I said.

"Oh, don't be so fucking ridiculous, Nouschka."

"I like that story."

"Because you are perverted."

"No! It's so, so sweet. I love Vladimir. I love him so much, I think about marrying him." I was already drunk on my gin.

"You should be thrown in the insane asylum."

When Misha was fifteen in Moscow he used to have a friend named Vladimir. He was a thin boy with long chestnut hair that he wore behind his ears. He would wear a red shirt that went above his belly button and he had a necklace with a pendant of a heart hanging from it. Every day after school he would stop by Vladimir's building. Vladimir lived in an apartment on the sixth floor. He would stand at the top of the stairs calling down encouragingly, so that Misha didn't change his mind about coming up. Vladimir would give him blow jobs.

Misha would close his eyes and pretend that Vladimir was a girl.

"Tell me about the time he wore a bra."

That was my favourite part. Vladimir put on a bra one night and put a different-coloured gym sock in each cup. Misha got a hard-on right away when he saw Vladimir in that little white bra. He never saw anything so lovely. And he squeezed the socks and whispered, "Sweetheart," into Vladimir's ear.

"The cold was different there," he said, instead of telling me the tale. "It made you crazy."

He took my hand and I hopped off the bar stool. We walked to the centre of the dance floor together. Misha was fun to dance with because he was so big. I loved his dancing style too. He would stand in one place and move his hands around and clap them in different spots. He would snap his hands to his side and kick a foot behind him in some sort of a flamenco move. I don't know where he learned that move. Any other kind of dancing was capable of giving him a heart attack, I suppose. I liked to dance slow dances with him. I hugged him and clung to him tightly as we danced. I hung off his neck like a tragic little monkey.

"Oh, don't ever leave me. You smell so good. You're so fat and lovely. Like a baby. Let's get married and teach our children to tap dance. They'll be a sensation. Can we get a wee dog and name him Gazou? We can feed him sherbet and apple pie. Let's never make our children learn the alphabet. The alphabet is for cowards!"

"Nouschka, you can never handle your drink."

"Don't say that, my darling."

Right in the middle of my wild declaration of love, I noticed Raphaël Lemieux walking into the club. He had grown up across the street from us and had been the greatest figure skater anyone on Boulevard Saint-Laurent had ever seen. We all thought he was going to the Olympics. But he lost his marbles and jumped off the Jacques Cartier Bridge. He became perhaps as famous for surviving the incredible fall as for his skating. It was in all the papers.

He had been in the Pinel Institute for the criminally insane and had only recently been released. Everybody in the club was quiet for a minute. He actually got the opposite reaction that I did when I walked in. People needed a second to see what kind of mood Raphaël was in. If he was in a bad crazy mood, then he was liable to pick a fight with anybody who made eye contact with him. He'd get into fights just as an excuse to pull out a gun that everybody said didn't actually work but was frightened of nonetheless.

He had picked up some weird activities while in the psych ward. The old ladies were rather alarmed when Raphaël showed up at a knitting circle in the church basement. He'd learned to knit while on the inside to calm down. He was working on a scarf that was about eight feet long. He did tai chi in the park with a group of senior citizens. It was something they did in the common room at Pinel. It looked like a ship had sunk and these were the passengers, slowly sinking to their grave at the bottom of the ocean. It was impossible to figure Raphaël out. Many had tried and none had succeeded. Don't try now!

Raphaël walked straight up to the bar. He was wearing a suit that was made out of blue, shiny, old-man material. His pants were hanging low because he had no belt on, and you could see his underwear. His jacket was so small that when he leaned forward and put his elbows on the bar you could see the tattoos on his wrist and on his belly. He had a sparrow on his wrist. The kind that fifties prostitutes used to have.

A cat hurried out from the backroom behind the counter. Everyone knew this one and called out, "Monsieur Moustache!" The cat leapt up onto the stool next to Raphaël. It leapt as if it had a wire on its back and it was in a play where it had to fly. Raphaël held the cat up and kissed it all over its face. He leaned forward and ordered from the bartender. Patrick brought him a brandy Alexander.

I was sober all of a sudden and my heart was beating in a strange place in my chest. I liked the idea that Raphaël had gotten released from the mental institution. It was mythic. He was the first person my age to have been committed, so it seemed to confer some sort of status. He was a handsome raving lunatic. For some reason Raphaël was the only person in the place who I felt I couldn't go up and talk to.

Misha asked if I was ready to go. I nodded quickly. I left holding Misha's hand. I told myself not to turn back and look at Raphaël. I would murder myself if I turned back. But I did anyways and at that moment, abruptly, he turned and looked at me. Our eyes met. Misha pulled me out the door.

❊❊❊❊❊

Trying to get Misha to have a hard-on was a circus-like enterprise. It was like a scene from one of those crazy foreign films that they played after midnight. He undid his belt as if he was sitting down for a big steak dinner. The lining of his coat was black with blue butterflies stitched into it. You could only see them when the light was shining on the lining at a certain angle.

Misha was smoking a cigar. He exhaled little girls in pyjamas who ran as fast as they could and crawled behind the couch and under the lampshade, playing hide-and-seek.

I always gave him a hard time. He liked that.

"Take off your bra."

"No."

"Take it off, baby."

"No. I can't. It's impossible."

"Why not? Just for a second. I need to see your tits."

"I'm really afraid that I can't do that."

"Yes, you can."

"You won't think of me in the same way."

"Yes, I will. I'll always think you are just the sweetest thing that ever lived."

"I don't believe it."

"It's true. Now take off your bra."

"Do you love me?"

"You know I do."

"Do you love me more than any other girl? Even more than the girls on television?"

"I don't give a shit about those girls."

I unclipped my bra from behind. I took the straps off one by one. He moved his chair closer to the table.

"Now what are you going to do with me?" I asked.

"I just want to eat you up. You're a little piece of cake. There's no one I've ever wanted to fuck the way that I want to fuck you."

"What about when I get old and ugly. What will you do with me then?"

"I won't be around then."

He grabbed both my legs and pulled me off the table and I landed in his lap. The grey of his suit pants was the colour of stones made smooth by the river. I always felt like a small child with him.

"Come over here, my darling. Come and sit on Daddy's lap. What would you do if you didn't have my kisses? Would you be so, so sad? Would you be able to get out of bed in the morning?"

"Yes, I guess I would. I could find someone else to kiss me easily."

"Who told you to be so, so pretty? You're going to send me to my grave early."

"Kiss me."

"You're going to have to beg."

"Kiss me, please, please."

Then he kissed one of those kisses that makes everything in the world seem okay.

There are things that are permissible in sex that aren't permissible elsewhere. You can smack each other and tie each other up and pee on them and strangle them. That's when love shows its face. When love takes off its clothes and has a drink. It sometimes takes the most appalling forms. It made the night seem like it was going to last forever.

In movies, sex was always a lot cleaner than it was in real life. No one ever found a receipt stuck to the back of their leg. No one ever still had brown sneakers on. They never asked for a glass of water from the kitchen. They never felt guilty afterward and wept.

Misha gave me a bath. His bathtub had enormous feet. A magic spell had been cast on it. It used to be a lion. The light green tiles on the walls had pink roses in the middle.

He said I was filthy and didn't know how to bathe properly. He scrubbed my hair with shampoo. I had lit a cigarette and he poured a glass of water on me, extinguishing it. He wrapped me up in a towel that had all the different sharks in North America on it.

Sometimes you don't realize that love is love. You think it must be nobler. You think it must involve someone better-looking. Especially since all the time when you're watching television, you are just watching good-looking people hooking up.

I thought he was ugly. I liked to stand next to him in the bathroom in front of the mirror. I liked how different we looked from each other. No matter how many times you were kissed, or someone bought you drinks or swore you were the one, or you spent your last five dollars on new lipstick, you couldn't be sure that God found you pretty.

He reminded me of a dancing bear that Gypsies had dressed. He lay in bed with his shirt off. His stomach was so enormous that it seemed like something out of a fairy tale. If you cut his stomach open, little children would crawl out.

*****

Just as Misha was dozing off, I decided it was time to get home. I started to get dressed quietly so that he wouldn't notice. I put on my coat.

"Why don't you stay for the weekend?" Misha said, opening one of his eyes. "I've had a hard week. I would love it if you spent the weekend with me. I wouldn't give a damn about any other crappy thing that ever happened to me for the rest of my life if you just stayed for the weekend."

I didn't answer. I just started tying my shoes.

"Just pretend to be this fat old man's girlfriend for one weekend. There's a bakery by the river that I discovered has magnificent cakes. You should come with me and I'll buy you some."

"I have to make an early start of it tomorrow."

"No, you don't. Sometimes you stay until dawn, but you never spend the night with me. You and your brother can't spend the night apart from each other. It's ridiculous. You aren't children anymore."

"It isn't that. It doesn't have to do with Nicolas."

"When you were little you tied each other's shoes and held hands on the bus. And when you were feeling down, the other one would say, 'Chin up, little guy.' I know all this. But that was because your parents weren't there. But the world won't fall apart if you spend the night away from each other. You are old enough to have a real boyfriend."

"Don't tell me what I'm thinking. If I say I have an important thing to do in the morning, then I have an important thing to do in the morning. Jesus!"

I was suddenly annoyed at Misha. It seemed as if everyone had told me to stay away from Nicolas that day. Even myself.

"The boyfriend doesn't even have to be me," he continued. "I'm too old and ugly for you. It isn't even only my hair that has gone grey, but it is also my skin that has gone grey too. I look in the mirror and I think, well, how does it feel to be the ugliest man in the world, my friend."

I kissed his fat cheek as I buttoned up my jacket.

"I, for one, find you insanely sexy."

I didn't really get the point of moving out. I loved our cozy room. I always felt happy there. I had no idea why everybody was so eager for me to be as miserable as all the other lonely adults going around.

CHAPTER 7

My Brother Is Always in Jail

I CRAWLED BACK INTO THE BEDROOM THROUGH
the window. We used the door and the window indiscrimin-
ately. A white cat with beige spots that I'd never seen before tiptoed off the bed and down the hallway, like a naked girl heading
to the bathroom after she's had sex in an unfamiliar apartment.
Nicolas was there sleeping on the bed fully dressed. I realized
that he had probably been out on some sort of score.

He had a little boy named Pierrot, who he wasn't able to
pay child support for. Pierrot was the result of a relationship
Nicolas had with a girl named Saskia when they were fifteen
years old. He started a life of crime soon after the baby was
born, in an attempt to be responsible, I suppose.

It wasn't that extraordinary that Nicolas had chosen this
path. Being a criminal was an obvious job option for someone
during the recession. It paid about as much as working the cash
register at a bakery, but you got to work your own hours.

All the proper thieves in Montréal came from the east end.
They were trained by uncles and fathers who were in the trade.

They were organized and had proper capers. They controlled the drug trade and robbed banks and made good money.

Nicolas was the kind of thief who ended up on the cover of the *Allo Police* newspaper. Like the pimp who had gotten beaten up by his prostitute and was now pressing charges. Or the teenager who had invented a new kind of hallucinogenic, called Grandpappi's Penis because you couldn't get an erection while you were using it.

Sometimes Nicolas would put on a ski mask and rob a gas station. It was easy in winter because it was nothing to break into a place wearing a ski mask and then to leave and blend in with all the other people wearing ski masks as they went down the street.

Nobody had more than thirty dollars in the cash register. But that was enough for Nicolas. He would do a holdup, stick the gun in the back waistband of his pants and then go to Guy La Patate and order a souvlaki and a Coke. Then he might use the rest of the money to see a movie and come back home and climb into bed as broke as the day he was born.

He had never been arrested for anything serious. People were always calling the cops on Nicolas for things that weren't even crimes. There was a woman who called the police on him because he was practising karate moves in her backyard in just his shorts and T-shirt. The neighbours called the police because he was singing a Jean Leloup song at the top of his lungs in the shower.

Once we were at a restaurant and he yelled at the waitress that she was a tease because she wouldn't bring the ketchup over. The cops showed up five minutes later.

It was nothing for the cops to be at the door looking for Nicolas. It was the only time that we would get up early. The cats would fall off whatever bureau they were sleeping on. Nicolas would pick us up these Chinese dumplings in Chinatown on his way home after being booked. He would be home sometimes before we'd gotten out of our pyjamas.

I curled up in Nicolas's arms. I turned and looked him in the face. He opened his eyes.

"You wouldn't believe what I got up to today at the Ukrainian Centre."

Nicolas didn't answer. He just stared at me with a strange, unhappy look.

"What?" I asked.

"*Est-ce que ça te dérange?* We don't even know our mother's real name."

I flipped over, not wanting to hear what Nicolas had to say next.

"I bet she hasn't even thought about us for years. I bet she doesn't give even two shits about us."

"Don't do this again. It's insane. Whenever something is bothering you, instead of dealing with it, you go on a rant about our mother."

When Nicolas was little and was mad at Loulou, he would lie on his bed and whimper, "I want to go live with my mother." It seemed impossibly strange. Where in his head did this missing of our mother exist, since it seemed not to exist in mine?

"She's real. That's what you don't understand. She's out there drinking tea out of a porcelain cup that matches the teapot. She's scratching lottery tickets. She's watching television. It creeps me out to the bone. It's unholy."

"What do you want to do? Find her and make her love you?"

"She fell for Étienne's charms. It's her fault that I'm stuck being alive."

"You blame her for everything."

"You blame her for nothing. Which is even worse, because everybody deserves to be blamed for something."

We didn't say anything to each other after that. We just lay there with our hearts beating. There is nothing as frustrating as being consumed with rage over someone and knowing that you aren't even on their mind. You want your enemy to be engaged in a struggle until the death with you. Otherwise you are fighting yourself. I mean we are all essentially only in wars against ourselves, but we don't like it to be so painfully obvious.

I could hear the family of mice that had moved into an old dollhouse that was for rent in the basement, moving their furniture around. I was curious if he'd seen Pierrot earlier. It was always such a disaster, so maybe that was why he was in such a bad mood. There were all these things that I had wanted to say to Nicolas, but I couldn't because he had been so worked up. I had wanted to tell him about signing up for school. And I wanted to tell him about the beauty pageant just to get it out of the way. Tomorrow so many other things would happen. How on earth would we ever catch up? I wondered. Then I drifted away.

CHAPTER 8

Bon Voyage

Nicolas was reclining on his bed in his underwear and a T-shirt the next week while I was getting ready for my first day of school.

"Let's go see a movie at the library," he said.

Unless Nicolas had just held up a gas station, they were the only types of movies that we could afford since they were free. Nicolas had always liked those black-and-white silent films when he was little, where the woman looked as if she had a toothache.

"You know I have school."

"So that's it. You are kiboshing our Tuesday movie nights?"

"I'm afraid so."

"You're always working now. You're no fun anymore."

"Oh, for crying out loud. We've had enough fun for one lifetime, don't you think? You didn't want to sign up for school with me, remember? You were absolutely adamant about it."

I headed out of the room. Nicolas got dressed as fast as he could in order to come after me. He wiggled into his jeans like a raindrop coming down the car window. He put on a black jacket that was way too small for him. It made him look like a matador. He followed me outside. He suddenly grabbed my bicycle keys out of my hand and held them up over his head. I started whacking him with my purse. We started wrestling and fell on the ground. I sat on him, slapping him with my hands, while he laughed hysterically. Somebody passing by shot us a look of utter disgust.

I suppose there was something a bit freakish about our relationship. We hadn't changed the way we acted very much at all since we were seven.

Nicolas got on his bicycle and rode next to me. We rode our bicycles in the middle of the street. The cars behind us kept honking at us to tell us to move out of the way. But we didn't move. We still owned that street. We loved blocking traffic. We rode with our arms off the handlebars and our arms stretched out while holding hands. It was a trick that we'd learned years before. Nicolas stood up on the seat of his bicycle. He loved risky behaviour more than anything else. Ah, the things that Nicolas had to do to feel alive. It was beautiful.

My night classes were going to be in the old school building on Rue Saint-Denis. I rode up onto the sidewalk outside the building. The lampposts out front had been planted when Loulou was a young boy. They had grown up and were now almost as tall as the buildings.

"I'll see you later," I said to Nicolas as I chained my bike to a pole.

Nicolas stopped a man in a business suit who was passing by.

"She's tossing me aside. She doesn't care whether I live or die. She thinks that she's better than me. *Elle est conne, monsieur!*"

"You interfere with all my plans," I said. "I knew that you

were going to do this. You don't realize that you're doing it. You don't know why you're doing it. But you just do it."

He was about to protest some more when a fourteen-year-old girl wearing a T-shirt with a fleur-de-lys on it came up and asked us for an autograph. We just got quiet for a minute and signed the back of a ripped-open envelope.

Nicolas sat on the bench outside the school. His hair was all messed up, but it didn't matter. He was able to pull off bed-head in a way I had only seen babies do. He looked so innocent. I almost felt bad about leaving him behind.

"Fine. Fine. Fine. I'll wait for you here."

By the time I got to the third floor, I looked out the window at the staircase, and the bench was empty. He could never sit in the same spot for very long. I was so distracted by the idea of going to school that I didn't care where Nicolas had gone to.

*****

I squeezed into one of the little wooden desks in the classroom. These desks had been around since the Depression. They had the small holes in the tops of them where the ink bottles used to go. I guess they were from when the children used to write with feathers. They had to lure ostriches at the zoo to the fence so that they could pull feathers out of their bottoms.

As soon as everyone settled in and the teacher began to talk, I realized that I was glad that Nicolas wasn't in school with me. I knew that he would never be able to sit through this. He would never be able to accept that he would have to do all the very ordinary things that everybody else did. It had been drilled into our heads that we were extraordinary. But it wasn't really true. We were only as extraordinary as the next person. Or, anyways, we had to do all the things that everybody else does to become something.

Dreaming too big was the cause of much horror on Boulevard Saint-Laurent. The street was filled with people whose dreams had gone bust. It wasn't always drugs and bad childhoods that brought them this low. It was ambition. There was a whole group of fallen Icaruses sitting under the blazing fluorescent lights at the soup kitchen. Their jackets were half blown off by the fall. They had the complexions of clowns whose cigars had just exploded.

Étienne Tremblay and his children were supposed to be geniuses who never did anything ordinary. Certainly nothing as pathetic as going to night school to complete a high school diploma. We ought to be up in the wee hours composing philosophical tracts on the banality of happiness. But those days were all over, weren't they? I was just a girl who worked in a magazine store, looking for a leg up.

Lord, we had been snobs. We took on friends once in a while when we thought that someone was charismatic. When we got disappointed or bored we would toss them aside. There was no one in the classroom whom Nicolas would even deign to make eye contact with. But I liked that everyone was so different. I wanted something new. I looked at these faces and knew that the unexpected was already happening.

There was a man who slicked his hair back into a black wave. He had probably been good-looking when he was a teenager. There was a pretty girl about my age except she was a completely different style. She wore a supertight tracksuit and about twelve pieces of gold jewellery, including a stud in her nose.

The man beside me had a checkered hat on the desk, next to his opened notebook. The hat perfectly matched his checkered jacket. I thought this was remarkable. He was also a doodler. He drew skinny horses all over the margins of his notebook, which generally was something that only young girls did.

I drank a cup of coffee at the break and made conversation with everyone. They were all from other neighbourhoods and took the bus downtown to go to school in the evenings. These were all sorts of people who were trying to figure out this world, so that they could have apartments and they could support their families, so that they didn't have to be afraid, so that they could feel proud of themselves.

A woman told me that she was going to get a business degree and that she was going to open her own flower shop. How lovely. How wonderful to have a plan and to have something to work toward. She asked me if I knew what I was going to do. I said no.

One of the guys asked me if I wanted to go for a drink later, but I wasn't interested. It would make it a pain in the ass to come to school when our relationship didn't work out—which it inevitably wouldn't.

The subject after the break was Québec History, the bane of every high school student in the province. When the teacher handed out the battered textbooks, I opened mine immediately. I looked at the cartoon drawing of Jacques Cartier, the explorer who discovered Canada. He was wearing a ridiculously tiny black hat and looked so proud that he had finally managed to get to this new land. I felt the same way. I was here! I was back in school again. I was as anxious to turn the page and find out what happened next as Jacques was.

CHAPTER 9

The Lineup for the Guillotine

I ACTUALLY DIDN'T EVEN FEEL LIKE STILL BEING a beauty queen by the time the day of the parade rolled around. I just wanted to work on homework that weekend. But I had to go. Before the parade, a hairdresser brushed and fixed my hair for over an hour. It didn't have much of an effect because it was messy again five minutes later. The white dress they gave me went down to my feet, so I could still keep my blue Adidas sneakers on. I had a long black robe with tiny stars all over it and white ermine trim.

A skinny white cat with black spots over its eyes hopped onto my lap. It looked like a little kid dressed up as Zorro. I kissed it a dozen times and realized that I was in a good mood.

I had gotten away with having a secret from Nicolas. There was never an appropriate time to tell him I'd hidden the whole thing from him. Especially since he was kind of upset about me going off to school almost every night. I left a note on the table saying I'd gone off to be Miss Montréal in the Saint-Jean-

Baptiste parade. I snuck out and prayed that he would wake up
and read the letter long after the parade was over.

The entire city was already drinking beer for the holiday of
Saint-Jean-Baptiste, our patron saint. The parade started moving down Rue Sainte-Catherine. The marching band came first.
They were playing those xylophones that you hold balanced on
your hip. The music was so beautiful that it was aggravating.
It made me feel like I had to pee or release something. They
started playing the theme song from a television show and the
crowd went completely wild. Kids were standing on kitchen
chairs and milk crates with their arms akimbo and rocking back
and forth.

There were clowns all around me. Québec was lousy with
clowns. They were smoking cigarettes and drinking empty bottles of champagne. Their eyebrows were drawn on their foreheads so that they looked perpetually raised. They wore tuxedo
jackets and spats. One carried a briefcase that smoke was coming out of. There was one who opened an umbrella over his
head and confetti blew everywhere like rain.

I stood up on the seat of the car. My dress was blowing all
over the place. The driver said that I should sit down because
he didn't think that he was insured for that kind of behaviour. I
started throwing blue and white candies from a basket into the
crowd. Little girls ran to the side of the car and put out their
hands for me to shake. They were surprisingly sticky.

"My people! My people!" I cried out as I waved.

All the old Polish women were standing in their little black
boots, their heads covered in kerchiefs. They watched as if there
was nothing whatsoever unusual happening.

Nicolas showed up. How could he not? He rode next to the
car on a ten-speed bicycle, insulting me. He had one hand on

the side of the car so that he could keep up with me. I started kicking his hand with my foot. He was drinking a plastic cup of beer while he was cycling. Some men started whistling at me, which really set him off.

"Blow some kisses!" Nicolas yelled at me. "That's what you're paid for!"

"Don't be an idiot," I answered. "I'm not being paid. Get lost, will ya?"

He was addressing the people in the crowd and telling them I must have bribed the judges.

"This is your queen? This is the most beautiful girl in the neighbourhood? Have I died and gone to hell? Come on, people!"

An old man from the Shriners Hospital tried to catch him. Two clowns on a double bicycle chased him around and around the car. A police officer came on a motorcycle to herd Nicolas off.

"*Vive le Québec libre!*" Nicolas yelled with his hands up in the air and then he sped off.

I watched Nicolas cycling away. I was annoyed with him. Now the parade would seem boring without him. I felt like climbing on the back of the bicycle and going off wherever he was going.

✳✳✳✳✳

As I was heading home later that night, fireworks were going off in the sky. They looked like there were construction workers soldering the heavens. They sounded like a necklace had been broken and all the pearls were falling on the ground.

People were sitting on their kitchen chairs on the rooftops. Montréal summer nights were always lovely. The breeze was perfect. You could make a paper airplane and throw it in the air in Saint-Léonard and it would fly all the way to the Quartier Latin.

As I turned up Boulevard Saint-Laurent, away from the crowd, the fireworks were reaching their peak. I passed a black cat in the alley. It was trying to do some sort of fancy tango with a piece of ribbon.

As I stepped in, Nicolas jumped out from the kitchen, grabbed me by the waist and spun me around. He was wearing a paper crown from the Valentine hot dog joint and was drunk. He danced me around the living room and spun me down the hallway. He had got himself all worked up.

"Pass me the caviar!" Nicolas was screaming. "Why won't anyone pass me the caviar! Okay, okay. Who stole my Grey Poupon! We are kings and queens. The kings and queens of beauty."

"Let me go," I begged.

"Adam's waiting for you in the bedroom."

"What! How'd he get here?"

"I invited him. I told him you'd been pining for him."

"You're crazy. I'm going to go throw him out right now."

"Suit yourself."

"Fuck you."

Nicolas hurled himself down on the living room couch. A calico cat was sleeping on its back, like a girl in grey stockings with her skirt pulled up over her hips.

*****

It was practically impossible to avoid Adam because he was such good friends with Nicolas. They would sit squashed in the loveseat in the living room, waving their arms maniacally over their heads, excited by their idiotic ideas. They could talk and talk for hours. He got on my nerves. Every time we had sex I would always promise myself not to ever do it again.

I had no idea where they met, because Adam grew up in Westmount, the wealthy English neighbourhood. René Lévesque had ranted long ago that there was no reason why the English in that neighbourhood should be running the show and had put a stop to it. They were still pretty damn rich though. Adam was charming and spoke perfect French. Like many anglophones in Montréal, he actually spoke French better than we did. They knew exactly which verbs to use in the same way that people knew which utensils to use while eating at a fancy dinner. It was very proper because they learned it from books. They didn't know slang or how to curse. They didn't know how to do anything other than be proper and reserved. It was a state-sponsored, dry-clean-only French.

Adam's family lived in an enormous house with a beautiful garden in front, which a gardener worked on every day of the summer. Once, Nicolas had driven me past it, just so I could get a look at it. His house was part of a walking tour that people went on during the summer. Adam had been one of the most successful children who had ever existed. He had gone to elite private schools and had had an unnecessarily comprehensive education.

He had music appreciation lessons where they would ding a xylophone while he tiptoed around the room trying to get better acquainted with the note. He took fencing lessons where he wore a mask over his face and yelled, "En garde!" He took wilderness survival lessons and he got to have wee badges with fires and bears' heads on them sewn onto his sleeves. He took tennis lessons where he called out, "One love," and took home trophies. He took photography lessons where he would walk around taking pictures of flowers and pigeons and would develop them in a sink in the basement of city hall next to other overprivileged children.

Here was the result of all that education, lying on my bed with a white shirt unbuttoned, his arms opened in some sort of posture that was halfway between benevolence and unconsciousness.

"Get out, Adam," I said as soon as I walked into my bedroom.

Although he had a noble way to describe it, Adam was slumming. He got a social assistance cheque at the beginning of the month, but he would spend it in a single day. He'd sit on a bench and drink a thirty-dollar bottle of wine while reading Romain Gary's *Les Mangeurs d'étoiles*. It aggravated me that I was attracted to him.

"Why can't you just love me, baby?" he said.

"Because you're ridiculous. And you get on my nerves."

"I think we should get married."

"Why?"

"I saw you in the car as Miss Montréal and it turned me on."

"That's hardly a reason for two people to be together."

"Can I at least sleep over?"

"No."

I flopped down on the bed, kicked off my running shoes and lay next to him. The black cat Johann was purring like it had engine trouble. His tail kept reaching round like an arm scooping up all the poker chips off the table.

"You drive me crazy, Nouschka. Why can't we just spend the rest of our lives together? Do you know how cool we'll look in the history books?"

"Ridiculous."

"What is this novel that you're working on?" he asked, pointing to my school notebook that was lying on the floor next to my bed.

"It's not a novel. It's a brief history of the fur trade. It's called 'Raccoon Hats and Cabin Fever.'"

"Write about our great love affair. How there was never anything like it in all the history of Montréal."

"No, that's not true. We haven't even got a relationship. Now you're making me unhappy."

"You're mistaking happiness for unhappiness. That's why the French are so melancholic. Everything beautiful makes them cry. They invented existentialism as an excuse not to love their wives."

"I thought it was because one of them was upset about not making the soccer team."

Adam threw back his head and laughed.

"Why won't you marry me?" he cried.

"I can't marry someone English."

"I never feel like myself when I'm speaking French."

"Who do you feel like?"

"Jean-Paul Belmondo. I feel like I'm in a French film, which means that you are unfaithful!"

"It's not possible for me to be unfaithful. I can't be. I told you, we're not in a relationship."

"It's a shame. You'll only learn to love me when I'm gunned down by the Parisian police."

He climbed over me off the bed and stumbled over to the closet. He dragged out a toy piano and sat down on the floor in front of it. Adam was always trying to get in our family act, always composing scores for Étienne to consider for a comeback album. This time he started playing a tiny twinkly

Mozart tune on it. I don't remember what it was called. He was just tickling the keys. It sounded like change being put in the peep-show booth. Like belt buckles unbuckling. His ridiculous production was turning me on. Adam always succeeded in seducing me.

"What's that called?" I asked.

"'The Mouse with a Broken Heart Finally Has Its Day in Court.'"

"That's beautiful."

"What? The tune or the title?"

"You are. You're beautiful."

"Just give me one single kiss and I'll go away."

"I don't think so."

"One fucking kiss and then I'll leave you alone. It's because I haven't been kissed in a while. There is scientific documentation that proves the body needs kisses. I just need one. Then I'll go find a high school slut to have sex with."

We kissed for a long time. I couldn't stop once I'd started.

"You give the greatest kisses on the planet," I said. "They should hire you at the palace to kiss the princesses."

He kissed me again. He put his hands underneath my dress, grabbed my hips and pulled them toward his own.

"*Tu m'aimes?*" he asked.

"I'm mad about you. I've never been as crazy about anybody as I am about you. Touch me. I feel so pretty when you touch me."

I couldn't believe how stupid I was being. I wished that I could eat my words as they were coming out of my mouth. It wasn't the sex that I was going to regret in the morning. It was going to be all these ridiculous words.

He squashed into the single bed with me. We were finished making love by the time Nicolas came into the room. He crawled into his own bed. Adam was the only guy Nicolas didn't toss out on his ear.

There were a million and one things that I liked about Adam. The way he smelled like black licorice. The way we curled up together. We were always so peaceful when we just lay together. He still had his suit jacket on. His pants were around one ankle he hadn't been able to kick his shoe off of.

Nobody was as fetching as Adam when he was sleeping. He slept in his clothes in odd positions, sometimes halfway off the bed, as if he had been shot to death in a duel. No one sleeps like young sociopaths meditating on the wonders of being themselves.

We all passed out in the same room; odd as that might sound, it seemed natural. Nicolas pushed the pile of clothes half off the other unused twin bed and crashed in it, the way he always did when Adam slept over.

Adam's suitcase was next to the bed. He clearly needed a place to stay. I never trusted love as a motivation for someone wanting to sleep with me. The cat's purring made the sound of a motorboat's engine, taking us off into the deep, deep waters of sleep. While the cockroaches put on their minuscule armoured plates and helmets and ventured out on the counter, looking for cookie crumbs.

✸✸✸✸✸

My flight instinct got crazy the next day. I kept trying to kick Adam out all morning, but he wouldn't go. I threatened to call 911 because he was taking so long putting on his shoes. Nobody else minded that he was there. He declared that he was going to make eggs florentine. You never knew when he was going to decide to whip up a plate of eggs florentine. It could be at five in the afternoon. I found it irritating, but Nicolas and Loulou clapped in delight.

I was about to tell Adam to get out again, but he turned on the old record player and put on Jacques Laframboise, a popular Québécois crooner who had walked in front of a train one night. The song was about his wife, Madeleine, who cheats on him all the time. We all started singing along to it no matter what else we were doing.

"This is a formidable record collection. You should have your own radio show called *The Loulou Tremblay Hour*! You're an archivist! In a hundred years this apartment is going to be a museum. They won't move a thing."

Loulou beamed because he was proud of his trash. Adam looked at me and winked. I smiled back. I found his arrogance attractive despite myself. Rarely had such confidence been seen on Boulevard Saint-Laurent. He had imported it from Westmount, all sparkling and glorious, like Marco Polo returning from the East with the first plate of spaghetti and meatballs that anyone had ever seen.

I liked that he was full of possibilities. I wanted to be full of possibilities too. I wanted to travel the world and be an intellectual too. I liked what he was throwing away. Most of all, I wanted an education. I was envious that he had one. As the music blared, I realized that it was time to go to work at the magazine store.

I didn't know why my temper was so short with them all these days. I calmed down as soon as I was out of the apartment and in the lobby. I stopped for a minute to breathe and then went outside, feeling that I had escaped the noisy Tremblays.

CHAPTER 10

Growing Up Naked

I STEPPED OUT OF MY BUILDING AND SAW A CREW of film people standing next to a beat-up van. One of the crew members had a camera on his shoulder, and a girl was holding a clipboard. A man with a microphone in his hand and a tape recorder in a leather bag approached me. He was wearing a blue polo shirt and jeans. He had thinning black hair that he combed upward and glasses. He looked a few years older than Nicolas and me. He looked very eager.

"Who the hell are you guys?" I instinctively put a hand out in front of my face.

"My name's Hugo Vaillancourt. I'm a filmmaker. I was to do a brand-new Tremblay family documentary. Sort of in the spirit of the one that Claude Jutra made a dozen years ago. You know the one! *La famille Tremblay dans l'hiver*."

"Nobody cares about that documentary anymore."

"You're kidding. That documentary was like . . . I don't know the word . . . classic . . . genius. I watched it every year when they played it at Christmas. It's like eggnog to me. Do you know what I mean?"

"I don't, but you're making me very uncomfortable."

"The way your family interacted. There was so much warmth. And funny! You guys were hysterical. You were like everything that's unique about being Québécois."

They never realized that hundreds of people before them had said just the same thing. People who came up in the supermarket while you were looking at the rows of canned soup would say what giant fans they were of Étienne Tremblay and how some of their fondest memories were of watching us on television at Christmastime.

I started walking down the street. He started following after me, waving his crew along. He had known that Nicolas and I would never cooperate if he asked us in advance. That was why he was outside our door with all the cameras.

"I've been pitching it as an idea for *Le Téléjournal*," Hugo said. He was kind of breathless from having to talk while running after me. "They're looking for a topical hook. But I saw the photo of you on the cover of the newspaper and I thought, The time is now. And if I don't start on this right away, well somebody else will. That would kill me. I've had this idea in my head for years, since film school. It belongs to me."

Someone from the crew hurried in front of us, to film while we were walking. Another girl stuck a boom mic between us from behind.

"What photo are you talking about? Actually, never mind. I don't want to hear about it. I really can't be standing here talking. I've got to get to work."

"Can we film you at work?"

"No!"

"Can I see if Nicolas wants to talk?"

"Are you insane? You can't talk to him. You know this. You must know this!"

"Yeah, I guess I'm a little intimidated by him. Do you think that's crazy?"

I looked at Hugo. He seemed like a nice enough guy. Judging from his pudgy belly, he had never missed a meal in his life. His kind mannerisms implied that he had had a perfectly normal, happy middle-class upbringing. This led me to believe that he couldn't actually handle the Tremblays. He had only seen the Tremblays on television and had no idea what he was getting into. He had never encountered narcissism quite like that embodied by my father. And he certainly had had no prior experience of the sort of hysterical fits that my brother was capable of.

He was after a fairy tale, but there was only tragedy, chaos and squalor behind the doors that he was knocking on.

Every time I said anything, Hugo held a large microphone up to my face. The other members of his crew were following us down the street. It was drawing attention. And despite the fact that I had been recently riding in a convertible and waving wildly at everybody passing by, I suddenly felt a deep, deep need for anonymity.

"Nobody cares about the Tremblays. Everything that there is to say has already been said."

The neighbour was beating her Indian carpet violently with a broom. One of the birds burst off the pattern and flew into the air. It circled around my head and went down the street toward the river. I followed after it and the crew went sadly back to their van.

The first thing you saw when walking into the magazine store where I worked were all the piles of newspapers by the

door. I was on the front page of one of them with my robe
and sceptre. The headline read, NOUSCHKA LEADS SAINT-JEAN-
BAPTISTE CELEBRATION.

The article beneath the photo was about the referendum
that would be held in the next year for Québec to separate. I
hoped people would concentrate on that and never mind me.
I stared at the photograph. There was my face right next to all
the Québécois cinema stars screaming at me from the covers
of magazines. Those guys had so many problems. They had
been molested by their managers. They had been forced to sing
Christmas carols so often that they couldn't enjoy the holiday.
They had had to pass themselves off as twelve for six years in a
row. They had been addicted to cherry bombs. They were wonderful. I wished I hadn't been a minor celebrity, so that I could
enjoy this world like everybody else.

I went behind the cash to await the customers. There were
lucky dollar bills Scotch-taped to the wall, alongside some old
Polaroids of shoplifters from twenty years before. The owner
had stuck photographs of babies under the glass of the counter.
There was a photograph of the owner's four-year-old son dressed
in a suit for a wedding. He looked like a Mafia don.

I had worked there since I dropped out at sixteen. Nicolas
would come into the store all the time and sit on the other side of
the cash, reading *Le Soleil* newspaper. It was one of those newspapers that have articles about alien landings and women who
gave birth to dogs. We had read those since we were little kids.

Porno magazines were a big seller. At first I would get shy
when people asked for them, but eventually I got used to it.
I met millions of people while working there. The men who
stopped by would hit on me and say that I was wasting my time
behind the counter and that I should go to Hollywood and

become a movie star. It made me think that there was a paper-back bestseller that they had all read called something like *1001 Compliments*.

One guy kept pulling quarters out of my ears. He pulled out about four dollars before I told him to knock it off. He was going to pay for his magazine and milk that way.

Today they were bothering me more than usual, buying the newspaper and asking me to autograph the front page.

"Little Nouschka Tremblay! Montréal's sweetheart! What the hell are you doing working in this hellhole? I can't believe it. It's like Brigitte Bardot working the cash at the Supermarché Quatre Frères!"

"Yeah, it's just like that," I answered.

"Shouldn't you be married to a millionaire?"

"The minute one walks in and asks me, I'll say yes."

"Ha, ha, ha. You're funny."

People figured that when you were in the public eye they could walk up to you and say anything that they pleased and you would have to listen and smile, which is what you pretty much ended up doing.

Raphaël walked in without looking at me. I felt like someone had just pulled a fire alarm. My heart started beating like crazy and there was almost a ringing in my head. He was chewing on a toothbrush while flipping through magazines in the rock and roll guitar section. He had a half-smoked cigarette butt behind his ear and a Remembrance Day poppy in his jacket lapel even though it was five months away or seven months ago—I wasn't sure which. Two dogs were on the sidewalk waiting for him. One of the dogs was a good-looking German shepherd. The other was a hound dog that looked like a man who had lost a lot of weight but hadn't had time to buy himself a new wardrobe.

He picked up the newspaper with me on the front cover. He held it up for me to see.

A police officer passing by outside spotted Raphaël and came in. The officer asked Raphaël if he could search him. When Raphaël consented, the officer patted him down and confiscated a doorknob that he was carrying in his pocket for some mysterious reason.

"What is this, a weapon?"

"Actually, it's for opening doors."

"Wise guy."

I was about to go after him down the street when the telephone rang. The phone was covered in stickers advertising restaurants that no longer existed. I walked over to the wall and picked the receiver up. Nicolas was on the other end, yelling.

"Channel ten, motherfucker!"

I hung up the phone and climbed up onto the counter in order to turn on the television that was balanced on a thin metal shelf. A little black cat with white paws fell off the counter and whined. It looked like a boy at a funeral whose suit was too small for him. I glanced down at it for a second until it righted itself and then I flicked on the television.

The news was showing footage of me in the parade. Then it cut away to old footage of us on television talk shows, a "best of" reel. I put my hand over my mouth. We'd been out of the spotlight for a long time and now look what I'd done. There we were, up on the television screen, seven years old and singing for our supper, trying to distract the city from how we had come into this world. I suddenly remembered the film crew and how enraged Nicolas would be if he knew of it.

Our father never cared about anything other than his career. The only time he had any use for Nicolas and me was when we added to his TV performances. Étienne bought me a little black beret to wear and gave me a daisy to hold in my hand. He was going for the look of Faye Dunaway in *Bonnie and Clyde*. Étienne was a master of image manipulation. It was a gift. Or maybe it was a side effect of being one of the most shallow men to walk the face of this earth.

Étienne would get me to read a poem that I had written. The audience would ooh and aah, and sometimes they would laugh their heads off. Delightful, how delightful, talent certainly runs in the family.

But Nicolas often refused to go on. He was unpredictable. Once he styled his hair with Crisco at the last minute and nobody could get it out. Once he went on wearing a T-shirt that he had custom-made himself, with lightning bolts on it. Once he said he would only go if he could demonstrate his karate moves and be given six Milky Way bars. Étienne could tell right away that Nicolas was too difficult to work with and stopped having him on after a while.

Nicolas would give long-winded answers to the interviewers that would break off into lies and silly flights of fancy. He liked to complain about all sorts of things. The audience would go wild when he complained about how our gym teacher made us do running backward laps. Nicolas thought they were all beneath him, laughing at his idiotic jokes.

"I would like to either drive a snowplow or be a politician," Nicolas said.

"And what does a politician do?"

"They meet with the foreign ambassadors. They make it so that Québec can be our own country. I think that will be a very good thing because we will make our own laws."

Nicolas became a favourite with separatists because of the

opinions that he voiced when he was seven. René Lévesque quoted a line from one of my poems in a speech on Québec separatism and then we were immortal.

Back in the seventies, Étienne thought that if Québec separated from Canada, it would infuse his career with new life. He thought that he would be able to write the new national anthem. He spent weeks working on a victory song. People would stand in the streets and sing his song the day after the referendum. It would be the first song to be sung in a free Québec.

But we didn't separate. And then the next year, Étienne got arrested for having an affair with a fourteen-year-old girl named Marilou, who was round and plump and blond like a baby and who nobody on earth could resist. She was on the front page of the newspaper. She was trying to parlay the scandal into a modelling career. She ended up in a root-beer commercial and Étienne had to serve eight months in prison.

Chapter 11

Papillon

THE NEXT MORNING, WHEN I WENT INTO THE kitchen, I saw that Nicolas had cut out the photograph of me from the front page of the newspaper and had stuck it up on the fridge with magnets on every corner. He had written, "Bravo! Bravo! Bravo!" all around the photograph.

I knew that the crew would for sure be going to see Étienne. My father would not turn his back on them. He would be ecstatic and want to expound all his ridiculous thoughts until the tape ran out. He would show them baby photos of us if he had them, but I was quite sure that he did not.

I was distracted from these thoughts as the day unfolded. Something much more interesting happened. I saw Raphaël three times that day.

In the morning, as I was about to leave the lobby of my apartment, I noticed him through the glass door, sitting on the front stoop of his mother's building. He looked like he hadn't washed his hair, because it stuck straight up above his head. He was wearing a suit jacket but no shirt underneath and purple track pants with yellow piping down the sides. He had a pit bull that was carrying a Cabbage Patch doll in its mouth. The dog had a face like a fist. It would put the doll down for a moment and bark like someone trying to plunge a toilet.

I moved out of the way to let an exterminator pass. He was there to see about an infestation. A puzzle box had spilled and the pieces were multiplying and living in all the cracks. I pushed on the door, trying to open it, even though I was supposed to pull on it. I had no idea how something like this was possible since I had lived in the same building my whole life. I felt so self-conscious when Raphaël was around that my IQ dropped a hundred points.

As soon as I turned the corner, I took a pocket mirror out of my purse to make sure that I had looked all right. What the hell? I thought to myself. I had never felt that anxious around a boy before.

Then, in the afternoon I saw him at the grocery store with a white Pomeranian that had a face like a chewed-up toothbrush. The small dog was sitting in the part of the grocery cart where you ordinarily put a baby. The dog was trembling with excitement, wanting to hop up, like he was waiting to add a detail to your anecdote.

Raphaël was wearing enormous sunglasses. Nobody in the store would dare say anything to Raphaël about having a dog in a place where you sell food. He opened a bottle of beer while in line at the cash and drank it while flipping through a magazine about homes and gardens. They just wanted him to get in and out of the store as quickly as possible. It was hard to imagine what would happen with a guy who looked like that, if he was provoked. There was this feeling of an electrical storm everywhere he went.

Then, after work I saw him at the Portuguese café. He was drinking a cup of coffee and reading *Papillon*. You came out of prison incredibly buff or with an addiction to paperback novels. Raphaël would buy paperbacks that the homeless people were selling for fifty cents each on the street corner. He walked down the street with paper bags filled with books like groceries.

I got two cups of coffee to bring home, one for me and one for Nicolas. I looked over at Raphaël again while I was in line, and he was scribbling on the front page of his book. He got up to leave and left the book lying on the table. After I watched him leave, I went over and picked it up. I opened up the book and read the inscription: "If a broken fool with broken teeth and broken tonsils were to go all the way out of his way to say hello to her, what on earth would she say back, I wonder?"

I slapped the cover of the book down, startled, as if I had just opened up the door on someone changing and quickly closed it.

Was that a message for me? It had to be. I looked at the book cover, which was a photograph of a hard-ass dude with a butterfly tattooed on his chest. He refused to tell me no matter how I begged.

CHAPTER 12

Good Morning, Nouschka Tremblay!

I HATED BEING WOKEN UP BY THE NEWS ON THE clock radio. I always meant to change the station to one that only played music. But I hadn't gotten around to it, although I had been meaning to do it for three years now. My laziness was astonishing sometimes. I lay there listening to the voice speaking.

"A chansonnier is different from a rock and roll singer because he is also a poet, he is also a philosopher, he is also a medium through which the people are able to voice their own fables, their own fears, their time and zeitgeist. That's why Étienne Tremblay was so important for the separatist cause."

I felt watery all of a sudden, as if I had been turned into a puddle on the bed. It took me a few seconds to realize that they were talking about us on the radio. My body always seemed to realize it first.

"Tremblay's luck changed the day after the 1980 referendum."

"Yes, that's true," another voice said. "While he was in prison, his manager, who was also his on and off girlfriend, took whatever was left of his money. He signed these terrible contracts that a lot of musicians signed in the sixties and seventies that saw them getting nothing for their work. Really just pennies when their songs are played on the radio."

"What will your documentary tell us that we don't already know?"

"I'm focusing on the entire Tremblay family. Because for a long time they sort of represented the beauty of Québécois culture—the warmness of it. And we grew up with them. When I watched the documentary as a kid, I wanted to change my last name and go and join their family. Who didn't want to be raised by Étienne Tremblay? It just seemed so magical. He would sing to you while he scrambled up eggs in the morning."

I recognized the voice of none other than Hugo Vaillancourt, that documentarian who had followed me down the street the other day.

"Have the Tremblays gotten it together at all? What I mean to say is, do you find this to be an optimistic documentary? Do you think that the family will sort of come out of the funk that they've fallen into and see brighter days?"

"Goodness no. No! We are witnessing the downfall of an era. These aren't the right times for dreamers. The Tremblays as a family were invented by the subconscious of a people prior to the first referendum. They are a direct result of a revolutionary, surrealist, visionary zeitgeist. They are wandering around now like animals whose habitats have been destroyed."

I switched off the radio and buried my head under a pillow. A cat peeped in the window. It had one white paw. One night it had decided to dip it into the reflection of the moon in a fountain to see what would happen.

The doorbell began buzzing. I didn't know where Nicolas was and Loulou was too deaf to hear it. I put on a tiny orange

kimono that had seen better days and ran to get the door. When
I opened it, a little old woman from one of the apartments
upstairs was standing there.

"Nouschka, they're talking about you and your family on
Radio-Canada." She said it in a very concerned way, as if it were
something that I really needed to know about, as if she had
smelled smoke coming from the apartment.

"*Merci, merci, merci*, Madame Choquette," I said.

Then I slammed the door. I didn't even get down the hallway when somebody else rang the buzzer.

"Go away!" I screamed.

I never thought that Hugo would get any funding for this
documentary or that it would actually happen. Occasionally
someone would say they were going to write a book or make a
film about Étienne, but in the past ten years, nothing had ever
come of them.

There was a pounding on the window. I pulled the curtain
aside to yell at whoever was there. It was Nicolas. Instead he
was ready to yell at me.

"This is so you, baby. You started this with your beauty
queen stuff."

"Oh, so what. So they're making a documentary. How bad
can it be?"

I didn't regret the pageant because it had brought Raphaël
into my store. Everything thrilling in life had its costs.

"They can edit it to make us look like total assholes. They
have degrees in how to make everybody look like assholes.
They'll capture us as we really are this time. Mark my words.
Mark my words, Nouschka. You do some very embarrassing
stuff that you might not want documented."

Adam's head suddenly popped into the window frame, next
to Nicolas, like someone unwanted trying to make it into a

photograph. They were both drinking coffee out of paper cups with silhouettes of bullfighters on them. It was coffee from the Portuguese place and it always made Nicolas completely insane. Coffee from there was like crack for Nicolas.

A kid we knew walked by with a boom box on his shoulder.

"Hey, are they looking for actors?"

"No, it's a documentary," Nicolas said, shooing the boy away. "Come on. Don't be so stupid so early in the morning."

"I think it's exciting," Adam said. "You should require it to be in black and white. It's always more beautiful that way."

"It's hard enough being a goddamn criminal without a documentary crew following you around."

"I always hear people bitching about that," I said.

"I know, right?"

We both started laughing. The kid with the boom box met up with someone on a bench. They turned the ghetto blaster way up.

"You think I care whether anybody anywhere knows anything about me? Then you don't know a thing about me. Look at how little I give a damn!" He started doing his crazy moves. People always gathered around to watch Nicolas dance. He suddenly got all loose and then all stiff. If you wanted to see what joy looked like, you only had to look at Nicolas dancing. He started doing a disco move, reaching his right hand down practically to his left foot and then stretching it back up into the opposite direction to the sky.

"You really shouldn't let my brother drink espresso," I told Adam.

"I have learned that the hard way."

I felt less anxious all of a sudden. The worst of it was over. He had found out and here he was dancing in the street.

CHAPTER 13

The Lazy-Day Revolution

ADAM LOVED THE ATTENTION WE WERE GETTING. Adam had every intention of being on the news when he got older. He hadn't figured out what he was going to be famous for. At one point about a year ago, when they first met, Adam and Nicolas had formed their own political party. It was called The People's People Party. Now they crawled in the apartment window with some posters of themselves that they had made at the photocopy store and were going to put up. Nicolas had suggested that they deface them with moustaches before they put them up around town. I had finished getting dressed when they held the posters up for me to see. They had combed their hair to the side and had these fake serious looks. This amused them to no end.

"We actually look really good as politicians," Nicolas said. "Do you think that politicians attract a lot of ladies?"

"No," I said. "You can't sleep with anyone or do drugs, or they do an exposé on the news."

"That sucks. What man doesn't like a crack pipe and a

couple underage girls after a hard day of campaigning about public schools?"

"That's the problem with the world today," Adam stated. "You can't reap any rewards."

"This is the stupidest political party ever," I said. "You're going to add crack and whores to civil liberties."

"Give me liberty or give me death," Adam said.

"It's beautiful in its simplicity," Nicolas added, nodding.

"Let's go campaigning for our revolutionary party today!" Adam cried. "All we ever do is talk about it."

"All right," said Nicolas. "Let me go take a crap and then borrow a car."

So far, their revolutionary tactics had largely been confined to soliciting sex from women who were obviously middle-class and clearly not prostitutes. Adam had been questioned by the police a couple times, but they always let him go. They could tell from his manner that he was an upper-class kid. Rich people weren't responsible for petty crimes. They were responsible for the great crimes that took hundreds of years to commit and were, therefore, unpunishable.

Nicolas came back twenty minutes later. He was wearing a pair of giant old-lady glasses.

"These are my counter-revolutionary glasses," he said.

"*Counter-revolutionary* means you're against the revolution," I said.

"Are you sure about that?"

"Look it up in the dictionary."

"The dictionary is obsolete," Nicolas said. "They don't even have the definition of *cocksucker* in it. Our first act of government will be the public execution of René Simard."

"Why? Just because you don't like him?"

"His music ruined my childhood."

"I thought your first act was going to be banning soccer."

"I have to wait awhile for that one. There are some soccer fans out there."

Nicolas was mad at soccer in general because he had been kicked off the team in Grade Eight for showing up late. He was going to be an irrational dictator. He had also suggested banning fanny packs because he thought they were ugly.

We whistled when we saw the car parked outside the building. Low-lifes sometimes hung around old people for pocket money and their cars. You'd see these junkies driving old Coupe de Villes and wearing alligator shoes. Nicolas borrowed a Cadillac from an old lady he claimed was named Madame Prèsdelamort. In exchange, he would sit with her at the doctor's office and repeat what the doctor had just said, but louder.

"You likey?" Nicolas asked.

"You look like a seventies cocaine dealer."

"A seventies porn star. Porn stars from the seventies used to live in this area and bought a lot of the buildings. But then they got older and impotent and got laid off. So they couldn't afford the upkeep. That's why this whole area is actually falling into total disrepair."

"Where do you get this stuff?" I demanded.

"A lot of Québécois do well as porn stars. It's because we all have really big dicks."

For some reason Adam and I laughed at that ridiculous joke. We were going to be laughing a lot that afternoon. I could feel it. I looked at my first pile of homework on the floor next to the bed, which I was supposed to finish. I had promised myself that I would be really diligent about it, unlike when I had originally gone to school. I decided that I could put it aside just once.

We were dressed in the way that only nineteen-year-olds can dress. I had on a blue shirt that tied behind my neck and a silver skirt that stuck out like a tutu and black cowboy boots with purple stars on them. Nicolas had on a pink velour jacket over a yellow T-shirt that had a drawing of a panda bear on it and purple track pants with green stripes down the sides. Adam had red sweatpants that were cut off just below the knees and a light blue dress shirt that had been washed about two thousand times and was threadbare. Adam was also wearing his suit jacket and tie.

Nicolas got into the driver's seat. I scooted into the middle and Adam got into the passenger seat after me. The car kept jerking wildly because Nicolas was having trouble with the enormous stick shift.

Once we got onto the road, we bounced along like crazy. The shocks in the car were terrible. All the streets in Montréal were always all broken up from potholes because of the long winters. If you were drinking coffee, it ended up going all over your lap. Children would sometimes get carsick just going three blocks. We were pleased with ourselves. We thought that we must have looked like gunmen who were riding into a town on the Western frontier with prices on our heads and there wasn't a damn thing that anybody could do about it.

I can't remember who suggested that we head toward our old elementary school. It had to have been Nicolas. The school was a giant brick building with gargoyles of twenties schoolchildren over all the doors. There were cages on all the windows.

We had hated school so much. Just being near it filled us with a horrible feeling. The teachers were always chastising us for not having our gym clothes or school fees. Loulou was too old to be on top of anything.

We parked right outside the schoolyard fence. It was lunch-time and the sound of children was almost as deafening as the ocean. School was out, but they all went there for day camp. They were singing their skipping-rope tunes—wee tunes of resistance that had been passed down from one class to another. They were probably singing Étienne's skipping-rope song:

I skipped out on my education
I was too smart for school
I skipped out on my bill payments
I was too cheap for those
I skipped out on my landlord
There were roaches in the sink
I skipped out on my court date
I have no time for prison
I skipped out on my woman
But she came and dragged me back
It's been one year, two years, three years . . .

Adam reached over me to the back seat and grabbed a bull-horn from off the seat. I couldn't even imagine where they had got it. But Nicolas and Adam were the type of boys that made friends easily and they were both thieves, so just about anything could appear in the back of the car or out of their pockets.

"Time to disseminate some knowledge," Adam said matter-of-factly.

We opened the sunroof. Adam stood on the seat with his bullhorn.

"Your teacher cannot search your locker without a warrant. Your teachers are part of a systematized, codified attempt to lower your self-esteem."

I was amazed that he could get these statements out without cracking up. We would never have been able to do that in a million years. Nicolas used to start laughing while ordering a loaf of pumpernickel bread because the woman who worked there had a picture of the pope on her kerchief.

"You are sheep. Your brains are being fattened for the slaughter! They are teaching you lies! Lies!"

The children all started gathering at the fence like fish trapped in a net. Their buttons were in the wrong holes and the backs of their skirts were tucked into their underwear. Children their age were in awe of teenagers. We inhabited a brief period of time during which we mocked all authority and we could get away with anything. We were screaming and yelling as we gave birth to a new generation. They hung on to the gates, staring up at us, utterly transfixed. I stood up, stepping onto Nicolas's bent leg like it was a footstool.

"My dick, Nouschka! My dick!" he yelled.

Adam handed me the bullhorn.

"Only prisoners are forced to line up," I cried. "You have been imprisoned without due process of a trial. You have committed no crime."

"Do not fear your hallway monitor," Adam yelled. "He doesn't actually exist. Just like the boogeyman. If you stop believing in him, he will disappear."

The children started screaming and yelling. Finally, finally there was some chaos in their lives. We had showed up like summertime. Their applause sounded like a forest fire.

"You are not alone in your struggle. All over the city, children are rising up to plan a revolt. Arm yourself. You have a constitutional right to bear arms."

Nicolas stood up and squeezed in next to Adam. He took the bullhorn from him and held it to his own mouth.

"Bring us the principal! I want Mr. Edery!" Nicolas yelled.

The principal was obviously on holiday, but the summer camp monitors came running toward us. They looked terrified, as if we were rabid dogs. They were waving their arms around in the air. One was blowing his whistle like it had some sort of supernatural power. An overweight counsellor with greying hair came outside the schoolyard and lumbered toward us as if he had just attached his legs.

Adam and Nicolas dropped back into their seats. We jolted back and forth a bit while Nicolas screamed hysterically, trying to figure out the stick shift, and then we sped away. Adam put his arm around me. It made me happy and I was in love with him. Or I was having such a good time that I mistook this good time for love. When you're nineteen, almost every day is a day of wine and roses.

"Do you think they called the police?" I asked.

"Who gives a shit?" Nicolas said. "I have dirt on all those teachers. At least eight of them molested me."

"No, they did not!" I screamed in laughter.

*****

The sun was going down. The pink clouds in the sky were delicates soaking in the sink. We were parked on Boulevard Saint-Laurent, crammed in the front seat, eating Vietnamese takeout, romantic poets having a rest after a good day of making asses out of ourselves.

Adam turned on the radio. It was the same interview from the morning. They played the news on a loop unless something new happened during the day, and apparently nothing had.

"I can't believe it!" Nicolas exclaimed.

The interview came to an end. They put on one of Étienne's recordings where he just talks while his musicians play behind him.

"Do you ever think about how weird it is that this guy is your dad?"

"Étienne's a jackass," said Nicolas. "He's not really our dad. Who gives a shit about Étienne Tremblay? Why are they playing these shitty songs? I'm going to write one myself about a guy whose wife cheats on him with the Hydro guy. I can't stand his average-Joe business."

My dad was drunk. He had just come home from a fight with the boss. He asked the boss for a raise, but the boss said no! So he came home and made love to my mother, Josephine.

I was conceived on a Thursday night!

I was born in a saucepan. My mother was cooking up a big frying pan of gravy. And she gave birth to me without turning away from the pan. I fell smack onto the kitchen floor. I lay there with the family dogs looking at me.

Étienne had a deep and gravelly voice. I felt his breath against my face as his words got louder.

Everyone expected me to pick up scrap metal like my dad. Or to go on welfare. We never had a book in the house, but I wanted to be a poet.

The funny thing was that I forgot for a second that it was Étienne who was giving the speech and I got goosebumps all over my arms. I always liked his political ruminations. It made me happy just like everyone else who was listening to his ranting in their kitchens. Unlike Nicolas, I was able to enjoy Étienne Tremblay even if he'd completely neglected us as children.

"Wonderful," said Adam. "He's wonderful and you guys are wonderful."

"What are you going to do once we separate, Adam?" Nicolas said. "You'll be exiled, that's for sure. An English lawyer—ridiculous. I can't imagine why any English person would bother staying in Montréal. You'll have to leave with the rest of the exodus."

That remark stung Adam. He wanted to be one of us, but there were just so many ways in which he was different.

One of these wretched black cats that looked as if they'd been struck by lightning one night and were now perpetually crooked walked by. His thoughts were broken things. The cat was looking at the sunset. Who ever believed in such a pink? Such a pink was terrifying even for grown men to look up at. It was terrifying to have the responsibility of living in a world that was filled with so much wonder.

CHAPTER 14

All the Best-Looking Girls Are Crazy

I HAD TO MEET SASKIA AND PICK UP PIERROT. I was the go-between for Nicolas and Saskia. They would lash out at each other for days after meeting. I didn't like being in this position. She was the only person in the whole world who would dare to trash-talk Nicolas around me. She knew I had to sit and listen to it in order to get an afternoon with Pierrot.

They were in the park. White round petals were all over the ground as if the polka dots had fallen off a woman's dress. Saskia hadn't even put enough clothes on Pierrot really. He was wearing an undershirt with characters from the children's show *Passe-Partout* and jeans with butterflies on the knees and flip-flops. Saskia was wearing a T-shirt that had rows of moustaches on it and jean shorts. Her hair was gelled back so tightly that it seemed painted on. Her ponytail was made into ringlets that looked like telephone cords. She and Pierrot were eating chocolate ice cream cones.

"I don't know if Nicolas is the one. I ask myself that over and over again. I want all sorts of things. My mother didn't give me anything. I'm not talking about she didn't buy me cars or a fancy gold suit. She didn't give me any manners. She never told me to stay in school. She never told me not to have sex. Look at me now."

"I think you're beautiful."

"What do you see in that ugly Russian guy Misha? How could you suck his dick? I could understand if he was a millionaire and you do it for lots and lots of money. But he has nothing. His skin is bad too."

Pierrot was kicking his legs back and forth, not really listening to us.

"I'm not seeing Misha anymore," I said. "But you know, he wrote poetry all the time. You could get him a pencil and a piece of paper and a blindfold and he would write you a poem. You could give him any subject."

"Even my mother never dated a guy that ugly."

"He played the French horn and I like music."

"I want to marry a millionaire. I want to take some fertility drugs so that I can have triplets with a millionaire."

"Nicolas will never be a millionaire."

Saskia glared at me. No matter what she said about Nicolas, she had apparently not quite given up on her illusion that he could make her filthy rich somehow.

Nicolas had only had a couple of serious girlfriends. The first was a girl named Maude, but she wanted everyone to call her Jessica. She always had these wonderfully perverted stories. She had a best friend who had had sex with a German shepherd. She had big black eyes, giant pouty lips and a faint dark moustache. Her head was too big for her skinny body. She wore boys' undershirts with no bra. She drank beer and wore a navy blue pea jacket from a vintage store and cut her hair short and tucked it behind her ears. I thought she looked a bit like Mick Jagger and I had never seen anyone so beautiful.

Then Nicolas met Saskia. We'd both known Saskia in high school. She had just immigrated from Czechoslovakia with her mother. Saskia wore a red acrylic sweater with patterns of white chess pieces on it to school every day. She always tied her scarf around her waist instead of her neck. Saskia's face always reminded me of a boiled egg because it was so round and pale. It was a very Eastern European–looking face. If you found this look attractive, then she was drop-dead gorgeous. If you didn't, then she wasn't.

Nicolas and I ran into her at the swimming pool one day. She had on a white bikini and we noticed at the same time that she had huge breasts and was a bona fide fox. It was a shame, I remembered thinking. I thought that if she had stayed in Czechoslovakia, she might have been a movie star. She would have married a high-ranking Communist. Instead she ended up in Montréal with a bath towel wrapped around her waist, making out with Nicolas up against a chain-link fence until the lifeguard blew the whistle at them.

She sounded like a man when she sang. The first time I heard her singing along to the radio when she was over one day, I didn't like it, but it grew on me. We liked the way Saskia sang Michael Jackson songs. Her accent made any rock and roll song that she sang seem like a strange ditty about the war. As if she was on the back of a truck with a goose on her lap and a machine gun hidden in a basket with loaves of bread. She worked as a checkout girl and housewives were terrified by her accent.

Nicolas for some reason—maybe because she was the only girl who wasn't wildly in love with him—was mad about Saskia. He got Saskia to go out with him by promising that he could get her a record deal through his dad's contacts. She was an ambitious, clueless lunatic. They had broken up twelve times and got back together before she got pregnant. They named their son Pierrot because of how he looked in a little black cotton hat that someone had given them as a present.

Pierrot was a typical kid of a single parent. He always seemed frazzled. He acted like he had just stepped off a school bus and realized that he'd left his lunch box on it.

As I sat next to her, Saskia started doing her makeup on the bench. She drew black Cleopatra lines around her eyes. Pierrot looked straight ahead sadly. They had fallen out of love with Nicolas, but I never could.

"Do you have my money? Jesus Christ."

I gave her every cent that Nicolas and I had, which unfortunately came to seventy-three dollars. He owed her about two thousand. I then asked her if she could actually give me back three dollars.

"You guys are pathetic."

"I know. I know. But Nicolas really wants to see Pierrot. It's driving him crazy."

"I'm going to take Nicolas to court for the back payments. Will you tell him this?"

"Yes, of course. Of course."

"Life, it is not a joke."

＊＊＊＊＊

After I handed over the money, Saskia let me take Pierrot off to see Nicolas. To make the afternoon special, Nicolas let Pierrot ride the mechanical deer that rocked back and forth outside the supermarket. Every time the deer gave any sign of letting up,

Nicolas would drop in another quarter until all his change was gone. Pierrot ended up nauseated and sitting on the curb with his head between his legs.

He'd slipped into one of his quagmires and there was nothing we could do to pull him out. He sat on the bench between us as we tried to cheer him up.

"Would you like me to tell you a story about a lion who loses all his mane?" I asked Pierrot.

"It is a book to help children cope with Papa losing his hair?" Nicolas said gloomily.

"Don't you remember that storybook?" I asked.

"I'd rather kill myself than go bald."

"You'd look good with a toupée."

"Would you, Pierrot, would you like to hear the story about a lion?"

"No, I don't like lions. They scare me." Pierrot shook his whole little body to show his disgust even with the idea of lions.

"Don't be ridiculous," Nicolas yelled. "We're not in Africa. When are you going to meet up with a lion?"

"I saw them at the zoo. They were eating bloody meat."

"Well, that is fucking disgusting, granted."

"Do you want to hear a story about a wee mouse who hangs around with Benjamin Franklin and discovers electricity?"

"I remember that movie. *Le Journal de Montréal* gave it one star."

"Pierrot, sweetheart, would you like to hear the story of a car named Herbie that could talk?"

"Don't even get me started on Herbie. He couldn't talk. He honked his horn. My friend has a horn that beeps when he doesn't push it. I don't see anyone making a movie about his car."

"Are you finished?"

"I'm just saying, you can only go so far, psychologically speaking, when you're dealing with a car."

"How about the story of Benji? Tell him a story about Benji saving the day."

"Stop polluting his head with that American shit. Benji never fucking saved the day. What are you talking about?"

"Didn't he prevent the Russians from developing the atom bomb first?"

"Are you drunk?"

"Benji saves the day. That's the point."

"Tell him the adventures of Snap, Crackle and Pop. Tell him how they saved the day. Making some noise in a bowl of cereal."

"Don't be stupid. What about the three little kittens who lose their mittens?"

"Sounds riveting. I'm surprised they haven't turned that into an opera. What happens to them after they lose their mittens?"

"Their mother gets upset."

"Oh fuck, Nouschka, you had to go and mention his mother. We're trying to get off that subject." Nicolas glared at me. Sure enough, Pierrot sat with a huge frown on his face and tears streaming down his cheeks. He always wanted to go back to his mother's house, where everything was done in the way he liked it. I could tell that Nicolas felt utterly rejected by his son.

I held Pierrot's hand as I walked him home. He kept looking in the opposite direction, as if he had no idea that anyone was holding his hand. He ran into his apartment without even saying goodbye. Sweet Pierrot Tremblay, the saddest boy in all the world, was not buying what we were selling. We still lived at home, in a tiny kingdom that we had spent years building. But it was so poorly defended that these days a four-year-old could take it down with a wooden sword.

CHAPTER 15

Pour Iodine on My Knees
and Call Me Sweetheart

Y̲OU COULD ONLY TAKE ONE HOT BATH A DAY IN
our apartment because it took twenty-four hours for the tank to
fill up again. I was in the bath Saturday morning about a month
after the parade. My nylons were hanging from the shower
rod by their tippytoes. Adam came in and started taking off his
clothes.

"What are you doing?" I asked.

"I'm going to be a great philosopher one day, Little
Nouschka Tremblay."

"There's a very fine line between being a person who
changes the way that his contemporaries think and being an
idiot with bad hair and an unpublished manifesto."

"That's funny! And you shall be famous too!"

He climbed in with me. We were sitting in the bathtub with
our knees pressing against each other.

"Just because you're in the bathtub with me, don't get any

funny ideas. It doesn't mean that I'm your girlfriend or anything like that."

"Did you and Nicolas used to take baths together?"

"We didn't have a mother, okay?"

"Neither did I, really. I spent most of my time with my
nanny."

"Still, you had one. Mine was just Val-des-Loups trash."

"That's terrible. Your mother was Lily Sainte-Marie! I like
that song."

We both started singing it.

I bought her a drink and she threw up on my shoes
I took her out dancing, but she was too young to get into the
    club
I bought her a book of poetry, but she didn't like to read
Lily Sainte-Marie!
Her hands were always dirty
Lily Sainte-Marie, the first pretty girl born in Val-des-
    Loups since 1883.

Adam got out of the bath, tied a towel around his waist and
started combing his hair straight up. He considered his blond
hair to be one of the natural wonders of the world. When he
was done, he looked like someone who would give bad advice to
the dauphin at the French court. I drained the bath and was sitting on the toilet lid in my underclothes, painting my toenails.

Nicolas walked into the bathroom. He leaned against the
wall next to the medicine cabinet, wanting to hear what we were
talking about, I guess. It was amazing that we could all squeeze
in there.

"Do you know that my nanny always turned off the radio

when Lily Sainte-Marie came on?" Adam said. "She said it was the saddest song in the world. I never got why that song made her cry. I thought it was funny."

"What was she like?" Nicolas asked suddenly.

"My nanny?"

"Yeah, what was she like?"

"She was really shy. She hated having to order meat at the meat counter. She used to collect the labels off of wine bottles and paste them into a book. She asked if she could have a cat. She always played the lottery. She had bumblebee patches on her jeans."

"What else?"

"If I had a tiny scratch on my knee, she would cover my entire leg with iodine so it was completely orange. She liked canned spaghetti."

"Was she beautiful?"

"No."

It was an awfully strange question to ask. I looked over at Nicolas. He looked oddly focused. He usually got impatient when anyone rattled on about anything, because he was anxious to be the one doing all the talking.

"You couldn't even really see what she looked like. She wore her bangs down in her face."

"Well, you were very lucky to have a nanny, weren't you? Wouldn't it be possible that without her, you would have walked into the street and been hit by a car? I was hit by a bus when I was five and I broke my arm. I could've used a nanny that day. Singing her cheery songs."

Adam and I were both stunned. I had never heard him turn on Adam that way.

"What are you so angry about?" I asked.

*****

When we were about eleven, Nicolas and I used to sometimes speculate on the whereabouts of our mother. We didn't talk about it in the house because we didn't want to upset Loulou. But it would pass the time as we walked to school.

We understood why she had left us. We had seen enough after-school specials to know that it was because she had been too young to take care of us. But we couldn't figure out why she wouldn't come back for us now. She was older and we weren't babies and we were able to do so many things by ourselves. We got dressed on our own and rode the metro everywhere.

Once, we decided that she was in medical school in Poland. We imagined her weeping as she did tests on white mice. And when she was finally a doctor, she would come back for us. We imagined her removing our tonsils and then giving us little bowls of Jell-O for dinner.

Sometimes we would look into the mailbox, just peeping, just hoping that there would be a note from our mother in there, something that would give us a clue about where she might be and that would give us a more concrete idea about what was keeping her away. But then as we got older, we just figured that she didn't want to come back. She was happy with her life, wherever it was. I tried to accept this, but Nicolas never did.

CHAPTER 16

Your House Is on Fire,
Your Children Are Burning

I WAS ON MY WAY TO SCHOOL. PIGEONS SHIFTED back and forth from one foot to the other, like old ladies with bags of heavy groceries in either hand. I was dressed up for class. I had a vinyl jacket with a horse on it and a pink dress shirt with a butterfly collar. I had a grey skirt and Wallabees. I thought I looked like the most no-nonsense girl on the planet.

I walked by a store that sold religious statues mostly to put in your front lawn. They were all crowded in the window. Some were on boxes and chairs in the back row. They were like people watching a parade. I felt peaceful looking at them. It was like they had all gathered to look at me and that the world just had to be full of grace.

I turned when I heard a car honk its horn. Nicolas leaned way out the window in order to talk to me as he was driving. He had on a polyester shirt with a print of buildings on it with the suit jacket he'd bought at the Salvation Army. His jacket was completely covered in cat hair.

"Hey, can you come check out this house with me?"

"No, you can see perfectly well that I'm busy."

"I want to see something. What, are you a snob now? You think that you're too good to spend the afternoon with me? I'm sorry, does Miss Boulevard Saint-Laurent have some sort of contractual obligation to fulfill? Will they take your plastic tiara away? Your free coupon for a meal at le Palais de Bombay? Have you used up your discount coupons for the amusement park? You know they sell those tiaras five for a dollar at the pharmacy."

Nicolas suddenly drove the car up onto the sidewalk, trying to run me over. I jumped backward, sticking my hands out in front of me as if to stop the car. I was startled.

"Get in the car, Nouschka," he said.

I took off running down the street. He jumped out of the car, which was half on the sidewalk, and ran after me. I was screaming at people who I passed on the street for them to call the police. Naturally nobody did anything. They knew to keep out of it. He grabbed me from behind.

I screamed and he held me against the wall. He was wearing a pair of pyjama bottoms with sharks on them. He was dragging me back to the car. One of my shoes came off. I was going to miss my class now.

My purse flipped upside down and my cue cards for my oral report spilled out and fell all over the ground. He wouldn't let me pick them up. I picked one out of a puddle with the tips of my fingers. When I bent down, he grabbed me from behind. This really enraged me.

"Why don't you help me?" I asked people passing by.

A man slowed down as he was passing us. He had a concerned look on his face, and he seemed to be thinking about stepping in.

"Don't try and interfere with me, sir, or you and she and everyone will end up dead. She's my sister. You don't want to get involved in this. It's been going on since we were born."

The man walked away, looking over his shoulder every few seconds. He was out of our hair, but then a police officer pulled over in front of our car. Nicolas was playing with fire because he was on probation for demanding that a librarian hand over the money she had collected in fines that day. We both sort of stopped moving as the officer came up to us. He was middle-aged, with greying hair, barrel-chested and intimidating. He didn't faze Nicolas in the least.

"Officer, she's mentally ill. You see, we were born as Siamese twins and I got the brain. I have to make all the decisions for both of us, on account of her faculties being so deficient."

"I'm a writer," I said in my defence. Even though I hadn't written a word.

"I don't care what either of you are," said the officer. "You're going to knock it right off."

The officer grabbed Nicolas by the shoulder, firmly. Nicolas let go of me and swung around to face the officer.

"She won a beauty pageant and it went to her head. She couldn't handle success. She expected us to bring her breakfast in bed after that."

"I'm sick of you bringing up that contest. Are you jealous?"

"Jealous! Officer, after she won there was a criminal investigation. It just didn't make sense."

"You two look familiar to me," he said.

"You saw him at the zoo," I said. "He reminds you of someone from the monkey exhibition."

"Are you two Étienne Tremblay's kids?"

We both stopped horsing around.

"I used to love you guys on television," he said.

He went and picked up my Wallabee and handed it to me. We smiled uneasily. We both walked over to Nicolas's car and got in it. We pulled away from the curb, Nicolas waving to the police officer to show that we were respectable and upstanding citizens.

As the gears shifted, so too did our spirits. It was amazing how fast our moods changed at that age. Two minutes before, I had wanted to kill Nicolas, and now we were two thieves on the lam who had outsmarted the law once again! But I was still slightly depressed and couldn't really feel good about being in the car.

We headed over the highway to the west side of town. The car picked up speed. I was worried; it felt like the bottom might fall right out. It was probably better easing down narrow rickety east-end streets, where you had to stop every couple minutes for a passing alley cat.

We turned off the highway and drove into a residential neighbourhood, down a street that was covered in huge trees that came together over the road and blocked out the sun.

There were identical houses on either side of the street. All the lawns were clean and all the cars were new. We parked in front of a red and orange brick house with light blue shutters. He was quiet finally. We just sat and looked at it. I was afraid to ask. I figured he was casing the place for some sort of robbery. In which case, sitting in front of it in broad daylight in the crappiest car in the city didn't seem like the most brilliant idea. Nicolas's knees were bouncing up and down and he was fluttering his fingers up and down on the steering wheel.

"What the hell are we doing here?" I asked.

"Forget it," he said. "I can't say it because it's something you ought to know about gradually. The shock of it might turn your hair grey."

"What? Say it or I'll kill you."

"I found our mother."

"Lily Sainte-Marie!"

"Noëlle Renaud."

I was suddenly afraid. I did not want our world turned upside down. I did not want to have any actual information about our mother.

"Oh, Nicolas. Leave her alone."

"I think we should meet her."

"You just go and stare at her every day?"

"Hey, you've got to stalk somebody."

"No, actually. You don't. I don't want to see her. I feel lousy. I don't even feel like myself. I feel shitty all of a sudden. It's like I have stomach cancer. I just want to go home. I feel like I'm disappearing. Oh, my stomach. Nicolas! Drive me back home. I don't feel well at all."

He put his hand over my mouth while looking straight ahead. It was five-thirty and she was coming home from work. She was dressed in a beige suit and comfortable white pumps. Her hair was dyed light brown and she wore her bangs in her face. She had nothing in common with Étienne.

We got out of the car. She saw us. We could tell from the look on her face that she knew exactly who we were. She looked uncomfortable. She looked nervous. Actually, she looked terrified. We were both quiet. We didn't even want to speak for fear that she would disappear. We got quiet the way you get quiet when you see an animal emerge from out of the woods. You know that the minute it notices your presence, it's going to bolt.

"Hello," she said. "Wow. What are you doing here?"

"We wanted to just say hello," Nicolas said softly.

"Hello," she said. "Do you live around here?"

"No."

"You two look so much like Étienne."

We just nodded. Lily looked around her. She looked up, as if to see if there was a helicopter up above that was going to lower a ladder down to her. We had probably popped up again and again in her dreams. But now, lo and behold, here we were on her lawn. I guess it was natural that she was befuddled.

"It was a long time ago. I was younger than the two of you are now," she said, almost as if to herself.

We nodded again. We all just stood there. She wasn't making any effort with us. She probably had rehearsed a million things to say to us. She must have. She probably had a soliloquy prepared. But she couldn't think of it right now for the life of her. I knew that Nicolas had said her name was Noëlle, but I couldn't help but think of her as Lily. That's what I had called her in my head for my whole life. Not Mother.

"Do you want to come in?" Lily asked.

Her house was very orderly. There were flowers on the curtains and on the tablecloth. Everything was new and had been bought at stores. Nothing had ever been dragged out of the garbage. We sat down around the kitchen table. All the chairs matched. She made some coffee. Nicolas and I felt painfully out of place. We were like kids who were showing up on the first day at a new school. She poured us all cups of coffee and set them down in front of us.

"How did you go about finding me?"

We didn't say anything. Lily looked at us and straightened up, gathering courage. She decided to launch into her defence.

"You have to understand what life was like for me when I got pregnant. Everybody in my town looked down on me. They treated me like I was so, so ugly. I just sat in my room, crying all the time. I was afraid of my father. The looks he would give me were so awful. I didn't even like going down to the kitchen because my dad would give me such a look. Sometimes he would slap me hard across my face."

She paused. We just stared at her, startled. She couldn't really do anything but continue.

"I couldn't go to school because all the boys made fun of me. They didn't believe that it was Étienne Tremblay who got me pregnant. They used to say that the school janitor was the father. Can you imagine that? Children are so cruel."

She raised her cup to her lips and it was shaking.

"My mother and I took the bus to Montréal to meet your grandparents. I left you two with them. They were very, very nice. My mother took me to go and get an ice cream cone by Avenue Atwater. It was so beautiful and exciting to me. All those people going by and all the windows. We stopped by a toy store and we saw all these dollhouses and train sets that moved around and little plastic trees. Oh, I had never seen anything like that in Val-des-Loups."

There was something horrific about the idea of her having an ice cream cone after having given us up. I just wanted it to end. I didn't want to hear her story. It had never occurred to us that she would see herself as the sad one in this story. Sure, sure, sure. She was the loneliest, most pathetic fourteen-year-old on the whole planet. But we had been listening to Étienne's excuses our whole life. The last thing that we expected somehow was another excuse. Although an excuse, of course, was exactly what we were going to get.

"You had much better outfits than I ever had as a kid. I remember this little black coat you had on once on TV, Nouschka. You had a daisy in the lapel. It was so beautiful. You looked like your father. Lucky for you two. He was a handsome man when he was younger. You were smart like him too. The things that would come out of your mouths!"

Nicolas and I immediately shot a knowing, wary glance at each other. She had loved us on television. The same way that everybody had loved us, which was the same thing as not loving us at all. We had had enough of that type of affection. What we needed was a love that was able to shine a light on who exactly we were, so that we could be people offstage. Then we would be able to be real. Then we would be able to grow up. Then we wouldn't be joined at the hip. This woman only knew what everybody knew about us. Of course she loved our persona. It was designed to be loved.

I wanted her to be proud of things that nobody but a mother could be proud of. I had wanted her to be proud of a story that I had written about a swan. I had wanted her to be thrilled when I dove off the high diving board. She should have been there to cheer when I learned my multiplication table. And I had wanted to be commended for giving the flea-ridden cat a bath all by myself. Those were the things that actually built character. They taught you that ordinary life was meaningful and made sense.

You could tell that she was a bit star-struck. We looked down on people that were star-struck. We couldn't help it. How could we not look down on people when they were looking up at us?

"I never, never would have been able to get to Montréal if it weren't for the two of you. After I went back to Val-des-Loups, all I could think about was getting back to the city. I was only seventeen when I came here to live. I looked after children for a while. But you know, that always made me sad. Now I work as a secretary. We sell accessories for used car lots. The little flags that go around them and those big blow-up snowmen flopping around in the parking lot."

She turned abruptly and reached into her bag that was on her chair and pulled out a binder, as if it would somehow save her from the topic of this conversation. It was filled with before and after photographs of parking lots where there could have been pictures of us as children. She closed it, knowing that she had to get on with her story.

"This is how I met my husband, actually. He owns one of these car lots. He's very successful. He does very well for himself. He's very conventional. He's very good." She paused. "I never told my husband about you. It's not that I'm ashamed of it. But I can't tell him now. He thinks that he was the first person that I had ever been with. That was very important to him. I really never thought that any man would ever love me. But he does. You can't tell someone a secret after you have kept it a secret for this long. He would think that I was a liar. He thinks that I'm a good person. It would change everything. He's a really good man. I've been happy with him. It was hard after Étienne Tremblay."

I noticed that she said our father's first and last name when talking about him. Even though she had had two children with him, they were not on familiar terms.

In an odd way, although we had dropped in on her, she was more prepared than we were. She had never come looking for us, but she knew that we would come anyways. She had been waiting.

I looked around. There were photos of children all over the fridge. Lily blushed when she saw me noticing them. This had never even occurred to me as a possibility. She had other children. Of course, her husband and children were real people with feelings. Not like us. She reached out for a second but then brought her hand back. Her hand was shaking. You could tell that she was restraining herself and that her instinct was to reach out and touch people who were suffering.

She was holding back because she wanted to protect her husband and kids. That wasn't fair, was it? She was choosing sides. At least we knew with absolute certainty that Étienne was incapable of loving anybody. He treated everybody else with as little regard as he treated us.

I looked at Nicolas. He usually slouched and crossed and uncrossed his legs when he was in a chair, but now he was sitting perfectly straight. He had beads of sweat on his brow, and his eyes looked almost black because his pupils were dilated. I don't think that I had ever seen him look that ill at ease.

Lily had been a nanny. She had given cookies to kids who weren't even hers. She ran around playgrounds putting Band-Aids on all the knees of all the children in the world. She was essentially sweet to every kid except us. This was going too far. I felt like picking up the kitchen table and throwing it across the room. Just so that she would know that I was a real person. Just to make it clear to her that Nicolas and I experienced unhappiness too.

Everyone thought that we had it better. Even when we were being dragged up to the guillotine, they would be envying our velvet jackets that we had picked up at the Salvation Army. They wouldn't think very much about the part about us getting our heads cut off. Imagine if she saw our living room? What would she think of it?

Lily, or whatever her name was, was starting to cry. But people cry for all sorts of reasons. They cry when they are startled. They cry when they are afraid. They cry to get out of things. People cried crummy alligator tears over their drinks. We were very, very suspicious of tears, having grown up on Boulevard Saint-Laurent.

She would never be our mother. We wanted to go back in time and tell her about nightmares, and about socks that were itchy, and about how spelling tests were unjust, and about how canned soup was creepy, and about how we felt scared first thing in the morning. We would never get that.

"Can you remember anything about us?" Nicolas asked.

His voice was very low and choked up and didn't sound like his at all. He was asking for a story about us before we could remember. We wanted something more than Loulou's absurd mythology. Most of his stories of us involved times when we were constipated and he had to give us castor oil. I don't know what Nicolas was thinking, though, as she had spent next to no time at all with us.

"Do you want to know which one of you was born first?" she asked.

"No!" we both said at the same time.

We didn't want that. We didn't want there to be any sort of difference between us. We didn't want one to be older or to have any advantage over the other. It was absolutely necessary that we be in exactly the same boat.

I realized that it was time to go. There was no need to drag out this painful meeting any longer. As soon as Nicolas saw me starting to stand up, he followed. He practically knocked the chair over, he was so eager to leave with me.

Noëlle walked us to the door. We stepped outside it and

stood there, looking at her. We weren't sure what we were supposed to do. It was customary to kiss twice upon parting in Montréal. Sometimes when I left a bar, I would go around kissing people I hadn't even spoken to or been introduced to during the night. What was a kiss other than a promise that the two of you would meet again and again?

She stayed inside the house. We waited, but she did not make a gesture; she didn't move at all. Her not kissing us meant that she definitely did not want us to come back. We nodded and turned and went on our way.

*****

We sat in the car outside her house. A family got out of their car across the street. They unloaded their grocery bags and carried them into the house. The whole family was pitching in.

"How do people live like that?" Nicolas said. He lit a cigarette.

It took me a few minutes to be able to say something. I knew that I was going to get crazy. I wanted to enjoy the blank numbness as long as I could. But then it came bursting out.

"You brought me out here without any warning just to set me off. You wanted to get me hysterical. You wanted me to get as hysterical as you do."

"Well, you never get worked up about it because you know that I'm going to be doing all the working up for the two of us. I mean, that isn't exactly fair either, is it?"

"You're being selfish. You just force me to go along with your stupid, stupid plans. What was the point of coming out here?"

"We had to get it over with, I guess. But I don't know, Nouschka. It was like I thought that maybe, possibly, something magical would happen. Sometimes I've thought about how I would tell her about all the lousy things that happened to us and about how lonely and unhappy she made me. And then she would just crumple up and die. Instead she just sort of made me feel shitty. Did she make you feel shitty?"

I didn't say anything. We were quiet on the ride back. This was almost impossible for the two of us to do. Talking to each other was like breathing. By talking we were able to keep track of every one of the other's thoughts. For once I didn't know what to say. I felt ashamed. The silence was terrible. We looked ahead.

"How did you know how to find her?" I asked.

"Adam gave me this address."

"Adam? Are you serious? How would Adam know?"

Nicolas pulled the car over. He turned toward me, preparing me.

"It's funny but I'd been thinking for a long time about hiring a detective to find her. But I didn't know whether detectives actually existed or whether they were just fictional, like in TV shows. But then a year or so ago I was talking to Laurence and he said that his cousin was a private detective."

"How much did he charge you?"

"I don't know. I never got around to paying him. He smelled like an old ashtray. He's friends with a lawyer who was able to pull our adoption papers. Or something. He gave me this old address where Noëlle used to work. I went and knocked on the door. Adam answered. That's how I met Adam. She'd looked after him. Anyways, Adam didn't know. I just told him later that I had been knocking on his door with the intention of robbing his house, which of course impressed him. You know how Adam is."

"She's the nanny he was telling us about? They watched us on TV together!"

I suddenly hated the two of them. Neither had loved me. They had sat next to each other on the sofa, cherishing my little black beret.

"She raised Adam! Adam of all people! I find that infuriating. I find that so impossibly weird. I can't even imagine it. I feel lousy about myself even picturing it. I can't believe that she put muffins and juice boxes into paper bags and wrote his name on them and gave them to him to take to school for lunch. And she took him to the zoo. And she put bandages on his knees. And she read him storybooks and kissed him before he went to sleep. Disgusting," I said. "I'm finished with Adam."

"Why take it out on Adam?"

"I'm breaking up with him as soon as we get home."

"I had nothing to do with it. Look, I gave up a very long time ago trying to get you to not fuck my friends. What was I supposed to say—don't fuck him?"

"No, you were supposed to tell me who he was."

"You got weird whenever I would bring up our mother. You would say, '*Laisse faire, laisse faire, laisse faire.* Don't bother me with that.' You never would have let me do this. I couldn't tell you. Because you wouldn't let me do it. I had to."

"You're a pimp."

"Are you crazy? Did you hear what you just called me?"

"You're a low-life. A degenerate."

"Ah, stop taking this all out on me."

"It's because I want you to realize why what you did is so creepy."

"I know. I know. But I couldn't get enough of him. When he told us stories about our mother, it made my heart beat so crazily and it made the blood rush through my heart. And it made me feel like shit. Like I was being poisoned. It's not my fault he fell in love with you."

I stopped yelling at him. I realized he couldn't help it. Our mother had been driving him mad our whole lives. He had had to find some way to get close to her. He could never let anything go once he got it into his head.

Now I understood the feeling that there was something that wasn't quite right about me and Adam. I was revolted that my sex life was somehow involved in one of Nicolas's schemes. There had never been any boundaries between Nicolas and me. Now he had created one by virtue of stepping over it.

CHAPTER 17

How to Woo a Degenerate

T HEY SAY IN QUÉBEC THAT IF YOU ARE CONCEIVED on a night when your parents are drinking, then you are going to be melancholic your whole life. If your parents conceived you the first time they ever had sex, then you will be lucky your whole life, and everyone you meet will fall madly in love with you. Nicolas and I found ourselves in this universe on an otherwise unmemorable night in Val-des-Loups.

Étienne left Montréal for the first time in 1973, to tour rural Québec. He despised it and was bored to death.

He was stuck in a motel room one night after a show. There was a movie playing on the television set. After ten o'clock, they played movies that were made in Québec. You would think that ninety-nine percent of the population were heroin addicts if you watched these movies. The *vedettes* wore winter coats the whole time and yelled at one another. These movies were so realistic that your own life kind of seemed fake and glamorous in comparison. If the movie had been better, he might have stayed in his hotel room that night.

Someone had given the drummer an address to a party. They decided to go check it out. Ordinarily Étienne would never have gone to a house party, but there was nothing else to do in these terrible, tiny small towns.

The party was in a white clapboard house. There was a field behind it without animals. There was a row of little undershirts on the clothesline. One was covered in strawberries, another with horses, and one had the teeniest bow at the neck. Étienne felt turned on by all the naked undershirts. They walked into the house without knocking.

The heavy metal was loud. You could do that in Val-des-Loups because there was nobody around for miles and miles and miles.

Almost the first person that Étienne noticed was a girl in a turtleneck sweater that looked like it would swallow her any minute. She had a plastic ring on her finger from a gumball machine. She was drinking a beer for the first time. She was fourteen years old. She may or may not have been beautiful.

She wore her black bangs down over her eyes. Étienne generally hated shy girls. They looked down at the ground when they talked to him. They were deathly boring because they were too afraid to say anything.

But then again, sometimes shy girls kissed you just so that they wouldn't have to talk. They hoped that they were pretty enough to get away with not speaking. Some shy girls were too afraid to say no. Even though you'd just met, they were terrified that you wouldn't like them. Once they let you feel their tits, they weren't sure what to do. They thought that maybe they weren't in the right to say no.

Étienne knew he could get this girl to sleep with him.

Étienne asked the girl if she wanted to go into a little bedroom at the back of the house to talk to him. She knew exactly who he was. The whole party did. Everyone was looking at him and pretending not to. She followed him to the bedroom. There was a forest on the wallpaper in the bedroom. The polyester bedspread was purple with gold roses. Ugly. They overdecorated their houses in small towns. Ugly.

Étienne liked young girls. They believed in his persona completely. What did he need with women who could see right through him? Lily Sainte-Marie looked like she was still afraid of the dark and spent her pocket change on candy. She looked like she still had to memorize the spelling of words at night.

She had little hands. She shrugged even though there was no reason to shrug. She just figured that she had to do something with her body. So she sat there shrugging and shrugging. He started taking off all her silly clothes. Her clothes didn't match and every piece was a hand-me-down. Ugly.

She didn't even really move during the actual act. She kept her eyes closed really tight and her mouth squeezed shut. She looked like she was holding her breath, as if she had just jumped off a diving board and her body was shooting straight down into the water.

She loosened up after losing her virginity. She was so excited sitting on the side of the bed that she wasn't even getting dressed. And she looked so young, like a kid that was expecting her mother to dress her. She climbed onto his lap while he was trying to tie his shoelaces.

She wanted to know if he would call her. She told him that if her father answered the telephone, then he should just hang up immediately. Lily Sainte-Marie told him that her father would kill him if he found out that she had had sex. She said that her father was strict and wouldn't even let her go to school dances. She wanted to know if she could come to visit him in Montréal.

She whispered that she loved him.

Étienne suddenly didn't know why he hadn't worn a condom. She had trapped him. She had caught him. He knew. He knew. He knew she was pregnant. He didn't know how he knew, but he knew.

He didn't want to throw down an anchor in this strange small town in the middle of nowhere. Where their symphony orchestra was a sixty-five-year-old man named Benoit, who could play *Peter and the Wolf* on his clarinet.

Domestic life took down people quicker than the bubonic plague. Étienne had struggled his whole life not to be a member of any class. A man without children doesn't belong to any class. He is a free man.

Étienne wanted to walk right back to Montréal. He climbed out the window and went back to the motel. He hoped to never see her again.

Anyways, all of this sounded better as a song. Our whole lives, from our conception onward, had been a romantic take on a narcissist's asshole behaviour. Our lives were a fiction. I had swallowed it all. I had believed it more than anyone.

CHAPTER 18

Goodbye, Prince Hal!

IT WAS GHASTLY. HORRIBLE. THE WORDS THEM-selves were meaningless; I was just saying the requisite number of them so that I could get to the end of the conversation. And when I somehow got to the end of the conversation, then Adam would be out of my life. He knew that too, so after everything was said, he still kept talking nonsense rather than leave.

"I was raised by the mother of Little Nicolas and Little Nouschka. It's amazing in a way. I don't think that it's creepy at all. On the contrary, it means that we were fated together."

"Give it time," I said. "When it occurs to you just how weird this is, you'll never want to touch me again, that's for sure."

Nicolas came in and was eating an apple. Adam was packing in slow motion. He acted as if his sweater was made of cement as he dragged it off the floor and put it in his suitcase. He flung it in violently.

"This isn't fair. I've done nothing but worship the ground that you walk on. That's where I went wrong. I should have been mean to you. I should have just yawned when you were talking. That's what the ladies like. Do you know how many girls are out there, lining up to go out with me? There will be riots on the streets."

I looked over at Nicolas, who rolled his eyes to register his disbelief that there would be any riots.

"I'm the one who leaves girls. They aren't the ones who leave me. You think you can do better than me. You can't. God damn you, I'm special."

At this, Nicolas got up and walked out again, embarrassed for Adam, I suppose. Luckily Loulou had the television on. He was incapable of hearing anything while the television was on. A marching band could pass right outside the window and he would miss it entirely.

Maybe the saddest thing about Adam leaving was that I wasn't going to miss him. How did I know for sure this wasn't love? Feeling oddly pissed off at someone for reasons that you couldn't put your finger on was surely somebody's definition of love.

But no sooner than I started feeling sorry for him, I would think about what had happened and then find that I was enraged. I had never been envious of Adam. I had loved his magical stories from the faraway kingdom of Being Rich. I had never wanted his grand houses or private school education. But this was too much. He could not have our mother's love because that was something that rightfully belonged to us. That wasn't something that you could buy!

He was pulling out paperback philosophy books from under the bed. He had located odd little spots in the cluttered room where he could find his own space for his things.

"Will you give me five and a half seconds, Nouschka? Can we sit down for a cup of coffee? I know this is really fucking weird. In a way. But in another way, it's not that completely crazy."

He didn't really sound convinced of his own words. He was trying to get his head around the news himself.

"It isn't actually a reason for us to break up."

"I think it's enough of a reason actually. I don't want to think about you, or Lily Sainte-Marie. Noëlle, whatever her name is. I don't even want to think about Nicolas right now."

"You can't get away from him. You're two parts of a whole."

I suddenly wanted to murder him for saying it. I was glad again that I was throwing him out.

"Why would you say that? We're not the same person, you know."

"But now Nicolas isn't going to hang out with me either."

"What, are you breaking up with Nicolas or are you breaking up with me?"

"You're both breaking up with *me*. You're both rejecting me."

His coddled upbringing had ironically made him susceptible to the ragged glamour that surrounded us. I needed someone who could see through all that. He didn't realize that it was preventing us from doing anything with our lives. Adam would never be able to get me away from Nicolas.

*****

Nicolas shook hands with Adam at the door. Nicolas too just wanted him to go. His escapade involving Adam had come to fruition and was over. More importantly, we just needed to be alone. After Adam left, Nicolas stood there, not saying anything.

"Why are you so calm?" I asked.

"Honestly, Nouschka, I think that I'm in shock."

I looked at him. He probably was. After he had broken his arm when he was five, he kept walking around in a circle, telling everyone to relax and stay calm.

"She asked us to go away," he said. "She asked us not to ruin her life."

He looked to me for sympathy, but instead I was outraged.

"I can't even be under the same roof as you tonight. I'm going out."

"Oh, where are you going? Don't leave me here all by myself. Come on, Nouschka. Can't you punish me in some other way? I don't want to be alone tonight. It'll drive me crazy. Look, we can have a long, warm tête-à-tête about this whole fucking thing tomorrow."

I climbed out the window. He reached for my foot, but I was already running off down the street.

*****

Our mother had come and seen the city with its 1001 flavours of everything and had decided to leave us here. I walked through the street. All the neon signs were flirting with me. They said things like PARADISE! THÉÂTRE ÉROTIQUE! L'AMOUR! XXX! DAN-SEUSES NUES!

I went down a tiny alleyway. There were floral curtains on the windows of the cheap hotels, behind which prostitutes were pretending to moan in ecstasy. There were faded murals of old advertisements from the thirties on the walls for detergents and colas that didn't exist anymore. There were bits of red brick all over the ground because the buildings were falling apart. I stopped and looked at some graffiti on the wall that I had written with a can of spray paint when I was thirteen: NICOLAS AND NOUSCHKA WERE HERE WITH THE RATS AND THE FLOWERS.

I remembered writing that. It was so exciting. Nicolas had showed it to all the other kids in the neighbourhood because he thought it was so great.

*****

I decided to go and see Misha. I hadn't seen him in months. I hadn't even called. Because I was young and pretty, he was able to forgive me for so many things, but maybe this time I had pushed my luck.

I just wanted him to tuck me up in his big, fat arms and sing me some sort of idiotic Russian lullaby and chastise me for not eating well. He would yell at me for sleeping around. He was the only person who did. He would unbutton my sweater and then put all the right buttons in their corresponding holes. He once bought a bobby pin with a cloth flower on it and pinned it in my hair. He was the closest thing that I had to a mother and I wanted him to take care of me right then.

I went into the Ukrainian restaurant. Misha often ate there. We'd order plates and plates of food and it would still only come to three dollars. There were photographs of Russian performers on the wall. The women used more hairspray than anyone else in the world. They were covered in sequins, which made them look like glittering skylines at night.

Sure enough, Misha was eating at a table at the back of the restaurant. The top buttons of his shirt were undone, revealing a Star of David around his neck. When he saw me, he wiped his mouth with a handkerchief that was on his lap. I sat down on the chair across from him. He grabbed the leg of my chair and pulled me over to him. He gave me a big kiss on the mouth. I sat on his side of the table with my head on his shoulder.

The waitress came by to refill his cup of coffee. She stood there, giving me a dirty look. She thought that I wasn't any good. She thought that I was a gold digger, which I was, except I wasn't there for money. I was there because I knew that Misha had an abundance of love that he had saved up. He had stored it away under his mattress because he'd had no one to spend it on.

She started a conversation with him in Russian out of spite, I guess. I didn't really care. Then she glared at me and turned and walked away.

"That waitress thinks that I sleep with you for money."

"I wish that you would let me give you money; it would turn me on. I could pretend that I called an agency and they sent you over."

"But doesn't that insult you? Why would she think that? I think you are devastatingly sexy. Do you believe me?"

"I don't know why on earth you do, but apparently you do."

I started telling Misha the story about how Nicolas dragged me to meet our mother, and the waitress went up to the wooden sound system that was on a shelf on the wall and turned the music louder. Then she gave me a quick glance backward as if to say, "Take that. He won't hear you begging for money." The stereo was playing a Russian singer. He sounded angry. He sounded as if he was marching up a flight of stairs.

I didn't mind though. I liked yelling above the music. It meant that there was a point to raising your voice. It was like turning up a burner under a pot on the stove so that all the food could start cooking. My emotions were getting all heated and then turning into something wonderful.

"Do you know that song that my dad sings about my mother, well about Lily Sainte-Marie?" I yelled.

"Yes."

"Well, it's about a real person. Like I really have a mother. Well Nicolas and I really have a mother."

"Naturally you had to have come from somewhere."

"So a couple days ago we went down to see our mother. Nicolas and I borrowed a car and we went down to see our mother. We just showed up out of the blue, outside her door. I didn't even dress up or anything. I didn't even know that we were going until we were going—no, actually, I didn't even know until we were practically already there."

"And what did she say?"

"And she said that she didn't want us to mess up her life. She said that she had had to work really hard to get to Montréal. And we were just these spoiled little movie stars. She said that she had moved on and that we should too."

"She didn't say it like that, baby."

"Do you think that Nicolas is the most outrageous person on the planet, or what?"

"It was a good thing, I think. I am always for confrontation even if it destroys our lives for a time. It's good. You needed to see your real mother. The two of you were rejected and unwanted. Doesn't that make you feel free? You can accept it and acknowledge it. You are not each other's mothers. You can stop pretending. You do not have a mother. Your mother doesn't even want her husband to know about you. But it happens! We get through stuff like this. That is what we are put on earth for."

"So you don't think that Nicolas was in the wrong?"

"Nicolas is a young man and he is trying to figure out the world. And young men do stupid things when they are trying to figure out the world. When I look at things that I did when I was a younger man, I'm amazed and stupefied. Truly. You can't expect anyone to be noble. We are all sneaky. We are all cowards. We are all complete fucking idiots. And by the time we figure things out we are old and fat and our life is behind us, and no one learns from our mistakes."

I smiled. He always made everything sound like the first few lines from *A Tale of Two Cities*. He made every situation, no matter how outrageous, seem like a natural part of life.

"Isn't that a pessimistic philosophy?"

"No, because it means that it's all right that your parents were disappointing. Because of a terrible mistake you were born, and look at you! Look at you! This whole wonderful universe of things in one skinny girl."

"I feel like things have been different between Nicolas and me lately. It makes me feel lonely."

"Loneliness is a wonderful thing. I would never, never have learned to play the French horn if it weren't for loneliness. I would never have come all the way across the sea if it weren't for loneliness. I would never have become a semi-successful businessman. You've never been lonely in your life. You are retarded where loneliness is concerned. You've been ruined by too much love for your brother. You were ruined by love when you were a very, very young girl."

Who ever heard of having these types of conversations in North America? This was what they were coming up with during the Cold War. They weren't stockpiling nuclear arms. They were stockpiling these dark and deep secrets.

"You are okay, Nouschka," Misha said. He leaned over and took my hand in his. "You are doing all right. You are a good little soldier. You are feeling sad now because it is wartime. You are engaged in the greatest battle of them all: the battle to be yourself. It is the ugliest battle. Many of those we love will be killed. Nicolas is the only person who will really make you weep one day. But we always feel good after weeping."

*****

I loved that. I loved that Misha had once had everything taken away from him and then had gone on and shrugged it all off. He had built something beautiful out of nothing. Adam had everything but he would never have what Misha did. He opened up his fat arms and I sat on his lap. Because that was our ritual. We had a hundred ways to sign our contracts of love.

Irritated by this latest show of affection, the waitress came over with a pile of cookie tins. She stacked them in front of him so that he could choose one to buy. We leaned forward and looked them over. The cover of each tin was fancier than the next.

There was a bear sitting on a train, wearing a jacket and drinking tea from a very fancy teacup. There was a swan with a wicked look on its face, wearing spats over its flippers and a bow tie and a bowler hat. There was a ballerina with her hair up in a bun and the sourest expression I had ever seen. She looked as if she was dating a man for money and he was trying to kiss her cheek.

I pointed to the bear. Misha pulled five dollars from his wallet and handed it to the waitress. He then opened that box. He held the lid above him.

"A magic trick!" he called out.

He was always doing magic tricks. That was one of the truisms about dating older men. They wore cologne, they were always looking for food and they knew magic tricks. I was looking forward to whatever it was he was going to do. All the waitresses gathered around.

He popped a cookie into my mouth and his own and the waitress's. He held the wrappers delicately in his hands.

His hands were beautiful. Like many fat people who couldn't be bothered to move or articulate with their bodies, he waved his hands around with an almost painful expressiveness.

He took a lighter out of his pocket and set the wrappers on fire. They floated up and came down from the sky, like paratroopers that had caught on fire. And when the cookie wrappers went up into the air, we were all just like children. The magic trick wasn't to have the paper float up into the air, it was to make everyone feel innocent. The waitresses forgot about how they despised me for a minute and we all applauded.

I felt happy. Misha could make anyone feel happy. Maybe he was enough for me after all, I thought.

*****

Later that night I sat on the living room floor after having given him a blow job. I was wearing only a pair of black tights with holes in the toes and a black bra with a miniature red bow in the middle. I was sitting next to a lamp whose base was in the shape of a mermaid. She had huge, heavy breasts with gold nipples. Misha was sitting on a wooden chair with roses on the frame, looking at me.

"You're going to give me a heart attack. Literally. I can't be having sex with you anymore. Although you do have an adorable ass. But it will kill me. This is the last time I'm going to let you come over here, my darling."

I didn't take him seriously for a second. There was no way that Misha could ever resist me.

"Don't say that," I pleaded. "We should go on a vacation together. We can go tonight. We can rent a paddleboat and eat sausages. We've never been for a drive together. We can go off to sea like the owl and the pussy cat. We will specifically ask for a beautiful pea green boat. We can stay in a quaint hotel where people will never judge us."

He got up and went to sit on the couch. I got up and followed after him. I put my arms around him and kissed his cheeks.

"We'll have a little baby. A little Russian baby. He'll be very good at gymnastics, he'll wear his hair long over one eye and he'll wear track suits with gold chains. I would put honey on his pacifier. We'll name him Igor. It won't matter if everyone in his class hates him, because then he will come home and I'll kiss his little tears on his cheeks and heat him up some borscht."

"I'm not here to rescue you. You have to do all the things that kids your age do. Go to school. Leave home. Stop hanging around so much with your brother."

I stopped babbling and listened to what he was saying.

"Let me go, Nouschka. It's better this way. You're better off with a guy your own age."

Then I realized that he was serious. He looked pained and miserable to be saying it. I got up and went around the living room gathering up the articles of clothing that I had flung haphazardly around. I got dressed quickly. How strange. Just the day before, I was doing the kicking out. And like Adam, I just wanted to say a few more things before we got to *goodbye*.

"I have to hand in something for English class tomorrow. Will you write another poem for me before I go?"

"You should write it yourself. You are a born writer."

"The light from the two-dollar chow mein restaurant is the same colour as the moon," I said. "And the astronauts have turned into soap bubbles."

"Lovely, my baby," he said.

His voice was so full of regret that I almost didn't go.

CHAPTER 19

La Guerre, Yes Sir!

I KEPT THINKING ABOUT LILY SAINTE-MARIE OVER the next days. It made me sadder and sadder. What had I been doing onstage reciting revolutionary poetry and acting like I was at the top of the world? My mother was alive and well and she had not loved me.

We were at each other's throats after Adam left. It was just the two of us again. This was suddenly worse to me than having nobody. We started picking on each other over all sorts of tiny, stupid things.

One morning a week later, I glared at Nicolas over the breakfast table. Loulou was standing at the counter, busy mixing up batter for an angel food cake. Everything about Nicolas was bothering me. It seemed as if his hair hadn't been washed in a week. His stupid nose seemed to be taking up his whole face. I didn't like the way he smoked. He inhaled half the cigarette and made the filter sopping wet. It was grotesque.

"Stop giving me the stink eye," Nicolas said. "I'm just trying to eat my toast like a regular guy. Just your average Joe."

"You changed the settings on the clock radio."

"Where are you going with this?"

"I have a job and I'm going to school. If you're going to change the clock radio, then I'm going to be all screwed up."

"I knew that's where you were going. I am a man that doesn't even need time. And you, on the other hand, are very important and are very much in need of the time."

"I only want to be able to hear the alarm when it goes off."

He put the cigarette butt out in his egg.

"Why don't you put your cigarette out in an ashtray like a normal human being?" I asked.

"You're questioning my humanity now. This is grand. That's the only reason that you're going to school, isn't it? So that you can lord it over me."

"And another thing: don't use my toothbrush. I'm going to gag until there's no gag left in me if I find that you've used my toothbrush."

"I'm going out because you're driving me up the wall. You're just looking for things to get irritated at me about."

And of course he was right. That was exactly what I was doing. But I couldn't stop.

"Did you take five dollars from my pocket?"

"Certainly I did."

"You think that my pocket is a bank."

"Since when did you become a member of the bourgeoisie? When did this house become too small for you? When did you start needing a bedroom with a princess bed? You think you're too good for me. Well I'm too good for you."

He slammed his fists down on the table. Then he pointed his finger at me.

"Because just remember that the two of us were in the same stinking womb together. We were rejected by the same mother. You think that if I wasn't there, she would have said, "Oh look, a sweet little girl." Oh no, no, no. She put us both out together. She was disgusted with the two of us. Because you were born unwanted just as much as I was."

Nicolas was trying to put into words what I was feeling. I hoped myself that he would be able to do it. Then I wouldn't have to have all these strange thoughts that made me feel like I was worried about something but couldn't put my finger on what it was. But he wasn't getting it right. Or anyways he was sort of getting it right. He was right that it had something to do with him.

"You're just looking for someone to look down on. But why don't you just go look in the mirror? You want to pretend that you've done something with your life, although I can't imagine what on earth that is. Who do you think you are? Sitting there and criticizing me."

"Just don't change the settings on the clock radio."

"The clock radio actually belongs to me. So I can do whatever I like with it."

"Fine, but don't touch my shit either."

"Those striped socks that you have on, they're mine. I was planning on wearing them today, so I'd prefer if you took them the fuck off."

"Fine."

I pulled off the socks and tossed them across the table at him. One hit him in the chest and the other one landed in his coffee.

"Ah, disgusting. What's the matter with you?"

Loulou turned to us, holding up the cake bowl and spoon. He had no idea that we were arguing.

"Who's going to lick the batter?" he called out.

Loulou didn't know about us having gone to see Lily. I wondered if he even remembered the Lily Sainte-Marie story. We were much more sensitive to Loulou's feelings than we were to each other's. Whatever else, Loulou had woken up every day and made us breakfast whether we wanted it or not. The least that we could do in return was to pretend that all his hard work paid off and that it never crossed our minds to want our mother. We didn't want to confuse him terribly by having him get to know our personalities.

"You know what Saskia told me once?" Nicolas said, completely ignoring Loulou. "She said that the worst thing about me was you. That I never did anything without checking in first. That you were a control freak. And that it wasn't very fun having to date the two of us."

"And I suppose it's my fault you didn't put a condom on your dick."

Nicolas picked up an orange and threw it at the window. The glass shattered.

"Whoa!" Loulou said. "What on earth is happening now?"

I flung the cooled coffee from my cup at my brother. He grabbed the trash can and dumped it on my head, while I opened up the fridge and started throwing the eggs at him.

I ran down the hallway, and Nicolas chased me into the living room. He picked up a lamp and started swinging it at me as if it was a sword. I stood up on the couch. I threw a jar filled with pencils at his head. He pulled me off the couch and we were wrestling on the floor, smacking each other on the head.

Loulou came in with his hands in the air, yelling at us to knock it off. The teachers used to sometimes separate Nicolas and me in class because we would erupt into fist fights. We just went crazy on each other, slapping and kicking and pulling each other's hair. I think it affected the teachers' sense of propriety to see two children whacking each other brutally and then walking hand in hand two hours later.

I stood up and ran out of the living room and back into the kitchen. Nicolas came after me and slid across the table to cut me off. He knocked over a vase of flowers and the change dish and grabbed me by both hands and pinned me against the wall.

"Calm down, Nouschka. Just calm down."

When I stopped struggling, he let go. He straightened himself out. He grabbed his jacket and walked out the front door, slamming it without saying a word. I was so frustrated that I sat on the kitchen floor and wept.

The thing is that Nicolas and I were afraid to be without each other. And whenever you are dependent on someone, then you naturally start to resent them. Everybody is born with an inkling, a desire to be free.

We had tried all the other crazy, violent things that other people did to end their relationships. We had humiliated and belittled and smacked each other. But nothing ever worked. He was furious with me now. But he would be distracted in fifteen minutes by a pretty girl or a song on a jukebox that he liked and he wasn't going to be mad anymore. No matter what we said to each other, it didn't seem to mean a damn thing an hour later. It gave this strange sense of futility to everything that we did. As if each day had just been a dream that we were waking up from and had no consequences.

I went and sat down next to Loulou to watch television. Loulou was out of breath, as if he'd just run around the block. He always got that way when he was decompressing after one of Nicolas and my fights. I wasn't mad anymore, just tired too. Sometimes I thought that if I could fall madly in love, well, that would change things.

CHAPTER 20

The Best-Looking Criminal in Montréal

LATER THAT NIGHT, LONG, LONG AFTER THE argument, I was lying on my bed reading *Bonheur d'occasion* for school. The white cat was lying next to me, dead asleep. He looked like a lumberjack that had taken off all his clothes and was asleep in his long johns. Nicolas started making a fuss in the other room.

"Oh my God. It's Raphaël!" Nicolas yelled. "Nouschka, come quick. That asshole from across the street is on the news."

I walked into the living room. Nicolas and Loulou were sitting on the couch. When we had brought the couch home, it had had only a couple flowers at the bottom; now it was covered in wild, giant pink roses. Who knew that it would thrive in that spot? They were eating chocolate-covered marshmallows and watching the eleven o'clock news.

"Why do you always call him an asshole?"

"Because he's a snob. Once, I asked him to play soccer base-ball with us and he just stared at me and walked the other way. Who does that! I wanted to kill him."

"Be quiet. I want to listen."

The news cameras were filming outside Raphaël's house in Sainte-Agathe. They had raided the house earlier that day. He had about 145 dogs in his house. The city health inspectors showed up with trucks from the humane society to take away all his dogs. The cameras showed the inside of the house, which was littered with debris and feces. The furniture was all ripped apart. There were plates of dog food all over the bedroom floor. The news presented it as tragic for the dogs, which of course it was. But it was also a terrible shame that Raphaël had gone to pieces like this.

They showed all the dogs being taken into trucks. One of the dogs had a tie around his neck instead of a collar, and they all looked on the skinny, mangy side. His dogs looked like they had all the diseases that used to kill humans all the time in the old days. They looked like they had TB and syphilis and cholera. They looked like they had scurvy. They looked like pirates.

There was a close-up of a dog with droopy ears that made him look like he was wearing an aviator hat. The dog looked like a kid who has been warned not to open his mouth and complain one more time. It broke my heart.

Then they showed Raphaël being led out of the house into a police car. He was in as bad a condition as the dogs. He was dressed in jeans and socks. He sounded confused when an interviewer held a microphone up to his face for a comment.

"We're all equally anticipating the end of a venture we call life on earth. There's only 412 days left."

He was wearing handcuffs. He lifted both hands at once to brush his hair over to the side, I guess so that he would look good on television. His face was tanned except for the pale circles around his eyes, which came from religiously wearing sunglasses.

"Woo-hoo!" Nicolas yelled. "He's lost it!"

"He was always a little oddball, wasn't he?" Loulou asked.

"He was quiet," I said.

"His mother was really, really pretty before she got so fat," Loulou added. "I couldn't keep track of her kids. She named them all after planets. Wasn't there one named Neptune and one named Jupiter and one named . . . Pluto maybe?"

"His brothers' names are Paul, Samuel and Christophe."

"It's a shame. He wasn't such a bad-looking kid. And he knew how to skate. Remember all those swirly whirlies he did in the park?"

"Hey!" said Nicolas. "I knew how to skate too. There's a limit though. No man needs to be spinning around in a twinkly catsuit and touching his toes."

"You may have a point," Loulou said.

Nicolas and I used to watch him sometimes at the community centre. Raphaël was fourteen then. His hair was short in the back but he had long bangs. I think it was the style with figure skaters to have long bangs like that. Once, the lockers at the rink were closed because of a flood in the boys' bathroom, and I got to watch Raphaël getting ready on a bench beside the rink. He put gel in his hair and turned the hair dryer on and aimed it at his face until his hair stuck straight back behind him. He never had any expression on his face back then.

He wore an outfit that was cut down the middle to expose his nipples and his belly button. He had enormous feet and his black skates looked too big for him. I wondered if it held him back, having such huge feet.

He used to do a move where he spun on one leg while

leaning back and hitting his chest with his hands as if he was stabbing himself to death. Then he would spin in a huge miraculous circle, his arms wide, wide open as if he was showing someone just how much he loved them. And sometimes he squatted down with one leg straight out in front of him and spun with his arms straight up in the air as if he was a corkscrew trying to drill himself into the ice.

I had always been so amazed by Raphaël's skating. I would stand there, absolutely still, as if I was doing something that required incredible concentration myself, like balancing an egg on a spoon or walking on a tightrope. I felt like my stillness was somehow responsible for whether he landed his jumps. They were so beautiful that I couldn't bear for him to fall and spoil the effect.

Nicolas would sit watching me watching Raphaël as if I was completely out of my mind. Nicolas wanted to be my most favourite human being, which of course he was. But Raphaël was just a much better skater. We used to have a consensus about whom we were friends with. I never got to spend any time with Raphaël, because Nicolas decided he was definitely off limits. We wouldn't hang out with someone that the other person didn't like. This prevented us from having any real friends at all while growing up.

I was glad when the footage of Raphaël was over. Okay, so obviously I liked the guy. But I didn't like how crazy I felt when I was looking at Raphaël. I didn't know why people made like it was such a great thing to be wildly attracted to somebody. It felt like being a fish caught on a hook, reeled in whether you liked it or not.

The newscasters began talking about the chances of there being another referendum.

"Oh, turn this shit off," Nicolas said. "It's so boring and repetitive. Québec will never, ever have the guts to separate."

"It might be bad for the economy," Loulou said.

"I hate to be the one to tell you this, my darling old man, but we are rock bottom. We can't get any worse."

Nicolas shouting, "*Vive le Québec libre!*" as a rumple-headed kid had gotten as many *oui* votes as anything politicians said. He was still an ardent separatist, even if he had no faith in the government.

"Look at all those sideburned monkeys from the past," Nicolas said. "All these heart-attack-prone pseudo-intellectuals without a cause. These ranting syphilis-ridden lunatics, kicked out by their wives and showing up in filthy unlaundered suits to Parliament. If they hold a referendum this time they'd better win."

I had been listening to Nicolas's angry rants for years. Sometimes I thought that he wanted to separate from Canada out of spite and to mess things up. The apartment suddenly became tiny again. For the first time it came upon me: the absolutely natural desire to move out. It was weird to think it. Nicolas and Loulou were both sitting on the couch, totally comfortable in their own skins, having no desire to be anywhere else in the world.

CHAPTER 21

Requiem for a Drunk in a Top Hat

NICOLAS AND I WERE IN THE BACKYARD DRINKING coffee and reading the newspaper on the evening of our twentieth birthday, trying to enjoy the last bit of sunlight. The tiny courtyard didn't get that much light because other buildings surrounded it. Loulou was always telling us how lucky we were to have a yard. When we were younger we would sit out there on small chairs, drinking Coca-Cola out of teacups. There were empty coffee tins with spindly roses in them. There were jars with bean sprouts.

There was a pigeon coop out there that Étienne had built when he was a little kid. He had spent all his time as a kid, even in the winter, hanging out with the birds. It was beautiful. It was built out of old window frames. Some of them had glass panes in them. Some of them had wire screens.

The building was still surrounded by the pigeons and seagulls and sparrows that Étienne had invited. There was something magical about that. They were still looking for Étienne, his dwindling audience.

Loulou came out wearing a paper crown from a doughnut box. He was sad when we didn't laugh. He missed having babies in the house.

"You twos were just so, so damn cute whens yous were little wee things. You looked almost as cute as your father. Now that was a beautiful baby! Lord oh lord! That baby was striking. Bus drivers would stop their buses and come right out on the street to look at him. Women would go insane. I was afraid he'd get stolen in the supermarket by crazy women."

"Oh fuck," said Nicolas. "Could you speak plainly or not at all?"

Loulou figured that since Étienne had been so successful, there was no way that anyone in our family was going to be successful again for the next hundred years. So there was no point bothering with us or encouraging us to do much.

We didn't really get to be the babies. Étienne was the one who was marvelled over. He was the one who threw tantrums and who had erratic behaviour. He was the sensitive one who needed to be complimented all the time. Everything he did was evidence of his genius.

"Look, old man," Nicolas said. "Today happens to be my and Nouschka's twentieth birthday. Which is a monumental occasion. This is not Let's Get All Fucking Gaga About Étienne Tremblay Day, like every other day. Okay? And that goes for you too, Nouschka."

"What did I do?" I asked. "I'm just sitting here."

Nicolas watched me as I read the paper. He kept staring at me, not moving an inch. I was acting as if I had no idea whatsoever that Étienne came by on our birthday. We could almost count on our hands the times that Étienne had come by since he had got out of prison. But he never, ever missed our birthdays. Nicolas hated how excited I would get to see him.

Étienne was as famous for his fall as he was for his songs. There were articles in all the magazines about how Étienne was living in a rooming house on Rue Saint-Dominique and had lunch each day at la Mission in Vieux Montréal. Nobody could believe how broke he was. It was almost miraculous.

He didn't even try to hide or blend in. He dyed his hair black in his sink. He continued to dress like he had gone home with the bridesmaid at a wedding and was walking home in the morning in his fancy clothes from the night before. Étienne's top hat had sailed above everyone else's head along Boulevard Saint-Laurent for years. It made everyone else seem dowdy and ordinary.

God knows why I got worked up when Étienne visited. I always anticipated something that never happened. He got drunk and he gave us the crappiest gifts on the planet. When we were twelve, he gave us both a secondhand porcelain doll. The doll's hair was messy, which had given me the strange impression that it had been sleeping in bed with Étienne.

When the doorbell rang we all went back inside. I answered it, cool as a cucumber. I opened the door and there he was. My heart skipped a beat. It couldn't help it! Sometimes Étienne looked magically youthful. He looked eighteen when he was forty. He was wearing a navy blue sweater vest with red diamonds on it, and he was carrying a beige cat that he had brought as a gift for Nicolas and me. The cat looked like a sweater that had dried on a coat hanger and was now stretched beyond all recognition. I don't know why, but it seemed like he had stolen the cat from someone's yard.

"A cat?" Nicolas said. "You brought us a cat?"

"This is no ordinary cat, my darling children. This was once Cleopatra herself. She demanded to be overly pampered when she was alive, and now as punishment she is forced to spend the rest of her days as a disdained and yet adored creature. Who wouldn't mind spending their life as a cat? Why, at my age I have a veritable envy of their flexible spine. Never mind the use of books of philosophy, never mind Marcus Aurelius or Kierkegaard. This creature is able to meditate on the wonders of the universe with a simple piece of string."

His bearing undermined his verbal pyrotechnics. He seemed incredibly nervous and was acting as if we were going to mistreat him. He shied away from my glances.

When Étienne sat down at the kitchen table, he didn't even seem to be able to deal with the chair. It kept tipping over to the side as if it was trying to throw Étienne right off onto the ground. He was holding a glass of water that was trembling like crazy. It was a glass with Tintin on it that we'd got for free at a hamburger joint. I had never known this glass to have any dignity before, but it clearly didn't want to be held by Étienne. It shivered like a dog that was being taken to the pound.

Étienne reached into the bag that he was carrying and pulled out a large can of beer. He looked embarrassed that he was doing this. He looked in my eyes sheepishly as he raised it to his lips. The beer changed his entire demeanour immediately. After he downed the beer in a few big swallows, he started getting talkative. He looked around the room.

He was the only person I ever knew who had a twinkle in his eye. Or at least he acted as if he had a twinkle in his eye. Or at least I imagined that he had a twinkle in his eye. I found it charming, whether it existed or not.

We were having an early dinner. Loulou had made his special

spaghetti sauce. He put a salad bowl with tiny hot dogs in the middle of the table. When we were younger, Nicolas and I used to leap on those like wild animals, but we were all feeling a tad reserved that evening. During dinner Étienne started reminiscing about our childhood as if he'd always been around.

"Nico, remember you flashed that girl in Apartment 7 and her mother called the cops on you. Remember how you tried drinking a raw egg because you saw Rocky do it and you threw up on the carpet. You were so bad at spelling. The teacher said that she had never met anyone in her career that was as bad at spelling as you."

Nicolas and I looked at each other, insulted. Where did he get these memories? His memory was a shelf in a junk shop with things that should have been thrown out. Like plastic roses or old tins of crackers. We thought we had tossed these memories away, but he had gone through our garbage like a ragpicker in order to find them and here they were again. I wished that Étienne would go back to being vacuous and entertaining.

When he saw this wasn't winning us over, Étienne tried to make us feel sorry for him. He paused as he inhaled his cigarette in the way that only a Québécois can inhale a cigarette.

"I'm beat up. I'm physically and mentally exhausted." He exhaled loudly for effect. The cigarette smoke hung over his head like the little cloud that hangs over Eeyore. "I just feel like digging my own grave, lying in it, letting it fill up with rainwater and drowning myself. I don't have any money. When I'm at a bar, people expect me to buy them a drink, but I don't even have money for that. I like to have my cup of soup at Dunkin' Donuts and that's all."

I reached over to put my hand on his shoulder to comfort

him, but Nicolas interceded and gently pushed my hand away.

"What the hell are you on about, old man?" Nicolas said. "You want to borrow some money? We're all fucking broke. The whole city's broke."

"Did you know that I performed in France once? They couldn't pay me to go back."

"Well, those days are over, aren't they?" Nicolas said.

Nicolas wasn't giving me a chance to respond to anything our father said. Étienne was quiet and looked awkward for a moment. Then he raised up his can of beer into the air.

"My beautiful, beautiful children. Today is the luckiest of days, isn't it? Today I had two children instead of one. Nineteen years ago today."

"We're twenty years old," Nicolas said. "Twenty!"

"Of course, I'm just feeling flustered today because I'm full of ideas. I'm excited. I get inaccurate when I'm excited."

"What are you excited about?" Nicolas asked. He narrowed his gaze, suddenly suspicious.

"There's a very tasteful reporter named Hugo who wants to do a segment on us all. He's doing a special on all the old rowdy gang. Where they are now."

"What the hell?" said Nicolas. "Who in the hell is Hugo? You know how I feel about Hugos."

"You don't even know where this conversation is going, my boy. Hugo has some interesting ideas. I've been looking for a venue to express some of the ideas that I've been developing. I think it would be a good vehicle for me to launch my album. It'll be a concept album. Part song, part memoir. Between my songs I'm going to read bits of my life story. This documentary will be broadcast nationally. I want to have a scene of myself standing on the bridge in Parc La Fontaine, reciting the lyrics to 'Pamplemousse vert.' It will be lovely, no?"

"*Putrid* would more likely be the word I was looking for," Nicolas said. "What do you need us for?"

"He's pitched the whole family. You're not going to leave your own father high and dry, are you? I thought that they could just film us doing something normal. We can be shown eating sandwiches. You two can be roller-skating in the park. You'll look so cute, *n'est-ce pas?* We can take a paddleboat around the pond with the swans in it."

What a lovely portrait he was painting for a seven-year-old Nicolas and Nouschka. He hadn't been clueless. Some parents didn't know how the hell to act, but Étienne had just proven that he knew exactly how a happy family would spend an afternoon. We had never actually done anything like that together.

Nicolas looked over at me and saw the stricken look that I must have had on my face. He motioned to me quickly that he was going to take care of this. As he stood up, Nicolas's chair fell over behind him. Étienne stood up at the same time. They looked so much alike. Étienne's skin was darker and his black hair was thinning, but other than that, the resemblance was uncanny.

"Are you out of your mind!" Nicolas said. "And why are you bringing this up on our birthday? This is supposed to be a private celebration, not a business meeting."

"I'm sorry I wasn't able to do certain things for you, Nico. I've never been sure what it was that you wanted from me."

"Advice! Why don't you give us advice! Why don't you take an interest and try to guide us once in a while. You know? Guide us through these troubled times."

"I can do that. Let me give it a shot."

Étienne looked like giving us advice was completely out of his depth. I think he would have preferred something a little more concise—like picking up our laundry or mailing some letters for us. But he decided to go before he revealed by virtue of his sitting there that he had no guidance whatsoever at the tip of his tongue.

"So no documentary then?" Étienne said as he was getting his coat.

"I don't think you realize it," Nicolas said, "but I dream of slicing the throats of these types of idiots. I would relish stabbing them in their hearts with a salad fork."

"My dear boy, you have always had a startling inclination toward hyperbole. It's truly remarkable. It would even be remarked upon in the courts of Louis XIV."

"Why don't you ask Noëlle if she wants to be in the documentary?"

"Who?" Étienne said.

Étienne looked to me for help. I was always the one who was able to talk Nicolas into performing when we were kids. I decided to take Nicolas's side. Étienne didn't even know who Nicolas was talking about when he mentioned our mother. I didn't want to pretend that we were a loving and close-knit family. There was something horrific about it. It shone a light on something I wanted kept in the dark.

"Nouschka, *fais-moi un sourire.*"

"No," I said quietly.

"Fine then. I will ask them to leave. For all I know, they might be recording this unpleasantness right now."

We were suddenly confused. There was a jarring inconsistency between what Étienne was saying and reality. He was talking about the documentary film crew as if they were here in the room, when clearly they were not. Nicolas grasped the situation before I did and said, "Where are they?"

"They're out in the hallway."

Nicolas went and threw open the door, and sure enough, there was the documentary crew. They were standing with their equipment, crammed together in the hallway. They weren't even really ashamed.

"Should we leave?" Hugo asked.

Étienne was immediately in character. He would know how to salvage this moment. He probably felt protected now that the camera was on—the only thing that truly adored him and never let him down. Everyone in the crew positioned themselves quickly and started taping.

"Well, my darlings," Étienne said, turning to bid us adieu, "who can believe that another birthday is here? Celebrate your youth, my darlings. Blow out your candles and make sure that you wish for immortality."

The cat slipped out the door after Étienne.

Nicolas slammed the door behind them. But we could still hear them as they departed.

Étienne began to sing an old song about an elephant that gets a peanut stuck up its nose. I hadn't thought about that song in a long time. I always assumed the song had a deeper meaning, although I had no idea what it could be. Now as an adult, I still didn't know. How could you not love someone who came up with songs like that? That was the trouble with people with talent. That was the reason that they got away with murder.

"I am done with that man," Nicolas said for the millionth time in his life.

I started to laugh. I couldn't help it. Yes, he was here again trying to use us. It somehow never prevented me from enjoying the show. I never took Étienne seriously or got outraged at him. Nicolas was the only person who made me livid, and he could do that pretty easily these days.

*****

Later that night I found an undershirt with anchors on it stuck between the mattress and the wall. The tag said LACOSTE. It was obviously Adam's. I inhaled the shirt deeply. It still smelled like him. I went into the bathroom with it. I took off all my clothes except my underwear and put the undershirt on. I stood in front of the mirror and watched myself put on some lipstick.

"I'm finished with you," I told myself as I puckered my lips. "I've lost all respect for you. Look, we had a good run. I just think that it was a mistake."

I put a towel on the floor and lay down on it. We could never masturbate in our own bed because the other one was there. I imagined that Adam was going down on me. I imagined Hugo was filming me through the window, encouraging me to come. God knows who we became when we masturbated. It was like our desire was a spirit that possessed us and took over.

Nicolas started banging on the door. I couldn't even find a place in this apartment to have a sexual fantasy without Nicolas barging in. I stood up and put my dress back on over the undershirt and flushed the toilet.

I flung open the door.

"*Niaiseux!*" I yelled, with my hands flying open toward his face, like a startled dove.

"*Osti de conne!*" he yelled back.

I moved to my right to get around him, but he moved to his

left. And then when I went to my left, he went to his right. And so on and so on. There was no way that we could imagine how either of us could ever possibly find our way out of that apartment. We were just going to spend the rest of our lives running away from each other and bumping into each other. The tiny apartment was a labyrinth and Nicolas was the Minotaur in every closet and every room.

CHAPTER 22

The Owl and the Pussycat

W HEN LOULOU WALKED INTO THE APARTMENT, I noticed that he had confetti in his hair. I looked out the window. The street was blocked off and people were heading down toward Boulevard René-Lévesque. It was *L'Assomption de Marie.* It was always at the very end of summer. Everybody went to every kind of festival in Montréal in the summertime. We were always in party mode, having been temporarily granted clemency by the winter.

"I forgot the fair was today," I said.

"Yeah, it's right outside the door."

"Do you want to go back with me?"

"It's all that Catholic crap. You know I don't go for that shit."

Loulou had had enough with Catholicism when he was little. When he was a kid, everybody attributed everything to God. You couldn't ride a bicycle unless you said a brief prayer. They couldn't suck a lollipop in public until 1960. He had to comb his hair to the side and have a visible part until 1966. It was the way that God wanted it.

"My Christ of a coffee machine is broken, tabernacle of the chalice," Loulou yelled out from the kitchen. Even after the decline of the Catholic Church, the Québécois loved to use religious words in vain in almost miraculous ways.

I went down the stairs as a neighbour's cat climbed up them in the opposite direction. It was wearing a teeny bell around its neck that played a Bartók tune. I stepped out into the bright light and walked down toward the fair by myself. There were wires criss-crossing the street with lightbulbs suspended from them. At that moment, a little parade passed in front of me. A group of men in suits was carrying a float with a ten-foot Virgin Mary on their shoulders. I looked up at the Virgin Mary. Her cheeks were painted blue. There was a metal halo of gold stars around her head. Her fingers were pointed up as if she was trying to do a math problem in her head. She always looked calm. Everybody loved her. She was as secure as a sixty-year-old woman whose husband had never cheated on her.

A group of ten-year-old boys with white nylon wings on their backs followed the float while playing the trumpet. A parade of young girls who had just been confirmed walked by in lace dresses. They had been up all night collecting moths in a jar to make those dresses.

I walked around a bit. I wasn't surprised to see Nicolas. Wherever there was a crowd, Nicolas was bound to be hanging around. He was sitting next to a pretty seventeen-year-old girl in a miniskirt, trying to talk her out of crying.

I went to buy a candy apple. I couldn't help but buy a candy apple for Nicolas too. I wasn't angry toward him that day. That was the nature of love, wasn't it? True love just shrugged its shoulders no matter what sort of obnoxious action the other party pulled. When I got back to Nicolas, the girl looked up angrily at me. Whenever a girl was mad at Nicolas, she took it out on me. She jumped up onto her feet and stormed off. Nicolas shrugged as I sat down, and he put his hand out for the candy apple. We ate them as we took in the scene.

There were some rides in the parking lot. There were those cheap rides that they drive in on trucks from one day-long fair to the other. The Ferris wheel looked like it had been set up by an eighty-year-old janitor.

The sun started going down. The red and yellow lightbulbs on the sides of the rides turned on. All of a sudden, everyone looked like they had black eyes. The calliope blared. The bingo machine sounded like an army of horses was coming. The angels were arriving to judge us all.

They were moving the Virgin Mary. She was teetering, on the verge of toppling, when I saw Raphaël. Good lord, I thought, what did you have to do in Québec to be kept in jail for more than a week and a half?

He was leaning against a car and was drinking from a giant can of beer. I loved those cans. You felt like a little kid when you held a can that big. You felt the same way as you did when your legs were hanging off the edge of an oversized chair.

Raphaël had on a pair of alligator shoes that made his enormous feet look even bigger. The laces seemed too thick for the dress shoes, as if he'd pulled them out of running shoes. He was wearing a white dress shirt that was unbuttoned. You could see that he had a tattoo of Jesus on his chest. There wasn't much scarier than a tattoo of Jesus. It meant that you were spiritually inclined. And if you were spiritually inclined around here, it probably wasn't Sunday school that got you that way. Rather, it was a combination of hard drugs and deep injustice to yourself. It was the last resort.

Raphaël's hair was already shot with grey, even though he was only twenty, and he was smoking a menthol cigarette. When he exhaled, the cigarette smoke looked like a girl doing rhythmic gymnastics with a ribbon. If you smoked menthol cigarettes, people wouldn't bum them off of you. He knew all the tricks for being alone.

Once, years before, I had run into him and he had the biggest hickey on his neck that I had ever seen. But I never knew him to have a girlfriend. Now he was just staring right at me.

And I smiled back: a smile that I knew he couldn't resist. You should beware of motherless children. They will eat you alive. You will never be loved by anyone the way that you will be loved by a motherless child.

Nicolas noticed me smiling at Raphaël.

"Oh my God," Nicolas said. "Don't talk to Raphaël. He believes in aliens and shit. I'm not even kidding. In high school he was voted most likely to become an axe murderer and stab his innocent wife in the fucking shower. No no no, he was voted most likely to end up with duct tape all over his mouth in the trunk of a car."

"I don't know. He seems kind of interesting."

"He doesn't believe in dinosaurs. For me that's a deal breaker. What? You don't believe in dinosaurs? Get the fuck out of here. That's just me. If you're going to fuck a guy who doesn't believe in dinosaurs, that's your own business. But it reflects poorly on me, being your twin brother."

"He does have a nice car though, no?"

"He just doesn't strike me as an upstanding guy, Nouschka. All joking aside."

Then Nicolas got up and walked away, like he just couldn't take it all of a sudden. There was something about Raphaël that caused me and Nicolas to separate. It was what elementary school teachers had been trying to do for a hundred years. Raphaël put his hands in his pockets and walked over and stopped right in front of me. We stood smiling at each other.

"What's with your brother?" Raphaël asked.

"Nothing."

"Did you see the horses earlier?"

"No. When did they have horses?" I asked, genuinely disappointed. "Show horses?"

"I was looking for you anyways. I saw your brother; I thought you might be around."

"Oh."

"Are you still banging that old guy? No. Well, that shit never works out. Kind of strange. You're an odd bird, Nouschka. I always liked you. Did you know that?"

"No."

"Did you get my Valentine's Day card?"

"When was that?"

"Grade Three, I guess. I didn't sign it. I just wanted you to guess it was from me."

"How am I supposed to remember something like that?"

"What was he, like, Russian mafia? I figured that he must be to go out with a girl like you. Did he buy you lots of stuff? Like clothes. Whatever it is that girls like?"

"No."

"Did you, like, win a beauty pageant or something? I thought I heard that. Like you were Miss Montréal or something. Then I thought, now she'll never go out with a guy like me."

"Are you confusing me with somebody else?"

"I doubt that very much."

"Look, I don't know what you're talking about. I like dancing. I like movies. I like that band playing right now. I'm no different from anybody else."

"So are you going to live on this block the rest of your life?"

"Are you?"

"I try to leave, but every time I do I get thrown in jail. I didn't realize it was illegal." He tossed his finished cigarette butt over my shoulder. "How many kisses do you think it takes to make a girl fall in love with you?"

"I never counted."

"Fifty?"

"Not that many."

"Thirty-five?"

"Don't be silly."

"Then how many?"

I raised up my index finger to indicate just one. He smiled. And then he pulled my face to his and we kissed.

It was all too late after that kiss. I already knew what his breath smelled like. I already knew what he looked like in his pyjamas. I already knew what he sounded like when he spoke in his sleep. I was already his girlfriend by the end of the kiss.

We went to get Raphaël's car. He drove a beat-up green Cadillac. A steer's skull was airbrushed onto the hood. It was a really shitty car, but the skull really distracted you. You didn't know what to think about the car coming down the street. It defied all your preconceived notions. The back seat was filled with paperback books. He had a suit hanging from a wire coat hanger so that it wouldn't get too creased. There were some dog toys and a box filled with dog biscuits.

When you hear that there's been an apparition of the Virgin Mary, you don't care where it is. You don't worry that it's in a bad neighbourhood. Or that in order to see it you have to go into a living room with shag carpeting or televisions piled on top of one another and busted-up couches and neglected babies crying in their cribs. The Virgin Mary trumps all that. You make your pilgrimage. It's the same thing with true love, which is just as rare.

*****

As we were driving he put his hand on my knee. I liked that. It was like we were already lovers. It was as if we had been lovers for a very long time already. It felt like we were a married couple. He ran out of the car and into a corner store to buy condoms. The door had so many bells that clanged together as he opened the door that it seemed to be waking up the entire neighbourhood. I liked that. They never rang the church bells in this city for anything exciting anymore.

We rented a motel room.

"Take your clothes off for me," he said as soon as he shut the door.

I felt as if my dress must have weighed hundreds of pounds, because I suddenly felt so much lighter. I was wearing these polka-dot underwear. I hadn't expected to have sex that night. They had been pretty once, but they had a tear and the lace trimming had come loose. When I took them off, I was so naked that I felt transparent. I don't think that I had ever felt so naked. I had on one single blue sock that was clinging to my foot for dear life. This was the first time that sex meant anything.

He took off his shirt and pants. He was really handsome. I don't know what on earth other girls would make of him, but I just found him so handsome. I would not change a single thing about his appearance. He was all skinny and fit still from having been a figure skater all those years. He didn't have any chest hair. He just had a black line going down from his belly button into his pants. I even thought that his ridiculously bad tattoos were so sexy. They were sort of beautiful to me. And whereas most people would liken them to drawings in ballpoint pen on the walls of a public bathroom, I would liken them to Renaissance paintings of serious girls holding ermines.

When he took off his underwear he reached out his arms and pulled me close to him. We made love on the pink flowers of the bed cover.

After I climaxed, Raphaël pulled out and took his condom off and came all over my tits. It was wonderful. He stepped into his pants and went into the bathroom. His pants were half down, below his ass, and he was walking on his pant cuffs. He came out with a cigarette in his mouth and a hand towel with orange roses and he wiped me off with it. I don't know why, but it was so tender.

*****

The curtains at the motel were covered in little pineapples. The trucks kept passing by outside, creating an infinity of sunrises and sunsets. It seemed like the world was orbiting really quickly. Shadows like black panthers crept in the window every time a car passed. This was what it must have been like to hang out in a motel room after robbing a bank, when you had no idea whether or not the police and detectives were surrounding the place or whether it was simply the night outside, which was filled only with crickets and lost keys.

The minibar was filled with tiny bottles of booze, like the ones that Alice in Wonderland found. They could either make your heart enormous or tiny. He turned on the light next to the bed so that he could set the alarm on his wristwatch. He turned the lamp off, but his body seemed to continue to emanate light as if he was incandescent.

Raphaël put his fists to his mouth and made a perfect mournful trumpet sound. When he closed his eyes, he looked like he just received a guilty verdict. Then he fell asleep. And like that, we were madly in love. They say that Jesus loves you, but will he come down and say that he loves you the most?

CHAPTER 23

All Perverts Great and Small

I WAS GETTING DRESSED FOR OUR DATE. I'D TOLD
Raphaël that I would meet him on the corner, but he said he'd
knock on my door. Why he thought he had to come and knock
on my door was beyond me. Our family had always considered
manners to be sort of on the phony side.

It made me nervous, because Nicolas had been insulting
Raphaël ever since I went off with him at the fair.

Nicolas came in the room. He took off his sweater and lay
down to rest in his undershirt. He had had that same undershirt with Papa Smurf on it since he was ten years old. He lay
there with his boots still on. He lit up a cigarette and watched
me while I buttoned up the back of my dress.

One of our own cats walked into the room at that second,
to see what was happening. It was Johann, a black cat with
perpetual bed-head. He looked like a splotch of ink that was
appearing through a pocket in a shirt. Nicolas looked at the cat
for a second as if he was going to pick a fight with it, and then
he turned back to me.

"Man, what a low-life," Nicolas said. "I mean low class. You might try and meet somebody who has a real job."

"You don't work at all."

"He has to punch a clock or he goes back to jail. Wow! He's a Fortune 500 man. A most eligible bachelor."

"You might like him if you got to know him."

"Frankly, I can't stand the motherfucker. I mean, who does he think he is walking around like that. I'll tolerate that kind of shit from those exiled Vietnam vets but nobody else. Did you know that the U.S. government cheaped out and gave the vets Edgar Cayce and *I'm OK—You're OK* books on tape instead of proper psychiatric treatment?"

"Where did you hear about this?" I asked.

"A library card is no cure for mental illness, that's for sure. When vets come back, they should not have library privileges. If I have to stand in the line for the bus and have a Vietnam vet behind me talking about Tolstoy, I'm just going to go move to the Northwest Territories. It's why I don't take public transportation."

"Why would you, when you can drive in style on your bicycle?"

"How do you know Raphaël hasn't been lobotomized? People with lobotomies don't know they've been lobotomized."

"So what if he has?"

"I should have known! You'll go with anybody!"

I tied a ribbon in my hair and wagged my head back and forth in the mirror to see if it would stay on.

"How do I look?" I asked.

"Really, in all honesty, he's a dick. I told you in Grade One and I'm telling you now."

"You didn't answer my question."

Nicolas would develop irrational hatred for people when he was a little boy and he would not let it go. It was very important for Nicolas to always be infuriated by someone. It allowed him to externalize some of the hatred that he felt toward himself.

"Why do I feel like your relationship with Raphaël is just to spite me?"

I stopped, startled. There was some strange truth in what he said, but I didn't want to explore it. Nicolas seemed to think that my relationship with Raphaël was a punishment for his having lied about Adam and dragged me to see Lily with no preparation. He couldn't believe that it didn't have anything to do with him. I also had a hard time believing that this relationship had nothing to do with Nicolas.

Everyone had always given Nicolas and me a hard time about sleeping in the same bed together and changing around each other. There was never anything about it that gave me a feeling of indecency or self-consciousness. But the idea that Nicolas had orchestrated my sex life creeped me out. Maybe it was about time that I wanted privacy. Even though *Le Journal de Montréal*, *La Presse*, and *Le Devoir* had all described us as precocious, Nicolas and I were late bloomers, emotionally speaking.

The doorbell rang. Nicolas sprang up out of bed and ran down the hall to the front door. The cat looked at its paws and frantically back at its body, as if it had just been transformed into a cat and couldn't accept it. I ran after him, but it was too late, Nicolas had swung open the door and was leaning out of it. Raphaël was standing there, expressionless, in sunglasses.

"Yes, can I help you?" Nicolas asked. "Are you here to convert us to Jehovah's Witnesses? You guys should put a little more something something into those magazines. Like maybe you should have a comics page. And some horoscopes. I'm just saying, if you're looking to attract more converts. Or have a telethon. Everyone loves a good telethon."

"Funny."

"Whatcha guys gonna do tonight? Drink some Kool-Aid with Jim Jones?"

"I'm here for Nouschka. Tell her I'm here."

"Were you here last night? Oh no, that was another guy."

"What's with you? Still sticking up fourteen-year-olds in the metro?"

"I'm going to let that go. But let the record state that I resent it."

I pushed Nicolas out of the way. He seemed resigned to being shoved aside. I trotted down the steps next to Raphaël. I liked the way Raphaël was dressed all in black except for a pair of brown running shoes with red laces. I don't think I'd ever seen him in the same pair of footwear twice. He put his arm around me as soon as we were outside.

Suddenly we heard Nicolas call out, "I'm looking right at you!"

We looked up and he was on the roof. It was sort of startling that he'd gotten up there so fast.

"Just because my sister's stupid enough to date you, it doesn't mean anything. I'm going to come and kill you one of these days."

"You talk pretty tough for an asshole all the way up on a rooftop," Raphaël called back.

"Just because you're fucking Nouschka doesn't mean you're fucking me."

"Doesn't he care what the neighbours think?" Raphaël asked me, actually looking shocked.

"They've heard everything," I said.

"He's disrespecting you, you know."

"I don't know how you can like me if you hate Nicolas. We're like the same person."

"No, you're not."

"We were having conversations before we were even born."

"You guys aren't alike at all. You're opposites."

"How so?"

"You love everybody and he hates everybody. Sometimes I don't even know which is worse, because I feel like both of you might want to show a little bit of decorum and equilibrium."

*****

We spent the evening in a motel. I threw my peacoat on over my underwear and went out onto the street and stuck my thumb out as if I was a hitchhiker. The minuscule twinkles were all over the sidewalk, reflecting moonlight. Raphaël got into his car and drove around the block. He was going to pretend to pick me up and then drive me to the outskirts of the city and rape me, or something like that.

A police car came around the block before Raphaël's car. The police officer got out and started asking all sorts of questions. He wanted to arrest me. The officer assumed that I was a prostitute because I had no clothes on under my pea jacket. Raphaël got out of his car and managed to convince the officer that we were just perverts. The police officer told us to keep it to the bedroom.

We went to a tiny underground restaurant that had mirrors on all the walls. It was one of those end-of-the-world Chinese restaurants. If you were a respectable citizen, you would never even notice that it was there. There were small bowls of water with rhododendrons floating in them on the tables. None of the menus had the right prices. They had the prices from 1975 on them.

I looked over at Raphaël. He had a pack of cigarettes in each of his pockets. It was a bring-your-own-wine joint. Raphaël unscrewed the lid and took a long drink right from the bottle.

"Disgusting!" he yelled.

We ate salt and pepper squid with chopsticks. The place was filled with actual prostitutes. One girl, who looked twelve, was wearing a fur hat and a T-shirt. She was so stoned that she couldn't tell whether she was hot or cold.

There was another girl with a turtleneck sweater and tiny shiny pants. She had ordered a plate of dumplings but couldn't eat them. She was biting her fingernails and looking out the window. She had a terrible cough, the way that pretty fifteen-year-olds who smoked in the wintertime and had sex with grown-up men did. The bottom of her face was all red around her mouth as if someone had been kissing her violently. A pimp was with her. He looked about eighteen years old. He had on a black sweater and sweatpants and poofy light blue sneakers.

There were horses on one of the girls' T-shirts. If you put your ear up against her chest, you could hear them galloping. It was here on Rue Sainte-Catherine that the most beautiful kisses in the world were grown.

Raphaël had stopped taking his medication. He told me that the drugs screwed up his perception of time. One particular Wednesday had lasted for a year. And once, three days went by in five minutes. He said he was looking out a window and saw a rose bloom and wilt right in front of him. And the drugs messed with his erections.

We both had this strange intensity when we were making

love. As if we hadn't quite figured out what it was for. As if we pinned too much of our hopes and dreams on it. I was thinking that sex could cure all sorts of things. But the girls here knew exactly what sex was worth. They knew that sex cost forty dollars and could be bartered down. If you took one of the girls up to a hotel room, and she drank a glass of water while sitting on the ledge of the bathroom sink in yellow polyester underwear, did it look much different than true love?

I wanted to tell Raphaël about my mother. I thought it was that time of the relationship where I could bring up serious things instead of just flirt and have sex. And I wanted to hear what he had to say about it. In his own way, he could be quite brilliant at summing things up.

"Do you know that Nicolas and I met our mother for the first time last month?"

"Really? How the hell did that go?"

"She didn't even want us there. There was this look on her face like we could destroy her life. We were, like, the worst things that had ever happened to her. She would have opened up her pocketbook and given us all the money in it, just to get rid of us. She looked like we were going to blackmail her."

"That's got to make you feel low-grade lousy all the time."

"It sort of makes me feel like I'm kind of creepy? Do you know that feeling that I'm talking about? It's hard sometimes to put it into words."

"You feel as if everybody has been given an instruction manual to how to be likable," Raphaël said, "but you didn't get it. And they are all sold out now. And if you are what you eat, then you must have surely spent the last few years of your life eating dog food and cat shit. Because when you look in the mirror, it is all that you see."

I wouldn't have used those metaphors exactly, but he had actually sort of captured that icky feeling. That's what it felt like when the little tank that contained your self-esteem was running on empty and you needed to somehow fill it up.

And that was what all the girls sitting in this restaurant were also feeling. They were very, very pretty, but they felt so ugly. They looked into their bathroom mirrors in the middle of the night because they had to pee for the twelfth time because of a bladder infection, and they saw ghouls and hideous things.

I didn't know what sort of memories had driven Raphaël to such insights. I was about to ask, but he had already stood up and swung his jacket on in a way that somehow implied that the subject was closed. He had no intention of delving into his own psyche that night.

"But you don't have to worry about how the rest of the world sees you. You just have to think about how it is that I think about you."

CHAPTER 24

It's Always Raining Under an Umbrella

R APHAËL AND I STARTED SPENDING ALL OUR nights at the motel. We couldn't go to his parents' apartment or mine if we wanted to be alone. We were blowing the little money that we had, but we didn't care. The belt slid from the loops of his pants like a snake through the grass. We lay facing each other with our foreheads and knees touching. We lay in the shape of a heart. I started to have the first inkling of why it might feel good to leave home and be part of a different family.

We left the motel one afternoon and went for a walk in the park. The clouds were like a group of sheep that was gathering to be shorn. There was a scent called Five Minutes Before It Rains. If you put it on your neck, whoever kissed you would cry.

All the people in the street had to rush up stairs and more stairs to close all their windows before the rain flew in. The laundry was being pulled in so violently that it screamed.

"Everyone to the lifeboats! Everyone to the lifeboats!" a boy was yelling.

Children who just wanted a few more minutes were still outside playing. Their mothers' voices calling them in were like pieces of paper. The wind crunched them up and threw them away before they could get to the children's ears.

Raphaël stood at the side of the pond and began throwing bits of bread into the water for the swans. They all started heading toward him. They looked like they were on their way to devour him. One stepped out of the water with its large black feet. It held its wings in front of it, like a naked girl with only her socks on, holding her hands over her privates. Raphaël turned toward me.

We started to feel a few drops of rain. We ran and climbed onto the merry-go-round just to keep out of the rain. We sat on a chariot that was being pulled by two zebras. Raphaël pulled a tiny box out of his pocket inside his jacket. It was a little brown cardboard box that had a drawing of a mourning dove on it.

"Let's get married," he said.

I felt a rush flood through my heart. I didn't know whether the feeling was love or whether it was the excitement you feel when you are doing something that you know is stupid but you are doing it anyways.

He put the ring on my finger. It was a mood ring. It was turning green and yellow. It was turning every colour in the rainbow. Sometimes I was so afraid of love. It gave you the feeling you had when you were shoplifting and you were walking out of the store with something concealed under your jacket.

There was a drug dealer who sold a kind of acid called Happily Ever After. That was the only time I had ever heard that term applied to anything in real life. Everything I knew about marriage pointed to it being a horrible, hateful endeavour.

And if there were any two people who would be incapable of a stable marriage, it had to be Raphaël and me.

It felt like I was doing something terrible when I said *oui*. But God help me, I wanted to see what was on the other side of that word.

The rain started coming by in gusts, like groups of frightened deer. We sat on the horses, holding each other's hands, and looked out at the world. It rained all day. Later it was reported that the rain had taken down a whole fleet of newspaper ships in the pond.

CHAPTER 25

An Angel in the Process of Becoming a Businessman

I WAS DOING WELL IN SCHOOL. IT WAS MAKING ME feel like I had a future opening up before me. I was tired of working at the newspaper stand. I was tired of every Tom, Dick, and Harry coming in and telling me who I was and acting as if I was their very best pal. And maybe I didn't need every man with a grocery bag telling me his theories of time travel.

I wanted to have a job that was farther downtown. I wanted to make a bit more than minimum wage, which wasn't even five dollars an hour. I was going to see about a receptionist job at the opera house downtown.

I looked through all my clothes to make sure that what I was wearing didn't have any holes. I had spent so many years perfecting a look of being cool that it was difficult now to go the other way around. It was hard to not look like a rebel. I spent fifteen minutes trying to comb my hair and make it look straight. Hopeless. It was far too in love with the wind. If I had a mother, I would know how to fix my hair.

The bricks on the metro wall were painted a bright blue and there was a mosaic of an explorer over the tunnel that the train travelled through. All the metro stations were completely different from one another, each having been designed by a different architect in the late sixties. Mad architects were all the rage back then. They had enormous moustaches and wild hair, and were considered geniuses. Étienne's generation had been a very busy one. The whole city reflected their strange talents and tastes.

I got off at the metro stop right underneath the opera house. I wasn't sure how the interview would go. I didn't have a high school diploma. I didn't know how to type. My English was shitty and they apparently had a lot of English clientele. But the job was certainly worth trying for. And it would make me feel like I was an adult, and that it made perfect sense to be getting married. Ha, or maybe I was just building up a case for when I told Loulou that I was engaged!

CHAPTER 26

The Collected Works of the Grim Reaper

LOULOU ALWAYS GOT DRESSED UP WHEN HE
went to visit our grandmother's grave. He had put on his fedora
and his navy blue suit. He was wearing a giant gold watch that
never told time properly. He had taken his weekly shower and
didn't have his usual vague odour of cat piss and dead things.
Instead, he smelled like the breath of someone who was sucking
on a hard candy.

It was September. It was already getting chilly. I kept waiting for the right moment to tell Loulou that I was getting married. I felt like I had to confess something bad that I had done,
as if I had been expelled from school.

We had to walk over the park on the mountain in order to
get to the cemetery. The police went around on horses. There
were old men who had their pants pulled up inexplicably high
and had plastic bags filled with apples hanging from their wrists.
Young people were sunbathing in the cold. Little children were

gathered around the brass statue of a lion. They stroked the lion's mane and blew into its nostrils. They begged it to awaken from its terrible frozen spell and come home with them.

Loulou was having more trouble walking than ever. He would stop, hunched over, and look all around him as if he was taking in the magnificent view, as opposed to being tired.

"Clouds don't look like much anymore. When I was a kid, you could look up and see adorable white goats running around. It was lovely. You see anything up there?"

"There's a naked woman taking a bath."

"You're a pervert, Nouschka. You and your brother."

There was a man on a unicycle balancing a hat on his nose. After the 1980 referendum, everyone with prospects left the city. Everyone here now was a direct descendant of a daydreamer. A disproportionate amount of people in the city were planning careers in the circus. We passed by the giant pond.

"There used to be puppet shows in this park all the time when I was a kid. Of course, there was a Punch and Judy show. There was also a Lush and Trudy show."

"A what?"

"Lush and Trudy. It was about a puppet who drank too much and cheated on his wife."

"Never heard of it."

"Well, it was very popular. There was a puppet named Putz, who wore a trench coat and exposed himself."

"What did they have at the big amphitheatre?"

"Oh! All sorts of things. There was a magician who was able to swallow birds and then crap them out of his ass, still alive!"

"That's disgusting!" I laughed.

"Oh no!" he said. "Look, swans!"

I'd heard his stories about swans for years. Loulou said that once when he was little, he passed by a pond on a rainy day, and a swan fell madly in love with his umbrella. Loulou said the swan decided that it wanted to marry the umbrella and keep it as his wife. The swan chased him all the way home.

I thought about the swans that were in the pond when Raphaël asked me to marry him. If things went badly, would I have a horror of swans? I wondered.

I looked over at Loulou. He was also lost in thought as he looked at the birds. The shape of his fedora was ruined, like he'd worn it in the rain. His brown tie was flying and twisting in the wind like a seal performing tricks. I suddenly realized, for the first time, how sad he was. He had never recovered from our grandmother's death. I felt sorry for him and didn't want to tell him about the wedding. He'd been upset enough for one lifetime.

He bent over to talk to babies in their strollers. "Have you tried Rogaine for your hair loss?" "Lost all your teeth? So have I!" "Come on, get out of there. It's my turn!" "I hope you're not drinking and driving."

Then he would look up at the mothers and laugh his head off. It was impossible for me to know what people thought about him.

"I went and bought a stationary bicycle. I rode it all day and I got nowhere."

He had to tell jokes to everyone. He was lonely. He wanted to get in all his talking for the day. He wanted complete strangers to love him. He was the last vaudevillian star in the world. It's harder to be funny when you're older. You've lost touch with the zeitgeist, to put it mildly.

"There's something I have to tell you," I said.

"Oh, what? What the fuck now? Jesus Christ. Here we go. Let me get off my fucking feet before you tell me."

"Raphaël and I are getting married."

Loulou looked like he was going to have a heart attack. He opened his mouth and shut it before he was finally able to compose a sentence.

"I hear people say that you're good-looking," he said. "Why can't you date a doctor or a lawyer?"

"It's too late for that. Besides, Raphaël's smart."

"You're just like one of those girls who gets kidnapped and falls in love with their kidnappers."

"That doesn't even make sense."

"And I think that he is slightly retarded, if I may speak freely," Loulou continued. "You were such a cute baby. Why did you settle for the first guy who asked you?"

"I love him."

"He'd better take a trip to the Wizard of Oz for a brain. On second thought, he should go there with a grocery list. He should ask for a backbone while he's there. And the ability to get a job."

"Oh stop. He can do anything when he wants to. Look how far he went with figure skating."

He was quiet again for a bit. He raised his shoulders and then dropped them, as if he was giving in to an argument.

"I think that if there was a weather report on his mental state, I would say eighty-five percent chance of crazy. He's a ticking time bomb. Is that fucker skating again a possibility?"

"No. He'll never skate again."

"He's too proud for the Ice Capades, eh?" Loulou shook his head.

We walked into the graveyard. If I had come on any other day, I would have stopped to read the tombstones. Here lies

Joachim Renault, who drank three beers then went to play hockey on the lake that was not quite frozen. Here lies Xavier Therrier, who never got over his wife having left him and just didn't have the strength to fight his fever. Luc Dionne, who was loved by all his family, died trying to rescue the family cat from a tree.

"I don't know," Loulou said. "Did I raise you properly? Did I not tell you two little assholes that you could be astronauts? Isn't that the philosophy? Tell your kids they can be dentists when they can't even pass third-grade math."

"Not really. You were obsessed with Étienne."

"You said such cute things on that radio show. I thought for sure you'd grow up and be a politician or something like that. You read all those pretty poems."

"I'm finishing school. I'm going to be a professional something or other. I want to maybe be a journalist, a political commentator, a writer. Something like that."

"You're sensible. Except when boys come around. Then you're fucking nuts."

I stood there second-guessing my decision to marry Raphaël, as I had done a million times that week. Maybe I was afraid to ever just be alone. Perhaps I needed to have a man in my life as a cowardly backup plan.

"What about that rich little Jew you were going with. Why not marry him? Don't tell me. He turned out to be gay, am I right?"

"Yes, you're right."

"I'm old, but I still know what is what, don't I?"

He looked around to see if anyone had heard his joke, but everyone there was lying six feet under the ground.

Loulou let it go at that. A proper parent would have been able to end it all there. Loulou could never get angry or lay down the law with Nicolas and me. He just stopped seeing us when we became adolescents. How could I avoid getting married young? This way I could start a brand-new family, where everyone would notice me.

CHAPTER 27

Nouschka Tremblay Says, "I Do!"

WITH IMMIGRANTS COMING FROM ALL OVER, IT was awhile before they settled on what would be the appropriate marriage ritual in Montréal. You carried a rooster under your arm all the way around the house of your betrothed. You rode a white horse over a chalk line in the street. For a while, if you jumped over a tool box, you were married.

I knew I was young to be a bride. Québécois did everything so young. We lost our looks young. People died at forty-nine from drinking and lung cancer and a steady diet of white bread and Jos Louis cakes. Getting married so young was like robbing a bank or getting a tattoo.

We weren't having a Catholic wedding, since Raphaël refused to set foot in a church. Nicolas had had a field day with this, saying that it was because Raphaël had been born in Hell and would start puking blood if he tried to enter a house of God. We got married in Raphaël's cousin's living room. It was a medium-sized apartment with ceramic tiles on the floors in the hallways and lots of tacky vases with fake flowers in them. The carpets in the living room were thick and nice to run your toes through.

I had a baby blue dress with cloth flowers all over the front of it. Raphaël's second cousin had made it for me. At first I was disappointed and wouldn't put it on. It looked like a pile of Kleenexes on a nightstand when you are sick. But oddly it looked really good on.

Strange relatives of mine were there. They were all square and pale. One of them had a glass eye. We hadn't seen them in years. I didn't even know how Loulou had managed to track them down to come to this.

Loulou came over to continue to try to talk me out of marrying Raphaël, who was standing on the other side of the room. He made sure to turn his back to Raphaël, in case the man I was about to marry was able to lip-read.

Loulou was holding a paper plate with a piece of lasagna that he had probably found while snooping in the fridge. As he was lifting the fork up to his mouth, he leaned over and said, "You know, what's a guy like that going to do for a living? Don't you want a guy who can support you? Why don't you go for a guy with steady work?"

"Knock it off, will you," I exclaimed angrily. "Can't you see that it's too late?"

I walked away from him and over to Raphaël and his mother. They weren't exactly having the most normal conversation themselves.

"Raphaël, this means you're a big boy now. You're really grown-up if you're getting married, huh?"

"Oh please don't make me feel like shit."

"Raphaël has always been guilty," Véronique explained to

me. "He always felt guilty about everything. He would feel terrible about going to school in kindergarten."

"The reason I would feel guilty about going to school," said Raphaël suddenly, "was because you cried every morning that I went for the first week. And all those guys started crying too."

"Well, they were sad to see their big brother go."

"They just started crying because you started crying."

Raphaël was his mother's favourite by far. In this neighbourhood, it was a curse to be your parent's favourite. You just sort of wanted to keep under their radar. It was like being picked out as a favourite by a psychopath who went by the name Mr. Mom in prison.

Raphaël's younger brothers didn't look anything like him. They all had their heads shaved and were wearing turtlenecks, as if they'd agreed on a uniform for the wedding. His brothers had always been out of step with whatever was going on. They missed school field trips. They would show up at school on holidays. Once, they got a ticket for calling 911 too often to find out what street they should go to to see the fireworks.

Raphaël's family was much bigger than mine. He had the type of family where people claimed to be related to one another even though they clearly were not. If you inquired a little, you would find out that their parents had lived across the street from each other in the fifties or that they had worked in the same restaurant for twenty years.

A cat that was annoyed by all the commotion leapt up onto the bureau and slipped into the mirror and disappeared.

At that moment, Raphaël's father walked into the living room. He had his thin black hair slicked back. He was with a new girlfriend. She was skinny and was wearing heels that made her taller than anyone else in the room. He tucked an envelope into Raphaël's inside pocket. He kept whispering to him while his hand was on Raphaël's shoulder.

Raphaël's father had been the greatest figure skater to ever come out of Saint-Pierre-de-la-Laundrette. He fixed cars for a living. His whole life had been devoted to making sure Raphaël went to the figure skating championships. He had been so disappointed that Raphaël had prematurely ended his skating career that they were barely on speaking terms.

Raphaël wasn't saying anything back. He fiddled with a white paper napkin with a print of roses on it that was tucked into his breast pocket. I didn't like how quiet he was being.

Someone gave us five dollars in an envelope that had a drawing on it of me and Raphaël naked and having sex. He had mixed up the wedding with a stag party. He thought there were supposed to be strippers coming out of a cake.

Loulou kept giving the guys playing guitars dirty looks. They had begun playing "Stairway to Heaven" even though they had been specifically instructed not to.

Raphaël used the music as an excuse to walk away from his father. He had a bottle of beer in each pocket of his jacket. He took out one of the bottles and opened it with a key chain, walked over to his best man and put his arm around him.

It was the first time I had ever seen the guy who was acting as his best man. No matter how much time I spent with Raphaël, he still had best friends who would come out of the woodwork. They were always being released from prison and then going back in for something else a week later. The minister was a friend of Raphaël's as well. He drove a truck around downtown and served hot dogs to street people.

Nicolas arrived with a bottle of orange soda in his hand.

Someone went up and safety-pinned a carnation to his sweater. Then they let him be.

Nicolas wasn't speaking to anyone. At one point Raphaël walked by him and he said, "Why are you all gussied up?" Raphaël didn't even turn his head.

Étienne wasn't there. But he never showed up at stuff like this. He thought family gatherings were destructive to the soul. But I had hoped that he would make an exception and come sing his wedding song. There was a bar from one of his songs that people used to shout at weddings back in the seventies. For once I wanted him to just show up in his former glory. Who could actually get Étienne Tremblay to perform his wedding song in the living room at their wedding? It would be better than having a five-tier wedding cake with blue roses on it. It would be better than having a ten-thousand-dollar dress and tables covered with crab cakes and cheese soufflés.

The minister, looking at his watch, motioned for everyone to gather around.

Someone put a Charles Aznavour song on the record player. It's what I wanted played while I went down the aisle if Étienne didn't show. There was all this laughter and excitement coming from the front door. I knew what it meant right away. Suddenly no time had passed. It was just as if it was 1972 and who could believe it was Étienne Tremblay in the flesh? Here he was, right before us, the same size as all of us.

He was smoking a Gitanes cigarette and grinning wildly.

"Turn this shit off!" Étienne cried.

It was magic. I should have known the whole time that all I had to do if I wanted Étienne to come was play Charles Aznavour. He had a heightened sense for Charles Aznavour. If you put on a Charles Aznavour record anywhere in the city,

Étienne would pop out of nowhere to yell at you to take it off the turntable and break it in two. He hated Aznavour because he was so much more famous and respectable. And he made all the old people cry.

Someone turned the record player off immediately, the needle making a loud scratching noise. I clapped my hands in delight.

Étienne looked fantastic. His hair was combed back. Lord knows where he'd got the suit he had on, dark grey and pin-striped. He had a burgundy tie and a matching burgundy carnation as a boutonniere. His boots were polished shiny black. He looked healthy and well fed. You wouldn't have known that he had spent the last decade in rooming houses, writing unreadable poetry.

All Étienne needed was for the whole room to declare their undying love for him and he was fine.

"I'm here to walk my daughter down the aisle!" he cried out.

Étienne burst into his wedding song. The band started playing it.

> *I bought you a mille feuille*
> *I took you to the downtown movies*
> *I brought you dancing at the Saint-Petit ballroom*
> *I spent twenty-five cents on polish for my shoes and three*
>   *dollars on drinks*
> *Now I am broke and can't court you anymore*
> *So come on and marry me, goddamn it*
> *Come on and marry me*
> *Nobody better is coming*
> *Come on, marry me, goddamn it*
> *Just spend your life with me.*

I wondered what the minister would make of this song. I looked and he was tapping his feet, seemingly not able to believe that he was seeing Étienne Tremblay up close and singing. Everyone in the apartment joined in. Everyone forgot their problems. Except for Nicolas, whose face had fallen. He couldn't believe that all the evidence that Étienne was a loser had just been swept under the table. He was the only person on earth who was angry with Étienne anymore. Étienne took me by the elbow and walked me down the hallway into the living room, right past Nicolas.

The room was so small that almost everyone had someone on their lap. If you were sitting on a couch, it would be rude not to have someone on your lap. There were kids standing on the coffee table. The minister asked Raphaël if he'd like to say his vows.

I wondered whether or not Raphaël would say anything in public. He was always so quiet.

"I used to watch a lot of old black-and-white movies because I couldn't sleep. And there were all these idiots dancing on rooftops and I wondered what on earth they were on about. But now I know. They were trying to show how it felt to be in love."

He put his arms out and did a lovely tap-dancing jig. He had had tons of dancing lessons as a kid in order to improve his figure skating.

I put my hands over my face. What could I say that would equal a tap-dancing vow. Luckily he had met his match. I was good at public speaking. And it just so happened that I was as in love with him as he was with me.

I took a folded up piece of paper out of my shoe. I always felt a thrill when I was about to read out loud what I had written.

"In the Bible, it says that God invented the universe in

seven days," I started. "But there was actually an eighth day, and on this day God created all the strange things that have no purpose other than making life more awesome."

I knew that this wasn't exactly the kind of thing that you should feel comfortable saying around a minister. But he already knew Raphaël and me, so he must have known what he was getting into when he agreed to participate in our wedding. And since he didn't interrupt me, I went right on.

"On the eighth day God invented the sound of rain and electricity. He invented roses and tattoos of roses. He invented city beaches and goldfish. He invented spots on cheetahs and made the legs on women longer than they needed to be. He invented trumpet players and haikus. He invented tiny old men that serve espresso, and wild flowers in abandoned lots. He invented constellations and neon lights. He invented being ticklish and exaggerating. He invented snowflakes and dinosaur bones for us to dig up. And, most importantly, he invented a little boy on Boulevard Saint-Laurent who would be the greatest figure skater and the greatest kisser the world had ever seen, and he named him Raphaël Lemieux."

I stuck the piece of paper into a nearby vase. I kissed both my hands and then blew the kisses at him. Then he grabbed me by the waist and pulled me to him.

"You may kiss the bride," the minister said, even though we were already doing just that.

Nicolas caught the bouquet out of reflex, because it came right at his head, and he immediately looked disgusted with himself. It was a bouquet of carnations. I was looking forward to him making a toast. He had made good ones since we were little. He would stand on the chair in the kitchen and make a toast with his orange juice. Our food would get cold because we'd be waiting for Nicolas to finish. Everyone quieted down as he held a glass of champagne over his head.

"May you both live five hundred years!"

There was absolute silence in the room, as people waited to see if Nicolas had anything to add.

But then I was relieved that he didn't say anything else. He could have gone ahead and told the truth. He could have said how this was the end of Nicolas and Nouschka. I didn't even know how I would have reacted to that. I might have wanted to call the whole wedding off right then and there. I would have flushed my wedding ring down the toilet and pretended that none of this had ever happened, and we would go back to sleeping on our little mattress by the window for the rest of our lives.

When it was clear that he wasn't going to say anything more, everyone put their arms up in the air and cheered. My heart tried to jump out of my chest like a startled bird. Good times are always so much more wonderful than you can imagine. And bad times are always much worse.

The band started playing music. A young girl was doing some sort of drunken dance with her eyes closed. An old man was dancing next to her. He had a jet black toupée that didn't match the white hair on the sides of his head. He leaned back as he danced, as if he was about to go under a limbo stick. Loulou made the music of a tuba and marched side to side.

The kids were crammed onto the chesterfield, drinking red wine from plastic cups and eating sandwiches made from white bread cut into triangles. Their patent-leather shoes were jutting in front of them. A thirteen-year-old boy with a faint moustache made the effort to stand up. He walked a few steps to the window. Smiling, and with his eyes closed, he peed out the window.

There were transparent balloons with teensy white stars on them, which had floated up to the ceiling. The dogs were yanking at their ribbons.

It would have been nice if Lily Sainte-Marie was there. She didn't even know that I was getting married. I wondered what would have happened if I had sent her an invitation. For a second I fantasized about her standing there with tears in her eyes.

Raphaël was sitting on a chair, drinking a beer. Once he started drinking, he could drink for days. He just smiled at me. I went and sat on his lap. Someone came and took our picture.

"Are you happy?" he asked.

"Yes."

"You don't sound so convinced."

Raphaël put his arms around my waist and interlaced his fingers. It looked strange to see his wedding ring. His right ring finger had a tattoo of a clover on it. I kept looking at the ring to remind me that we were married. The stone on my wedding ring was like a drop of dew on a leaf.

From the couch, Nicolas asked Raphaël if he could have his porno magazines now that he was married. Raphaël ignored him.

Nicolas had put one of the carnations from the bouquet in his hair. I could tell that he was feeling unloved. He was crossing and uncrossing his legs. He kept getting up to leave and then coming back.

I was listening to one of Raphaël's relatives tell me about a hotel that they had stayed in in Cuba. I saw Étienne walk over to Nicolas. I stepped away from Raphaël's relative to try and get to Nicolas before our father did. Surely Étienne would be careful not to upset Nicolas. Surely he would have the sensitivity to know that Nicolas was feeling lousy.

"You think that you have lost your child," Étienne said, putting his hand on Nicolas's shoulder.

He had decided to bring up Pierrot! Maybe Étienne was right. Maybe Pierrot was on Nicolas's mind more than I was. Nicolas and I were both waiting to hear what he had to say. Given the speaker, it was going to be either brilliant or horrific.

"But really, children don't really belong to us. We all disappoint our children. But you know that. You know that better than any of us. That's why people loved you so much when you were a kid. You had convictions even when you were a boy. You were the voice of the people's discontent. You were a cynic. You know that everything is bullshit. It's a hard burden to carry."

Nicolas looked up at Étienne. He actually looked sort of moved. All the vodka that he'd mixed with his orange soda had weakened his defences.

"I haven't seen my son in months," Nicolas said sadly. "This is something that matters to me. I don't care if he hates me. I just don't want him to say, 'I never saw my father growing up.' I don't even know where Saskia is. She's so crazy. She could be anywhere."

"We're in the same boat, my boy."

Nicolas looked shocked. He stood up, shrugging Étienne's hand off his shoulder violently.

"Are you insane?" he exclaimed. "We're not in the same boat. You walked out on your kids. Mine was stolen from me. Do you get the fundamental difference?

"Where's the documentary crew? You were obviously expecting them. You probably got the day wrong. Or maybe your last performances on the street corners weren't worth the film that they were recorded on."

Nicolas had a sort of genius for recognizing ulterior motives. It was the sort of quality that you would probably want to live without. It was probably better to go around the world being duped by everyone's shit.

Everyone in the wedding party stopped whatever it was that they were doing and stared at Nicolas. They were waiting to hear what Nicolas had to say next. Nicolas didn't say anything though. He kicked over a table with plates of sandwiches and stormed out the door. Raphaël held me tightly so that I couldn't jump up and run after him. Struggling, I finally got out of his clutches and bolted out the door.

When I got outside, a bunch of kids who had left the wedding party had surrounded Nicolas. He was on the verge of doing something stupid and inappropriate. Children can always sense that and they go mad for it. A beige cat came down the stairs like caramel seeping out of a Caramilk bar. Hugo and the film crew were out there filming quietly.

Raphaël came out of the building behind me. I knew he was there before I saw him.

"What's the matter, Nicolas?" Raphaël said. "You can't let anybody have a life?"

"You're trying to take her away. You don't give a shit that any of us were here before. I knew from the second I saw you that you were bullshit. You have this weird idea that Nouschka belongs to you."

"She does belong to me. I don't give a fuck that you met her earlier."

"When we met earlier? Like when we didn't have brains? When we were just heartbeats with thumbs? Do you have any idea what that means?"

"It means nothing. Because shit changes faster than anybody can imagine. All of a sudden, every day, people wake up and have completely different lives. Get used to it."

"I don't like you," Nicolas yelled back. "I don't like you and your false prophesying."

Nicolas tried stomping on a balloon. It kept jumping away from him. He yanked the carnation out of his buttonhole and threw it into the middle of the street. He picked up a newspaper and wildly tore it into pieces. There was a moment when it almost seemed like he was going to rearrange the sheet of paper into a great bird that would take flight, beating its huge wings, into the sky. The children gathered around to see if he was going to pull it off. But there wasn't going to be any magic that day.

This kind of fighting had always served Nicolas well when he was in elementary school. It had terrified the other children. He was a bit like a moth working up its courage to touch a lightbulb. I got distracted just watching him.

Nicolas took a piece of cake out of a kid's hand and smashed it in Raphaël's face. The boy started crying at the top of his lungs. Nicolas picked up a glass and tossed the contents of it after the cake.

Then Raphaël smacked Nicolas in the face. It happened so fast that I thought I'd imagined it. Nicolas spun around and fell. I ran toward Nicolas as if I could catch him. When he hit the pavement, his nose was bleeding. I felt like I was the one who'd been hit. Humiliated, weak, Nicolas stood up without me. He shook himself a little bit to make his clothes go straight and to knock the experience off.

"Nouschka, I'm fine," Nicolas said shakily. "I'm fine. I'm feeling fine."

He turned and walked down the street. I called him back. He kept fixing his hair. Nothing in the entire universe could cause him to turn and look back at that moment. He was miles away from where anyone could hear him. Off he went, defying every law of physics that I knew. Raphaël had separated us somehow. I didn't know exactly who I was. I was terrified.

"Oh, something like this is bound to happen at every wedding," a woman who had come out behind me said. "At mine, my cousin was trying to get everyone to quiet down for a toast, so he set off the fire alarm with a lighter. Then he couldn't turn it off. Ruined the cake."

When I stepped out onto the stage as a kid, I used to feel tiny, tiny. I couldn't see the audience and everyone would hush. Their voices were suddenly blown out like birthday candles. And there I was, the Little Prince all alone on a tiny planet somewhere in space.

Raphaël wiped his face off with a napkin and then tossed it in the trash. He put his arm around me and walked me down the sidewalk. We just headed down the street, like nobody else mattered.

Hugo's van pulled up just as the fight was over. Étienne came out of the front door and went with his arms opened toward Hugo and the crew as if nothing had happened, and to welcome them to the celebration. I waved goodbye to Étienne and he nodded, obviously preoccupied at the moment.

A lot of the wedding guests had left the apartment and gone to sit in the laundromat across the street. There were some on the terrace of the legion hall. You could see members of our families for blocks away, farther and fewer apart, like marathon runners who had fallen behind in the race.

"Change is good," Raphaël said.

"I don't like it. I think that everyone should eat off the same plates their whole life. And you shouldn't ever change your kitchen chairs. I don't like when people talk about moving to new cities. Everybody should stay exactly where they were born."

"What are you worried about, Nouschka? You shouldn't be worried, baby."

Who are we other than our roles? I had gone directly from being Nicolas's twin sister to Raphaël's wife. For that one second earlier I was alone. And it was atrocious. It was unfathomable. Just being one's self, utterly abandoned, with no man wrapping his arms around me like a straitjacket.

A photographer in a car drove up next to us. He took a couple photos. I didn't think anything of it.

I was happy now, I guess. Who can tell what certain emotions are. Happiness, terror, joy, hatred—they're all so incredibly alike. We walked for a couple more blocks to a building that Raphaël had signed the lease for. He had put all the money that he had on the first month's rent. I was glad that he had done it on his own. I never would have had the courage to sign a lease without Nicolas. We walked slowly up the stairs to the new apartment. The moon came down low over the buildings. A housewife came out on her fire escape and pushed it back up into the sky with a broom handle, and bats flew by.

Raphaël was too drunk to have an erection. I sat on his face while he was still dressed in his wedding suit, a white carnation in his lapel. And that is how a marriage is consummated on Boulevard Saint-Laurent.

Chapter 28

Days of Beer and Dandelions

THE PHOTOGRAPH THAT THE MAN TOOK ENDED up on the cover of a tabloid. What with the attention from the documentary and a wedding, how could I not have expected to land in the magazines? It really was a lovely photo. I even bought myself a copy. The problem was, of course, that the tabloids were in our life; they were impossible to shake. They were waiting for an arc in the story. They were ecstatic that we were married. But now the only thing that could make them happier was if we divorced. The trick to outwitting the tabloids is to lead a well-adjusted, serene life, which I hoped to do.

I was moving out that day. I was in the kitchen, wrapping up my favourite teacup in newspaper. Loulou was wearing a yellow toque with the logo for the Boston Bruins on it. Sometimes he liked to wear it to be controversial. Younger men would scream obscenities out their car window at him. He was having trouble opening a can of peaches, quite possibly because his can opener was at least twenty-five years old. I flung my arms around his neck.

"Oh, for crying out loud, Nouschka. You're moving around the block. You're too emotional. You'll be an alcoholic by the time you're forty."

*****

I walked into my room. I was surprised to see Nicolas there. He was wearing the same outfit from the wedding. Nicolas gave me a look that indicated that he knew I wasn't expecting to see him there.

"You can run but you can't hide. What's the deal? Are we, like, mortal enemies now? Are you going to cross the street and duck into a store when you see me from now on?"

"How could you even ask me that?"

"Well, we were getting creepy close anyways, right? I think that you were cramping my style. When people see us together they always expect us to start tap dancing or something. I've got to go out on my own."

He had come ahead of me so that he could already start packing. He wanted it to be clear that he was leaving me and not the other way around. He had a gym bag that was filled with clothes and sunglasses.

I started putting dresses into my flowered vinyl suitcase. Everything else there belonged to children. We couldn't really bring the plastic horses on the windowsill or the mobile of birds that we had cut out of the pages of a children's magazine, or the shoebox full of Hot Wheels cars.

I suddenly felt full of incredible doubts. The entire city had told us over and over again that we were lovable and special. Why didn't I just remain a child like they had wanted!

"Actually, do I have a tie anywhere among my things?"

Nicolas said. "I might actually need that. I don't know. I don't want to just get married and settle down right away like some people. I need to make my first million before I do that."

It suddenly felt as if we had been at war for a hundred years. I wanted to surrender, to throw in the towel and just let Nicolas have his way, whatever his way was. But that wasn't even an option now.

We walked out of the apartment together and stood on the sidewalk, just staring at each other. For a moment it felt as if we were waiting for each other to call each other's bluff. We didn't say anything. As soon as we went in different directions, it would be the end. We just turned and walked off like duellists who, after a certain amount of steps, wheel around and fire bullets into each other's hearts.

✳✳✳✳✳

Our new apartment was in a building that was surrounded by a wrought iron fence that looked like something a girl had doodled in a notebook. There were twenty doorbells on the door of the building, with names next to some of them written in pencil or stuck on little bits of red tape.

Raphaël was being sweet to me that evening. I sat on the new bed next to my suitcase, waiting for the whole world to tumble down while he stood at the stove making spaghetti sauce and smoking a joint. But it didn't. There is nothing in the world as pretty as the smell of marijuana and spaghetti sauce. If you wanted the simple things in life, then you could be happy. He had already started working as an orderly at the hospital. This delighted me because Loulou's prediction that Raphaël would never work had proven to be false. He had been given a pile of pamphlets on studying to become a nurse. I thought it was a good idea. I wanted our lives to be normal, because for me *normal* meant that anything was possible. It meant that I could continue going to school. It meant that I could find a job that I liked to do.

Raphaël was a bookworm. One of my favourite things was to lie in bed and listen to him tell me about books that he had read. He had enormous bony feet. I liked that I could look at his naked feet all the time. I liked that I was married to somebody with those feet. He was reading a detective novel by Simenon.

"He goes home at night and weeps. He thinks that if he can figure out why it is that people die, then he can figure out why it is that people are born. He was born not of woman. Instead he was created out of garbage: an old trench coat and some scraps of pornography and leftover bones from a dog. That's what Maigret is made of. When he solves crimes, he is really making his confessions. It is only by solving crimes that he is able to prevent committing them."

Every two people, when they grow intimate with each other, begin to construct their own language. For Nicolas and me, our grammar manual had a chapter on advanced sarcasm, a chapter on absurd associations, six chapters on humour, a chapter on inappropriateness and an appendix on bragging and general know-it-all-ism.

In the manual for Raphaël and my language there would definitely be a foreword on flattery, a chapter on mysticism in a downtown environment, one with words to help define the existential condition, a chapter on pseudo-intellectualism and a 1995 afterword on the conjugating of dirty French words.

I didn't like to read books after he had told me about them, because it always seemed that they would never be quite as good.

He got a book at Ben Noodleman's pharmacy. Mr. Noodleman gave out tiny candies in prescription bottles to kids for Halloween until some mother complained. The book was called *How to Keep Your Love Life Alive* and had been published in 1973. Raphaël was determined to try every trick in the book.

He climbed in from the window. He declared that he was a pirate and that he was coming in to ravage me. The tip of his shoe got caught on the radiator and he fell on the floor. We tried making love in our little shower. The flow from the faucet was so weak that one of us was always trembling and trying to get under the warm flow.

He took all the petals off a rose. He scattered them on the floor around the bed. It looked as if someone had been stabbed and ran out of the room. He carved our initials into the wood slats of a bench. I don't think that he could have done that to a tree—the trees on the block were spindly and had tiny black gates around them.

He talked this limousine driver into driving us around and around the block on his hour off. He got this old man from next door to come and sit on the couch and play classical guitar while we slow-danced around the coffee table.

He was wearing a tie when he came to dinner, even though the shirt that he was wearing had permanent sweat stains under the armpits. He had a huge silk handkerchief tucked in at his neck. We had a spaghetti dinner. He put it on a big plate and put it in between the two of us. I'm not sure if he got this idea out of his paperback book or *Lady and the Tramp*. He ate much faster than me, being an athlete and all, so he ended up eating most of the spaghetti and I got hardly any. He lit up so many votive candles, which he bought at the Polish grocer's, that I was seeing black dots in front of my eyes the rest of the night.

We spoke on different pay phones so that we could have phone sex. I sat in the phone booth in the library with the glass door closed while talking in whispers. He spoke from the phone booth on the corner. He had to shout out dirty things above the noise of the trucks.

He came home with a cardboard box shaped like a heart. When I opened it, there were heart-shaped chocolates. They all had the most repulsive centres. I tried to guess the flavours.

"Cough syrup?" I asked.

"No, cherry."

"Powdered toothpaste."

"Mint."

"Dried-up jam on the side of the jar?"

"Close, strawberry."

"Bruised plums?"

"Marzipan."

"Burnt butter?"

"You're right, caramel!"

There was a feeling, when we were together, that we were little kids dressing up as adults. That the universe was something that we drew with crayons and there was no such thing as tragedy. Maybe he had taken a book about time travel out of the children's public library when he was seven, and he had skipped over all the difficult parts and here he was.

Where did he get all this crazy-assed knowledge? Maybe I was just being wilfully naive. Like those women who married Mafia guys and their husbands kept bringing them home mink coats even though they claimed to work at the bowling alley.

The winter winds were arriving outside, sounding like children stationed under the puppet theatre and trying to make thunder and lightning with pots and pans and rattling paper bags. He was making shadow puppets of wolves on the wall. They were just outside. That's why we built the city: to keep out all the wolves.

CHAPTER 29

The Rise and Fall of Nicolas Tremblay

It would have been a happy time except that
I was always conscious of the fact that I had not spoken to
Nicolas in three weeks. We had never spent twenty-four hours
apart before our fight at the wedding.

I had just ditched him. I wanted to see him again, but how
could I face him? A month in the life of a twenty-year-old is a
very long time. You can become a completely different person
during that time. You can grow so distant from a person that
you can never quite catch up in your friendship. It was like falling behind in school.

If Nicolas was actually able to stay mad at me any longer,
then it would change everything that I knew about the universe.
Surely there had to be one constant thing about this world.

I brought it up to Raphaël before he went to work one
night.

"Nicolas is always going to be Nicolas," Raphaël said. "He's
probably got to go through a period of not being himself—just
so that he can be sure that he really isn't anybody else. Or he

wasn't just himself by mistake. But then he'll go back, you'll see. And then we'll have a shitstorm of Nicolas, don't worry."

For a second I was annoyed at Raphaël for not worrying along with me. I remembered how Nicolas had warned me that Raphaël was one of these lame-ass philosophizing types. And I thought, man oh man, my brother was right. Why didn't I listen to him and refuse to have anything to do with this jerk? But then I sighed. Being mad at Raphaël wasn't going to help this situation at all. None of it was his fault. I went back to worrying.

A few days later a twelve-year-old in a yellow and black striped sweater knocked on my door and said that Nicolas was waiting for me down on the corner. And then the boy buzzed away, off to smell some flowers.

Knowing how impatient Nicolas was, I ran around the house, scrambling for my peacoat and some shoes. I hurried down the stairs and onto the street. I started running but I was a little bit scared of how quickly my heart was beating, so I slowed down and walked.

I kept fixing my hair. As if I was on my way to a first date and was feeling insecure. I even stopped and looked at my reflection in the window of a car. I think I was wringing my hands as I walked. Trucks were bouncing along beside me on the street like they had thunderclouds in the back. What if Nicolas said he didn't ever want to see me again? Whoever said that twins can read each other's minds was wrong. I never had any idea what Nicolas was thinking.

Nicolas was standing on the corner, waiting for me. He put his hands over his eyes when he saw me coming toward him. He ran around and hid behind a skinny tree, all Inspector Clouseau–style. He picked up a piece of newspaper from the ground and then hurried to the bench and held it up in front of his face with his legs crossed, reading it. I sat down next to him, and each time we made eye contact we blushed.

He was wearing a green ski jacket over a brown acrylic track suit. I think he wanted to prove that he looked good in anything. He dressed like a toddler that had snuck out the back door while his mother was preoccupied doing the laundry.

"Well, here we are," he said finally.

"Fancy that."

"Just the two of us, like old times."

"Yup."

"I never gave you a wedding present."

"If you promise that you aren't going to talk shit about my husband anymore, that would be the best wedding gift that you could give me. You know?"

"Oh, you should have told me. I could have saved three dollars and ninety-nine cents."

He reached inside his jacket pocket and pulled out a small blue music box. When I opened it, it began to play the tune "Il était un petit navire"—that song about a young sailor who is about to be eaten by the other sailors because they've run out of food. Why had anyone ever invented songs? They made your heart all crazy.

I loved it. I'm not even sure why I started to cry. Maybe it was partly out of relief. I had imagined this meeting 360 different ways and I was just glad that I didn't have to picture it anymore.

"Do you like it?"

"It's the most wonderful thing that I've ever been given in my whole life."

"Oh, don't overdo it now! You sound like a numbskull. It's nothing. It's nothing. It's nothing. Don't get so emotionally crazy, please. I never met anybody who cried the way you do."

"I missed you."

"Are we good? I don't want there to ever be bad blood between us. You're the only person who loves me."

"Loulou loves you."

"Loulou's too busy worrying about his gastric problems to really love anybody. I'm a bum without you. I'm like a guy on a trapeze who's hanging by his knees with nobody to catch. I mean that's no kind of act, is it?"

"No, it isn't."

"I'm a bonehead without you. I'm a bungler. I'm a booger eater. A backwater bigot. A lonely pickled egg floating in a pickle jar. I feel like shit. I miss you, okay. You wanted to know if I would miss you. Well, I did. There you go. You're a stronger man than me, Gunga Din. You win. You outdrew me."

I laughed. It was funny because Raphaël had never said anything like that to me. I knew Raphaël loved me, but I sometimes got the feeling that if I left him, he would be perfectly all right about it pretty soon afterward. I'd never met anybody that was as good at being alone as Raphaël. Nicolas would actually go nuts if I left him for good.

"I missed you too."

"What a softie! Promise me that you won't ever abandon me. Don't move away or anything like that."

"I would never do that."

"He has to stay here as a condition of his parole, right?"

"Where would we go?"

"Somewhere where I could never find you again."

"Okay, I promise."

He looked content as he folded up the promise I'd given him and tucked it away in some deep, inner pocket.

"I need some normal clothes," he said.

"I'll say. You're getting downright eccentric."

"You want to come shopping with me now?"

"Oh, all right. I only have about five dollars though."

"That's great!"

Nicolas was in a particularly good mood. He called out random insults to people as they passed by. He stopped an Asian kid with a pocket protector and beige pants.

"Don't ever change, man," Nicolas said to him. "I love everything about that look. Seriously."

There was a mural of the big bang outside the Salvation Army. Nicolas stood up on a bench to throw a beer can over his head into the garbage. His aim was really nice. It was lovely to see.

Nicolas was usually aiming a little bit too high. He always thought that he would be able to do things that he didn't quite have the talent or ability for. He broke his nose once trying to ride a unicycle.

When we pushed open the door of the Salvation Army, so many bells rang that it sounded like the king had just died.

Nicolas went to the men's section. He started trying to pile every suit jacket from the rack onto the crook of his arm. A fifteen-year-old store clerk gave him a funny look because he was making a mess.

"I'm going to a job interview on Monday."

"Yeah, sure," I said.

I wasn't sure why he always had to claim that he was on his way to a job interview. It had probably become a nervous tic. The way some people had to laugh after everything they said.

"I had this friend named Maxim," Nicolas said, raising and dropping his shoulders in a black jacket that looked too small. "He found out that he was one-eighth Native. So he goes on a spiritual quest. Because that's what all Natives do when they are eighteen. And then they rename themselves. So he does this. He roams through the wilderness outside of Boucherville. And then he comes back and his name is Daniel."

"So?"

"So? Are you retarded? He's supposed to have a name like Sleeps with the Fishes or Little Itchy Ass. Not Daniel."

"Just stop. You're being racist."

"How the fuck am I being racist?"

He went into the changing room to try on a grey suit.

"Remember my friend Xavier?" he yelled from inside the stall. "He lost his job as a teacher because he was teaching the kids to play Russian roulette or something like that."

"Yeah, something like that. Something like that . . . Do you have any idea what Russian roulette is?"

He came out of the changing room in the suit. He actually looked really handsome in it. I gave him an enthusiastic thumbs-up.

"Why do they call Russian roulette *Russian roulette?* Because Russians are bastards. There are these Russians who own a wallpaper store near the library and they shortchanged me. After that, Russians were dead to me."

"Understandably so."

I walked over to a long green chesterfield with upholstered, buttoned armrests. It looked like it could fit a family of eight people on it. It was made when the Catholic Church was still in power and everyone had up to ten children. They needed a gigantic couch so that they could all fit on it together. I sat down, waiting for Nicolas to get his regular clothes back on. A cat's tail waved above the arm of the couch like an elegant hand in a black glove waving goodbye.

Nicolas came out of the stall and walked over to a cart of fur hats and started trying them on, one after the other. I shook my head at each one. Every one of them gave him the effect of looking completely insane. Not that he would mind, but the police would stop him for sure if he was wearing one of those hats, using it as grounds to search his pockets. He held up a wire coat hanger with ties hanging from it.

"Remember Sébastien?" Nicolas asked. He couldn't stop his nervous chattering. "Turns out his mother put Pepsi in his bottle when he was little. Now he has, like, jitters all the time. He has epilepsy. He's suing PepsiCo. He's going to be a millionaire."

I asked the fifteen-year-old worker if he could turn on the television so we could make sure it worked. There was a rerun of *Chambres en ville* on television. Nicolas changed out of his suit and picked up a beat-up copy of *Une saison dans la vie d'Emmanuel* from a pile of paperbacks and sat, squished, next to me. We sat through two episodes, resting from the energy of having come to a store and found a new outfit. It was nice to sit on a couch. It was the closest we had been to being home together for a long time.

"Do you remember that time Loulou came to our parent-teacher interviews dressed in a tuxedo?"

I started to laugh. Our favourite thing was remembering stupid things that Loulou had done when we were children. There were memories that cracked us up every single time we told them to each other again. Like the time we got kicked out of the zoo because Loulou had brought along a plastic bag filled with steak bones and table scraps to feed to the lions. Or how we were once dilly-dallying on the way home from school, and Loulou called the police and told them that Nicolas had been kidnapped. Loulou wanted to see if there was a way to put Nicolas's face on a milk carton, just to teach him a lesson.

"Remember the time Loulou cut out the picture of Tony the Tiger from the cereal box so you could wear it as a mask on Halloween?" I asked.

We laughed. Nicolas had to put his hands on his stomach because he was laughing so hard. I had to look away from him to stop laughing. If we laughed too long, they would think that we were stoned and throw us out of the store.

"Remember how Loulou used to hold his hand up high in the air and get us to kick it? I'm not sure what he was training us for."

We had been together so long these memories were as important to history as Stonehenge and the *Mona Lisa*.

He brought a suit with him to the cash register. I counted out my change for the five dollars it cost. I held up my one-volume encyclopedia. The woman shrugged and said it was a quarter.

Outside the store, a robin hopped by. It looked like a fat man with a red scarf tucked into his waistcoat. It looked like it knew what it was doing with its life.

"You have a court date, don't you?" I asked. "That's why you're getting a suit."

"Saskia and I are going to court about visitation rights and all that. I'm sick about it. I don't even like to talk about it, it's making me so fucking nervous."

"It'll be okay. It'll go fine."

There was a photograph of Nicolas sleeping on top of a bar in the tabloids the next week. It was quite extraordinary that Nicolas had managed to get himself in such an awkward situation. But Nicolas was given special privileges in bars around the neighbourhood. If anybody else was up on a table, you could be sure that the owner would throw them the hell out. But if Nicolas was up on one, dancing drunkenly, it was good for business. People knew that they were hanging out in the right place at the right time.

Nicolas liked to make a spectacle when he was out. But he didn't drink during the day. He was only going to AA as some sort of plea bargain that his lawyer had made for him after he was caught stealing a family-sized bag of Ringolos from a corner store at two in the morning.

But the tabloid saw the scene as a sign that Nicolas had begun to travel down some terrible road.

For a second, I thought, how bloody ridiculous. But then I felt an uneasy premonition in my belly. Maybe the media were the ones that were right. Perhaps they had been paying closer attention to Nicolas than I had.

CHAPTER 30

The Last Public Performance
of the Tremblay Twins

I DECIDED TO GO ALONG AS A CHARACTER WITNESS
for Nicolas on his court date. I put on a green dress with a fancy
lace collar and brushed off all the cat hair from my long black
coat. Saskia wouldn't have a chance against us. She didn't know
how to be professionally adorable.

As we were walking to the courthouse, Nicolas and I even
felt sort of cocky. We were going to be back on top of the world
again. I felt happy that there was finally something that I was
going to be able to do for Nicolas. It was going to be like old
times. When we were together, no one could pick on us.

"You look great!" I said.

"So do you."

"You look like one of those old-fashioned gentlemen from
Les filles de Caleb."

"You look like you should be in Paris, seducing their
president."

Nicolas had a legal aid lawyer that he had spoken to on the phone. He met us outside the courtroom. He didn't look as confident as we did, but I ignored that.

The judge wanted to know why Nicolas had no record of employment. Saskia's lawyer pointed out that Nicolas didn't even have a high school diploma. He brought up an arrest from the year before, for a petty theft that hadn't seemed serious at the time.

Nicolas went up on the stand to defend himself. He was flustered and didn't know what to say. He just kept shrugging and smiling, hoping that the judge would be converted to our belief that his life of petty crime was no big deal.

Nicolas suddenly seemed out of place. I saw him through everyone else's eyes. He somehow looked more seedy in his suit than if he had just showed up in jeans and a sweater. He looked like a businessman who had just walked out of a strip club at three o'clock in the morning in a strange city and needed to find his way back to his hotel room. Why hadn't we spent more time looking for a respectable outfit? We weren't able to take anything seriously when we were together.

Saskia was dressed tidily in a burgundy suit and looked infinitely calm. She had a regular job as a receptionist now. She had gotten her shit together and we hadn't.

Saskia's lawyers brought a copy of the tabloid with the photo of Nicolas on top of the bar. To show that it was not just Saskia's opinion that Nicolas was a fuck-up. It was actually newsworthy.

I went up on the stand to answer questions from the lawyers. I was sure to describe how Nicolas loved Pierrot and wanted to help raise and educate and set him on the proper path. I said that Nicolas was loving and funny. They all just stared at me, waiting for me to finish so that they could get on with business. I looked around the courtroom. Nobody was falling in love with me.

The judge said he didn't see how he could grant any visitation rights to Nicolas since he didn't have a residence or a job. In addition, the judge told Nicolas he owed Saskia three thousand dollars in child support. This was an impossible amount of money. He sat on the bench outside the courthouse in his five-dollar suit and wept.

CHAPTER 31

The Devil Never Loses His Receipts

I GOT THE JOB AT PLACE DES ARTS. THEY HIRED me despite my terrible English. Étienne always said that we shouldn't bother to learn the language of colonialism. Loulou was hopeless and couldn't speak a word of it. I would answer the phone at the theatre and say something like: "There will be evening-time presentations down the line in the season that comes just after winter . . . with the blossoms in it?" But surprisingly, people didn't let on that my incompetence bothered them.

I really liked the job. I was always busy and having to figure out something new. I would completely lose myself in the task at hand. I hadn't known how great this could feel. Since I had grown up around so many unemployed people, there was never anyone to tell me how awesome work was.

In the evenings, when I left, the hallways were always still filled with girls from the corps de ballet. They sat on the floor with dour expressions on their little faces and their eye makeup smudged. Their skirts looked like they had toilet paper sticking out of their tights, and their toes stuck out of holes in the feet of their stockings. Their spines poked out of their backs, like great lizards. There was a girl in a tutu smoking a cigarette by the fire exit. Her knees were all bandaged up, as if she was a porcelain doll that had been shoddily repaired by a child.

In the café, the devil was sitting at the counter sipping an espresso and making notes in his ledger book. He was a good-looking guy of about forty. He had flecks of grey in his hair, which had the effect of making him look rather distinguished. This was where he did his best business. All the ballerinas wanted to sell their souls. There was a nineteen-year-old girl with bandages all over her toes who had sold her soul that afternoon, just to get out of the corps. She wanted to execute a perfect pas de chat.

They thought fame would make them happy. They wouldn't have to feel bad about having been teased in Grade One. No one would ever break up with them. When they rode a metro packed with people, they would be different. When they brought their clothes to the laundromat, their underwear would be special. There is nothing so wretched as being human. It's inevitable that you would, at some point, try to be something a tiny bit more. The trick is to come away from fame unscathed.

One of the artistic directors of the theatre caught up with me as I was walking through the building. She had very straight blond hair and was wearing a gorgeous black power suit. Her high heels made a deafening roar as we walked down the corridor together.

"Nouschka, you seem to be fitting in very well here."

"Thank you," I answered. I was so pleased that this sophisticated lady liked me.

"You and your husband should come over for dinner some-time. You can meet my kids."

"Okay. I guess so. I'm not sure if we can do it soon; my husband's on tour."

"What does he do?"

"He's on tour with the Ice Capades."

"*Wow! C'est le fun! C'est incroyable ça!* Well you'll have to bring him over when he comes back!"

We were turning in opposite directions. I was going toward the metro and she was going toward the underground parking lot. We kissed each other on both cheeks. Then we put our hands on each other's shoulders and smiled at each other for a couple seconds. I was starting to pick up a lot of ritzy manner-isms from her.

Of course I had lied about Raphaël being in the Ice Capades. There was no way that I could bring Raphaël to a dinner party. He could never just put on some regular clothes and act in a superficial way and make small talk at a dinner. He would sit there in a tank top with all his crazy tattoos showing. And if he said anything at all it would probably be something vaguely au-dible about the illusion of linear time. Nicolas was the same damn way. He always had to act in an obnoxiously idiosyncratic way.

I realized that I was capable of things that Raphaël and Nicolas were not. They were too committed to the personas that they had created when they were fourteen years old. Because they had both felt that they had been taken advantage of and exploited. When they were teenagers, these personas gave them an aura of toughness and of being unapproachable. Now they made them seem sort of mad.

What would the ballerinas think if they got a glimpse of us all at home? If they saw what your actual quality of life was like after you sold your soul to the devil for a little fame: Raphaël in the bathroom underlining passages in *Cujo*, Nicolas having trouble with a tie while getting ready for a court date, Étienne lecturing at a café to a twenty-one-year-old fan.

I was worried about going home. I stopped at a movie theatre and sat in the darkness, just watching the images, not really following the story. I was in hiding from the world. It was an American film. I had seen the actor in another movie. In the other movie he had been a spy in the Cold War and the Russians were on to him. Now he was in a dystopian world. He was reading the newspaper and drinking a coffee while people all around him got arrested. Look how easy it was for him! Surely Raphaël could role-play for dinner parties! But I knew that he could not.

CHAPTER 32

You Can Skate a Figure Eight
for Eternity

THE DAYS STARTED GETTING SHORTER. THE SUN
was bright, but it wasn't warm anymore. It was all used up and
would have to be replaced with a new bulb. The maple leaves
were coming down like girls jumping out of hotel windows with
their dresses on fire. All the ice cream stores had put curtains in
their windows, as if there were deaths in the family.

I looked in the closet for a warmer coat. I finally came out
with a woollen overcoat. I tried it on. Moths flew everywhere
around me, like I was in a little snowstorm. It was me. I let winter out of the box.

*****

While I was digging I found a pair of Raphaël's skates. It was
silly that Raphaël didn't skate anymore. I wanted to encourage
him. I bought a light blue skating skirt at the secondhand store

and put it on over some grey tights. I stood in the living room
with my arms spread out.

"Let's go skating," I said.

He looked up from his novel and studied me.

"All right," he said.

God help me, I was pleasantly surprised. It really was a perfect night for skating. The snowflakes were lovely and lit up by
the coloured traffic lights. They were like the tiny windows of
Gothic cathedrals.

*****

Raphaël and I had tied on our skates and were waiting in the
hut next to the rink for the ice to be ready. The caretakers were
clearing it of snow with a Zamboni. There were loads of kids
sitting around us, sipping hot chocolate. Their jackets were
unzipped, revealing their long johns covered in prints of snowflakes. Raphaël put some quarters in the vending machine with
daisies on it. Some chocolate milk trickled out into two cardboard cups for us.

Raphaël put down his cup to sign autographs for a bunch
of little girls. There was a photograph of him on the wall by the
cash, winning the junior championship. I wasn't sure who'd recognize him five years older and scruffy-looking. But all the girls
were in a line and in love with him. Their teensy-weensy hearts
were beating in their chests, like birds held in fists.

Usually if someone recognized Raphaël on the bus or in a
café, he would give them a dirty look and yell something like,
"Raphaël Lemieux is dead!" But how could he lose his temper
at little girls with sweaty curls pasted on their foreheads, and
plastic foxes on their rings where the jewels should go.

I saw a guy named Rosalie waddle over on his skates. You couldn't even really see Rosalie's face because it was almost entirely covered with hair. He had a thick beard that covered his chin and cheeks up almost to under his eyes. He wore a leather cap and a leather jacket with sheepskin lining. He had a pot belly similar to that of a very pregnant woman.

There were motorcycle gangs all over Québec. Rosalie was a member of the Bleeding Sparrows. They changed their names to girls' names to show how tough they were. No one would dare comment. Their gang controlled all the illegal activities in the neighbourhood. They were always making the cover of *Allo Police*. They seemed much more violent on television than they did in real life, where they really left you alone unless you wanted to start dealing cocaine. Then they would bury you alive or something like that—otherwise they seemed pretty nice.

Raphaël got along with people in gangs. He never reacted to anything strange that was put in front of him. If a guy walked up with a tattoo of a third eye on his forehead, Raphaël acted just like a pleasant bank teller asking him what she could do for him. He was a Zen master in that respect.

"Hey Raffi, man. What's going on with you, my brother? Shitty that your dog business got raided."

"I'm married now."

"I fucking hate marriage myself, but you've got a beautiful wife," he said, nodding politely at me. "Your father's music changed my life. It made me who I am today. I was a fucking animal before I started listening to that shit."

"Great," I said.

"What racket you in now?" Rosalie asked, turning back to Raphaël. "I'm looking for someone to sell shrooms in your neck of the woods."

"That's too much excitement for me. I'm going to try to just keep a low profile. I'm going to try to be a regular sort of guy."

"Come on. You can't make money that way. Look at your girl. Don't you want to buy her a fancy jacket? Or some earrings? Girls pretend that they don't like that shit, but deep down, they're all resentful of you if you don't buy them shit."

"You would know," I said.

"Try this. You are going to be so impressed that you're going to need to sell it."

Rosalie took out a mini Ziploc bag of mushrooms, crushed the bag and then poured the crumbs into the hot chocolate. Raphaël liked getting high. He would take any sort of drug. He said that he had developed a taste for them in the psychiatric institution when he was a boy. Raphaël gave me a sip and it tasted horrible, like chocolate dirt. After I handed it back, he knocked the remainder back.

"You've got to be prepared for alternative ideas of how to get by. Because it's going to be way better to be in the woods when the results of the referendum come in. If it's a *oui*, you can be sure that there's going to be some bloodshed. The Canadian government is already moving out all the warplanes from northern Québec for when they come and slaughter us."

Rosalie had a tattoo of a rose on his right hand, which meant he was a separatist. Raphaël didn't care one way or the other about Québec independence, but he was always up for talking to somebody about a money-making scheme. Maybe it was because he was Québécois. It was part of our heritage to get into idiotic rackets and petty crime like robbing doughnut stores and bringing in cigarettes across the American border.

We Québécois had to be particularly careful about the risk of joining motorcycle gangs. It was in our blood. Like an untended garden turned into weeds, neglected boys in Québec turned into Bleeding Sparrows. I looked at Raphaël and noticed that he was on the verge of becoming one of those guys. Had I not been paying attention? Had he been shaving less and less? Had he been wearing his sunglasses more and more? Had he been putting on weight? Had he been wearing leather vests? Had he been wearing T-shirts with eagles and wolves on them?

He already had loads of horrible tattoos. His hair had been growing long lately. I couldn't let this happen. I simply couldn't be married to someone named Lucille. I would have to distract him from becoming a Bleeding Sparrow.

A Petula Clark song began to play on the loudspeaker. That meant that the ice had been cleaned and we could go back on it.

"It's time for The Magic Hour Spectacular Ice Show!" I called out.

Everyone turned to look at me. I realized that I had stuck my arms straight in the air and that they were still up there. I dropped them to my sides. Then I stepped through the door that led to the ice.

Petula Clark always made me happy. Étienne always claimed that he had dated her, so on some weird level I thought of her as my mother. I started making up a skating routine to the song. I put my hands over my head and started spinning. I noticed that people were coming out of the hut to watch.

I skated with a petite hop, as if there were holes in the ice. This was my really fanciest move. I put the tips of my fingers on the side of my head, like a heroine from a silent film. I wasn't a bad skater myself. Everyone in Montréal had spent a great part of their childhoods on an ice-skating rink.

Raphaël skated around and around me, as if he were tying me up with a rope, encircling me with his outstretched arms.

A circle of children had formed around us, with their brightly coloured ski jackets and toques pulled down over their eyebrows. You might not know it to look at them, but they were the world's most discerning figure skating audience.

I almost stopped skating to watch Raphaël myself. There was something unsettling about it. It was like sleight of hand in a card trick. He was doing things that weren't properly human. When he skated backward it was as if he were disappearing. As if he were slipping away—back into the past. As if he were unravelling. He disappeared into the falling snow. He came out of the darkness like an image appearing in a Polaroid. His skates made the sounds of sharpening knives. They left patterns on the ice, like a genius solving physics problems on a blackboard.

Then Les Colocs came on the loudspeaker, singing and cursing. Raphaël started skating more violently. He was doing a mad sort of dance, flailing his arms in the air and twisting his body from one side to the other. These didn't seem to be North American emotions. He was really giving a full-on performance. Especially considering that he always swore that he never ever wanted to perform in public again. Maybe it was the drugs that were making him lose his mind.

He took off his hat and rubbed his head with his hands viciously. Then he fell to his knees and slid across the ice. He stayed there, with his head hung down, looking at the ice. When he didn't get up, the little girls realized that the show was over. They began skating around themselves with their palms out in front of them, like orphans asking for change.

The only person there who had snapped a photograph was a seven-year-old girl with a yellow camera. Ha ha ha! I thought to myself. The tabloids and the documentary crew had missed this! One of the loveliest performances that anyone had ever seen. Later, at home, we shook the snow off our clothes and sat in the kitchen as our hair got wet, warming back up.

Nobody was watching me when I was taking a shower. No one was watching me as I trimmed my pubic hair with a tiny pair of nail scissors. No one was watching as I drank milk right out of the can. No one was watching as I lay in bed in an undershirt, reading *Gigi* by Colette.

No one was watching as Raphaël cracked his knuckles. No one was watching as Raphaël washed the dishes with a wire brush with pink bristles. No one was watching Raphaël when he was biting a hangnail off the side of his finger. No one was watching as Raphaël poured himself a cup of tea.

He was going through those strange silent movements. The numbness of the drug was overtaking him. Every now and then a second would slow down and he would get stuck in it. And it would take him, like, five minutes to rip open the bag of tea. But then time started moving again and he was fine.

"I feel like I can't feel the roots of my hair. Do you know what I mean?"

"No, but I didn't drink any of that Bleeding Sparrow brew."

"True," he said, pointing his finger up in the air, as if we were engaged in a very thoughtful debate and he was conceding that point. He stayed frozen in that position for about two minutes. He looked like a Leonardo da Vinci painting.

"I can't believe I skated like that," he said, as soon as time started moving again. "What was I doing? All those tacky moves! I was stoned out of my mind. Why didn't you stop me!"

"Because you were so beautiful."

"I was like a gay kid left at home alone with his mother's clothes."

We laughed as we got ready for bed. They were outside, looking for us. They were demanding an encore. They were banging their shoes on the floor. But we could not hear them. We were not listening. Little Nouschka and the Kid Who Figure Skated Really Well were being themselves.

Chapter 33

Matadors Won't Take No for an Answer

It was Raphaël's birthday. Earlier that day we'd seen Étienne. We hadn't spoken to him because he was in the middle of being filmed by Hugo. He had his arm around the butcher and was extolling the virtues of salami. I'm not even sure the butcher understood French. He seemed like one of the immigrants who were so confused by the language issues that they had given up on talking altogether. They just made gestures to indicate that they were happy with this world.

Raphaël and I had thought it was sort of funny. But now we were going to meet Raphaël's father and his father's girlfriend at a steakhouse in the east end that was near their house, and so I was miserable.

"How come you hate your dad so much?"

"He's one of those guys who wanted to be big shots but then never were. He's always judging everybody. He thinks that if he can criticize people and point out their flaws, that means that he's better than them. Anybody can be critical. Most people just have the decency to shut their mouths about it. He can't even really look at me since I stopped skating. It's not his fault, I guess. He had a lot tied up in the whole endeavour."

It's harder than people imagine to break the habit of having parents, so we were still going. We were squashed onto a blue leather bench on the bus. Some of the greatest love poems in the world were written on the backs of those seats. A row of advertisements lit up above the windows. They advertised soap, drug rehabilitation centres, laser eye surgery and the Catholic Church.

I had never been to the restaurant before. I thought it was beautiful. There were mirrors everywhere and framed drawings of famous bullfighters on the walls. The ceiling was covered with tin roses and had once been painted gold. The gold had chipped off and some of the roses were now black.

I had a feeling that things weren't going to go well. His father, Fernand, actually approved of me. He didn't know me at all, but he knew that I had been on television. It conferred a certain status on me and he was obsessed with status.

His father and his girlfriend, who looked like Tinker Bell, were waiting for us at a booth with red leather seats. They stood up to say hello. They were all spiffed up. His father's girlfriend had on a tight sweater over an enormous pair of boobs. Raphaël told me once that his grandmother had left him a trust fund but that his father had spent it on getting his girlfriend these top-of-the-line boobs. This sort of seemed like something that Raphaël might make up. She wore ridiculously high heels, which gave the impression of a child standing on something wobbly to reach a top shelf. It was hard to imagine what on earth she was thinking. She had a pretty Uzbek accent.

His father was wearing high-heeled boots too. After we all shook hands, we sat down.

"What did you guys do with the car that I gave you?"

"It's in the shop," Raphaël said.

Raphaël's car had broken down a week after we got married. We couldn't afford to fix it, but the mechanics didn't mind it being in the lot. It was the type of car that men liked to come and look at. I found it so tacky now that I almost fell into a depression every time I looked at it. It was only when I was looking directly at it that I could truly grasp how hideous it was.

"Have you ever been here before, Nouschka? This place is famous. They can't tear it down even if they wanted to."

"Is that so?"

"You have to make sure to order the veal cutlets. That's what they're known for."

"What if she doesn't like veal cutlets?" Raphaël asked.

Everyone was quiet for a second. Raphaël was going to make sure it was a difficult evening. He had indicated that he had no intention of playing nice.

"Then she'll order it here and she'll change her mind about it. You get certain negative things in your head and you insist that everybody go along with them. Nobody's allowed to enjoy anything."

I ordered chicken and fries. His father looked at me as if I was a complete fucking idiot, then turned to Raphaël.

"What's the news? Your mother said you were planning on being a nurse. What are you doing? I slaved all those years so that you could be a nurse. Why not be a stewardess or a waitress? Or a high-class fucking call girl? Come on. Nouschka doesn't want you to be a nurse."

"Everybody at the hospital likes Raphaël," I said. "He has a knack for talking to sick people and making them feel that everything is going to be okay."

Fernand paused to look at me. I wasn't supposed to inter--
rupt. Due to the complacent nature of his girlfriend, I don't
think he was used to women talking. He turned his gaze back
to Raphaël.

"Aren't you going to take your sunglasses off? Fine. Be a
wise guy. Be original. Be unique in your very own special way."

Raphaël just sat there on the other side of the table. Leaving
his sunglasses on was, granted, a provocation.

"Is he still reading all the time?" Fernand asked me. "All
those idiotic novels with dragons on the front. They create
mould and cockroaches go in between the covers. He used to
always read on the toilet. It's a terrible fucking habit. It gives
you piles."

"He loves reading. Readers are a rare and wonderful breed.
I've never heard of anyone not liking a reader."

"What's the point? The point of reading all the time is that
you get good grades. Here's a nerd that doesn't even do well at
school. Have you ever heard of such a thing?"

"He's very bright."

"Of course he is. He gets it from me. Not his mother. I
didn't mean to get her pregnant. But I fully accept responsibility for it one hundred percent. I stepped up. She's not even my
type. Nouschka, you know that his mother is not even my type."

"I find Raphaël's mom lovely," I said. "She looks like a boot-
legger's sweetheart."

"What else are you going to say? The point is that I didn't
waste that many hours for my son to be a nurse. You only had to
figure skate for a few more years, you fucking idiot. Then you
could be a newscaster—or a judge. Something intellectual, for
fuck's sake. I'm embarrassed to tell people about what you're
doing now." .

Raphaël didn't say anything. This was probably a ritual that they had established a long time ago when Raphaël was a little boy, where he would just sit there and listen to his father's litany of insults. It was sort of an enchantment, a spell that turned Raphaël into a stone.

"They should just have the senior figure skating championships," I said, trying to lighten the mood. "They wouldn't be allowed to make any jumps. You would score points for getting all the way around the rink."

His father ignored my comment. "I used to put all my money into paying his coach. He was really top of the line, that guy. He was the sort of coach that these upscale, hoity-toity fucking people get. But I went ahead and I talked him into taking on Raphaël. He said that Raphaël had the right look about him. That he could be on peanut butter jars and stuff like that."

He stopped to look at Raphaël. As if he needed to get a proper look at the face that ought to have been on peanut butter jars. Raphaël told me once that trophies didn't mean anything. What was going to be a big deal were all the sponsorships that were going to come in because Raphaël was a good-looking kid. He only had to get on the Olympic team and he would get to be on cereal boxes. Maybe he would be on the Nutella chocolate spread. There was nothing you could say that would dissuade the Québécois from believing that chocolate spread was good for them. If Raphaël could get on the side of the jar, they would be millionaires.

"Raphaël said you were a beauty queen?" Tinker Bell asked me suddenly.

She also didn't seem to be listening to Fernand. I wondered if anybody really listened to anybody else. Maybe it had just gone out of fashion.

"Sort of," I said.

Tinker Bell looked at me skeptically, as if she couldn't believe that someone who dressed like me and didn't bother with her hair could possibly be a beauty queen. I was certainly not her idea of pretty.

"Look," I explained, "they just needed a relatively decent girl to sit in a car for a couple hours and not expect to get paid for it."

"My cousin was a beauty queen," she said. "They didn't want her to be in the competition because her father was in jail for selling drugs. But all these people sent in money to the local news so that she could go. She ended up marrying a man who was thirty-five years older than her."

I thought we should all immediately shut up and listen to this fantastic girl's fantastic story, but Fernand continued.

"I had to get the community centre to help pay for those lessons. I had to go and beg and humiliate myself and say, 'I am a man of limited means. I fix cars. I can't afford all these lessons.' And they helped me out. I've never asked for handouts. The city gave him a scholarship. Everybody wanted to see this little working-class kid skate like an angel."

He stopped ranting for a second to watch his girlfriend pull a maraschino cherry off a toothpick. It was as if he was trying to cheer himself up with her good looks. Unfortunately it didn't work.

"His coach was so disappointed by his quitting that he left the country. I mean, the man was a saint. He invested so much time. It was like he had been waiting his whole life for Raphaël. It was finally his chance to get to the Olympics. He was almost a second father to him."

I was surprised that Raphaël had never told me about this

coach. I looked over for him to shoot me some sort of explanatory expression, not that I had any idea whatsoever what such a gesture would look like. But Raphaël wouldn't make eye contact with me. He had such a peculiar pale and blank look on his face that it made my heart jump in shock. For a split second, looking at his features, I thought that he looked dead.

"Well I guess they achieved some things together that they can still be proud of, right?" I said, still kind of distracted by Raphaël's expression. "Raphaël won a lot of trophies."

"You can't live through your kids. That's a lesson to everybody. Your kids will break your heart. You have no one to blame but yourself for your life. So I finally left him alone, after all the whining, after all the theatrics. And look how he turned out. I finally let you have your own way and you're mopping floors. It's a *cercle vicieux.*"

"No, it isn't," Raphaël said.

"What?"

"It isn't a *cercle vicieux*. You're not using the term correctly."

Everyone was quiet. We all looked at Raphaël. Everyone knew he was eventually going to react. His father was waving red flags like a crazed matador in front of him.

"There was nothing physically wrong with you that kept you from winning medals. You need a bloody therapist on-site when you're training a kid. I swear to God. I tell people over and over again when they say, 'Fernand, what is it that makes a successful skater': It isn't in the knees. It isn't in the elbows. It's right up here." Fernand pointed to his forehead with his finger.

It happened so quickly, we didn't see it coming. It didn't seem like a movement that beings existing here on this planet were capable of. Sort of like when cats lifted themselves up into the air in order to alight on a cupboard. Raphaël had been sitting so absolutely still that it didn't seem as if he was capable of movement anymore. I had never in my whole life seen someone pull a gun on someone else. I'd seen his handgun before, when I was looking through a box in the closet for shoe polish, but it had never seemed real.

Raphaël did have the natural stealth of a figure skater. Sometimes he would move up behind me and grasp me so quickly and quietly that he was holding me before I even knew that he was there. And now, Raphaël was holding a gun up against his father's temple.

"Eat your words. Eat your fucking words."

His girlfriend started murmuring epithets in Uzbek. Thank God we didn't have words for this sort of situation in our language. The rest of us were dumbfounded. I started grabbing our things. I just knew that we had to get out of there. At least before the waitress came back. I didn't think for a second that Raphaël would pull the trigger. I just didn't want him back in jail.

"You will die a sick death in a chair," Raphaël said. "You will rot to pieces right in front of everyone you love. Because my hatred will kill you. When you sit at home watching television, I will actually be hating you to death."

I was trying to make sense of Raphaël's words. I pulled on his arm gently, trying to see if he was through. Raphaël's father just stared at him, aghast.

"You should respect your father. It isn't right," Tinker Bell said in English.

"I am done with this," Raphaël said. "You are dead to me."

＊＊＊＊＊

Raphaël was shaking with rage as we rode home on the bus. I didn't know whether he wasn't talking because he didn't want to cry or to explain himself, or what.

His father might have had a point. Often assholes do, if you can get past all the bullshit and the lack of tact. Perhaps he was only asking what everyone wanted to know. Why had Raphaël quit and gone mad? I mean Raphaël's dad was a bona fide asshole, but he was just, in some way, trying to figure out what Raphaël was upset about.

"Why did you do it?" I asked suddenly.

"What? Pull a gun on that dick?"

"No. Why did you stop skating?"

"Because I didn't want to do it anymore."

"But why like that? Why all of a sudden? Why would you jump off a bridge just so that you didn't have to skate?"

He stuck his hands in his pockets and then brought them back out and stared at them. He then put his hands over his eyes. He exhaled heavily. He slid his hands down to his cheeks and just stared at me for a moment.

Fernand was always an asshole. But I reflected on what he had said that evening that had upset Raphaël so much. Raphaël would sometimes talk about tournaments that he had participated in in the city as a kid. He would tell me about some of the incredibly idiotic training techniques that Fernand had come up with, like doing jumping jacks blindfolded. But he had never ever mentioned having a fancy coach.

It seemed so strange that he had left something like that out of his autobiography. And I realized that if he left that part out of his life story when talking to me, he left that part out when he was talking to anybody: to doctors, to therapists, to whatever oddball friends he had happened to encounter along the way.

Nobody could understand why Raphaël had gone from being a dedicated little champion to leaping off the Jacques Cartier Bridge. His psychology was a mystery because they didn't have the full picture. Something had happened that he couldn't bring himself to speak about. It was like a curse. He had to wait until somebody came along and guessed it.

"How long did it last, the thing with your coach?"

"It went on for I think two years, but it seemed like it was my whole life. We started travelling around to different competitions in small towns in Ontario. We were always on the road, staying in dumpy motels. My dad said that I would have no problem winning because English-speaking people can't skate. I didn't know how to get out of the situation, which probably sounds sort of stupid and weird, but it's the only way that I know how to explain it."

He took his sunglasses off and looked at me. He looked apologetic, as if he should have told me a long, long time ago. He never cried and I knew he wasn't going to now. I put my arms around him.

"I wish you could have told me all this years ago. Then it wouldn't have been a secret."

"I was always envious of you and Nicolas and the relationship that you guys had."

"Why?"

"Your desk was right in front of me. Remember how you always sat next to each other in class? And we were in the middle of a test. You looked over at his test and you filled in something very quickly for him. I imagined what it would be like to have you next to me, filling in all the answers for me."

"You should have asked me out way back then."

"You would sit on the bench, inside the same jacket, reading from the same comic book. Whenever you tried to turn a page, he'd slap you and you slapped him back. When I saw the way that you were with your brother, I knew that you were the only girl in the city that would have a heart big enough to love me."

We got off the bus to walk the rest of the way home. We didn't care that it was winter. At least it meant that there was no one on the street. It seemed as if Judgment Day had just happened.

We walked down Rue Sainte-Catherine. We passed hundreds of tiny stores that were closed for the night: a tiny drugstore named Quebodeaux after its owners, a grocery store with its windows plastered with specials, a French bookstore with a framed photograph of Michel Foucault in the window, a *boucherie* with a pig painted on the glass door. We passed a store with prosthetic limbs in the window. I never saw anyone go in. Perhaps it did a brisk business after World War I. They sold mechanical hearts in the back. You could go in and have your broken one replaced.

Up above all the stores were cheap apartments. All the blue lights from the television sets. As if the inhabitants were up late, being visited by the Virgin Mary.

Love is like this small room where a child brings you to show you all their treasures. First the child shows you all the new toys that are bright and shiny and top of the line. But then she shows you all the stuff that has ended up at the bottom of the trunk. There are dolls with eyes that wobble, hair that is falling out of their heads, and dirt behind their ears. Their fingertips have been chewed off by dogs and they have been drawn on with ballpoint pen. It has been so long since they have been held or anyone has told them that they are lovely. They lie at the bottom of the toy chest, hidden and ashamed. You are either going to be disgusted by them, or you are going to be so filled with love for them that your heart almost breaks.

I took his hand in mine.

*****

I woke up late that night. Raphaël was standing at the window with no clothes on and smoking a cigarette, looking cool and tough. Boys are good at personas. There are a certain number that you can get at the drugstore, like costumes before Halloween. Being cool is pretending that you're not afraid of anything. But everybody is afraid. Everybody is afraid.

I remembered that in school we thought Raphaël was snobby because he had won medals and had a sweater that was covered in patches. But he wasn't proud. He was terrified. That was what the look on his face was. But nobody guessed it. It was a curse to have a face that was impossible to read.

He climbed back into bed later. Although he held me tightly as we slept, we did not make love that night.

CHAPTER 34

The Most Dangerous Man on
Boulevard Saint-Laurent

EVEN THOUGH I TRIED TO TALK TO RAPHAËL, HE grew more distant. He poured himself a glass of whiskey when he came home in the evening. He took off his clothes whenever he was drunk. After two drinks he'd be standing in the apartment wearing only an undershirt and underwear. There was a halo over his head when he drank. You could see him warming up and start to glow.

He stopped eating dinner. He cooked himself up some magic mushroom tea one night. He drank it out of a mug with the comic-book hero Lucky Luke on it. He sat on the other side of the kitchen table, winking at me.

I noticed that he never reacted to a single thing on the TV. And he always had totally random expressions on his face. He once looked like he was in terrible pain. I asked him what he was thinking and he said that he was trying to figure out where he had put his keys.

*****

I woke up and Raphaël had his gun in his hand, pointed at me.

"Who are you?" he asked.

I kicked him in the stomach with my bare foot. I picked up a tiny teacup that was on the bedside table and flung it at his head. Then I stood up in front of him and slapped him as hard as I could. He reached out and whacked me across the face. What a smack!

We stood staring at each other, as if we were waiting for something to happen. It was as if we were both trying to wake ourselves up from this awful dream—this strange dream where we were married.

I started to laugh my head off because nothing happened. This was reality. This was my world. I was stuck, married, in a tiny apartment. We were uneducated. We had no prospects. We were a typical sixties Québécois couple living in the nineties. We had thrown our futures away. We would be doing the same thing fifty years from now. The difference was that we would be uglier. We would argue with each other on Friday nights.

He looked at me some days like I was a hostage that no one was paying the ransom for. Marriage was disgusting, wasn't it?

Later that night I lay in bed studying for history class. Love is cursed in Montréal. Samuel de Champlain's wife cursed it. She was twelve years old when she had to marry Champlain. She was repulsed. She wanted to go right back to Paris, where she could drink *chocolat chaud* and fall in love with boys named Bruno. They told her in France to just go limp and then she would have a darling baby to play with. Every time he went near her, she screamed at the top of her lungs.

Champlain's beard was shaved into the shape of a heart and

his sleeves were the puffiest that money could buy. He knelt down at her bedside in his flea collar and wept and felt alive. Her rejection was like a drug. He had never seen a pale little face like hers. It was just like the hole that you cut out of the ice to go fishing.

He liked making her angry. There was nothing so beautiful as that girl thrashing about and pouting her round little mouth, which was like a drop of red wax sealing an envelope. She ran into the woods one night, wearing only her petticoats, which looked like frost on glass windows. The mud coughed violently beneath her feet, like an old man clearing his throat. Her little fists were clenched and her little knees knocked together. She pulled out her hair and shook her locks.

She started spitting out horrible, wee, adorable, unthinkable curses. She hoped that the Iroquois would kill Champlain. She hoped that every other married person was just as unhappy as she was. You could still hear her curses on very cold days. When the wind was like paper airplanes being thrown at your head. When the wind was like walking through plates of glass.

CHAPTER 35

Mon Oncle Loulou

And poor Nicolas! What on earth was he up · to every day? I should not have let him out of my sight after the court case. Before when Nicolas was upset, we would talk about nothing and everything until he felt better. We would pace around the block until the sadness got bored and stopped following us. Who was helping him feel better now? Who could replace me? I kept expecting to look outside the window and see Nicolas leading some rag-and-bones orchestra of disadvantaged kids down the street. They would be banging on old laundry buckets and blowing into recorders and kazoos, playing the most sorrowful version of "Alouette" that anyone had ever heard. But Raphaël was a handful and I was working and going to school. And then the real snowfalls began.

There were trucks everywhere trying to make sense of it, all day and night they worked, carting away massive containers of snow to dump into the river. The cars were completely buried under piles of snow. People shovelled them out for hours only to find that they wouldn't start. The roofs of elementary schools caved in. The statues had piles of snow on their heads, so angels looked like they had fur hats on.

It was hard on old people. Some of them just died. They couldn't get their rickety grocery carts down the street.

Loulou had been living all by himself for the first time since the thirties.

I had promised to take him to the Friday drop-in clinic. When I entered the apartment, Loulou was wearing a pair of pants that had stains on them and a checkered lumberjack jacket. He had a white scarf with an orange maple leaf knitted into it around his neck. He said he had come in from the cold and didn't feel like taking his jacket off because it would be so much trouble to put it back on.

The clinic was an old apartment in a building. All the old bedrooms had been turned into consultation rooms. The walls were covered with wood panels and the linoleum had blue snowflakes on it.

There was a poster of a heart on the wall, held up with thumbtacks. There were little names of the parts of the heart with arrows drawn to them: Aorta, Obsession, Right Ventricle, Sentimentality, Pulmonary Artery, Pathos, Pulmonic Valve, Sadness, Romanticism, Delusion, Love, Hatred, Superior Vena Cava.

"What's the matter with you?" I asked Loulou.

"I get dizzy when I stand up. I have the feeling that the whole room is filled with steam and clouds. I'm tired all the time. I'm always crapping my pants on the way back from the grocery store. My toes are blue. When I wake up in the middle of the night, my sheet is drenched with sweat. I'm so depressed I could shoot myself. My right knee doesn't work."

Loulou was always trying to impress on Nicolas and me the fact that he was old and that he had serious health issues.

But we could never believe it. We were too young. We didn't really believe in death and there was nothing that anybody could do to change our minds about it. I still didn't really care about his condition that day. I was preoccupied by my own problems.

"I've been feeling confused about life," I said.

Loulou looked up at the ceiling and sighed deeply.

"I'm not sure if I understand this whole marriage business."

"You went and got married. Everybody warned you."

"Can't you tell me something more than 'I told you so'?"

"Well, once you marry somebody, you have to get to know them. People are filled with all sorts of strange characteristics. One of the terrible things that happen to people in this lifetime is that we fall in love. There's no dignity in love. It's ugly and it's crazy. You chose to marry somebody with demons. Now you have to deal with all of those demons."

"Maybe I should just move back home."

"No one on earth can tell a person to leave their husband or wife. Don't ask me about that, Nouschka. That's something between you and God."

"I thought you didn't believe in God."

"That doesn't mean He won't come strike me down. You're not a little kid. You have to pay the consequences. When you get to be my age, you look at a kid that's seven years old and you know it already. You say, 'This kid is going to have trouble paying his rent his whole life.'"

"And me? What did you see when I was seven years old?"

In these clinics you waited so long that it seemed like a miracle when they finally called your name. We were so flustered. We started looking around us as if we had important documents and briefcases that we couldn't accidentally leave behind.

Loulou was so lost. This was his call for his big audition. It took him so long to shuffle into the room. He moved slowly, turning side to side like a windup toy trying to move in a straight line.

He took his sweater off. He was stuck for a while with the sweater halfway off his head. He looked like a turtle that had pulled its head in. He was wearing a thin gold chain with a tiny cross on it. It was the same chain that he had had since he was a very small boy. It still fit him.

"Raise your arms."

"There's a woman upstairs from me who is deliberately running the shower at the same time that I'm taking one, so I can't take warm showers."

Like any old person who lived alone, he just wanted to tell the doctor about everything that had happened to him lately. It felt so good to be able to talk to someone that he just didn't know when to stop. He was like a hungry person eating.

"I'm worried that there's a Q-tip stuck in my ear and that's why I can't hear anything."

"I examined your ear canal and there's nothing in there."

"There are junkies in the neighbourhood. They break into my apartment and steal my heart medication."

"You can go to the pharmacy for a renewal."

"I bought a microwave from the neighbour's son. It doesn't even work. I put a bag of popcorn in it and I sat in front of it for seven hours, waiting for it to pop."

"Mmm-hmm."

"I've been waking up, lying on the kitchen table."

"You sleepwalk?"

"I have no idea how I got there."

I would instinctively try to stop Loulou from talking about something that couldn't possibly be of any interest to the person he was talking to. It always hurt his feelings, so this time I just decided to let him go on.

The doctor wasn't responding to anything that Loulou said, no matter how wild it was. The doctor looked as if he was above all the elderly oddballs that came in. They all lived in tiny apartments with mismatched plates. It was his job to keep these people alive, but there didn't seem to really be a point to their being alive. Loulou had been giving away part of his paycheque for years in order to sit in this cramped room and be looked down on by the doctor. This was our lauded free health-care system that we bragged about to the world.

"She used to be on television, you know."

This always got people's attention. The doctor glanced around at us, vaguely interested, but then he lost focus again. He seemed absolutely exhausted and overworked. Anyways, how could he possibly recognize me in a wet fur hat and combat boots with scuffed toes. He was English. He watched American television. They had no idea whatsoever what happened in French Québec.

"Nouschka spoils me. I raised her myself. She had a red raincoat that was so cute. I never knew anything about little girls. I don't know what on earth you're supposed to tell a girl to stay out of trouble. She ran around wild. Little boys' mothers would come and complain that she had been playing doctor with their kids. I thought for sure that she had a career in medicine ahead of her, because she played doctor so much."

He laughed really loud so that he didn't have to notice that no one else was laughing at his terrible joke.

There was a knock on the door and the doctor stepped out for a moment to talk to the nurse, making us wait again.

"What was I like when I was seven?" I asked. "You were about to tell me."

"You were always fretting about Nicolas. When your brother broke his arm, you cried for three days. You were always worried that we were all going to die. You were worried about the neighbours' cats. Just worry about yourself. You don't have to worry about the whole world. It doesn't do it any good."

That suddenly made me sad. He was right. All that worrying hadn't done anything for anybody. It certainly wasn't helping Raphaël. The doctor walked back in, interrupting my melancholy.

"Do my feet look blue to you?" Loulou asked.

The doctor glanced at Loulou's feet for a split second and then went back to writing on his pad.

"Are you voting *oui ou non*?"

That got his attention. The doctor looked up at the old babbling lunatic, whose *oui* vote could put an end to the life he was enjoying. English speakers had an absolute horror of separation, and scores of them had left after the first referendum. Loulou smiled innocently at the doctor.

CHAPTER 36

The *Titanic* Sails at Midnight

O<small>NCE IT WAS COLD, IT WAS IMPOSSIBLE TO</small> imagine that it had ever not been cold. Arguments lasted longer. They hid behind couches and under the table. They stayed in the corner like a sulking child waiting for you to ask what was wrong, so that he could start complaining all over again.

On New Year's Eve I wanted to go to the Ukrainian Ballroom. I went there every year.

Raphaël put on a black sheepskin hat, a thick woollen peacoat and a long scarf with red and blue stripes, which he wrapped around and around his neck.

I had on a coonskin hat. You bought them at the back of the tiny tourist shops, along with wallets made out of sealskin, toy polar bears, maple syrup and miniature Indian braves. I put on my black coat.

I reached into my coat pocket and pulled out a little matryoshka doll. Misha had given it to me. There were always things that were left in the pockets of your winter coats from last year. My last winter was so far away that it was like a childhood memory that I had completely forgotten. I was going to time-travel that night.

Sometimes I would be pulling on a pair of tights and I would remember a past adventure. I would remember a time when I was at the cheap repertory movie theatre. And the boy next to me walked his two fingers up my legs and under my skirt. And put his fingers inside me.

I always ran into boys I had slept with. They would do things that clearly acknowledged that we had slept together. They would wink in a stupid way. They would smile a giant smile. Or do some sort of bad moonwalking on the opposite side of the metro.

At the entrance of the club, there were mounds and mounds of coats hanging from the coat racks. The rose-patterned radiators were spray-painted gold. The water inside them was boiling hot. If you touched them, your hand would be scorched. If you left your hat on them too long, it would catch fire.

People were getting on stage to sing popular songs, while the policemen's band played along. They were cheaper than a regular band. They all wore navy blue uniforms. I think that they gave a portion of their pay to burned children.

The old people were wearing paper crowns. They were dancing by taking two steps forward and two steps back. They were wearing their fancy suits that they hadn't worn since the holidays last year.

There were passed-out children everywhere. They were lying under tables. They were lying in amongst the piles of coats. Like moths with folded wings.

The waitresses started passing out toy hats. Everyone was putting on plastic top hats, or yellow paper crowns, or red cones with ribbons cascading from the top in ringlets. They were blowing little plastic gold bazookas that were shaped like tiny trumpets. I put on a gold crown. People were giving one another New Year's kisses. A girl with a red dress came up and kissed me. A man dressed in a light blue suit came up and kissed me.

We were obsessed with kissing in Montréal on ordinary days, but on New Year's, we took it to a whole other level.

Raphaël was drinking at the bar. He knocked back another Scotch. Each Scotch weakened his immune system and lit him up like a lightbulb. Girls kept planting their kisses on him like he had just rescued their village from a giant. I looked over at him and laughed. He looked sort of annoyed. I mean, some truly filthy and beautiful things came out of his mouth in bed, but out of it he sometimes was oddly puritanical.

It was so pretty. Before I was married, all those many months ago, I would have probably ended up going home with someone there. I missed the feeling of being able to go home with just anybody. I missed the feeling of not knowing who you would end up with by the end of the evening. I missed having fried eggs on a cracked plate with a pattern of a peacock on it with a stranger that I'd had sex with the night before. It was impossible to be married so young at the end of the century.

"I can't stand it here. Let's go."

"Oh for God's sake, Raphaël. It's New Year's Eve. Live a little bit, will ya?"

Everyone at the bar was talking about the referendum. It was becoming more and more likely that it was going to be called. We had been looking forward to this since we were children. A lot of us had been raised by separatists. Other countries had declarations of independence written by men with white wigs and tailcoats and buckled shoes. Ours was written by men with bell-bottoms and sideburns and tinted sunglasses and enormous butterfly collars.

The Canadian government was telling us that we couldn't use their money anymore if we separated. Why did they think we cared? We would have dollar bills with roses on them. We could have René Lévesque, his comb-over slicked on top of his bulging forehead, with a cigarette in his mouth, on the five-dollar bill. And Gilles Vigneault with his navy blue sailor hat, white sideburns and big nose on the twenty.

It was a bit of a shock, especially given the context of the conversation, to see Adam standing there. I didn't understand why my English ex-boyfriend would be in my part of the city. He knew that I spent every New Year's Eve at the Ukrainian Ballroom. There wasn't much point to being there if you weren't in love with me. Here he was, dressed in a tuxedo, the bow tie undone. He was looking at me intently, waiting for me to notice him.

I touched Raphaël gently to indicate that I was leaving him for a second. I made eye contact with Adam as I walked to the bathroom. I passed a bulletin board that had crudely coloured butterflies held down by push-pins. I went to the upstairs bathrooms. I knew that no one would come up here, because most people didn't know about the bathrooms. They were the children's bathrooms for the daycare in the building. There was no secret corridor in this neighbourhood that Nicolas and I did not know about.

The echo of someone singing a Patricia Kaas song was coming down the hall after me. It was like she had fallen down to the bottom of a well and was continuing to sing nonetheless. She was becoming smaller and smaller. I was hoping that Adam was following me.

I looked at the tiny sinks and the little toilets and the door-knobs that were close to the ground. The change in perspective seemed to really throw me. It gave me the feeling of being in a funhouse. I had been coming here for years. When I was very small, I had never noticed that there was anything different about this bathroom. I had fit perfectly. Adam walked in behind me.

There was something absurd about his outfit. It was almost as over the top as the paper crown I had on my head.

"I didn't want to just come up to you because I heard that your boyfriend might be a little bit mad and somewhat irrational."

"Did Nicolas tell you that?"

"Might have been."

He smiled. We were wary of each other. Every time I had been with Adam, it had the breezy lightness of a one-night stand. It had never felt as if there could possibly be a heaviness between us. And here it was. I had been feeling so brash and confident and wild and glamorous out in the hall. And now I felt like a schoolgirl who had been caught cheating on her home-work. I was shaking the same way that I had when we visited Lily. He was filled with stories and knowledge about my mother that had the possibility to floor me.

"It's strange what happened, isn't it?" I said.

"Yeah, I thought that it would stop feeling odd, but it didn't. I feel sort of like we're brother and sister, but then I don't. I mean, that isn't quite it. Then I realize that I don't have any siblings myself, so I would actually have no idea what that felt like."

I went and sat on the wooden board over the radiator. I hoped that it would warm me up. Adam followed and sat next to me.

"But I sort of felt that by staying away I was keeping something from you. That I had something that you wanted. Nicolas used to ask me all these questions about Noëlle, but how did I know that she was your mother? I just answered off the top of my head. The thing is that I was at a family dinner back home and I started thinking about you. There was stuff that I should have told you about her when we were breaking up."

We were talking in the bathroom because we were aware that what we were doing was somehow illegal. We were somehow intuitively ashamed. What would Raphaël think if someone whispered to him that Adam and I were alone in the bathroom together? He would surely imagine that we were fooling around or fucking or flirting or having some sort of conversation that was the equivalent of sex. But it wasn't true. We were doing something that made us feel even dirtier. We were talking about my mother.

"What do you want to tell me about?"

"Like about how she would lie in bed with me and tell me stories."

"What kinds of stories?"

"Stories about twins."

"She told you stories about twins?"

Without even thinking about it, I put my hands up and pointed to my chest, as if to ask, "Stories about me?"

"Yes, there was a boy and a girl."

"What did they look like?"

"What do you think? They had wild black hair and they were so lovely that people would slam on their brakes to get a better look at them."

"Did you add that, or did she?"

"Noëlle did."

"Were they personable? Were they charming?"

"Sure, sure, sure. They were very funny and very adorable."

We had begged Loulou to tell us stories. He would lie on the bed and try to read us a picture book. But Loulou had only gone to Grade Three and the effort would put him into a deep, deep sleep. He would take up all the space in the bed, so that we were scrunched up against the wall. Then we would spend ten minutes trying to push him off the bed. He would inhale so deeply that he would suck all the oxygen out of the room and then let out these brief sorts of snores. We had always had to tell each other stories. Which we would find unsatisfactory. Then we would get into squabbles.

Those were our stories Adam heard. We were meant to be the ones who heard those stories.

"Tell me one of her stories."

"My favourite one was the story where the twins get lost at sea."

I perched anxiously on the edge of the radiator, waiting to hear it.

"They were on a big ocean liner. They were on their way to the World's Fair in Paris. But on the way, there was a ferocious storm."

"The ship sank."

"Exactly. It didn't stand a chance."

"Were the twins okay?"

"There was a cello case. They climbed up onto the instrument. They floated on it for weeks."

The conversation itself was just like a cello on the water, and it was going in whatever direction the current took it and was drifting out farther and farther into a strange ocean.

"All alone? How did they have anything to eat?"

I kept asking him these questions to egg him on. I did not want him to stop.

"They made good friends with a pelican that would bring them fish. There was a hundred-year-old turtle that taught them their school work so that they wouldn't fall behind."

"Who else?"

"There was a walrus that was always trying to get the girl to marry him."

"Did she return his affections?"

"No. But she would make daisy chains to go around his neck."

"Were they happy?"

"I mean, they were affected by melancholia the way that anyone who is stuck on a deserted cello island would be. They missed going to school and riding the city bus and having tea parties with their friends, stuff like that."

"Was there any hope of rescue?"

"They put letters in bottles and tossed them out to sea. Then the bottles washed up on the shores of France. They were published in a collection that won the Prix Goncourt!"

"*Oh mon dieu! Quelle histoire!*"

I clapped my hands because it was a marvel of a tale. I had tears in my eyes. My heart had slowed and I had stopped shaking. Adam and I had always wanted to swap our memories, as if we were kids trading cards at the back of a school bus. He had wanted to have a memory of being famous. And I had wanted a memory of feeling secure.

I think he realized that he didn't actually want my memories. They were the type that mocked you as you grew older. They were like ex-lovers who had dumped you. Adam's, on the other hand, got better with age. They were memories that you could blow on gently, like a dying ember, and they would light and make you feel warm and wonderful.

And now he had managed to bring us even the voice of our mother and spread it out at my feet like a fantastical tapestry from another land.

Adam put his arm around me because I was crying. He wasn't doing it in a romantic sort of way. I realized that I had actually stopped being attracted to every boy I met. I had just thought it was a myth that people might only ever be attracted to one person.

"So you're living at home again now?" I asked when I was able to wipe the tears from my eyes.

"Yes, for now. I've returned to the rest of the world but I just can't seem to fit in. It was a lovely place, your make-believe kingdom."

I looked at the clock on the wall. It was indeed almost midnight.

"Oh, I've got to go. I've got to make it back. If I don't get back and kiss my husband by New Year's, then we'll have bad luck in bed all year."

We laughed.

"I'm going to go out the back way. I don't want to risk running into Raphaël. He's a hair-breadth from going over to the dark side."

Suddenly the blaring music that was coming from down the hall stopped. There was a woman's voice on the loudspeaker telling everyone to get ready because midnight was about to be here. Her voice cracked and she sounded like she was a hundred years old. Everyone started whistling and cheering. I hurried down the corridor, my boots making fantastic noises, like a herd of wildebeests.

Then a drum roll sounded and everyone yelled, *"Dix!"* I could see the giant open doors to the ballroom. I could see all the people with their sparkly top hats. *"Neuf!"* they were shouting at the top of their lungs. By *"Huit!"* I was halfway across the ballroom. *"Sept!"* I was almost up to Raphaël. At *"Six!"* I flung my arms around him. He was happy to see me and held me in his arms. I yelled out the rest of the numbers with everyone in the room.

We held our plastic flutes of champagne up in the air. Heaps of confetti blew all around our heads. I was buoyed up by my new memory. For a little while, it was going to feel as if this memory were really mine. The same way as when you snort a line of coke, for a few moments you believe that you are experiencing real happiness.

Raphaël put his arms around me and lifted me off the ground. As he spun me around, I raised my arms up in the air to catch all the silver and gold squares of confetti falling from the ceiling. The music was booming. Raphaël had one of his big smiles on his face. He rarely smiled, but when he did, it was beautiful and enormous.

We could have our own memories. How hard could it be? Wasn't our wedding a good memory? Even with Raphaël's fight with Nicolas. Even if it had cost about three hundred dollars and everybody had pitched in for it, and there were plastic forks.

This night was another happy memory too! Happy memories were easy to come by.

*****

I was sitting on the toilet seat, singing a song and staring at myself in the bathroom mirror. I was feeling confident. I was glowing like a girl with a lovely childhood. I was feeling very pretty. I couldn't wait to open the bathroom door for Raphaël to see just how lovely I was. How lovely was I? When I crossed the street, people would slam on their brakes just to get a better look at me. I knew that he wouldn't be able to resist me tonight.

I tiptoed out of the bathroom on my stockinged tippytoes. I started getting undressed in an extremely suggestive way. My shoe hit the window. It rattled. I paused for a second to make sure that I hadn't broken it. I flung my bra across the room. It ended up hanging from a nail on the wall. It was perhaps a tad dangerous to be performing a strip show while I was this drunk.

But when I climbed into bed he just wrapped his arms around me and closed his eyes. I felt really, really exposed and awkward after my performance. But what was a little humiliation if one day we could have sex again? The snow was falling outside. I wondered if, when Noëlle told that tale to Adam, she had imagined Nicolas and me squished up with them on the bed too. We would all fall asleep together on that tiny cello as it rocked up and down and back and forth on the waves.

CHAPTER 37

Nicolas Tremblay Plays by His Own Rules

Nicolas hadn't seen Pierrot in months and he had stopped bringing him up. Nicolas's spirits seemed to have risen, though. Or in any case, Nicolas started to act as if his spirits had risen. Whenever something was really bothering Nicolas, he got this weird version of happy, which was more like hyperactivity.

I put on my coat and hat and boots and stomped off through the snow to find Nicolas on a windy winter day. I couldn't hear myself think because the wind was so loud. It took forever just to get to the corner store because my boots kept getting stuck in the piles of snow that I was trudging through.

By the time I found Nicolas at the Portuguese bakery, my eyelashes were frozen and I couldn't feel the tips of my fingers, even though I had gloves on. My tights were covered in slush right up to my knees. I pushed open the glass door and hurried inside. The tiles on the wall were all blue. They served pastries that were as hard as rocks, and teeny tiny cups of espresso that could make you completely insane.

Nicolas was sitting at a table. His big overcoat was slung over the back of his chair. There were some young guys sitting with him at his table, listening to him avidly. One waved his hands around madly whenever Nicolas made an interesting point. The other boy had a fine moustache and a cast on his wrist, which he had drawn little ships all over. I guess that if his childhood had been better, he might have become a sailor. There was a big puddle underneath them from the snow that had melted off their boots.

Nicolas's head was lowered as he talked to them. He had a piece of paper with a diagram drawn on it. As I approached the table, he quickly folded up his paper and stuck it into his pocket. He smiled at me as if he wasn't doing anything at all.

"Hello, sweetheart," Nicolas said. "Here she is, ladies and gentlemen: my marvellous sister. We once had a fabulous show together. Unparalleled."

Nicolas stood up and started walking in an exaggerated manner, and then he got slower and slower, until he bent over and hung forward like a windup doll that had petered out. I stared at him for a while. Then I stood up, walked over and stood behind him. I turned an imaginary key around and around on his back. He stood up and started moving again. Everyone in the café applauded. He was doing it for my benefit, of course.

It was a routine that we'd performed on the talk show *Midi plus*. We had these routines stuck in us like refrains from songs that we couldn't stop singing, or nervous tics. Anyways, this time it was fun to do one of our old shticks together.

Nicolas brought me over to a table in the corner where we could talk alone.

"You're miserable. That's why you came looking for me, isn't it? You can move back home if you want."

"No. Raphaël and I are doing fine."

"I saw your husband reading the newspaper in his pyjamas at the Polish breakfast place. He was making one of the waitresses nervous as hell. And you're going to tell me that your marriage is okay?"

"Things are really good between us; just the other day I said that it was like we were still on a honeymoon."

"God, how tacky."

I didn't want to let Nicolas think that it had been a mistake to leave home. I didn't want to admit it to myself. I wanted to keep moving forward, even though it might be awful and strange and difficult.

"Why are you lying to me?" Nicolas asked. "You think that I'm going to judge you? You think that I'm going to give you a hard time about your relationship not working out? There hasn't been a relationship that worked out on this street since 1973."

"Do you want to do something together?" I asked. "We could go see a movie or a show?"

"No, no, no. I'm through with that Everyman shit."

"So what does that mean? You want to go read philosophy or jump out of airplanes?"

"No. What I think we should do is pay our mother another visit."

"Oh no, that's not a good idea."

"Come on, Nouschka. We can't just leave it the way we left it."

"No way, Nicolas."

"You're afraid of your own mother?"

"First of all, she's not really our mother; Loulou is. And I'm not afraid of her. She expressed that it wouldn't be appropriate for us to go and see her, and I'm not."

"Fuck that. Why does she get to have the final say? This time I'm going to show up at dinnertime and I'm going to scream my motherfucking head off until she comes out and falls on her hands and knees and weeps. What do you think about that?"

"I think you should calm down, Nicolas."

"I am going to show up on the lawn and I am going to masturbate right in front of all the children. After I have gone back to the city, an army of ugly, dirty boys that nobody will want will sprout out of the ground."

He tapped his index finger against my chest.

"We have to go back there, Nouschka."

A woman passing by looked at him. He pointed his finger at the woman and she immediately jerked her head away.

I thought about telling him the story about the floating cello. My idea of who Noëlle was had changed now that I knew she was a storyteller. I had always thought that Étienne's attraction to her was one hundred percent based on her being young. But maybe she whispered something into his ear that had made her seem completely unique and different from all the other girls crammed into that house in the country. Maybe she told him that he looked like a pirate who had lost his treasure map.

Somehow I liked that idea. I think that all kids—no matter how acrimonious their parents' relationship is—want to believe that at the point of their conception, their parents had been in love.

But this sort of wistful thinking wouldn't cut it for Nicolas. What he was looking for was something real. He wanted change. He wanted confrontation. He seemed to be offering me a choice, or a dare, rather. I could either go with him to see our mother, or he was going to stay at the lovely Pâtisserie Gourmande and continue orchestrating his mad Children's War.

"Everyone is always telling me about what a shitty parent I am. But why do my parents get away with bloody murder? Why do I have to come up with three thousand dollars? Why do I have to prove myself? She's a terrible parent. She completely abandoned us, so why don't they take her kids away? Will you explain that to me? Why does she get to have Little Fishstick and Dumont or whatever the fuck their names are?"

"Did you just call her kids Fishstick and Dumont?" I started laughing.

"I don't know what their names are. I'm just guessing."

We started laughing hysterically at these two strangers out in the world, who we could think of in a hundred ways but never as siblings.

"But that's what they looked like in the photographs, no? Didn't they look like a Fishstick and a Dumont?"

We laughed so hard that we cried.

"That doesn't even make any sense," I said. "You've completely lost your noodle."

"My bananas have fallen completely out of my banana tree."

Nicolas was wearing a OUI button on his pea jacket. I pointed to it. He took it off and put it on my jacket. We were still fighting on the same side of that war. But I wasn't ready for Lily. Maybe once I had lost everything like Nicolas had, then I would be able to face her again.

CHAPTER 38

Love Me Under the Dirty Moon

ALL I SEEMED TO HAVE THAT NIGHT WAS Raphaël. We hadn't made love since he told me about what had happened to him as a little boy. When we were first married, he would come home and start kissing me and trying to put his hands up my shirt before he had even taken his coat off. I would scream bloody murder because his hands were so cold.

But the worst of it now was that he was obsessed with me having an affair. He wasn't in the mood to talk to me.

I was standing naked at the bathroom sink, feeling at a loss as to what I was going to do if we broke up. I took my black sweater and a red leather skirt off the hooks on the back of the bathroom door and put them on. I put some makeup on. I had promised to go to the bingo hall with Loulou. I picked up my boots from beside the front door, sat on a kitchen chair and pulled them on.

Raphaël walked into the kitchen. He was drinking instant coffee out of a teacup. He leaned against the counter and watched me.

"Where are you going?" he asked.

"The bingo hall."

"Bullshit. Look at you. No one dresses up like that to go to the bingo hall."

"What are you trying to say?"

Raphaël had started asking me all these detailed questions. He was trying to sink my battleship.

He sat down and lit up a homemade bong he'd fabricated out of a 7UP bottle. The smoke swirled inside it, looking like a mermaid trapped in an aquarium, banging on the walls. After he exhaled, he pulled a pair of yellow underwear out of his pocket and held them up.

"Where the fuck did these come from?"

I blushed because I had taken them out of somebody else's laundry bin. He took my blush as confirmation that I had received them as a gift. He went into my closet. He ripped all the pretty dresses off the coat hangers, shoving them into a huge garbage bag. He tossed the bag right out the window. I sat on the side of the mattress, speechless.

I knew that we were one fight away from splitting up. So I just let him act crazy, like I was watching a television show.

The next morning, as I was waiting for the bus to go to work, I looked back up at the window and saw Raphaël standing in it, watching me. When I finished my shift, I saw him sitting in the restaurant across the street from the magazine store.

That evening he came home early from work. He walked right past me and threw open the window and looked down the fire escape to see if someone was running down it. The cold air rushed in. It made me feel incredibly naked, even though I had my clothes on. I just decided to ignore him and continue reading. He sat next to me on the bed. He held up one of the pillows to his nose and inhaled. He kissed me really hard. Then he almost pushed me away and went to the kitchen to smoke a cigarette.

He thought it was weird that I was wearing perfume. He thought that it was because I was trying to mask some other smell. He dumped my purse out on the kitchen table. He was perplexed because there were about twelve half-used tubes of lipstick. A girl who sold for Revlon had given me her samples.

It was driving me batty that he kept trying to put two and two together. I got caught up in his madness, I suppose. I started going through his things too. I was trying to find out what he was up to.

I found a notebook in his underwear drawer. I took it out and opened it. On the first page, he had written "The End of Beginnings." I had no idea what it was about lunatics that made them almost sound like geniuses. I sat on the edge of the bed to read what was inside. He had written down all my comings and goings. He had noted that there was somewhere that I snuck off to at 4:20 every day. I was frightened. I put the notebook back where I'd found it. I wished I had never seen it. His defence mechanisms were leading him down a dangerous path. He had made a mistake trusting someone once, and now he was examining me under a microscope. How could anybody withstand that kind of scrutiny?

If you want to see yourself the way the devil sees you, then read your sweetheart's diary.

Nouschka was moving a strand of spaghetti into the shape of a heart.

Nouschka was in the bathtub for an hour reading Anna Karenina.

Nouschka bought a postcard of a boxer, although she had no intention of mailing it to anyone.

Nouschka put her teacup on the windowsill. The cat jumped up and drank out of it, but Nouschka didn't say anything.

Nouschka was crying while reading the newspaper.

Nouschka stopped outside the building and just stood there for a few minutes before coming upstairs.

Nouschka put her hand out to see whether or not it was raining, even though it clearly wasn't.

It almost seemed like I was reading about someone I had never met. It was the sketch of a Russian novel—except the author hadn't yet come up with the tragedy that would befall the female protagonist. But even I could see that she was already dissatisfied.

I decided to try harder to prove my love and to somehow get our relationship back to the way it was just a few months before. Later, I went into the bathroom while Raphaël was leaning into the mirror and shaving. All I had on was a pair of green woollen tights and a lavender bra, which must have been from the fifties, from the thrift store. It was the prettiest thing I owned. He made love to me every single time that I took my sweater off and was wearing it. I sat on the toilet with the lid down. It was a feat, because even though we had the heat pumped up, it was still always cold in the apartment. I was pouting my lips and tilting my head in a way that I hoped was attractive.

"Raphaël?" I asked, as sweetly as I could. "Do you think about me when you're riding the bus? Do you think maybe we'll go on a holiday together by the seashore? We could bring some Polish sausage and beer. Do you find that half the characters in books remind you of me?"

I was trying to get him to compliment me like he used to.

"What I wonder sometimes is why a girl like you would go for me. Unless maybe someone put you up to it."

We were both quiet for a spell. We just stared, trying to figure each other out. We were wondering what the other's game plan was.

"I'm pregnant," I said.

And after that night, I was.

CHAPTER 39

Pin Your Heart on Your Jacket

NICOLAS WAS OUTSIDE THE MÉTROPOLIS. HE WAS
scalping tickets to music shows. He always did that on Friday
nights.

The thousands of lightbulbs on the marquee were flick-
ering on and off. Whenever a light in our kitchen would blow
out, Loulou would tell us to take a ladder and go and get one
of the bulbs from the Métropolis sign. It was a staple in his
stand-up routine. He looked sort of picturesque under the marquee, looking off into space with a stern expression, his hair
swept back. That's why all the girls in high school had always
been in love with him. He sort of looked like a tortured gang-
ster from a sixties film noir. The crowd had all gone inside to
see Les Colocs, and if he had any tickets left, they weren't worth
anything anymore.

"What's the news?" he said when he saw me walking up.

"I'm pregnant."

"Ohhhh, why?" Nicolas yelled, throwing his arms up in the
air. "We're supposed to be trying to put this family out of its

misery. We're sluts, we have ADD and we're separatists. We shouldn't be procreating."

He was grinning though. We both started to laugh for no reason, or perhaps at the fact that we were inflicting more Tremblays onto this world.

"I thought that wearing spandex all the time was supposed to render a man infertile," Nicolas said. "Just please don't let the little fucker figure skate. You know I hate that shit."

"I'm going to buy him one of those all-white outfits. The ones with fringes under the arms."

"You wouldn't! Think of all the poor kids in China who are in sweatshops being forced to make sequins for those outfits."

We started cracking up. He was sort of happy that I was in the same boat as him. It was like when he had dropped out of school and I had done the same. He usually did stupid things first—like smoking and drinking and having sex—and then he felt all weird and guilty about them until I did the same. Then they just seemed normal. He always liked when I followed him down. If you think that that is an awful quality, well you are probably right, but you can't have a very high opinion of love.

"You must be hungry," he said. "I was hungry all the time when Saskia was pregnant. Also, I had morning sickness, because I vomited when she told me."

"What else can you tell me about being pregnant?"

"You'll want an ice cream sundae."

We went around the corner to a café that served sundaes year round. It was a tiny, cozy place that we'd liked since we were kids. The walls were painted pink and there were paintings of blue skies with clouds. There were plants in the petite jars on the shelves; their roots were swimming around in the water, like some nineteenth-century etching. The chalkboard had a dozen different names for ice cream and specialty coffee; the bottom halves of the words were all smudged.

He took a wad of cash that he had made that evening out of his pocket. There were an awful lot of red two-dollar bills padding out that roll. He peeled a couple off the top and handed them to the waitress.

"Two sundaes."

The waitress had an afro, the back of which was white with chalk powder from leaning on the menu board. She put scoops of vanilla ice cream into the bowls and then poured hot caramel onto them. The sauce melted the ice cream immediately. We waited for a moment to see whether or not the hot caramel might have the power to melt away all of winter.

"When I get the three grand together," Nicolas said, "I'll be able to see Pierrot and we can let the kids play together."

I wasn't going to try and argue that getting three thousand dollars didn't necessarily mean he would see Pierrot again. We were just going to sort of celebrate the possibility of being good parents. Getting pregnant while we were young and unprepared meant we were old school. I had written a paper on family life in Québec before the Quiet Revolution in the sixties. During *La Grande Noirceur*, when the Catholic Church controlled the province, Québec was famous for its birthrate. Girls everywhere got pregnant too young. You would see them skipping rope with their pregnant bellies. You would see them in the children's section of the library, using their huge bellies to prop up their books. There were seven or eight carriages parked outside every store. The sound of all the rattles shaking at once could drive you mad. Every house smelled like pissy and shitty diapers. You had to wear rubber boots because of all the porridge spilled on the floor.

There were babies in baskets in all the doorways. Once, a woman came home with a baby wrapped in newspaper, sure that it was a little piece of ham that she had bought. Babies were always crying. Mothers could do nothing to make them hush, because all the lullabies were written in English.

As we looked out the window, Étienne and the camera crew passed by. He had cut out a heart from a piece of red construction paper and safety-pinned it to the lapel of his jacket. I don't know what he was trying to say. He was getting experimental.

Étienne was holding up his hand as if to claim that he was the one who had come up with the idea of having snow this year. And maybe it was. Maybe Étienne hadn't just invented Nicolas and me, but maybe he had created the whole world.

I guess, since he was my father, it would make sense for me to go out there and say hello and tell him that I was pregnant. He had other things on his mind right now though. Clearly. To go up and talk to him would be like interrupting a performer in the middle of a play. How lovely to be in a production of your life instead of being in your life itself.

CHAPTER 40

The Children's Brigade

THE WINTER WIND WENT AWAY LITTLE BY little. I put away my coat with the big buttons with the faces of grizzly bears on them. Children started coming out of hibernation. They seemed dangerous to me now that I was pregnant.

A child wrote its name on the wall with a black crayon. The child wrote that it was in love with someone named Roger. Every day there was something new written by this child on the wall. What could you do? You would have to put out a trap with a candy in it to catch the child and break its neck.

A kid made mud pies in aluminum dishes with tiny stones on top to decorate them. They were all over the back stairs.

I opened the mailbox and marbles poured out. There were orange plastic soldiers hanging by strings from the bush. There was Monopoly money under the windshield wiper of the car. There was an egg carton filled with bean sprouts on the windowsill in the stairwell.

The circulars had all been turned into diminutive ships and

were sailing off on the sea in the pond in the park. It was an armada that had snuck up on us during the night.

Soon they would win. One day, with their plastic swords, their cork guns, their snowballs. They were amassing an army and stockpiling weapons. We just weren't paying attention.

*****

On the way home from work, Raphaël and I found ourselves stopping to stare at children when we were walking down the street. It was as if each child might be ours and we were trying to recognize it.

I noticed someone taking a photo of us across the street. They had begun taking photographs of our family no matter what the hell we were doing. There were photographs of us eating sandwiches in the park. I ignored the man and kept walking with Raphaël, staring at babies.

We had no idea what the connection was between the baby that was inside of me and the kids who were running around. We weren't really convinced that because I was pregnant, it followed that I was going to have one of these odd little creatures.

Anyways, the baby was so teeny at this point that I didn't even know where it was most of the time. It was like Pluto. We knew that it was way, way out in the universe, because somebody told us that it was. And we took them at their word. We really had no empirical proof of that ridiculously small planet ourselves.

"When I was little, there was an old man who worked at the corner store," Raphaël said. "And he had tattoos of butterflies on each hand. I thought that he had been born with those tattoos."

It made me happy when he said that. He remembered something beautiful about being a child. Raphaël seemed to be much better since he had found out that I was going to have a baby.

We lay in bed talking.

"What are we going to name it?" I asked.

"I hope it's a girl. I wouldn't want to be responsible for bringing another man into the world."

"Let's name her Fleur, after the skunk with the long eyelashes."

"Let's name her Nouschka. I love your name."

"Let's build her hundreds of snowmen and make sure every snowman has a hat on its head."

"Let's never ever make her wear a woolly, scratchy sweater."

"Let's not tell her about death for a long, long time."

We didn't have a philosophy of child rearing. But like every couple who are expecting a child, we thought that we would do it differently. We would do it our own way. We would be the parents that we hadn't had. People who have had bad childhoods are always excited when babies are on the way. They make the mistake of believing that just because they know what a horrible childhood is, they will know the opposite.

CHAPTER 41

Horses

THE NEWS SAID THAT THE PARTI QUÉBÉCOIS WAS postponing the referendum. It didn't seem like anything actually ever happened in Québec. History was something that happened elsewhere. I mean, they hadn't changed the French store signs since the thirties. The things that were written on the bathroom walls had been scribbled there in 1964 by wild girls with beehives.

But then again, I was pregnant. That seemed like the kind of thing that could never really happen either. I was walking home from Place des Arts when I suddenly felt numb and absolutely still. I put my hands on my belly. The strangeness of it just struck me. Everything all around me, even the beetles, was filled with grace.

There was a bunch of doves flying around outside. A magician had passed out drunk and he had left his top hat upside down. Doves had been flying out for hours.

I had started to have creepy dreams. I had a dream where I had a baby that was made out of plastic, and I put it on the radiator and it began to melt. I had a dream that I traded the baby for a bag of cherries at the grocery store and then regretted it intensely afterward. In one dream I had a baby that had little duck feet, and it paddled sadly back and forth across the bathtub. I dreamt that I had given birth to a wee calf, and I had to take the calf for walks at night so it could eat the neighbours' roses.

I went to see the doctor for the first time. I was only three months along. The fetus was a small drop of amber with a heart that was already a million years old. I stood on the scale at the clinic. I held up my pink T-shirt that had the letters for the rock band Indochine ironed on it in glittery letters. The doctor said it was normal to still be skinny.

"Oh," I said. I felt about five years old.

He gave me a photocopied page with different charitable organizations that I could call if I needed help. I went to see the Grey Nuns and they gave me a plastic bag filled with clothes. I laid them on the bed. There was a sweater with a monkey holding a banana on it. I couldn't even look at it. It broke my heart. I put the clothes in the bottom drawer. I decided to just not think about the baby. It was just a piece of macaroni with a heartbeat, after all.

I had started to be terrified of the baby. I imagined a young boy with curly black hair, smoking a cigarette. Maybe he would sit by himself and read sci-fi novels. I worried I would have a kid who was bad at school and afraid of everything.

Then one morning I was making coffee and I suddenly felt as if I had just stepped off a spinning ride at the amusement park. I was sick to my stomach. I went into the tiny bathroom to throw up. I looked at the reflection of my face in the mirror above the sink. The colour had drenched out of my face. Ah, I thought. So the baby has decided to launch its first attack. The first time you really, really notice someone is the first time they hurt you. When you realize that they have the ability.

There wasn't a single woman in my family that I could ask any advice from. It was sad to have to just read pamphlets that the doctor had given me. I brought it up to Raphaël when he sat down for breakfast. He was wearing his pyjama bottoms and reading the paper. He put it down.

"What do you think that you are missing out on by not having a mother? Someone to help you put your lipstick on? That would be something, because you really don't know how to put lipstick on. You, like, put it on half of your mouth and then get bored."

"I just wish that I had a mother to talk to about things right now."

"You're lucky that you didn't have a mother, because you didn't have to listen to shit about your horoscope."

It was strange that he made that comment about horoscopes, because he himself checked his religiously in the newspaper every morning.

"Yeah, but Véronique did all these practical, responsible things for you."

"My mother was always combing my bangs and then the comb would scratch my nose. I hated that. It's like, my bangs are fucking straight enough, woman!"

I laughed despite myself.

"I'm serious," I said.

"So am I. Mothers are overrated. The smell of their perfume gets on you and just lingers all day. They wake you up in the middle of the night to check if you are breathing. They make you wear shoes with buckles. You shatter all their hopes and dreams and they never let you forget about it."

"I think that if I had had a mother, I might have done a lot of things very differently."

"If you had had a mother, then you wouldn't have married me."

"I would just like to know what I'm supposed to do with a baby."

"Ask Loulou."

"Loulou doesn't know. Once Loulou forgot us in the grocery cart at the store. The delivery guy brought us home."

"How can he be so absent-minded?"

"He's old."

"Why does it seem like Loulou's been old since, like, 1924? Has he been old since he was twelve years old, or what? Anyways, I know what to do with babies; don't worry about it."

"How do you know what to do with babies?"

"My little brothers were always swallowing stuff. They used to swallow the house keys and shit. I would have to give them the Heimlich manoeuvre. I'd just go around the table, giving each one of them the Heimlich first thing in the morning."

"You know how to change diapers?"

"I can change diapers in twenty-three seconds. I have the Montréal junior championship."

"On top of skating? That's very impressive."

Then I threw my hands up in despair. "Maybe I'll go ask Nicolas."

"What are you talking about? Nicolas never raised his own kid."

"Well, I haven't seen Nicolas in a while anyways."

"We saw him two days ago."

"Yes, but it was only for ten minutes and then he had to run. It's hard to get him to spend any time with me."

"Because he's punishing you."

Raphaël was sort of miffed at Nicolas. We'd run into him at the grocery store and he congratulated us on the baby and suggested we name it Chef Boyardee if it was a boy. I wasn't sure what had annoyed Raphaël more: Nicolas's stupid joke or how hard I had laughed at it.

"Well, if he has no advice about the baby, at least he remembers being a baby. Do you know that Nicolas remembers having been in the womb? He remembers not having any eyes. He said that my foot was in his face for five months." As I was talking, I started getting dressed. I was tying my shoes as fast as I could. "I know that it can't possibly be true, but imagine if it were. That would mean that Nicolas would know exactly what on earth the baby was thinking right now."

I was getting very excited about the prospect of having a highly conceptual, nonsensical conversation with Nicolas. He wouldn't be able to give me any advice, but at least he could distract me from worrying, which was probably even better.

"Fine," said Raphaël. "Let's go see my mother."

*****

We went over to the building that was across the street from the one I'd grown up in but might as well have been a thousand miles away, because we had never had the courage to knock on each other's doors.

I sat in the living room with Véronique while Raphaël sat in an armchair, fidgeting and crossing and uncrossing his long legs. I, on the other hand, felt relaxed around his mother. Véronique was overweight, but she was undeniably beautiful. That's why she had four kids with different fathers. Her round face was as soft as clouds. She sat on the couch, wearing an orange kimono covered in blue butterflies. I sat on an armchair across from her in a ski jacket and a black and white striped sweater dress. Raphaël stood up and began pacing around the room. He was wearing a track suit, maybe because he wanted this visit to go quickly.

"You've been good to him really. You don't sleep around. You haven't put on any weight even though you're pregnant. That's one of my main problems, really. I've always put on weight during the first few months of my relationships."

Raphaël grunted in dismay. "Véronique, why don't you tell Nouschka about what a free spirit you used to be? I can never get enough of those stories. Those stories are delightful. Tell her about how some random guy took your picture on the street. I love that story, Véronique."

"Stop calling me Véronique."

"Please just explain to Nouschka how you cut out coupons from a *circulaire* and then bring them to the store to trade them for diapers."

"I've been dyeing my hair black in the sink. It takes three packages."

"Focus, woman!"

"Raphaël used to be so good with all his little brothers when they were babies. He's a natural with babies. Raphaël used to sing the song 'Marcia Baila' by Rita Mitsouko and that was the only thing that would put them to sleep. It was so cute."

Raphaël sighed and smacked his forehead. Véronique had no intention of stopping. He went into the kitchen.

"He'll never be able to hold a job for very long. There are just some men that are like that. I wish that I could help you out with some money, but you know that I just absolutely can't."

She hurried into the other room and came out with one of his trophies.

"He put these outside the house once in the garbage can. I went and got them back when he wasn't looking and I hid them at the back of the closet. I think that he liked figure skating, to be honest. He's just too hard on himself. Every time he likes something he gets very upset."

"Tell her why I'm really like this, though," Raphaël said. He had walked back in the room with a tall glass of water in his hand.

"It's because he's a Scorpio," Véronique said.

"I didn't have a chance, you see." He handed me the glass of water even though I hadn't asked for it. "Could you just tell Nouschka how to burp a baby? Can you be useful? Go ahead, begin. I don't have all day. I have no idea what you'll say to her if I leave you alone together."

"Even when he was little, everything upset him. He was extraordinarily sensitive, you know. Even the doctor said he's extraordinarily sensitive."

"In reference to what? A diaper rash? Has anyone been around asking questions about my past?"

"No."

"Why did you answer so quickly?"

Véronique immediately looked apprehensive because she knew that he was acting strangely. Her seismograph for picking up an oncoming quake was much more sensitive than mine.

"I don't want you to tell anyone about my childhood, Véronique. You got that?"

Raphaël left the living room and headed toward his bedroom. I think that Raphaël was always afraid the tabloids would dig into his history or interview his coach and learn his secret.

Or maybe he thought that if they thought long and hard enough about him, they would just be able to figure it out.

I sat in the living room with Véronique, as it sounded like Raphaël was tearing apart his room.

"He was always a kind of maddish. But I think that it was his coach who didn't treat him right," she whispered. "Did he talk to you about that? I can't bring it up. He gets bananas."

While Véronique was talking, Raphaël came back in the room and started going through all the photograph albums, removing pictures of himself as a child. There was a photo on the living room wall of Raphaël at about twelve years old, wearing a big brown fur coat over a red turtleneck. He had a bit of a moustache above his lip even then. Even in one where he was wearing a plastic cowboy hat and standing behind a white cake with pink frosting, he looked troubled. Véronique put her hand up as if to say she was going to keep her hands clean of this mood.

Raphaël put the photos in a plastic bag, which he shoved down the front of his pants. He took my hand and led me out of the apartment. As if there was some reason to be in a hurry.

As he was walking down the street, he checked to see if the coast was clear, then threw the bag into a public trash can.

The next day he gave me the binders filled with his school work. He asked me if he could trust me to shred them.

"Of course," I said.

He left the apartment, off on some other mission. I started taking out the pages of math equations. I ripped them into four or five pieces, then threw them in the trash. I was sure that he was going to complain that it wasn't a professional job.

I found an oral report that he had read in front of the class. I remembered that day. No one could hear what he was saying, because he was mumbling.

HORSES
By Raphaël Lemieux

Horses are generally large. They are bigger than many such animals. Many such animals that are too many to name. Among which are the pig, dog, cat, rabbit and chicken. People are fond of horses because they take you many places on top of them. You will sometimes find a police officer riding on top of one. Horses are very fast and win many races. They cannot break a leg like you or I. I broke my leg last year and was not shot. This is unfair. They do not need gas like a car. Their children are called fouls.

Raphaël was right to destroy all the evidence of who he was as a little kid. Nobody wants to be reminded of what they could have been. If there was a time machine invented and we could all travel back in time to see ourselves as children, we would never recover.

CHAPTER 42

My Husband Is Crazier Than Yours

I WENT TO LOOK FOR RAPHAËL AT THE POLISH Social Club a few days later. He hadn't come home the night before. There was a woman singing on the stage. She strummed a ukulele and pouted her lips abruptly as she said each word, as if she was spitting out sunflower seeds. It was a style of French singing where you spoke the words really emphatically, as if you were lecturing a child.

A cat was in the corner, yawning. It looked like an insomniac in striped pyjamas.

Raphaël was drunk. He was sitting with a blond girl on his lap. I walked over, took a drink off their table and threw it on her. Everyone was startled and started to laugh, even the girl, who shook the beer off her hair like a wet dog that had just come in from the rain. I had thought that we were happy again. It had been the loveliest thing on the planet. That was the last time we were happy in the city.

After that night Raphaël would check his horoscope in the mornings as if he was checking his stocks. He bought six different

newspapers and had a Spanish man help him translate the horoscope from a paper from Mexico City.

He started laughing at odd times. There was something a
little terrifying about people who laughed at a joke too long or
at jokes that weren't funny.

"Are you going to work?" I asked him as he was leaving the
apartment one night.

"No. I'm all washed up. I've got a Grade Eight education.
The only work for me is robbing jewellery stores. And my
heart's just not in it."

"Weren't you going to go back to school, for nursing?"

"There's a reason for you to go to school. You write all those
clever essays in your notebooks. You know how to do something
like that. It is very hard for a person to go to school once they
have rejected the linearity of time. It presupposes that we are
moving forward through time and that a gradual accumulation
of facts is necessary. Some of us are going backward through
time. As such. We are unlearning loads of information."

He walked out the door. He frustrated me the way that
Nicolas did. They didn't act as if they would ever be twenty-
five. They didn't have any sort of long-term plan. They were
just trying to get through the day. They were often involved
in plans that weren't actually plans. Complicated plans that left
them exactly in the same place that they started out. They put
on all sorts of costumes and affectations, but they couldn't get
away from the idea of who they were as children. Nicolas was
Peter Pan. Raphaël was Captain Hook. But it was the same old
story being told by a slightly different character.

It would be okay—we could make it—if we both did something small every day to make sure that we were getting our

lives together. I wanted to have some fun in life too. I didn't want to have to do all of the work while he got to go mad. I didn't like to be like the ant, all industrious and worried, while Raphaël went around being a grasshopper, all wild and upset and singing at the moon. I felt terribly selfish thinking this way, but I couldn't go down with Raphaël. I had to have my own trials and tribulations. Jesus, I was twenty years old!

I walked into the kitchen one night. Raphaël was naked and running a magnet from the fridge door that was in the shape of a piña colada all over his body. He wanted to see if he could detect any magnetism. I glanced at the workout sheet he'd put on the fridge. He had been up late the night before and had apparently done three thousand sit-ups. He told me that he thought that some scientists had put a transistor in him when he was a little kid so that they could monitor the effects of child abuse. He said they were writing a book about him. He was going to ask at the hospital if he could have his whole body X-rayed so that they could find the receiver and remove it.

Try as I might, I could no longer make sense of Raphaël's behaviour. In retrospect, I should have done something. But he had been to the doctors and that hadn't worked. His family was useless. What other options did I have? There was a cult around the corner, where a twenty-seven-year-old who wore a pair of pants without a belt lectured about macrobiotics. There was a hypnotist above the legal clinic who wiped away all your problems for sixty-five dollars. There was a tarot card reader on the first floor of our building. None of them seemed like viable solutions.

Instead I hid some extra money from my paycheque in a

tin with roses on it under the bed. I didn't want to admit to myself why I was hiding it. I was hiding it in case I left Raphaël. I had started to do it since I found out that I was pregnant, just in case. But, actually, I knew that he was going to fall apart. I looked around the room guiltily when I was done. No one was there.

CHAPTER 43

Cyrano de Bergerac Is Alive and Well and Living in Montréal

FOR FRENCH CLASS WE WERE ALL SUPPOSED TO write a book review and then go up in front of everyone and read it out loud. Instead of writing a run-of-the-mill report, I decided to get creative. My story was a retelling of *Cyrano de Bergerac*. In the original tale, he feeds all these wonderful and romantic lines to his friend to recite to a girl named Roxane, who he has a crush on. In mine, Cyrano comes up with the tackiest and crudest come-ons possible—something that I was an expert on, having grown up on Boulevard Saint-Laurent.

A couple of students in the class who were going to school to get bigger unemployment cheques slept through the tale. But the others laughed and clapped at the end. The girl my age with giant gold hoop earrings almost fell off her chair and started whistling during my reading. After the class, some of the students came up and told me that they had really enjoyed the story. The teacher took my hand and said that I certainly had a way with words, not unlike the original Cyrano. She wanted to know if I planned to continue on to university after I graduated. I told her I did. She was the first person that I had said that to. I liked the sound of it.

I walked home with a skip in my step. Oh okay, so they were only twenty-four people. They were not exactly literary critics or a crowd of refined aficionados. But it was the first audience that I had captivated on my own. They were not Étienne Tremblay fans. I hadn't written the story to somehow neurotically capture my father's fickle love. I had written it for myself. I felt very good about it, indeed. It was something that I could get better at. And if you don't have something to try and get better at when you are twenty years old, you are lost.

*****

I got home. The referendum was back on and it was going to be in the fall. There was an article in the newspaper talking about how there was going to be a rally of Québec artists and poets to speak out for separatism. I saw that Étienne's name was on the list.

Oh là là! I thought. What would Étienne do? He wouldn't have anything prepared. I had seen his notebooks in recent years. He was incapable of sustaining a thought for more than a few lines. His brain was like a bucket with holes in the bottom. It would suddenly be filled with brilliance, but that would all quickly leak away. I didn't want him to make an ass of himself. He had been such a great orator. I didn't want him to go out with a whimper. Oh, who knows why I cared, but I did.

I took out a pen to jot down some notes. Why did Québec want to separate this time? We were the original descendants of the losers of the war between England and France for Canada.

We had been shit upon for generations. But we were proud and we had finally built our own culture in the sixties. We became urbanized, and in apartments we sat up late reading philosophy books. We got rid of the church, but we stuck to our nationalism. Many of us wanted to leave Canada.

In 1980, after the loss of the first referendum, our premier René Lévesque had famously said, *"À la prochaine fois."* Then Québec didn't sign the new constitution that was drafted in 1981. René Lévesque had the Québec flag flown at half mast.

Finally, a few years ago, Québec made some propositions for constitutional amendments. We wanted it in writing that we were distinct, that there was something weird and special about us. Since we didn't have our own country, at least we could have some sort of other protection. But Canada said no. They scoffed. We had asked for a consolation prize and they had laughed in our faces.

If they didn't think we were going to react badly, they were mistaken. We were going to react badly, Nicolas Tremblay–style. We were leaving this damn country that went around calling itself the greatest country in the world.

We were packing our bags. There was nothing that they could say now. Now they were trying anything to make us stay. Like a lover who was trying to talk reason into you as you were throwing your clothes into a suitcase, they went from saying soothing, reconciliatory, sweet things to calling you a complete idiot and telling you that you'd regret it for sure. Well it was too late for all that.

We would go off on our own. We just wanted to speak French in peace. We wanted to whisper dirty things to our loved ones in French. There was a certain kind of love that could only be expressed in this way.

There was no difference between the expressions *I like you* and *I love you* in French. You could never declare love like that in English.

We loved in a self-destructive, over-the-top way. A way that was popular in sixties experimental theatre and certain Shakespeare plays. We loved like Napoleonic soldiers in Russia, penning beautiful letters while seated on the corpses of our dead horses. We were like drunk detectives who carried around tiny notebooks full of clues and fell for our suspects. We were crazy about the objects of our affection the way that ex-criminals in Pentecostal churches were crazy about Jesus. We went after people who didn't know we existed, like Captain Ahab did. We loved awkwardly and hopelessly, like a wolf ringing a doorbell while wearing a sheepskin coat that is way too small for him.

How could you explain that in a political platform? I wondered. I began to write a speech for Étienne. The only way that we would win the referendum would be if the speech-makers came out. Only poetry could win the vote.

They didn't want to hear these words from a young, silly girl, pregnant with her first child. They wanted to hear it from a man with a huge nose and wild hair. Who tossed women aside and went out into the fray. Everybody wanted Cyrano to show his ugly face and scream his beautiful words. We all knew what a revolutionary looked like, the same way that we knew what a lover was supposed to look like. I knew that I was writing this for Étienne to read. I used to be his mouthpiece. Now he'd be mine.

CHAPTER 44

Turn the Radio Up

RAPHAËL SAID THAT HE WANTED TO GO OUT AND have some fun with his gorgeous pregnant wife. He watched me getting ready. He was drinking Scotch out of a glass. I put on my red dress and was leaning over the bureau to look in the mirror while putting lipstick on. He was wearing a shirt that was the colour of robins' eggs. The sole was hanging off the bottom of his shoe. It looked like an alligator with its jaw hanging open.

"Mirror, mirror on the wall. Who's the fairest of them all?" I asked.

A skinny girl in a wife-beater T-shirt in Saint-Henri appeared in the mirror. Her stepmother was yelling at her in the background.

"I don't know why you even spend one second fixing yourself up," Raphaël said. "You look fantastic all the time. I am going to draw you eight hundred hearts on a piece of paper. And I'm going to mail it to you. And you're going to open the mailbox and the hearts are going to fly right out of it like hornets coming out of a hornets' nest."

"That's sort of beautiful, baby," I said. It was actually something that my Cyrano might have said.

I put the lipstick down and turned around with a flourish to indicate that I was ready to go. I was willing to forget everything. If there was one thing that I knew how to do, it was to live in the moment and have a kick-ass time.

"Look at you! I have to take you out into the world. I have to let other people look at you because it's only fair. You're so pretty it's breaking my heart just to look at you. I think that I can see your aura. Glowing out of you."

"What colour is it?"

"The colour of daffodils, I think, except pink."

We went dancing at the Armenian Confederation Ballroom. He sat on a chair as I danced the sweetest, tightest lap dance in the history of mankind.

We probably looked like the most romantic couple on earth, like we were having the best time that any two people could possibly have. Really, we were going someplace where the music was loud, loud, loud, so that we didn't have to hear the anxious mutterings of our psyches. And if we partied and went out dancing and made love often, didn't it mean we were okay?

When we got home, Raphaël told me not to turn on the lights yet. I stood in the dark as he ran to the window and opened the blinds. He told me that he was certain we'd been followed. I told him that he was imagining things and flicked on the light switches. But for once he actually turned out to be right. Even a crazy clock is right twice a day.

A week later I saw a photograph of me dancing against Raphaël at the ballroom on the corner of the cover of a tabloid. But that wasn't the worst of it. I opened up the magazine, and inside there was a blown-up photograph of Raphaël as a little kid wearing a silver spandex tuxedo and matching top hat. He had a gold medal hanging around his neck. His father was standing next to him, looking like the proudest man in the world. As I stared at it, I realized that it was one of the pictures that Raphaël had thrown away. In fact, the entire page was covered with photos that Raphaël had crammed in the bin that day on our way home from Véronique's house. Someone had gone into the garbage and taken out his secret history. I never thought they would go that far.

According to the writer, Raphaël was a tortured genius. He had gone mad doing pirouettes. They found some doctor to say that training children to be professional athletes was a form of child abuse. Supposedly, figure skating was one of the few professions that could lead you to catatonic despair. Space travel was another one. Maybe now that he was with Nouschka Tremblay, he would get his life back on track and he would join the exhibition circuit. I wondered if there was a possibility that Raphaël wouldn't see this magazine.

A patient in the hospital ended up showing it to Raphaël. He said he couldn't understand why Raphaël was working as an orderly if he was in a magazine. He brought it home and tore it up in front of me as he carried on frantically.

"I'm going to spend the rest of my life standing in front of this garbage can, tearing myself up. I'm going to climb into the garbage truck myself and just get the fuck out of here. Just be taken and not worry about this shit anymore. Who do they think they are? I'm going to eat my fucking fists."

Sometimes it was hard to figure out who the press was going to be smitten with. Raphaël didn't fit into the ordinary, day-to-day life of the city, but he fit into the mysterious world of the tabloids beautifully.

You could have a graduate class on him at Université de Montréal. The prerequisites would have to be Russian Realism, The Death of the American Dream, The Bad Guy in Henry James, French Postwar Existentialism, and Seventies Independent Cinema. You could write your thesis on a man like him. The story wasn't going to go away in a day. It was going to be drawn out, like a love triangle on a soap opera.

He chased a photographer down the street. He took off his jacket, threw it onto the photographer's head and then knocked him to the ground. He yelled at everyone who had stopped to view the spectacle that he had every intention of breaking their fucking necks. He walked home in just his undershirt. Everybody got out of the way. He stopped at a store to buy a carton of milk. When he was looking through his pockets for change, the guy at the store told Raphaël to just take it.

He gave great quotes to interviewers who called him up at work, telling them that they were parasites and the like. That's exactly what the tabloids wanted to hear. They liked their heroes to play hard to get. And to be honest, I thought that having a concrete enemy was doing Raphaël some good. He could stop waiting for demons to come out of the woodwork.

There was a photograph of Raphaël smoking a joint in the park. He was incredibly worried that his probation officer was going to see the photograph and have him thrown in jail or committed again. Which was actually a legitimate fear, I suppose. I wonder if it's more comforting to a schizophrenic to have legitimate fears or imaginary ones.

He got into a scrape in the hospital elevator with a man

who came in right after him with a camera in his hand. It turned out that the man was there to photograph his newborn baby. The hospital suggested that he take a leave of absence. Raphaël walked into the apartment wearing his scrubs, looking distraught.

CHAPTER 45

Running Away from Home

I T WAS WARM OUT. THE TATTOO OF A ROSE ON Raphaël's arm had grown new leaves and buds and completely surrounded his bicep. My stomach had finally grown big enough that people on the street were able to tell that I was pregnant. I wasn't sure how I felt about it.

At work my boss kept laughing and telling me not to lick the envelopes because it would cause my baby to have birth defects. And then she yelled at me for carrying boxes of programs into the office. She said that she would never forgive herself if I had a miscarriage. Finally she told me to take some leave and promised to give me my job back whenever I wanted to come back to work. I was at home during the day with Raphaël.

"We're going to the country," Raphaël said. "We'll be safer there."

"No, we're not."

I didn't even look up from my math textbook. I hadn't left the island of Montréal since I was seven years old and visited Étienne in prison. There was just tundra and nothingness out there. I did not want to go into the wilderness, where you were all alone under the stars with nothing to distract you from your thoughts. If you lived a certain way downtown you could get away without having one of your own thoughts for weeks.

"We have to leave tonight," Raphaël said. "I don't want to be taken away and be incapacitated. They'll fill me up with drugs so that I can't even tie my own shoes. I'll never be able to support my family."

I had no intention of leaving the city and living in the boonies. I was outraged. I had put up with all his craziness all winter and I had to draw the line somewhere.

"Well it's been nice being married to you, baby," I said. "But I guess we'll have to get a divorce."

His face got red, but he didn't say anything. Instead he launched into action, throwing stuff randomly into a suitcase. He mostly seemed to have packed underwear, an alarm clock and a copy of the novel *Comment faire l'amour avec un nègre sans se fatiguer.*

"Goodbye!" he yelled.

He walked out the door. I sat there listening, but I didn't even hear the sound of his boots going down the stairs. I knew he was standing outside in the hallway, waiting for me to run after him. Finally, he flung the door back open.

"We've got to get out of here now. Stop being a crazy, irrational bitch. Please! I've fucking had enough of this. You've got five minutes to put your things together."

"I'm not putting any of my things together."

"Fine, you don't need any of it. It's all cheap, crazy crap anyways."

"Who do you think you are? Talking to me like this. Do you think I'm going to just sit here and be insulted by a washed-up figure skating schizophrenic? You are sorely mistaken."

"They'll all survive without you, you know. Your family."

I burst into tears. I felt horribly homesick. I wished that I had never left home and that Nicolas and I still lived together in the same bed.

"I feel guilty and terrible," I said.

"You want to believe that everything and everybody will go to hell when you're gone. It's all about your ego."

"Fine," I said. "Let's go. Just let me pack a few things."

I took off the dress that I was wearing and tossed it out the window. I threw my shoes out the window. The coats went down to the ground like descending birds of prey. A homeless man stopped, put on one of my hats and walked off. There were understudies everywhere getting ready to play my part if I left.

I dropped the drawer filled with utensils out the window in order to make a point. It woke up the whole building. I threw the plates. The little glass and ceramic people lay without their heads on the street. Some of them frowned sadly and closed their eyes and whispered their last words. I took Raphaël's ten-speed bicycle and pushed it out the door. It rode itself down the stairs miraculously. It was as impressive as when Kermit the Frog rode a bicycle in that movie.

Raphaël walked out the door and headed down the stairs with our suitcases. I followed him down in my undershirt and underwear. I'm sure I looked ridiculous; everyone could see my protruding belly. I followed him out onto the street. People leaned out the window to watch, but they didn't seem to worry very much—or think that they should come down and help us.

I lay down in the street in front of the car. I knew people did that kind of thing—but I didn't know that I was one of those people. I was so afraid and confused that I almost wanted to let Raphaël run the show, but he was completely crazy.

An older woman wearing an orange housecoat came out of the building. Her white hair was held up in senseless directions with bobby pins. She started walking toward us with her cane.

"Yes, Madame," Raphaël said fiercely. "Can I help you? Can I help you? This isn't a show. If it was a show, I would charge admission and you couldn't afford it. So go back and watch *La Petite Vie*."

"I'm going to miss *La Petite Vie!*" I said from the ground. "I hate you. I used to be a beauty queen."

"Here we go. Here we go."

I was suddenly terrified about Nicolas not being able to find me. I thought that if I could just stop anywhere to leave a message for Nicolas, it would be okay. It was just impossibly awful for me to leave the city without telling him. I had promised him earlier in the year that I would never go.

"I just want to go to the pharmacy. I have to go get some aspirin."

I knew that my excuse wasn't believable though. Raphaël called me out on it right away.

"Are you crazy? You don't get headaches. You just want to have a chance to call Nicolas."

"You're always making me choose between you."

"Our relationship always suffers when you start obsessing about him. You can't be a wife. We have to have our very own little family. I get to be number one just for once."

"I always make you number one."

"Not really, Nouschka, my darling. Not really. You pretended that you chose to be with me at the wedding. And maybe you were, for just that night, but you've been slowly, bit by bit, trying to get back to Nicolas. But time moves forward and not back. And don't you realize that all the successes in time travel are so that we can move forward?"

I sat looking at Raphaël, trying to grasp the gist of what he just said.

"If we were to go back in time, it would be disastrous to civilization. There would still be dinosaurs running around. And there would be no Beethoven or Sigmund Freud. All of our encyclopedias would be obsolete because they would be encyclopedias of the unknown."

I shook my head at him in an uncomprehending way.

"You got married to me," he said, putting his hands gently on my shoulders. "You can't go back to the way things were before. Have some respect for the present."

He was right. He was completely mad and even he could see that I couldn't go running back to Nicolas.

A scrap-metal truck passed by. They were building space-ships out of fences and grocery carts. They wanted to be the first Québécois to plant a fleur-de-lys on the moon.

"Do you still love me?" I asked.

He paused and sighed. "*Voyons donc*, Nouschka."

We left the city in the night. Nicolas and Loulou and Étienne were all on the island, having no idea that I was leaving. I felt in my purse. I had brought along the tin that was filled with money.

CHAPTER 46

In the Land Where I Was Born

W<small>E DROVE DOWN THE HIGHWAY, PAST ROWS OF</small> farmhouses that looked like a line of lunch boxes on a bench at the back of the class. The radio was playing a late-night show. The DJ's bosses were asleep. Otherwise, surely, he would be fired for playing music that was so profoundly sad. The notes from the piano were like raindrops falling on the lake.

We drove past the exits to towns named after saints. There was Sainte-Julie, who was conceived one Christmas night when her father swore he'd put a condom on. There was Saint-Jacob, who woke up after a night of heavy drinking to find that a tattoo of the Virgin Mary had miraculously appeared on his arm. And Saint-Martin, who got up in the middle of the night to get a glass of water, and when he turned on the faucet, beer came out.

Nicolas and I were conceived in a small town like this. But I was tired of believing the Lily Sainte-Marie creation story. It made no sense to me. It was easier to believe that a cow was licking maple syrup off a stone for an hour until the stone began to cry and stretched out its little arms in the air. Or to believe that a wolf gave birth to Nicolas and me under the rotten floor-boards of one of the rotten houses in Val-des-Loups.

The house was down a path in the woods. The headlights illuminated the woods, like a spotlight that shines on the stage before the circus begins.

It belonged to one of the Bleeding Sparrows. I expected it to be a dump. On the contrary, the house was made out of wood and was painted white and was really pretty. The rent was only three hundred dollars, because there was no work in the area. I had never been in a house that size. There was a green Indian carpet with salmon pink flowers. There was a couch with deer all over it, and framed needlepoints of deer on the wall. There were actual deer out in the forest. You could hear them making the sound of pulling off their boots.

The mattress let out a cry when I flopped onto it. Raphaël was burning sage and waving it all over the room to get the evil spirits out as I fell asleep.

Raphaël threw his clothes into the garbage bin behind the house. Why he did this, I have no idea. Maybe he thought they had bad karma. In a pair of jean shorts, he drove to the local dump and filled a paper bag with clothes. Someone had thrown out an entire wardrobe from the seventies. The collars on all the shirts were too long and the buttons on the jackets were gigantic. Raphaël came into the kitchen wearing a pair of bell-bottoms and a polyester undershirt with a red and brown tweed pattern on it. He was wearing a pair of flip-flops on his enormous feet. None of the shoes at the dump were big enough for him.

I liked his style. It was like we had gone back in time to before we were born. Raphaël had proven his thesis that you could indeed move backward in time as well as forward.

"I need some sort of outdoor work," Raphaël said.

"You don't even know what that means."

That evening, Raphaël asked me to pass him his red jacket as he pointed to a black one on the back of a chair. I passed him the jacket and he seemed happy with it. I guess he didn't subscribe to the idea that words belonged exclusively to their definitions. That, or he was reading a different dictionary than the rest of us.

"I'll be back in a couple hours," he said.

"I'm going with you."

"Suit yourself. But I'd rather you not interfere with my transactions."

I had on a skirt and a turtleneck that was too big. My hands kept getting lost in the sleeves. I grabbed my boots and put them on.

"Are you going to be a drug dealer?"

"No. The guy who owns this house is doing two years in Kingston Penitentiary for that sort of thing. That's why we get to stay here for so cheap."

"It's so lonely though."

"I'm going to get a guard dog to help with that."

Part of Raphaël's probation conditions was that he wasn't allowed to have a dog. It was worse than all the drugs. That he was getting a dog was a clear sign that he was going down the same old path he'd gone down before.

As we drove, we passed the one Chinese restaurant for fifty miles. Old women still wore their hair in beehives out here. The teenagers were always being killed hitchhiking home from heavy metal concerts in the city. Half the dogs were named Princesse.

"You can't have a dog, you know," I said.

"Don't Daddy know it to be the bitter truth. But Daddy gonna take care of you, baby-child."

On principle, I ignored guys when they chose to talk like forties pimps from Chicago. We drove down the highway. We passed all the black-eyed Susans weeping about how badly their boyfriends had treated them. But we had no time for them.

CHAPTER 47

The Wild Roses of Québec

T HERE WAS A WOODEN SIGN THAT HAD THE word GYPSIES painted on it on the side of the highway. We drove down the path that was next to it. It led to a clearing where a group of white houses stood at the end of the road. They could all have used a coat of paint, but they were actually kind of pretty. There were motorcycles everywhere, which ruined the effect of it being a kind of a nice little enclave.

We stopped the car in front of the biggest house. There were all sorts of chairs and an old couch on the porch. There were pots of plants all over the steps. There was a small statue of an angel, which had enormous pores from having survived countless winters.

There was a very young girl with a blond mullet and a Mitsou T-shirt, which she had knotted under her underdeveloped breasts, sitting on the couch next to a boy who was covered with stick-on tattoos. Children always ended up looking and acting like their parents. Which was a thought I didn't want to be having right then.

We were going to see that biker named Rosalie, who lived here. He opened the front door and gestured that we should follow him. His hair was wet, as if he had just taken a shower, and he had on a leather vest. He walked us out behind the house to a cottage. He opened the door of the garage and there, unmistakably right in front of us, was a cage with a lion in it. He was telling Raphaël how a person could train a lion and make a fortune leasing him out to American film companies. And how people liked to get their photographs taken with lions at fairs and birthday parties.

"What's its name?" Raphaël asked.

"Michelangelo," Rosalie answered.

At which I rolled my eyes as violently as any human being could. Raphaël turned away from me, so that he didn't laugh. He came and stood next to me as we looked at the lion.

The lion looked heavy. It looked like a sweater that you had pulled out of a bucket it was soaking in. His belly slouched toward the ground as he paced. The lion's step was so quiet, however, as if it was walking on carpet in a suburban home. It had giant black gums and little brown spots all over its body. It had big amber eyes that were filled with so much innocence, it was terrifying. It was hard on some level to believe that the lion was dangerous, because it was hard to believe that it was real. It seemed like I was just imagining it. I jumped back when it raised one of its paws.

"I never imagined that a lion could have such big paws," I said.

"Yeah, it takes awhile to get used to. It's better to sell them when they are cubs like this. Before people have fully grasped the idea that they've bought a lion."

"Aren't you worried that the lion will eat your children?"

"He's totally tame. He doesn't have a mean bone in his body. If someone came and slit my throat, he'd probably just sit there yawning. I got to get rid of it because my ex-wife says she'll tell the lawyer and I'll lose visitation rights."

"That'll do it."

"She'll say anything about me."

While Raphaël was looking at the lion, I followed Rosalie back into his house. I was worried that Raphaël was going to buy that lion and try to fasten him into the back of the car with a seat belt. I didn't want to be around when he made such a decision. At least later, while I was being ripped apart, I would know it wasn't any of my doing. Rosalie sat in a leather easy chair and did a line of cocaine. Cocaine was popular in this neck of the woods. His cheeks were all flushed and he glowed, like a baby that was fat on breast milk and about to pass out. He started babbling.

He said that he came from a small town where all the women his age were named Charlotte, after a character on a television show that was popular that year. He said he had once cut his initials into a tree trunk and the tree died.

Three other Bleeding Sparrows walked into the house and came in the living room. A boy followed them. The boy, who was about four years old, was wearing nothing but diapers and a pair of red cowboy boots.

"Your husband is, like, the deepest dude that I ever met," one of them said. "Once we smoked mescaline. We were in our underwear. And he taught me all these rules. He taught me about the physics of the universe."

He was wearing a bright yellow tank top that was almost exactly the same colour as a dandelion. Because they wore sunglasses, it was hard to know how stoned they were.

"Oh that's nice."

They all seemed to have at least three tattoos of roses a piece. There was an entire rose garden sitting right there in front of me. He had never promised me a rose garden, but here it was.

"What kind of freaky weirdos buy lions anyways?" I asked.

"I'll take him," Raphaël said, walking in.

For a second I thought that he meant the lion, but I saw he had a huge German shepherd following behind him. I never thought I'd be relieved that we left there with a dog.

CHAPTER 48

Are You There, God? It's Me, Nouschka Tremblay

As WE WALKED BACK TO THE CAR, I TURNED AND waved to the bikers.

"I want you to ask yourself a serious question," I said, once we were out of earshot. "I want you to ask yourself whether you think that what Québec needs is another biker?"

"I'm not a biker. I'm just visiting a few of my business associates."

"Do you know what business associates do? They wear suits and have briefcases, and you meet them in boardrooms and you give presentations. They don't walk around in black tank tops and have designated tables at strip clubs. They don't start their meeting by bragging about their oral sex skills."

"How would you feel about changing our names?"

"I don't like that. What are you going to change them to?"

"I always feel fantastic with a new name. It's like a brand-new suit. I feel like a new man. How about Marguerite? Arnaud Marguerite."

"I don't think I'm one hundred percent in love with that stupid name, to be honest."

"You're not being open-minded."

"I think I've been reasonably open-minded enough for one day. I'm out here in Saint-Maurice-Fucked-Ma-Blonde, looking at lions!"

"If we stay out here for a year, then we will maybe make fifty thousand dollars breeding this guy, and then we can go back to the city and get back on our feet. We can buy a lot of fancy things."

"Now we're going to breed the dog?"

"Sure, why not? He's a champion."

"A champion how?"

"Would you like a brand-new fur coat?"

"No."

"What about leopard-skin seat covers for the car?"

"What about gold teeth? We should get matching gold teeth."

"Be serious, Nouschka. We can have our own house."

That's the problem with marrying young, isn't it? It's almost like one of you has to sacrifice your dream for the other. It was true that Raphaël's dream was a little bit more lucrative at the moment. But it was just money that was going to run out and then leave us off exactly where we were before. If I had a degree, it would lead me to all sorts of promising futures. But here I was in the woods, a thousand miles from school.

We climbed in the car with Champion the German shepherd. The dog was clearly ecstatic that we were taking it home with us. It kept toppling around in the back seat as we drove off. It finally squeezed its head behind Raphaël's seat and stuck its head out the window.

We stopped outside a grocery store. There were about a million signs on the front of the store window. The prices were written in big fluorescent numbers on white pieces of paper. There was a sign that was making a big, big deal about the price of milk. Raphaël went inside.

The dog kept looking anxiously out the window to see if Raphaël had come out of the store yet. Perhaps it thought that Raphaël might sneak out a back exit and run away from us all. The dog was trying to suppress a whine. I could tell that it was almost painful for it not to cry out. I wondered who had fallen in love with Raphaël quicker: me or the dog.

I watched the people walking out. They all looked Québécois. No one out here understood a word of English. Knowing how to speak English was a Montréal thing. There was a man with a handlebar moustache. Everything else about him was ordinary—everything except that moustache.

A woman with a brown trench coat that almost went down to the ground came out of the store. She was smoking a cigarette. Her children were all following behind her, each carrying a plastic bag with the word MERCI written on it in blue. They walked in a row behind her, like a row of pretty little ducks.

"Look at that woman," I said out loud. "She doesn't even know when to stop. Soon she'll need a school bus just to take her kids to school."

I could spend the rest of my life in this car, waiting for Raphaël to come out of the grocery store. There would be three kids crammed into the back seat, wearing different T-shirts and reading comic books and praying that their father would bring them out a bag of Cheetos. Their running shoes would kick the back of my seat, like a heartbeat.

The dog did a circle of joy when he saw Raphaël come out

of the store, pushing a cart with a huge bag of dog food and other groceries in it. He loaded everything into the trunk of the car.

"I always sort of saw myself as some sort of intellectual," I said as I watched Raphaël through the car window. "But here I am, pregnant, in the middle of nowhere, waiting for my biker boyfriend to come out of a grocery store."

As Raphaël got in the car, he handed me a plastic bottle of spruce beer. There was a lumberjack on the label with a tiny red toque on his head. We Québécois were always drinking spruce beer. Every time I drank it, I thought that this time I might like it, and every time I drank it, I liked it even less. I almost gagged after having a sip. I'd never felt as contrary as I did that day.

"I should have just stayed stranded on the island with Nicolas. I should have. We would have been happy with the pelicans and the swans. I should have just married the walrus. What was so wrong? Things were less complicated. All that Nicolas and I ever did was bitch about our lives. But maybe it wasn't so bad. Because everything off the island is worse."

"Are you talking to your mother?" Raphaël asked. "You talk to her all the time. Ever since I started seeing you, you were always talking to your mother. Maybe every time that you talk to her, she's probably somewhere—wherever she is—answering your questions. Did you ever think about that?"

I looked at Raphaël. Sometimes mad people could say such wonderfully astute things. They could wrap their minds around lovely possibilities that the rest of us couldn't.

"Let's not fight," Raphaël said with kindness. "Let's just see where this adventure takes us, shall we?"

"How long are we going to be out here?"

"I just can't be on the island right now. You know that we had a difficult history. They're all sorts of ways for places to be bugged, you know. I saw a documentary on the Cold War. Since Communism fell, they sold all their equipment cheap. There are warehouses full of wiretaps and headphones."

But then, of course, they ruined it by saying something like that.

He was wearing a giant gold watch. It didn't seem to tell the right time, but he didn't seem to mind. Maybe his broken watch told the right time in a parallel universe. He clicked on the ignition. Someone screamed out from the radio. The dog put its paws on the back of the seats and leaned its head forward between us like a little kid that was excited about wherever we were going.

CHAPTER 49

The World's Tiniest Tremblay

WHEN RAPHAËL AND I WERE IN TOWN A COUPLE days later, I bought a book at the drugstore about having babies. There was a photo of a six-month-old baby on the cover. It looked like a goldfish in a plastic bag that a child was carrying home from the pet store.

Once we got home I read the baby book in one sitting, engrossed, as if it was a gruesome thriller. After reading about all the things that could go wrong with a baby, I wanted to go to the doctor's to have an ultrasound or at least another checkup.

"The baby could have an umbilical cord wrapped around its neck."

"I doubt that very much."

"It might not have the right-sized heart necessary for it to go on living."

"If it doesn't, then there's nothing that we can do for it."

"But if I know that it has the proper-sized heart, then I can stop worrying about that."

He had come out here to live on the fringe. Going to have

an ultrasound at a hospital with some strangers looking at his unborn child was about as intrusive an activity as any a person could fathom. He would have to sit in a waiting room with all these people who seemed unconcerned by the fact that all of modern society was a hypocritical sham and an outrage.

"We might as well wear beige pants and eat with four forks."

But I insisted that I wanted to go. I'd made a doctor's appointment at the little hospital. Raphaël was in a bit of a temper because this was going to ruin his day. We sped down the highway. Someone out there had opened a pie and blackbirds had flown out and filled the air.

He stood next to me as I lay on the hospital bed and they rubbed gel all over my belly. It was so weird, that wee baby on the screen. It was right there with us, but it was like we were hundreds and thousands of miles away from it. It was like those photographs of aliens that were on the news. You needed more evidence. Sure, the photos looked sort of real. But, obviously, it was a hoax.

I looked to Raphaël for some sort of reaction. He had taken his sunglasses off, but he somehow gave the impression that he still had them on.

"Would you like to know whether or not it's a boy or a girl?" the nurse asked.

"Yes," I said. Raphaël shrugged as if to say he wasn't going to stop her.

"It's a boy."

And the baby was real. It was a baby boy and it belonged to us. There it was, alone in the dark. I didn't even know what to think. I felt like crying. I was too terrified to be sad or happy. For the very first time in my life I realized with absolute clarity that I was going to die one day. And then that feel-

ing was gone. I was back among the living. If I couldn't handle
the sight of that little baby, I could only imagine what the shock
must be like for Raphaël. There was no way he was going to
be able to handle having a boy.

Our eyes met. His face was still wiped clean of expression.
He didn't think it was anyone's business to know what he was
thinking. I hated that about him suddenly.

I had the photograph of the ultrasound in my hand as we
left the hospital. I didn't know what to do with it. I put it in
the glovebox of the car. Raphaël climbed into the driver's seat,
drinking a Diet Coke. He put the key in the ignition, then he
turned to me and smiled.

"Well, the baby's healthy! That's fantastic news! We'll have
to go out and celebrate. Isn't that what men and women do
when they find out that they are going to have a baby?"

"But we knew that we were going to have a baby before
now."

"But now we have documented proof that the baby is normal and is going to be just as cute as all the babies that you see
in the supermarket, so there is no reason for you to worry."

I didn't say anything.

"What's the matter with you?" Raphaël asked. "Why are
you sitting there looking so pipsqueaky and quiet?"

"I just thought that you would be unhappy about it being
a boy."

"You're the one who's nervous, sweetheart. I'm feeling fine."

"Really."

"I've never been happier about anything in my life. You
don't have to worry about anything. I'm your man."

"Really? Honestly? You promise?"

"If you ask me like that one more time, I have a feeling that

I might start to get pissed off. And stop trying to telegraph your own insecurities into my head so that you don't have to take responsibility for them. Okay?"

"Okay."

"Okay! Now! We are going to have a fucking celebration."

He leaned forward and kissed me on the forehead. I didn't really trust him for a second.

On the way home, Raphaël stopped at a general store on the side of the road. He bought a huge bottle of whiskey. I was frightened by this idea of celebrating.

He also stopped off at a Bleeding Sparrow's house. We'd been there before. A dealer who called himself Marie lived there. Raphaël said to hang on, that he wanted to go see about a roll of chicken wire for his enclosure. It seemed like this was something that he was making up off the top of his head. And he was acting in that stupid, overly energized way that boys get when they are on their way to score drugs. They practically started tap dancing. I figured that he was going to buy some cocaine from the guy. I decided not to ask. I just didn't want trouble. I just wanted to not give a shit the way that the rest of the twenty-year-olds without babies in the world did.

From the way he was dressed when he stepped out of the bathroom after we got home, I knew that he was definitely high. Raphaël would try any sort of drug. He took them as if they were the answer. He would stand there waiting for the effects of the drugs to hit him as if they were magic potions. As if he were suddenly going to transform into a cat or a bird, because he did not want to be himself. He was always such a lunatic when he got high. But it's always the people who act the most ridiculously on drugs who are the ones who seek them out.

He was all dressed up. He had on a white shirt and a black

suit. His hair was clean and combed back. He kept throwing his head back as he fixed the cuffs of his shirt sleeves, sort of like a racing horse. He was strutting about in a way that his dad used to do when he was outside Raphaël's building, checking out the passing girls. His asshole percentage had immediately cranked up.

He turned up the radio in the kitchen. It was starting to get impossible to think. I decided to just let the song do the thinking for me. It was sort of happy. I started feeling happy too. I gave in to the good mood. It was impossible not to.

"I think you're allowed to get drunk once when you're pregnant."

I knew this wasn't true. But he was the dad, so I decided to let Raphaël make that decision. Besides, I was still so young and I wanted to have a night out of drinking and dancing. I couldn't resist a party. He poured the whiskey right up to the rim of the glass. It kept threatening to spill over. The whiskey stung me like a bee. I felt my mouth swelling up. We were going to have a blast and have lovely hangovers in the morning and wish that we were dead. It would be wonderful.

"Put on something foxy. Like something that a magician's assistant would wear. When I was a kid and I would go to see magic shows, I always wanted to fuck the magician's assistant."

"Ridiculous."

Anything fancy that I had looked quite funny with my belly. I pulled a red dress over my bump. We were laughing.

"Let's go out, baby. A girl as pretty as you shouldn't even be sitting on the side of a bed in the middle of the jungle on a Saturday night with no place to go. Let's go out dancing and then I'll bring you back home and treat you right, show you that you married the right man."

"How are we supposed to go out? There's no place to go. It's the heart of darkness out there."

"Where there's a town, there's dancing."

✷✷✷✷✷

Raphaël brought me to a giant barn-like edifice that housed a country club's ballroom. There were a couple of ravens outside the club, dressed in tuxedo jackets with their hair slicked back. The club was filled with rich people from Montréal who had country homes for the summer. The ceiling was made up of innumerable arches. There were big balls of light hanging down all over the place. Imagine a sky filled with so many moons. I wonder if it would make us any happier. We would probably just get used to it. The dance floor was made of the shiniest wood money could buy and it was enormous. It was the size of a little city, like Detroit, or of a little sea, like the Mediterranean.

The mirrors on the wall were in a lousy mood. They made everyone look sad and tired. Which was surprising them, because everyone felt like they were looking better than they had ever looked. It was impossible to tell how old anyone was. The dancers were thin but they had hairdos from fifties commercials. All the couples were wearing strange glittery costumes and dancing the tango. When the music stopped they would just freeze. The women had big pink carnations on their dresses.

Raphaël told the hostess that he would give her a hundred dollars if she could find me a fat carnation to pin on my dress, so that I wouldn't feel left out. She just shrugged. No matter what he said, she just thought he was mocking her. She had encountered men before in this place who were in Raphaël's mood.

There were hundreds of tables with gold chairs on the sides of the dance floor. We sat at one of the tables and a waitress came over.

"Line up our table with glasses of whiskey," Raphaël told her. "We never want to be without whiskey, because we are in love and we are spending money and we are going to have a baby."

"Is it a boy or a girl?" she asked.

"It's a millionaire. In the ultrasound it didn't have a penis; it had an attaché case."

Raphaël watched the waitress as she walked away. "How do you like that? Why do people ask me these fucking nosy questions? Is that a normal question to ask? I never know."

"I think it's normal."

"Some complete stranger asking the sex of my unborn child?"

The cocaine had put him into a totally crazy mood. I'd seen him like that before a couple times. I kind of liked it. He always called me baby and sweetie and opened doors for me, and started acting like Elvis Presley coming out on a Vegas stage. He would get all confident and macho. He would order for me at a restaurant and tell me not to worry my pretty little head about anything.

He was almost about to get worked up again, but the waitress brought the drinks over. He knocked back another shot and that seemed to calm him down. He was encouraging me to drink as if it would cure me of a cold, as if the booze was the voice of common sense.

"I like these places that have tabs. It's classy. This is my kind of place," he said. "Let's dance."

He was sliding around the floor. I followed after him. I didn't think that we were allowed to fake tango. Especially since the other dancers had numbers on them. I couldn't tell if the other couples were angry at us. I couldn't really make sense of anything. We were so drunk that if we paid attention to anything other than each other, we would get nauseous and throw up.

Raphaël kept smiling. It was one of those ironic smiles. It was glued on his face. Whenever a smile is glued on someone's face, it seems kind of sleazy. But I was in love with him and you can't find someone that you love sleazy.

It was the smoothest floor that I had ever been on. I kept slipping because my shoe soles didn't seem to be working properly. I put my arms up in the air and he held my waist and just shook me from one side to the other. I leaned all the way back onto his arm, which he was holding out for me. I stood on my toes and waved my arms in the air as if I was a tree in the wind. He blew into my hair and onto my neck as if he was the wind causing me to move that way.

It really felt like we were doing some sort of ballroom dance, although this was impossible. We clung together. It was impossible for two beings to get any closer.

We seemed to fall over hundreds and hundreds of chairs before we got to the table. They made a noise like approaching thunder. I was so drunk that I was clairvoyant. But I wasn't a very powerful clairvoyant. I was only able to see into the future half an hour ahead of time. All I knew was that an argument was coming.

There were always these beautiful moments at the end of a relationship. Like the thick juice at the bottom of a pitcher of concentrated mix. Like the sky at sunset. They made parting so painful.

*****

I walked out of the ballroom into the dark of the parking lot. The stars were winking on and off, like girls making signals with their pocket mirrors. I realized that Raphaël wasn't with me. I turned around and Raphaël was having a fist fight with the bouncer. I don't even know how this happened. They wrapped their arms around each other and were trying to wrestle each other to the ground. After disentangling himself from the bouncer, Raphaël got into an argument with a guy in the parking lot who honked at us because he was pulling out of the parking lot and we walked right into his way. Raphaël banged on the hood of the car and told the driver to get out immediately in order to suck his dick.

The guy just started honking his horn more. I would be curious to know whether, in circumstances like these, God chose a side, and which side he would be on. Raphaël reached into the back of his pants and pulled his gun out. I had come to think of it as a toy of sorts, but I knew that it scared the hell out of other people.

"Are you crazy?" I yelled.

The driver's face went completely red and he put his hands up as if to say sorry. He put the car in drive and screeched off into the distance.

"I fucking hate that guy. How am I going to get to sleep at night knowing that there's a piece of shit like that walking about?"

"You don't even know him."

"I hate him like it's a malignant tumour inside of me."

"Do you want him to call the police and they'll come to our house and see that we have an illegal animal?"

If Raphaël were to let himself go, he would just go around getting into fights and intimidating people and smashing tin cans in their faces. When Raphaël got into bad moods, he tended to get into trouble. When he got into a really good mood, he also would get into trouble. If he got into any kind of a mood, he would get into trouble. The very best thing for him to do would be to stay out of moods altogether. I should have known not to go to the hospital and trust it was okay.

Raphaël swayed around drunkenly for a couple seconds and then stared at me, suddenly not caring about the guy. His eyes went all soft and stupid again.

"You make me forget about things. You know that. You're the only little body that makes me forget about all my problems."

I smiled. It would be a miracle if I didn't puke any second.

"I'm going to have to take you home and give you a beating. Would you like that? Would you like Papa to teach you a lesson that you'll never forget?"

"You're disgusting."

"You love it. Come here, baby. I just want to bite into your knee as if it were an apple."

"Are we happy? Are you glad that you met me?"

"I'm mad and hysterical and over the top in love with your ass. I don't have any money left. I spent my whole paycheque keeping you in ribbons and sexy underwear."

He drove the car with one of his hands around my neck. He just thought this road was going to lie down in front of him as he drove. Just like it was his bitch. Which is what it did. No matter which way he swerved the car, the road just lay down and took it.

CHAPTER 50

Tell the Revolution to Wait for Me

THE NEXT MORNING I WOKE UP TO THE NOISE OF Raphaël moving about the bedroom quickly. The sun was coming through a little hole in the blind, like the police shining a flashlight into a car where lovers are kissing.

"What are you doing waking up so early?" I asked. "Did you ever even take off your clothes?"

"Yes, we had sex, remember?"

Raphaël said he was going to see about buying some more dogs to breed. He was packing his suitcase in that terrible way of his that made no sense, piling it full of random things. It was almost as if he thought that packing was a superstitious, superfluous activity that you just did for appearance's sake, like wearing a tie.

"Don't leave me. Not right now," I said.

He said that he was going to be back before sunset, but I knew that he wasn't.

"Oh, what do I fucking care? Do me a favour. Leave me!"

Get out of here. I saw this shit coming. I saw this shit coming like the fucking five o'clock train."

"Why are you being crude. It's not attractive."

"You know what? You can't leave me. Because I'm leaving you. I've been on eggshells for months, wondering how you're going to psychologically tell your fucking left hand from your right hand."

I got out of bed. I started throwing my clothes on. I started pulling my clothes out of the dresser drawers and putting them on the bed.

"Come on. Come on," he said. "What are you doing?"

"I didn't get pregnant all by myself, you know. I've been fucking accommodating. I came out here to the middle of nowhere. I eat boiled hot dogs for dinner. I didn't even get to say goodbye to my brother. I didn't complain about anything. You want to go into business raising lions; I don't say anything. I tolerate bikers hanging around for two weeks. I put on a red dress. I went dancing. We have a good time and then you lay this on me. Do you have any idea how insulting this is? It's too much."

I started packing my suitcase on the opposite side of the bed.

"Sit your ass down. You're my wife. You can't leave me. Or else I can legitimately murder your fucking ass. You do what you want, Nouschka. I don't make you wash dishes. You've never even heated up a jar of spaghetti in the history of our marriage."

"You talk about what good am I for? What good am I for? How dare you ask! What good are *you* for?"

We were hysterical. We couldn't figure out who was leaving whom.

"How dare you threaten to leave me?" I screamed.

"I don't know what the fuck you're accusing me of accusing you of."

"All I know is that you're leaving this morning and you have no intention of coming back and you can't say it to my face."

"You're the one who's leaving."

"That's right. That's right. Just watch me leave first, and then have the nerve to say that I left you. You know that I could never leave you in this lifetime."

"Then what are you doing?"

"I'm leaving!"

"So leave."

"You would let me leave!"

Then we just started really going at each other. We were frustrated because neither of us was ready to be an adult and we didn't know how to be married. Because we were both terrified of the baby that was on the way. And we both knew that Raphaël was going to run away from it because he could. And I knew that I couldn't run away from the baby. I could run to the opposite ends of the earth, but wherever I went, I was still going to have the baby. I would fall madly in love with it, with a love that was enormous and unshakable, with a love that was six feet deep and would be buried with me in the grave, with a love that transcended our names and our beginnings and our ends.

He threw the armchair at me. I ducked. It hit the wall and made a hole in it. As I tried to get up, Raphaël came over and held me down on the floor. He held my hands in his hands, and his knees were on the sides of me. I don't even know what on earth I was screaming.

He let go of my hands for a second and I started slapping

him wildly in the face. As he leaned back, I got up. He jumped up too and pushed me up against the wall. He grabbed a kitchen knife and held it against my throat.

"If I killed you, then I wouldn't have any more problems. Would I? I have to have my head examined for having gotten involved with a crazy family like yours."

"What? You haven't had your head examined enough already? You're not worried about what this is costing the taxpayers?"

"You're pushing me over the edge, Nouschka."

"Whatever. Just hurry up and do it then, because I don't have time for this kind of shit. I've got things to do. Besides, I want to go get a new husband. If I get to Montréal early enough, the lineup at the food bank will have started. There's always a few lookers in it."

"Sure, sure. I'll go see if there aren't any girls being let out of jail for soliciting cops last night. Maybe they'll be hungry. I'll buy them breakfast."

"Why not? Dip into your savings."

We started laughing at this. He let go of me. We both collapsed on the bed. We lay there next to each other, breathing heavily.

"I wanted you to feel happy with me. But I've only made you feel the opposite. I've tried to be good enough for you. I can't do it anymore."

I didn't say anything. I did want him to leave. I wanted to get on with life. Being married to Raphaël would be like being married to a hurricane. I would have to be putting up storm windows and climbing up trees to rescue the dog. It was wonderful in a way to be so marvellously distracted, but it didn't leave you any time or boredom for being a person.

Maybe there was nothing out there. But I felt too young to give up on the world yet. I loved Raphaël, but I loved my life more. I loved Montréal more. And Raphaël would be back. Men always came back. Men always come back. When you least want them back, that's when they come back.

"Look, I'm going out to Saint-Raymond to see a guy who might want to go into business with me and I'll be back in two days."

"Okay."

"Okay."

*****

I left a note on the table for Raphaël, saying that I was back at our old place.

I hitchhiked to the bus station and caught a night bus back to Montréal. I looked out the bus window. The stars in the sky were like candles on the birthday cake of a one-thousand-year-old man. Somewhere in the night there were bears and raccoons with jars stuck on their heads. Like astronauts lost in space.

*****

Someone on the bus had a portable radio that they turned on. The chief negotiator for the separatist movement, Lucien Bouchard, was talking. Everyone on the bus quieted down to hear him. He was magical. He had gone into the hospital months before with a flesh-eating disease. Everyone thought that he was going to die, but he had his leg amputated and was walking in the Saint-Jean-Baptiste parade a month later. He had been spared from death so that he could lead us to having our own country. It had been so long since there had been miracles in Québec.

Everybody wished that he would take one of his suits and cut it up with a pair of scissors so that we could carry a tiny bit of it in our pockets. Give us a relic.

The Canadian politicians said that we were all going to lose our jobs. We were all going to lose our homes. We were going to lose our trading partners. Our economy would totally fall apart and we would never recover. But Lucien Bouchard said very calmly that it was okay. Just vote *oui*. Then we would be our own people. We could control our own finances and culture. We wouldn't have to go to Ottawa for anything. We would have a partnership with Canada. Not to worry.

He had turned the referendum around. *Oui* was climbing in the polls. And listening to Bouchard, I thought, okay, okay, okay. All that I had was five dollars in my pocket and two hearts beating inside of me. That was enough. I would have faith that Québec would make its own successful country. It seemed natural to vote *oui*, because since we were little, Nicolas and I had been taught by Étienne that Québec should be its own country. It was our family's religion.

I took out my notebook and started working on my speech for Étienne. Writing always took my mind off things. I wanted to think about anything other than Raphaël right at this moment.

As soon as the bus drove into the city, I started to notice that the signs and slogans had already been put up. People who wanted Québec to separate had tied great big signs saying OUI to their balconies. People who didn't want separation put big signs that said NON on their lawns and in their windows. The telephone poles each had signs that said OUI and NON right on top of each other.

*****

The first thing I did when I got off the bus was go and see Nicolas.

I climbed in through our window. The whole house smelled different. It smelled kind of rotten, the way a house smells when a girl hasn't been in it for a while.

The trees on the wallpaper had grown taller and many, many more blossoms had opened up on their branches. The drummer boy on the sheets had grown up. He was a tall, handsome teenager with a bayonet in his hand. The birds in the painting had migrated. They were now in the bathroom on the windowsill.

Nicolas was sleeping on top of the covers. He was wearing a puffy pink sweater and white briefs. I turned the small lamp on. Nicolas opened his eyes. He acted as if it was the most natural thing in the world that I had come back to him. He put his arms out. I fell into them.

Nicolas marvelled over my belly, which had gotten much bigger.

"You look like a fucking whale, but in a good way. I knew you were going to come back. I was just about to go look for you. I was trying to round up some people. I was looking to borrow a car. We were going to drive right out to Val-des-Loups and get you back. But you know how I feel about leaving the island. Once I cross the bridge I lose all my magical powers. So I just decided to think about you really, really hard and I knew you would come back."

"I'm exhausted; you can tell me about everything in the morning."

It felt good to smell his breath and his skin again. I wondered how it was that I had ever been able to be apart from him. He smelled like winter and tobacco and leather. He always smelled like fireworks had just gone off. I could feel Nicolas's breath falling and rising. My heartbeat slowed down to his heartbeat.

There I was, back in my room with Nicolas, just like nothing had happened at all. Except there was another teeny-tiny heartbeat in the room, and it was beating as rapidly as that of a little bird.

Chapter 51

Nouschka Tremblay Strikes Again

When I came back to Loulou's apartment from the grocery store the next morning, Hugo was there with his camera crew.

"I'm just going to set up here. You can come out and talk to us when you're ready."

"How did you know that I was back?"

"I gave the upstairs neighbour five dollars to give me a call if you came back to town. Everybody's very excited about your pregnancy."

"Ridiculous. You guys are going to have the most boring documentary on earth," I said and stormed inside.

"Could you walk in the building again, but slower and don't slam the door," Hugo called after me.

*****

When I got to the bedroom, Nicolas was wearing pinstriped pants, an old T-shirt of mine with strawberries on it and one of Loulou's old fedoras. His outfit was so mismatched that he seemed like an exquisite corpse drawing.

Nicolas pulled out a briefcase from under the bed. It was filled with four or five guns. I had no idea what you would call those types of guns, but they were bigger than the one Raphaël had. I did not want to see what I was seeing. He took out a gun and held it out straight and spun around the room with it, as if he was the arm in a compass looking for north. He was right in front of the open window.

"Put that away!" I yelled. I ran and closed the blinds. "Where did you get these guns? Are they for real? They look like movie props."

"I bought them from an Armenian, who got them from a Polish guy, who got them from a Moroccan, who got them from these Senegalese dudes that I sure as hell don't fuck with personally." I stood there with such a look of shock on my face. "Did you think that I just sat here waiting for you to come back? No, sir, I was very productive. What's your husband doing out there?"

"Breeding dogs."

"There's no money in that. I could have told him."

A preadolescent boy wearing a T-shirt with horseshoes on it and enormous running shoes climbed through the window. He looked like a criminal that had been shrunk in a dryer.

"This is my accountant," Nicolas said. He put his gun away and slid the briefcase back under the bed. "I promoted him last week."

"He's, like, eleven years old."

"I'm thirteen and a half," the boy said.

"He's a mathlete. Which is all the more remarkable because he was raised in a single-mother household. How much dough do we have saved up, Julien?"

"Fifteen hundred dollars."

"Brilliant. Fantastic."

"Open up the blinds again, Nouschka. It's like a morgue in here."

"Morgues are actually well illuminated," Julien said.

"That's why I have this kid around. I hate to mix my metaphors. I get the headache of a lifetime when I mix my metaphors."

"I can't stay in this apartment. What would happen if the whole place was raided?"

"Oh, no one's going to question you. Everyone thinks of you as being as pure as the driven snow. Your popularity ratings are through the roof. You look fucking adorable pregnant. Oh, they are eating you up."

I hadn't even unpacked my suitcase. I probably knew deep down all along that I couldn't move back into my childhood apartment. That evening I went back to the apartment where Raphaël and I had lived. The cups and plates were still in the dish rack from the night before we left; we had been eating spaghetti together. His jacket was slung over the back of the chair. I sat down across from it. It was eerie that he was missing. Whether Raphaël came back or not, the pretty little apartment was still here waiting for the baby to be born. But for now, I was going to live alone for the very first time in my life.

*****

I thought that I was going to have trouble getting back into school. I'd missed so many classes without notifying them that I would be absent. I just pointed to my belly and shrugged. The director didn't seem to have a problem with it since I had been doing so well.

Pretending to be a good parent isn't the same thing as being a good parent. This distinction seemed particularly important to me. Parenthood was something that the Tremblays ran from. They wrote you a love poem and put it under your pillow. They put on their black peacoats, slipped on their shiny shoes, flopped their hair back and ran out at midnight over the rooftops to freedom.

I thought that going to school was somehow part of being a good parent. Someone had to go through a lot of screwdrivers and screws and instruction manuals before they were able to build a rocket ship to the moon. I had to do a lot of practical stuff so that my baby would be able to daydream worry-free for years.

*****

Later that night I started working on a history essay that was supposed to have been handed in the week before. It was on Henry Hudson. Henry was a brilliant seaman and explorer. He was obsessed with finding a Northwest Passage.

Henry Hudson hired handsome, ne'er-do-well gentlemen instead of reliable mariners. He looked for men who woke up with prostitutes' ringlets all over their pillow and who spent hours getting dressed in the morning. He looked for men who looked the way that men were supposed to look. He took on men who had lovely turns of phrase. He adored men who seemed as if they should be extremely talented at something or other, although no one could figure out what that was. He took on men who showed up at his door with glorious smiles and notes from aristocrats and their mothers recommending them.

He went to great pains each time he went out on a voyage to assemble the crew that was most likely to mutiny against him. Of course they ended up mutinying. But the thought of setting out into the unknown with these men filled his heart with such a surge of blood that it made him weak with terror. It made him feel as if he was plunging to his death from a window. This is an incredibly unpleasant feeling, but you get addicted to it just the same.

CHAPTER 52

They Shoot Poets, Don't They?

I WENT TO PICK UP MY LEAVE CHEQUE FROM THE post office downtown. The city was getting out of control. The rest of Canada had thought that the separatist movement was a fringe element. Now polls were showing that there was a very definite possibility that we had every intention of leaving Canada.

The streets were suddenly filled with people from other provinces. Since we obviously weren't going to listen to reason, they were trying another tactic. They were going to come and get down on their hands and knees and pray for us to stay. The airplane companies had reduced prices of flights to Montréal by ninety percent to encourage everyone to go to Montréal to convince us to vote *non*.

A family walked past me waving paper Canadian flags over their heads. A man was holding a placard saying QUÉBEC WE LOVE YOU! DON'T LEAVE US! They might have thought to write it in French, but what can you do?

They were having a giant rally that day that was going to

outdo any of the ones that we had had. Well, that's what the English had going for them, wasn't it? They had numbers. They were actually proving to me, at least, what I had always known: that we were a minority that was in danger of being overwhelmed. Our culture could disappear and all that would be left of it would be little French-Canadian bobble-head dolls dressed in lumberjack shirts next to the polar bear clocks in the tourist shops.

I walked in the other direction. Nobody recognized me. There had been an article in the paper that morning saying that Étienne Tremblay had no right to be participating in the rally since he had been in prison and had been living a dissolute lifestyle. No one from outside of Québec had ever heard of Étienne Tremblay. If that didn't prove we were a distinct society, I didn't know what did.

That night I couldn't sleep. It was strange to lie in bed all alone. I woke up with a chill no matter what the temperature was. The baby was squirming around so much. It was tossing and turning all night. It kicked like the neighbour banging for us to keep down the music. But it only made me feel lonelier.

I hadn't heard anything from Raphaël. I really didn't know anyone who could vanish into thin air like Raphaël. I always heard girls bragging about how their ex-boyfriends were stalking them and wouldn't leave them alone. And about all the terrible fights that they would have when their husbands showed up. I was sort of envious. Anything was better than this silence.

I knew that I was as responsible for the breakup as Raphaël was, but I felt abandoned. And I wanted to feel sorry for myself. I sat on the kitchen floor and wept like a fifties housewife whose husband had run off with his secretary. Then I got bored and lonely. I couldn't exactly go out dancing, could I?

It was almost midnight, and I knew that Étienne would

likely be found at a twenty-four-hour diner called Madame Lucie. Hugo told me that Étienne had been eating at this diner all week. They had put a huge OUI sign in the window. Étienne thought that it was bold and that he should support the establishment. Hugo had filmed him from the outside, with the OUI poster in view. He had showed me the footage and asked if I thought it looked at all like the famous painting *Nighthawks*. I had just shrugged. I didn't like being asked whether or not my father was a work of art.

It only took me ten minutes to walk there. I saw him through the front window, illuminated by the restaurant's fluorescent glow. I slid into the booth, across from Étienne, as gracefully as I could given the enormity of my belly. There was a jukebox at that table that only had songs from the seventies. It had all of his songs on it, which was one of the reasons Étienne was such a strong supporter of the institution. There was one song about a turtle that was so slow, it took him eight years to go from Montréal to Chicoutimi. There was another song about a man who had twenty-five kids. Étienne sang their names really, really fast. Everyone would try to remember and sing the names in the right order when the song played on the radio. Sometimes Loulou would sing this song while mopping the floors: *"Rita! Marie! André! Mario! Sebastien! Eloïse! Louise! Louise! J'ai déjà dit Louise."*

It was probably a good thing that the English couldn't make out what these songs were going on about. There was a song about a man whose hat got blown off by the wind. It blew all the way to New York City. He ended up there selling Christmas trees for a living. There was a song about a lumberjack who went mad. It was a traditional song but Étienne had recorded a new version of it.

"Put on the song about the unhappy piece of tourtière that's in the fridge and nobody will eat it," I said as I settled in. I was nervous and my first reflex was to draw his attention away from my belly. There was no better way than to bring up his music.

The waitress came up and served Étienne a beer that he had already ordered. I watched him take the first holy sip. The one that makes you feel the same way as when someone is playing the trumpet in just the right way. It was as if he had been dying to take a piss and had just found a urinal. As he drank, his pupils dilated and the blue of his eyes disappeared.

Étienne put down his glass and looked hard at me, trying to figure out what on earth would be the perfect thing to say at this juncture. He wasn't an idiot. The man could intuit that I would be hitting him up for some emotions any minute now.

"I've been feeling a little bit blue," I said, getting to the point.

"People can't even look at me," Étienne said. "I remind them of the ravages of time. I am everything that they are going to lose. I am the inability of love to last. I had the most beautiful songs in the world—but this is something that you can't own. I sang them until they just stopped coming one day."

This was the only way Étienne could give advice: by describing his own hardships. His ability to feel sorry for himself was truly epic.

This was the kind of conversation that we had been having for years. It was fancy talk but nothing specific. Sort of like how fencers swirl their swords all over the place but never actually pierce one another through the heart.

"I don't know what I'm supposed to do with my life," I insisted. "I don't know how to go about doing anything. You see that I'm having a baby?"

"I heard," he said, nodding toward my belly. "I thought a lot about it too. You don't have to raise your children, really. They raise themselves. You're a writer, *pour l'amour de dieu!*"

It was out of the bag! Wanting to be a writer was the sort of thing you might be reluctant to admit, especially in Québec. Look at our very first great poet, Émile Nelligan, who went mad at twenty trying to write a book of poems about angels. That Étienne knew my secret was surprising to me. But he was good at intuiting what people's talents were. He was abominable at recognizing their feelings, however.

"You're too intelligent to be changing diapers. Why don't you give the child to your mother-in-law to be raised? Don't feel guilty if you have to do it. It's for a higher calling."

I wasn't sure that I had heard what I thought that I had heard. Étienne seemed to think that he was on some sort of roll. He just continued in the same vein.

"If you have a baby, you're supposed to be their slave from here on in? They come first? But why? If Jean-Jacques Rousseau gives birth to a sadistic petty thief, then the sadistic member of society is more valuable than the most important philosopher on earth. Rousseau should stop writing in order to worry about his waste-of-space son? No, children don't come first. A person's raison d'être must always come first. "

I was insulted. He was basically saying that Nicolas and I had been a waste of time and his talents. I was in an indignant mood that night. I started shifting toward the end of the seat in order to leave.

"I wrote you some notes for a speech," I said. "I don't know if you're interested. You're probably not interested. You've probably already prepared something. You probably already have something that you want to go ahead and say."

"Show me what you have," he said seriously, holding out his left hand. With his right, he reached into the inside pocket of his blazer and took out a pair of reading glasses.

"Fantastic, fantastic, my darling," he said, not even having read it yet. "You stick to this. You'll go far."

I looked at Étienne poring over the scrap of paper. All that he valued in me was that I was some sort of artist too. So I decided to forget for a moment that I was a human being. We were just two poets sitting at a diner in the middle of the night, discussing our work. It offered me a respite. Anyways, it was better than going home to be alone in my kitchen, experiencing emotions. It must be nice sometimes to have an all-consuming philosophy that includes not really caring about anyone other than yourself.

CHAPTER 53

Shake That Jar of Bumblebees

I TRIED TO FIND RAPHAËL. I CALLED HIS DOCTOR at the hospital, the one who had given Raphaël the job as an orderly. The doctor had no idea where he was. I called Rosalie's ex-girlfriend, whom I'd gone to high school with. She said that Raphaël would turn up eventually.

I didn't even know if I wanted him back. What would happen if I did find him? He would be back in the apartment, installing locks on the doors and wanting to change our name every morning. Our kid would come and say, "There's a monster under the bed." And Raphaël would say, "You're probably right, my son." And the house would be so full of night lights that it would seem like we were lost in the Milky Way.

Maybe I should have just considered my escape from the country a lucky break. I could be out there taking the damn lion for a walk. Imagine having to scoop that poop?

I had to go on with life regardless of the men in my life. I went the next morning to the university to talk to an adviser. I had never been inside the big building on the other side of the small mountain that is in the middle of the city. I stood in front of it, looking at its sprawling wings. There were hundreds of bicycles locked up outside the building. There were kids of all different races—Asian, black, Arab—hurrying down the hallways with their books and their school bags. The adviser was wearing a brown suit and had her hair swept up into the tidiest bun in the world.

"You were out of school for a while?"

"I had an unstable upbringing. I wasn't really encouraged to stay in school."

"Hmm," she said.

Then she just smiled as if it wasn't a big deal and we got down to the practicalities of me going to university. She told me that there was a good daycare at the school and there were loans and scholarships that were available to me as a single mother. She made me an appointment with a financial adviser. As she explained these very basic things to me, I realized that there was so much about society at large that I didn't know anything about.

I asked for an application and took away a huge book with all the courses in the French Literature Department. I didn't need Étienne to tell me I was a writer. My own sense of who I was had begun to speak up lately, even though it didn't speak that loudly. I was listening to it as best I could. I was not going to define myself by the traits that men found adorable in me. I was pushing myself to get on with life and to not chicken out. I warned myself not to be afraid of people who lived off of Boulevard Saint-Laurent.

As I read through the great big book of course descriptions on the metro back downtown, I was overwhelmed by excitement.

Jules Verne: Why bad science makes for wonderful fiction. Arthur Rimbaud: Why a sordid teenager is still being read today. Guy de Maupassant: A classic, but still dirty. Molière: Comedy in an age of very big wigs. Colette: A lady in a top hat turns Paris upside down.

*****

A parade of motorcycles passed by me as I waited for the green light outside the school. For a moment, Lord oh Lord, I missed Raphaël.

What sort of strange malevolent plots were the bikers up to? Maybe they were going to terrorize a kid who was selling his ADHD medication at school without giving them a cut. Or perhaps they were trying to get a corner on the bingo market. When they were done, they would head home, where they would go down on some long-haired, underage nymphet.

I felt the rumble of the motorcycles in my groin. I just wanted to throw my life away. I wanted to get my thighs covered in rose tattoos. I wanted to be making love to Raphaël. I suddenly pictured myself on top, riding him violently as he held my hips in both his hands, lifting me up and then slamming me back down.

They would know where Raphaël was. If I called out to them, they could take me to him. Even if I decided that I didn't want to get back together with him, I was still worried about him. I thought about going to see Véronique. But I realized that it was useless to ask her advice. She didn't even know how to talk about what had happened to him when he was a little boy. I felt like getting a bullhorn and going into the middle of the street and stopping the traffic and letting everybody know. If not for him, then for me. I didn't know how he managed to keep the weight of his secret when the burden of it was crushing me.

One of the reasons that I wanted to study literature was because it exposed everything. Writers looked for secrets that had never been mined. Every writer has to invent their own magical language, in order to describe the indescribable. They might seem to be writing in French, English or Spanish, but really they were writing in the language of butterflies, crows, and hanged men.

CHAPTER 54

Such a Pretty Mob

I WAS GETTING READY TO GO AND SEE ÉTIENNE read my speech before a crowd on Avenue du Mont-Royal. I was wearing a blue cotton coat with tiny white flowers on it over a white dress. My outfit was to match the colours of the Québec flag. I was delirious with anticipation. I knew that there were going to be a lot of people showing up. We were very into the collective experience in Montréal. There was nothing that we liked more than a pretty mob. I felt tingly and excited as I hurried down the stairs with a plastic bag hanging from my wrist. This was going to be more interesting than when I had been in the beauty pageant and had flung my hair about. Now there were things at stake.

I took the metro to get there on time. It was jam-packed with people and I loved the feeling that we were all headed to the same spot. I was just a happy sardine in a tin of other sardines.

The square was filled up with people. They stopped the traffic going in all directions. There was a bus that had slowed down, and people climbed on top of the bus to see. People were sitting on top of all the buildings with their legs dangling off the sides. Everyone had blue daisies in the buttonholes of their jackets and behind their ears.

Even if you weren't for separation, surely you would peep out your window to get a look at these cultural luminaries. Those broke philosophers in their old suits, driven in by their children from their small houses, in which they had been brooding over manifestos for years.

There were some university students talking about Che Guevara. There was something about revolutionary speech that worked when it came out of the mouths of young people. It was untempered and uncensored. A quality that, when there is a group of kids at the back of the bus, can be positively annoying. But when it comes to incendiary rhetoric, it can be quite lovely.

The old man next to me took out his teeth and wrapped them in his handkerchief and tucked them into his breast pocket. Then he began to enjoy a piece of fudge that was shaped like a maple leaf. He was going to enjoy that fudge no matter what damn country he was in.

My heart was beating like crazy. The crowd would be hearing my words soon.

I looked around for where Étienne might be. I saw that there was an artist's tent, so I figured he must be in there with those guys. People put their hands out to stop me as I was going in, but then they smiled and pointed me toward my father.

Étienne was smoking a cigarette furiously. When he was really anxious, he was able to inhale a cigarette in two drags, which was actually very disconcerting. A woman was trying to pin a carnation onto the lapel of his jacket. He kept swatting her hand out of his face. He kept forgetting what she was doing, and he kept mistaking her hand for a wasp.

I had never seen him look so distracted before a performance. He was looking at the other artists. They were shaking each other's hands, amazed to see each other after more than a decade. Étienne looked at them as if they were strangers. They had had very different fates than Étienne. They weren't living off welfare in men's hotels. Gilles Vigneault was there, and his songs had practically become anthems in Québec.

Étienne was wearing a suit that had seen better days. It seemed almost as if he had slept in it a bunch of times. He had probably pawned the lovely pinstriped suit that he had worn to my wedding. For the first time he looked like he was desperate to fit in. When you are young, you can dress in rags and stand on the table and piss in telephone booths. In a young person, these are the traits of a poet. But if you exhibited any of those behaviours at forty-five, people would think you were a degenerate.

He motioned for me to follow him. We went out the back of the tent and toward the metro. We sat on a bench inside the metro just to be away from the crowd. There was a river of people coming up the elevator from the underground train. We were sitting next to an old woman who was wearing a navy blue dress and a red apron with giant pockets to hold change in. She was selling roses out of big green buckets. We were sort of hidden away by all the fat flowers.

"Should I have had this suit dry cleaned?" Étienne asked me anxiously.

"No, I like it. It looks good. It looks more comfortable now, like you've been on tour and have been doing loads of speaking engagements."

I spit on a napkin and then rubbed off a splotch of something on his sleeve.

"But that's just it: I haven't been doing any engagements. These are lovely words, but can I deliver them with any sincerity? You know it's never just the words. The words have to be delivered with an arrogance. You have to believe in them."

"You haven't retired. You're always delivering speeches at the café."

"I don't think that I've ever had stage fright in my life—you know that? But I just have some terrible jitters. Do you know that? Feel my hands. For God's sake! I'm a nervous wreck!"

"Look at me. Remember when you were just a little boy in rubber boots delivering newspapers at five in the morning. And everyone said to you: you are not distinct, you are not unusual, you are not special."

"*Et moi, j'ai répondu: Oui, j'suis unique. Oui, j'suis distinct. Oui, j'suis spécial!*"

"You were born to do this. Of course you're wretched at most things. Everybody knows it. But that doesn't mean that you can't do this one thing."

Étienne held on to my wrist. He was listening to my every word. I was telling him what he needed to do in order to win the crowd over. I knew it exactly. The way that he knew exactly what I had to do to make the audience eat me up when I was very young and he'd fix my hair up with a bow or give me a daisy to hold.

"Look what I brought you."

I reached into the plastic bag dangling from my wrist. I had climbed into the back of the closet in the bedroom at Loulou's, looking through his old paraphernalia. I had found one of his old top hats. This one was worn out. That was probably why it had been relegated to the back of the closet. The fur was worn away from the side of it, and the top was beaten in. But somehow it was even better this way. I held the battered top hat in my hand for Étienne to see. It was a poem in itself.

When he put it on his head, I held out a tiny pocket mirror for him to take a look at himself.

"I can't stand mirrors," Étienne said. "They are always trying to convince me that I am an old man."

"Well, why don't you go out there and prove them wrong."

"Because I'm a handsome young buck, right? In my prime? Wait until they take a look at me. I'll be like that handsome and fabulous man in that story, who never ages. What was that gentleman's name . . . Ah yes, the fabulous Dorian Gray."

He took a tiny can of breath freshener out of his pocket and sprayed it generously into his mouth. He smiled with his giant teeth. He was quite happy that he still had every one, although the tops were grey. Then he gave me one of his big, wet kisses.

"This is such a lovely speech that you wrote for me, sweetheart. I can always count on you."

It struck me that I could never, ever say the same thing to him, but I decided to let it go. We walked out together. He went to the stage and I moved back into the audience to watch him. The crowd started whistling as soon as they spotted the top hat on its way. The audience. What a beast. A beast that screams it loves you and then lets you drown, like the sirens that called out to Ulysses's men from the water. Everyone was so visibly excited that there was an electricity in the air. I couldn't help but feel charged by it. How could you not give a glorious speech on this day?

"So. I read the papers. Some journalists are going to drag my past out of the closet to say that I don't have a right to speak out?"

He had a deep voice. His voice was a little bit raw from smoking so much. It gave it a sort of lovely effect now that he was shouting. It made him sound as if he had been weeping and that his voice was ravaged with emotion. He lunged forward when he spoke, as if he was going to grasp someone by the throat. He waved his arms out in front of him as if he was clearing a path through some tall grass.

"Well, go ahead. People have been talking about my past for years. Yes, I have been in prison. Not once, not twice, but three times. I'm broke. I've been a womanizer. I've been a drinker. I have more than once disturbed the peace."

The audience was quiet now, looking at Étienne uncomfortably.

"Now, since we are bringing my past out of the closet, let's go all the way back before those days. Let's go right back to *La Grande Noirceur*, the Great Darkness."

The audience let out a roar.

"My father never went to school. He had fourteen brothers and they were taught what their place was in the world. Good jobs went to the Anglos. Bad jobs went to the Tremblays."

Everyone cheered.

"And let's see . . . When I was a teenager I woke up with the tanks rolling down my street. I went outside to see what was happening and there were horses with police riding them, clunking me on the head with their batons. If you want to know why I started wearing this top hat, it was to hide *les grosses bosses sur ma tête*."

The crowd started laughing happily at their age-old grievances.

"They were treating anyone in a turtleneck sweater like a criminal. Give a frog a dictionary and they become a revolutionary and start putting bombs in mailboxes and asking for their own country. "

Someone screamed out, "We love you, Étienne." And there were whistles coming up from the crowd.

"And when the Trudeau government drafted the constitution in 1981, they didn't get Québec to sign. While René Lévesque was asleep, the other premiers got up and worked on the constitution at midnight. At midnight! While we were in our underwear, trying to convince our girlfriends to have sex with us. We were watching our *téléromans* and farting, and they were busy drafting a new constitution without Québec! Whenever I need a knife, I don't go and get one out of the kitchen drawer; I just reach around and pull one out of my back."

Here the crowd started stomping their feet. There were people on balconies who started banging their pots and pans.

"When we asked for a constitutional amendment all these years later, they called us ungrateful and ignorant and racist. They finally bought a *Dictionnaire Larousse* just so they could look up some words to insult us."

Everyone screamed. They were in heaven!

"It is not me who should be ashamed of my past, because I own up to everything that has happened. You, the Canadian government, should be ashamed of our past!"

There was only one more line to go and I could go back to breathing and enjoy his success.

"And look at my daughter, Little Nouschka!"

My heart stopped. He was going off script. For a moment I thought that he was going to acknowledge that I had helped him with the speech.

"She's going to give birth to another Tremblay any day now. Is there anything more miraculous than birth itself? Well, the most wonderful day in my life was when my two twins were born. How many men can say that they have had two miracles happen on the same day? It is like having lightning strike in the same place twice!"

That was it. The audience was applauding like wild. He had rediscovered the love of his life. I understood why Étienne had always been single. Étienne kept taking bows and flinging his arms back into the air. Once again I was a pretty prop in his performance. There was nothing interesting about me, other than that I got to stand in his shadow. He was going to be the genius in the family. He was always going to take the credit for the Étienne Tremblay Show.

And now he had no intention of leaving the stage, even though his speech was finished.

"If it weren't for my children, I'd have been no more than a drunken mop of a man."

Everyone laughed, but I did not like it one little bit that he was carrying on. From having watched his odd performances for the documentary crew, I knew that they were uneven, to say the least. It sounded like he was going some place interesting with his thoughts, but if he spoke for more than a few sentences, the sense would run out of them quick, like the flavour out of a Slush Puppie.

"I am a degenerate! Look at this nasty old suit! I couldn't even afford anything decent to wear to an occasion such as this!"

He was going to keep going. He thought the trick to winning over the crowd was to be self-deprecating. He had lost touch with the Everyman years before.

"I am not special. I have done everything that a dog would do. And yet here I am before you, calling myself a man. I mean really, am I a man? Or am I just a dog in a fancy suit. Bow wow wow! My colleagues and countrymen. Bow wow wow!"

The young men started laughing and cheering him on. Others started having quizzical looks on their faces.

I was cringing. Please, dear Lord, cut him off, I thought. I waved my hands at one of the organizers. He was too young and too intimidated to go out and interrupt Étienne Tremblay. I motioned instead at Gilles Vigneault.

Gilles Vigneault came up onstage with his arms spread out. He had his sailor hat on, a part of his costume that was as iconic as Étienne's top hat. Everyone started jumping up and down when they realized just what was happening. Two of Québec's most legendary chansonniers were sharing a stage.

Étienne usually never got onstage with anyone, for the simple reason that he was competitive with all these old chansonniers. Any attention that his contemporaries got would eat him up alive inside. He had spent many hours wishing in his heart of hearts that Gilles Vigneault had never been born.

Nonetheless, Étienne smiled at Gilles Vigneault. He turned to the audience and gave them the expression that they wanted to see. He gave them his giant, charismatic smile that they always believed in unreservedly.

Everyone started shouting, "*Une chanson, une chanson, une chanson.*" Gilles Vigneault waved his band out and spoke into the guitar player's ear. The guitarist began to pluck out a tune. He began to play "Lily Sainte-Marie."

The entire crowd immediately joined in. You could hardly hear the voices of Gilles and Étienne over the crowd's sing-along. "Lily Sainte-Marie." I hadn't heard that song since we'd gone to see her. I suddenly couldn't stand to listen to it. It was like listening to a lover lie when you know the truth.

It was insulting. I felt the need to get as far from that song as possible.

I turned and started manoeuvring my enormous belly through the crowd. Étienne didn't need me anymore. Now he was probably going to go out drinking with people who couldn't believe that they were out drinking with him. I had been feeling like it was my day too. But once they started playing that song, it was all over.

I suddenly felt sort of blue. It's funny how you can forget a feeling. I remembered so well being onstage as a kid, of course. But that feeling! I had forgotten that sensation that came afterward. I didn't even know what it was when I was a kid. But now I knew that it was the feeling that I had been cheated of something.

I wasn't actually that upset that Étienne hadn't thanked me, because I hadn't written the speech for him because I wanted anything in return. But when he had pointed to me in the crowd, for a moment I had thought that he was going to do something for me. That he had made a big to-do about the baby seemed now, in retrospect, especially hypocritical.

At the end of the day, when the audience went home, we were no longer a family.

What did you have if you didn't have a family? One morning a week from now, children would be lugging their erroneous atlases out to the corner and dumping them on the side of the road. The city would have to send a special truck around to pick up all the books, like they did with Christmas trees. Nothing was permanent.

I wanted to get out of there before this maudlin mood became overwhelming. At the point where the bodies became less numerous, I met Nicolas, who was also escaping from the crowd. Normally, it would have been difficult to find my brother in such an enormous crush, but we were the only two people who were hightailing it out of there. The song had the same effect on him as it had on me, apparently. We were like rats who met on the way out of a sinking ship.

We couldn't say anything to each other over all the singing. He put his arm around me and we walked away from the crowd. I felt better immediately.

"You wrote that speech for him, didn't you?" Nicolas asked me. We were far from everyone now. "He didn't even thank you. You're aware of that. You're such a sucker. I came here today to watch the man make an ass of himself, but now you've reinvigorated the fucker."

"But what about the cause? I thought you were a diehard separatist. You could have given a speech yourself."

"I would have said that we should not only separate from this country but from the entire planet. I would recommend that on the morning after the referendum, we all get into spaceships and orbit Jupiter. The world would never hear anything from a Québécois ever again."

"That would have been a lovely speech."

"I've been studying up on my radical revolutionaries."

"That, or you've been watching too much *Star Trek*."

*****

Halfway down the block, we passed the documentary crew. The cameraman was up close to the stage. But Hugo was standing back on a chair, taking shots of the back of the crowd with a small camera. He waved to us.

"Are you going to cut that last bit?" I asked him.

"For every few minutes that Étienne is brilliant, he spends hours and hours saying inane, inappropriate stuff," said Hugo, stepping down from his chair. "Or somehow kind of . . . just a touch sleazy or something. Sorry, I know he's your father. But we're going to have to throw out eighty percent of the footage."

In that eighty percent of Étienne's life was our childhood.

CHAPTER 55

Praying to Saint Lovely Mary Full of Grace

O<small>N THE EVENING OF THE REFERENDUM, NICOLAS</small> and I went and voted at the polling station in the basement of the Saint Lovely Mary Full of Grace Church. I knew that at some point every member of my family was going to be in that basement that night. And every member of the family was going to vote *oui*.

"It would be strange if it finally happened," Nicolas said. "Remember how when we were little, Étienne used to promise us all sorts of stuff if it did?"

I never took the promises seriously. He would say anything to get Nicolas to go up onstage. He told us to tell everyone to vote *oui*, because after the referendum we would ride on an elephant and take a trip to the beach and get a country house.

"I somehow thought that if we separated, Lily might come back and we could live somewhere clean, and we could invite people over for our birthday party."

I looked at Nicolas, understanding something for the first time. When he was a kid, he had been told that if he screamed and carried on, he would get to have a mother and a normal family life. And he hadn't ever stopped hollering, but he still hadn't got what he wanted.

I remembered Nicolas weeping after the last referendum. He was inconsolable. I wondered what it was that Nicolas was expecting if Québec separated this time. He would open the mailbox and discover a cheque from the government for three thousand dollars and an invitation from our mother asking us to come over for tea and cookies. Everyone who had ever watched us on television would be forced to line up and apologize. He would no longer hate himself and he would be a good dad.

Nicolas had the same sort of charisma that our father had, but he didn't want the entire city to love him. He just needed to feel that he was important to a very small group of people. He wanted a family.

But that night the *non* side won fifty-one percent. And Nicolas woke up knowing that nothing was going to change.

CHAPTER 56

The Pied Piper of Boulevard
Saint-Laurent

I T WAS HALLOWEEN. I WAS SITTING ON THE FIRE
escape. The man at the laundromat had his face painted white
with a giant black circle around his mouth and an orange nose
tied on with an elastic band. He was eating a sandwich and turning the pages of a television guide.

There was a knocking at my door. I climbed back into the
apartment and hurried to see who it could be. It was the neighbour Isabelle. Her baby was on her hip.

"Nicolas is on the phone. He says he needs to talk to you
urgently."

I had been waiting for the phone to be installed. Raphaël
had never wanted one. I didn't bother putting on any clothes. I
just walked down the hallway in my kimono over my underwear
with my pregnant belly sticking out. I started feeling anxious.
Nicolas Tremblay almost never used the telephone. I saw the
receiver off the cradle on the kitchen table. Isabelle put the baby

in its high chair. It started whacking its body back and forth, back and forth, as if it was in an electric chair. I was so glad I didn't have a baby to raise just this second. I picked up the receiver.

"Nicolas?"

"Nouschka. I need a favour."

"Where are you? I'll come meet you."

"Can you get us four masks from the costume store?"

"Why do you need those? What do you have cooking?"

I was being discreet while pushing him to give me the details because I didn't want Isabelle to hear. He was in such a braggy mood about it that he couldn't help but tell me. They were going to rob a caisse populaire that night. He was crazy on the other end of the phone. He kept shouting out his sentences. I couldn't believe that it was actually happening and right now. I wished for a second that he was dead, just so I wouldn't be forced to live through this.

"Eloi had the masks in a duffle bag and he left it on the bus. And the costume store's closing in fifteen minutes."

If it was going to take place, I was going along. If Nicolas was going down, I was going to go with him. The baby was trying its very best to be real. But it wasn't real yet. It hadn't even gotten around to being born.

"I'm coming with you."

He was like a tornado and everything around him was rushing toward him. Nothing could resist his pull. My ordinary problems didn't matter. Having to finish school didn't matter. Raphaël wandering in the wilderness didn't matter. Lily Sainte-Marie not even mentioning us in the confession booth didn't matter.

"You can't rob a bank with us. We'll come pick up the masks later."

"No, I want to come."

"What do you mean you want to come! It's all the way on the other side of town."

"I want to come."

"No."

"You'll get arrested. And if you don't get arrested, you'll end up celebrating all night at a strip club. Either way, I'm going to spend the night alone."

"Listen to you! Your hormones are all over the place. Fine. You can drive the getaway car. Great! You can't even drive."

"My driving is fine."

"Get a mask for yourself then too, idiot."

"What'd he want?" the neighbour asked, bouncing her baby on her hips.

"Nothing," I said.

She looked at the perturbed look on my face and knew that it wasn't nothing.

"You and Nico have always been getting into trouble since you were little. You're adrenaline junkies. You can't help it."

"Yeah, yeah. Do you have anything to eat?"

"You want some cake left over from Emmanuelle's birthday party?"

She opened the fridge with her free hand and took out a plate with a fat slice of chocolate cake on it. A cat stepped off the table. It looked like an accordion falling open. I shovelled down the cake, famished despite my nerves.

"It's because you were on television. You're always trying to recapture that high."

My stomach was already jittery and I had eaten the cake so fast, I was worried I might throw up on my feet. As I left Isabelle's apartment, the baby looked like it was trying to shake its own self to death. The mother picked it up and comforted it. No wonder Lily Sainte-Marie had given her children up to a passing Gypsy. I was going out with the boys tonight; I didn't care what they did. I put on a black dress with a red bow tied under the breasts. And my black high-heeled boots. I tried to stick my hair up with every bobby pin I could find. I found them at the bottom of teacups that were filled with change, inside teeny cough-drop tins and underneath the radiator. What was I thinking! Why the hell was I getting dolled up!

I had almost forgotten about the masks. I emptied out the jar of change onto the counter in the kitchen and looked through the pocket of my winter coat for money. I ran down the street to the costume store just as it was closing. I bought four cheap plastic animal masks. They were the only ones I could afford. I bought just a little cat snout for myself. I wouldn't be able to see through a mask if I was driving. Nicolas was right: I couldn't drive for shit. I put the snout on as I walked down the street.

When you're about to do something really stupid and you know it's incredibly stupid and it's the very last thing on earth that you should be doing, but you go ahead and do it anyways, that's when you realize that you are predestined to be a loser and there is nothing anyone can do about it, night school or not. Anyways, I didn't think robbing a bank was that difficult. Every second bonehead at the bar claimed to have robbed a bank. I felt pretty in my scrap of a mask, and when I felt pretty, I felt infallible.

*****

I went downstairs early. I was so nervous about the whole thing that I couldn't sit alone in the apartment.

If the *oui* side had won, the streets would have been filled with people. You wouldn't be able to drive a car downtown. The army would surely be here. The riot squads would all be out. Flags would be flying everywhere. Fireworks would have been going off all day. There would be people standing on top of cars, singing Gilles Vigneault and Étienne Tremblay songs. We would all be weeping that René Lévesque wasn't alive to see this.

Instead it was quiet. There was nothing at all to keep Nicolas from self-destructing.

*****

Nicolas came by half an hour later, driving a minivan. I suddenly realized with absolute certainty that I had to talk him out of robbing the bank. I climbed into the front seat, next to a teenager, and handed out the masks. One of the boys had on a blue suit jacket and track pants. One was wearing a striped sweater filled with holes. One had a velvet brown hoodie over a T-shirt with a unicorn on it. I wondered if bohemians had ever robbed a bank before.

"Where'd you get this car?" I asked.

"I stole it outside the Chalet Bar-B-Q. We told these old ladies it was valet parking." Nicolas held his giraffe mask and looked disappointed. "Why'd you have to get us these? You could have gotten us something more manly, like Godzilla."

"The Godzilla masks were pricey."

"When people see us, they'll just think we're dressed up for Halloween."

When Nicolas put the elastic around his head, I realized that this operation was completely out of his league. Nicolas's art of thievery resided in his ability to rob places that would simply never occur to anyone else on earth.

"How do you know how to rob a bank?"

"Jean-Pierre's dad was a security guard there for fifteen years."

"Who's Jean-Pierre?"

Nicolas gestured to the back seat. I looked. The rabbit waved at me. I turned back.

"Where did you find him?"

"He ran away from home. His dad always gives him a hard time because he can't pass English or he thinks he's gay. One or the other. He worked at the bank himself last summer. The whole thing's organized."

"Is that what you call an inside man?"

"I don't know. Is it? Who cares? Let's focus."

"The Caisse populaire was invented for people in a serious time of need," a boy in the cow mask said from the back seat. "Now we the people have determined this to be the hour of our need. Now we the people are about to make a withdrawal."

I stopped the van outside the bus terminal. I pulled the keys out of the ignition.

Was this the shitstorm of Nicolas that Raphaël had warned me was coming? Raphaël had had the right idea to get out of this crazy city. He had dragged me out and I had snuck off in the middle of the night to get back. How I longed to be in a small house in the middle of the country, turning the flashlight on and off in case there was some sad alien life form stuck up in his spaceship, afraid to come down. It seemed downright quaint.

"Did it ever occur to you that everything in an operation of this manner is exceedingly fine-tuned? You are disturbing the delicate balance."

Nicolas took his mask off and got out of the van and came around and stood in front of me. The others all took their masks off too and tossed them in the back of the van.

"You're going to end up in jail. This is crazy."

"How's it going to look if I have my pregnant sister giving me advice on the street corner? I'm nervous enough already. All I'm asking God for right now is that I don't have to take a shit in the middle of the robbery."

"You think you can't get away from this but you can. We can just go for dumplings and forget about it. Like everybody else in the city."

"I want to prove that I'm responsible enough to see my son. And if I have to rob a bank and bring the money in a duffle bag and throw it down in front of Saskia, then that's what I'm going to do."

"This isn't about Pierrot! This is still you screaming, 'Look at me, look at me, look at me. *Je suis l'enfant terrible.*'"

"Enough with the philosophizing, okay?"

"I was gone for two weeks and you went ahead and concocted this elaborate plan to ruin your entire life."

"You know, Nouschka, when you're not around, I don't just sit on the bed like a dog waiting for you to get home. I get up to stuff."

"Are you trying to get my attention? Because if so, then you can consider yourself successful, because you most certainly do have my attention."

"Why on earth would this be about you?"

"Why are you so angry?"

"I'm not angry." He started smashing his hands against the hood of the van. "I'm not angry! I'm not motherfucking angry! I'm not angry!"

He stood and looked at me.

"All right, maybe I'm a little bit angry. But in half an hour, I'm going to be rich and angry. Which is a step above being broke and angry. Just wait for me inside and I'll come meet you when it's all over."

"You don't have to get in that van. You are my brother and I love you more than anything and I don't want you to do this."

Nicolas looked like he didn't know what to say to this. A man walked past us and got into his car. As he turned on the ignition, music started blaring from his car radio. Nicolas started moving his body around to it. He started mouthing the words to the song, singing to the man in the car, who was trying hard to ignore him. He started clapping his arms in the air above his head and swinging his hips around in circles. Nicolas was the centre of the universe right at that moment.

All the boys had gathered at the window of the van to watch Nicolas once again making a glorious ass of himself. There was nothing that I could say. He was off to prove that the earth was round and that we were all morons for saying he was going to go too far and fall off of it.

He didn't seem to realize that the party was over. That everyone had gone home and was doing other things. Maybe he didn't have a life to go home from the party to.

"You're a pervert just like your dad," the man said from the window of his car as he drove off.

"Whoo-hoo!" Nicolas yelled.

The music drove off, and Nicolas suddenly sobered up. He turned to the van, opened the driver's door and climbed in.

"My gorgeous sister will not be joining us tonight."

He looked ahead over the steering wheel. A dark look had come over his face. He smoothed his hair back. He motioned for everyone to sit back in their spots and put their masks on.

He looked at me in a way I couldn't say anything to. It shocked me. He had suddenly turned a little dangerous.

"Let's go, *les gars!*" Nicolas said.

He pulled his giraffe mask over his face and the mask had its effect. I had no idea who in the fucking world he was. A mask is a face wiped clean of love. Not even God could recognize him.

I walked through the glass doors and went into the bus terminal to wait. I passed the sad-looking diner with silver tables. I went to sit on the orange plastic chairs that had television sets attached to them. My belly was practically touching the television set. I put a quarter in the television, but there were just politicians talking about the referendum results. There was nothing worse than waiting in places where people are meant to wait. Especially at that age. I had no patience for anything.

Maybe he would never come back to me. Maybe I would sit here until I was a little old lady.

I prayed. I wasn't interested in wishes. I prayed that Nicolas would come back to me. I prayed that Nicolas would come back to me. I prayed that Nicolas would come back to me. I prayed that all the magic of Boulevard Saint-Laurent would still be on his side. God does what he wants to with our prayers. All we can do is send them without an address.

I put my hands on my belly. I looked like any other person looking around and waiting for someone they loved to step off the Greyhound bus. All the girls with their ponytails done up prettily and their most becoming dresses. The ones that they wore when they wanted to look good but like they hadn't tried to at all.

There were so many people with their heads held back, wishing on the first star that came out at night. There was, generally, on average, only one star that you could make out because of all the light boxes with advertisements painted on them. But I asked that overextended star to look over Nicolas right now.

When he came through the doors, I was so shaken up that I couldn't even feel the fear anymore. The way that sounds are so high-pitched that you can't even hear them.

His face was flushed and he was carrying a medium-sized blue leather suitcase. He dropped it down beside me. His hands were trembling as he took a gold pack of cigarettes out of his pocket and kept trying to take one out, but his fingers were shaking too much. I didn't even know what to say.

"Is the money in that suitcase?"

He nodded and leaned back. He was a wreck. He handed me the pack of cigarettes. I took one out and lit it and stuck it in his mouth. I decided not to ask anything about the robbery, until he'd calmed down.

"What kind of cigarettes are these?" I asked.

"I don't know. We told everyone to empty their pockets and some jackass tossed in a pack of cigarettes."

"It has Russian letters on it. He probably bought them in another country."

"I didn't even notice. I thought they were Export A Smooth."

"Was it scary?"

"There was this old guy in line who passed out. I think he was having a heart attack. He had an envelope with his social assistance cheque. I took it out of the bag and told him, 'Relax, I'm leaving your envelope right next to you. I'm not even taking a cent out of it. Nothing's worth worrying about, *mon oncle*.' Jesus. Having a heart attack over a couple hundred dollars that the bank will replace. That scared me."

He threw the cigarette onto the ground and then leaned forward with his head in his hands. He stopped moving for a second, as if he was about to puke. Then he inhaled deeply and looked at me with a red face.

"Let's do something," he said, getting up.

I followed him like a scared child. He asked to check his bag at the bus station for two nights. He paid ten dollars. He put it under the name Monsieur Guillaume Ladamoiselle. As soon as we stepped out of the bus terminal, he stopped in his tracks.

"I'm never going to remember that fucking name. Why did I come up with such a stupid name?"

"How can we possibly forget a name like that?"

"Because it seems obvious now, but after a night of drinking it won't be."

"I'm pregnant. I'm not going to be drinking."

"You're half-mad with missing your lunatic boyfriend."

We stopped at a poutine restaurant. We just sat there for twenty minutes, not saying anything. When the police didn't barge through the restaurant door, we ordered food.

Nicolas and I were always chasing that first gravy high. At the grocery store we would buy packages with a sexy chicken with eyelashes on the wrapper. But gravy just didn't taste as good anymore. That night, however, the fries and gravy seemed to taste the way that they did when we were seven.

As we walked down the street we realized that we were going to get away with it. Why had I ever doubted him? We weren't going to grow old. We weren't ever going to feel any regrets. What on earth could change that? Not hurricanes. Not volcanoes. Anything seemed possible.

The sun began to set. The water of the river got all gold and shimmering. Maybe there was enough money in that suitcase to buy Pierrot's love. Then we would truly be millionaires.

CHAPTER 57

Raise High the Washing Machines, Strongmen!

WE WENT BACK TO LOULOU'S TOGETHER. WHERE
else was there to go in order to feel safe, other than home?

Sometimes after I hadn't been home for a period of time, I
was always taken aback by how filthy the place was. Everything
in the apartment seemed to have been inhaling cigarette smoke.
If you sat on the couch, it might let out a cough. The flowers
on it looked wilted and their petals had all turned black around
the edges.

Loud noises of pots and pans hitting one another were
coming from the kitchen. They sounded like cymbals being
smashed at the end of jokes. When I walked in the kitchen,
Loulou started organizing store-bought cookies on a tray. A fat
white cat walked down the side of the fridge like wax dripping
down the side of a candle.

Loulou was wearing a shaggy yellow sweater that looked
like it had been made out of endangered teddy bears. What was

left of his thin white hair was sticking straight up, as if the rest of it had been blown away like a dandelion's down. He turned toward me and put his index finger up to his lips.

"Be quiet, you'll wake the twins up. That's all I need. Them coming out in their pyjamas, saying they want some milk, they want an apple, they want me to turn the television back on. They won't leave me alone until I give them a spanking and then I'm going to be the criminal."

There was a small parcel on the table. It was wrapped awkwardly in blue paper. There was a bow stuck on top of it. I picked it up and looked at him.

"I got that for Nouschka. I slapped her on the back of her head because I caught her sucking the whipped cream out of the tube. But she gave me such a sad little look, I went and got her something. She's going to be so happy. She's been asking for that for a long time."

I looked at the box. It was heartbreaking. Whatever I wanted most as a child was inside that box. I had no idea what it could be. I didn't want to open it. I couldn't open it. How could you compare what you had really wanted with what you had? The shock of it might make you old immediately.

Nicolas walked into the kitchen in a pair of jeans with the belt undone, stretching his arms up in the air.

"Loulou, those cookies look awesome."

Loulou recognized Nicolas. His gaze leapt toward me. He was completely confused. He couldn't understand how he had lost fifteen years in a few seconds. How on earth were we fullgrown? He looked horrified. Then he looked embarrassed, because he didn't want to admit that something had just happened that was utterly beyond his comprehension.

Nicolas put a cookie in his mouth as he opened the fridge.

Beer bottles trembled in the door, like kids lined up for the diving board. He poured himself a glass of milk. He and Loulou stared at each other, not saying anything. Nicolas was in the quiet lull left behind by adrenaline and self-destructiveness. And Loulou probably knew deep down that there was nothing he could do for Nicolas anymore. The disconnect that had grown between them was apparent right now.

Up until 1932, unpasteurized milk weeded out the weak. Only the strongest little babies survived in Québec. The greatest strongmen in history were born in Québec at the beginning of the century. They swallowed boiled eggs whole. They lifted washing machines over their heads. They attached buses to their belts and walked down the street. Louis Cyr was the strongest man who ever lived and once lifted eighteen men on his back. Once milk became pasteurized, poets were able to live past three months. They were all over Montréal with their pale skin and giant eyes. The poets and the strongmen never had any idea what to make of one another.

CHAPTER 58

The Nicolas Tremblay Variations

WE WERE AWOKEN BY A POUNDING ON THE FRONT door. It was the loudest knock in the world. I'm surprised that the whole building didn't come down. It was as if they were banging with hammers. Nicolas and I woke up so violently, it was as if we had never been awake before. As if we had just been delivered from the womb and were shocked by our arms and legs. We didn't know how to stand or laugh or count to ten. Only the police ever knock on a door like that. Everyone knows that.

Nicolas leapt up, like one of those worms from a peanut brittle can. Everything seemed to be happening in slow motion, the way it does when you are falling off a chair. But Nicolas was achieving incredible feats in small increments of time. He had his clothes and boots on and he had stuffed his money in his pockets.

He tried to jump out our bedroom window, but when he saw cops waiting for him right outside it, he leapt back in. I even saw some police officer's arm reach into the window and try to catch Nicolas's foot.

There were police officers everywhere. They had surrounded the building. It was five o'clock in the morning. That's when they always had raids. Right when thieves were in the farthest realms of their dreams.

Nicolas tore through the house screaming. He went out the kitchen window and up the fire escape and into the upstairs neighbour's window. I guess he figured that he could shimmy up the fire escape and over the rooftops and escape the law the way he escaped from girls he had had sex with. His boots going up and down the stairs were making the sounds of children playing a manic clapping game. He was running in and out of doors like a ball in a pinball machine, waking people up. They came out into the hallways as if they could help him. They were going to be bone-tired. All day it would feel as if there were a little hole somewhere in themselves that sand was slowly draining out of.

The police caught Nicolas on the third floor.

I was looking up the stairwell. I ran back into the apartment and down the hallway to the bedroom, searching for anything incriminating. I saw the gold pack of cigarettes on the night table. I snatched them up, but as I turned, a police officer walked right in the door.

"Hand those over, Nouschka, sweetie."

A cat peeked out from behind the curtain like an emcee wondering if now was the right time to begin the show.

Loulou had quickly put on his best clothes so that he could show the police that we were clean-living people. He came out of the apartment with a framed photo of Nicolas and me when we were babies.

"Weren't they cute?" Loulou asked one of the police officers pleadingly. "They're good kids. They have good natures.

They're just always in with bad crowds. They were on the radio with their father. Do you remember?"

"Sure. Sure. I know who you all are."

A news van was pulling up on the scene.

"He was such a sweet, talented little guy," Loulou persisted.

At that moment, two officers escorted Nicolas out of the building. He was sort of making a fuss, but his heart wasn't in it. Every now and then he would jerk his arms. He wasn't actually trying to get away. He kept throwing his head back as if he was desperate to get his bangs out of his eyes. Maybe he knew that this was his last time to look tough. The law always makes an ass out of you. We knew that from Étienne's fiasco.

Nicolas's goose had already been cooked the night before.

The old man who had a heart attack had been taken immediately to the hospital. In the ambulance on the way, he began to slip away. As he was being bounced by the potholes, the old man uttered his last magical words. The paramedics leaned forward to hear what he was saying.

"It is okay. *Le petit* Nicolas was at the bank and he told me that everything was going to be okay. He got my envelope back for me. My wife is just going to go crazy knowing that I met him . . . He was so nice to me. *Il était tellement mignon quand il était petit!*"

We didn't know any of this at the moment. We had no idea how the police knew that Nicolas had robbed the Caisse populaire. We didn't know why I wasn't in handcuffs too.

A reporter ran up and put a microphone in Nicolas's mouth.

"You love it. You love it," Nicolas said. "Look, they thought they were somebodies. They thought they were better than us. Now they have nothing. Oh, isn't it lovely. Take him down a notch. It's entertainment. I'm not a character in a television

show. Tar and feather me. You stole my childhood. On top
of it you losers voted *non*! Throw me in jail. You animals, you
owe me. You all owe me. Where is my pay for having to spend
my whole life being a clown? Be sure to send a postcard of the
hanging to Grandpipi in Abitibi! "

Whatever else was said about him, you had to admit that
Nicolas had a lovely turn of phrase. He was quoted in all the
newspapers. In Montréal later that day, a twelve-year-old boy
in the smallest-sized combat boots the army could issue and
a jean jacket with gold stars ironed all over the sleeves put a
flyer up on a telephone pole and slapped it with a huge paint-
brush of glue. The poster was a mug shot photocopied from the
front page of *Le Journal de Montréal*. Underneath was written:
LIBÉRER NICOLAS TREMBLAY.

The next morning I was standing completely clueless in
front of one of the posters outside Loulou's house. I had been
standing there for ten minutes. I thought that there was something that I should be doing, but I didn't know what. I was
missing a compass and it made me feel dizzy. There was no
use in trying to call Raphaël. He was not to be found. I suddenly wanted to call Lily. Supposedly, mothers were like North
Stars that guided you when you were profoundly lost. How on
earth could I explain this situation? I walked over to the phone
booth. I looked up her number in the telephone book that was
hung from a metal ring. I first turned to the names that began
with *S*, but then I remembered that she would be under Noëlle
Renaud. It was amazing: her number was there, right where it
should be. What was even more incredible to me was that her
name had been circled with two different colours of ink. How
many times had Nicolas sat right here, thinking of calling her?

CHAPTER 59

That Strange Land, Ontario

THE FOG WAS MADE IN A FACTORY IN LAC-SAINT-Jean. They have the same old machines that were built in 1942. The same guys have been working there for fifty-five years. They have a good union. They carry the steel cans of ice cubes up a huge ladder and then dump them in the machine. Nobody needs fog anymore, but Heritage Canada saved the factory and kept it up and running.

I couldn't even see out the window as the train pulled out of the station. The tracks went west over nondescript land into Ontario. The train shook ever so silently back and forth like it was weeping in bed.

The fog magically went away as soon as I crossed the border into Ontario. You rode across it and there were jobs and decent, clean living and loads and loads more Protestants.

I probably wasn't even considered good-looking in Ontario. I certainly wasn't famous. It was no big deal to be tall. There were people that chose not to smoke. They spoke one language. Nicolas would probably come out of Kingston Penitentiary speaking perfect English.

This was the same prison we'd visited Étienne at years and years ago. Nicolas stuck out among all the other prisoners. His hair was flapping all over the place. He looked good and clean. His face looked sober and wiser. He looked relaxed for once. It was strange to see him in one colour and not some crazy getup. We held each other for a long time. I could have spent the whole hour just holding Nicolas in my arms. I felt perfect and complete. Finally we let go because we worried simultaneously about what the guards would think. We sat down on either side of the table.

"Have you heard anything from Pierrot?" he asked.

"No."

"Did you go to that poor old man's funeral?"

"No, I didn't know what his family would think."

We were quiet. The things that we had to say to each other were so gigantic that we didn't know where to start. We had no idea how this new situation defined or changed us.

"You look good," I said, breaking the silence.

"You're the only one that I miss," Nicolas said quickly. "But I guess that I can get used to it and then I can do anything. I was always so scared that I couldn't live without you when we were kids that I wanted to roll over in bed and strangle you. I don't mean that in a bad way."

"I know," I said. "Remember when I hit you on the head with a pot for no reason at all?"

"Poor Loulou. That sort of stuff confused the hell out of him."

"And remember when you poked me in the eye with that crayon?" I said. "I could have gone blind."

Nicolas put his hands over his face in disbelief.

"How did we ever survive each other?" he asked.

"Or do you remember that time we had an argument with a kid at the park because we said that we were identical twins?"

"And he said that his father was a doctor and his father said that it was impossible for a boy and girl twin to be identical." Nicolas laughed.

"Well, we proved him wrong, didn't we?"

"We did."

We both put our arms on the table, straightened up our backs and became absolutely still. We had this routine where we pretended that we were the mirror image of each other. We'd performed it on Gaston L'Heureux's show once, but we'd perfected a few versions of it over the years.

As we sat in the prison visiting room, we began to move very slowly, so that we could guess the meaning of each other's gestures more precisely. We both pretended that we had picked up a toothbrush and we began brushing our teeth. Then we both spat into a nonexistent sink together. We put our toothbrushes into their immaterial stands. We both picked up our imaginary combs and we pulled them through our hair. When we were done with our hair, we dipped the tips of our fingers into little invisible tins of wax. He twirled the end of his imaginary moustache. I twirled the end of mine.

And the most amazing thing about our performance was that we had identical tears streaming down from our eyes at the very same time.

CHAPTER 60

The Petit Prince Has Had Enough

I SAT ON THE COUCH NEXT TO EMMANUELLE WITH her arm around me. The baby was finally asleep. Emmanuelle's boyfriend came and squeezed in too. There was going to be a special segment on the news about *Le déclin et la chut de la famille Tremblay* as directed by Hugo Vaillancourt. Before we knew it, there was Nicolas in a prison uniform, his hair slicked back, smoking a cigarette, looking confident.

"Did you feel that you were missing out on anything as a child?" Hugo's voice asked.

"I had the best clothes," Nicolas started with a big grin, plainly feeling that he was going to dominate this interview. "I would have a cobbler make these adorable leather shoes for me. Because I have very particular feet. A doctor once called them *jazz feet*. We had this chauffeur named Gauguin. And Gauguin was always getting speeding tickets while driving Nouschka and me to school. Because we would say, 'Gauguin, Gauguin! Will you just drive this car and get us to school on time; we'll pay your fucking ticket.' Oh, we were raised very differently than

Papa. As Papa is probably very anxious to tell you, he was baptized in a spaghetti pot."

There was a cutaway to footage of Nicolas on the street corner, scalping concert tickets. Then there was footage of Nicolas and me fighting on the street corner. I wasn't even pregnant yet. We were horsing around. But they played the clip in slow motion and for some reason it came out looking brutal.

Then there was Raphaël yelling at a journalist. Raphaël held a garbage can over his head, threatening to dump it on all of Québec. I missed him. I didn't even care what he thought of this fiasco. What I really wanted was just him here next to me on the couch. Now that the other love of my life had been taken away, he ought to return.

Hugo's voice-over reiterated our family's loss of fortune. Next came Étienne looking tipsy and trying to stuff a hot dog in his mouth. You'd think that they might have had a bit of respect, seeing as how he had been a national hero a couple weeks before. But as usual, now that the referendum was over, he would end up being tossed away by the public. Then they played the end part of the speech I'd written him, where he'd gone off-script and ended up barking.

Nicolas was the one who had seen it coming. He had always known that the *non* side was going to win.

Then the camera was where it had never been before. Loulou had let them in and he probably told them his most complicated thoughts and his most colourful anecdotes about life in *La Grande Noirceur*. But they weren't interested in those. This was a case of a picture saying a thousand words. I felt sad for Loulou. When he was lonely he would garbage-pick. There he was, proudly displaying all the wonderful things that he had found in the trash: cracked vases, lamps with no lightbulbs, amateur paintings of trees. He had straightened up, but he had put things in odd places. There was a plastic kewpie doll in with the dishes, and a row of shoes on the bookshelf. They panned the camera slowly across the room, as if they were showing footage of a city that had been ravaged by a bomb.

This was our great secret. This was where we had grown up. This was what the childhoods of Little Nicolas and Little Nouschka had actually looked like.

"How did growing up without a mother affect you?" a voice asked Nicolas in prison.

"How do you mean? Well . . . yes," Nicolas stuttered, clearly taken aback by the question.

His nonsensical, witty repartee came to a stop. You had to give it to Hugo. He was asking new questions.

"I don't know," Nicolas said carefully. "Most of the guys in here have mothers. They show up on visitor's day all happy and shit. I mean, there are guys doing eight-year stints in here and their mothers treat them like they're saints and if they can just turn things around, they'll be the next prime ministers for sure."

Nicolas stubbed his cigarette out and looked up at the ceiling for a minute.

"So I don't have some coddling middle-aged woman coming in and telling me fairy tales about myself. And telling me how wonderful I am when I am clearly nothing but a piece of shit. I've always been a realist. Since I was five years old, I've been singing the sad, true nature of this terrible world."

There he was in the cage like Iago, speaking like a beautiful, bitter bird. Iago pretended to be a model of virtue and propriety, but at heart he was downright rotten. Whereas Nicolas wanted to be evil and hard, but he was really so soft and sweet and broken.

CHAPTER 61

The King of Boulevard Saint-Laurent

I WAS SITTING AT THE KITCHEN TABLE, WRITING an essay for school, when the clock radio went off by accident. I had stopped listening to the radio and tried to avoid newspapers. It seemed like every day they had a different angle on us. Today there was a leading psychologist trying to explain what factors had led to Nicolas's particular brand of insanity. He couldn't get away with just being another idiot who robbed a bank.

Now the radio hosts were laughing their heads off. They couldn't be talking about Nicolas. I didn't know what was amusing them so much.

"No, but really, he gave a forty-seven-year-old woman an asthma attack."

"It's not the lion's fault. He was just going for a stroll."

"I don't know how they're going to fit him into one of those little cages at the SPCA."

After this remark they laughed and laughed. They were so delighted with themselves that they couldn't stop laughing. They were just going to laugh and laugh until the weather report.

I ran downstairs and across the street to the corner store and picked up a newspaper. It was on the front page, and the store owner was talking about it with a customer. In the middle of last night, a lion had crossed the Jacques Cartier Bridge onto the Island of Montréal. Early-morning drivers had spotted him as he walked down the highway. Drivers at that hour were always seeing hallucinations at the side of the road and didn't know what to think. There was an aerial shot, taken from a helicopter, of the lion leaping over a car and heading to Chinatown.

The lion had strutted down Boulevard Saint-Laurent with his mane looking like it was slicked back. I could swear it was the same scrawny lion that I had seen in Val-des-Loups. Now he looked majestic walking down the street. Nobody could touch him. No one could tell him how to be. He was confident and calm. He took cool to a whole other level. When he yawned, his yawn was so enormous that all the little boys and all the little girls caught the yawn and went to bed.

It was time that there was a new *Roi de Boulevard Saint-Laurent*. He made everyone so happy. They were going to give him his own exhibition at le Zoo de Granby. One of the police officers who was the first on the scene affectionately named him René, because he said that the lion, with his thinning mane and enormous jowls, resembled the ex-premier of Québec René Lévesque.

There was something unsettling about that lion being here. I thought for a moment that I had better go check my bible. Because I was pretty sure that there was a verse in Revelations that said that a lion walking over the Jacques Cartier Bridge was a sure sign of the apocalypse. People all over the city were taking that lion for an omen. Some saw it as a sign that they should stay away from the casino that week, some as a message that they shouldn't get married. I was frightened. But I knew one thing for sure, looking at the photograph of the lion: Raphaël was coming back.

CHAPTER 62

Raphaël Lemieux's 115th Dream

I WOKE UP WITH A START A WEEK LATER. I HAD only a bra on. My belly was enormous. I was so tired that I couldn't even remember anything. I couldn't remember if I was a little kid in pyjama bottoms waking up from a nap. I couldn't remember if I was an old lady. I couldn't remember what point of my life I was at.

Raphaël was sitting in a chair in the corner of the room. He was drinking a glass of iced tea. He had showered. His after-shave smelled like licorice. His hair was combed back and he was wearing a suit. He had a gold ring on his pinky finger with a sparrow on it. My eye went to it as if it was an announcement. He looked like he'd been up all night. This worried me. If he had been up all night thinking, there was no telling what kind of crazy thoughts he had come up with.

Raphaël closed his eyes for several seconds. He was gone to the world when he did that. Who knew how long he was away in his alternate universe? He could be spending years in Narnia.

He might be involved in a terrible four-year battle. He looked exhausted and world-weary when he opened his eyes again.

I thought he looked dead handsome.

I still wasn't used to being awake. I felt as if someone had made me out of snow and I was going to melt soon, so what was the point? We had gone back to the way we were when we were little kids, where we couldn't say anything to each other at all.

"I've decided to kill my father," Raphaël said.

His gun was hanging from his left hand. He stood up and walked to the window and looked out. He seemed to be checking for something, but I couldn't imagine what. I wasn't sure if he meant that he was going to go kill his father right now. I somehow didn't think so. Nobody ever did what they said they were going to do right after they said it. You could procrastinate for years.

He turned back around and came and sat on the end of the mattress. He gave me such a strange look. He looked at me with terrible love for a second. He put the gun to his temple and pulled the trigger.

Chapter 63

I, Said the Sparrow

I WAS WEARING A BLACK SWEATER DRESS AND A peacoat. The baby kept kicking. The baby kept crying out, "Goodbye, goodbye." I kept opening my hand for Nicolas to take it as I walked down the street toward the funeral parlour. But there was just emptiness there. It was just an instinct that he should be showing up any minute to make me feel better. But he wasn't.

I felt as if I could hardly walk. We always imagine the sidewalk to be so strong. But it is hardly true. It could give any second. Grief turned everything to liquid. Grief could deny the reality of all this. All the bricks were holding one another up. But any second, they might just give up hope. They might stop seeing the point and then they would all come crashing down. And the windows and signs and beds and all the nonsense that we fill our apartments with would end up lying on the street. As if we had all been evicted from our homes at once—if we'd been foolish enough to think that we'd ever had one at all.

Someone else had called the police. They had heard the shot, heard me calling out *"Au secours!"* over and over again. Although I didn't have any memory of calling out to anyone at all. It was hard to remember. Everything had a make-believe quality to it still. And I was skeptical that it had happened.

The words CHAMPOUX ET FILS were written on the glass of the front door with gold letters. The son was a seventy-five-year-old man. He did everything by himself. There was no one as organized as these old men who had been doing the same tasks for forty years. They knew how to look terribly sad but also completely in control.

The place hadn't been redecorated since the sixties. There was something anachronistic about it. Even the hearse outside seemed old-fashioned. The driver wore a small blue sailor hat and a suit.

Some of the white tiles on the lobby floor were broken because so many people had walked across the lobby floor. Every day there were lines of people trudging up the stairs who were going through the exact same thing that I was going through.

I had already been here for three funerals. It made me feel a little bit comforted to know that I was at least some place that was familiar. Raphaël wasn't the only person on earth that had ever died. My grandmother's funeral had been here when I was five, but I could hardly remember it.

I could not make any sense of death. Even though death was just about the most ordinary thing that could happen to a person, it defied everything that I knew about the world. It was like anything could happen now. If King Kong had reached his hand through the window and snatched me up, I wouldn't have kicked up a fuss in the slightest. I would just have let him wrap me up in his fist and looked out at all the sights around me.

Everyone in the neighbourhood was there because it had been on the news. They were all crowding in and squeezing up the staircase. They didn't know Raphaël enough to really be devastated. In a meaningless world, they were desperate for a ritual. Everyone loves a sad little tune.

I had been trying to learn how to be alone. But there was a way of being alone that made you feel as if you didn't exist at all. That was too terrible. All these people in their black suits were squeezing in around me. It seemed as if all the people on earth were gone and all that was left of them were their shadows.

The room where the coffin was had light blue curtains on the wall. There were two vases of lilies on either side of the closed coffin. There was a photograph of Raphaël that had been taken on our wedding day next to the casket. There was also a photo of him from school. Who knows where Véronique had found it, seeing as how he had tried to erase all evidence of his past.

A cold, clammy feeling of dread came over me. It was as if my insides were all rotten and black. Someone asked if they could take my coat and I whispered no.

I looked around for someone to comfort me. Loulou was sitting on a chair. He was shaking his head in disbelief the way that he had when I told him that I was marrying Raphaël. He was never going to be able to understand Raphaël. This was just the cherry on the cake. He couldn't understand any of us as adults. He only really understood tiny babies who needed to have their diapers changed and their bottles put in their mouths.

Someone whispered to me that my father was here. Étienne was indeed standing in the doorway in a raggedy suit, holding a hat up to his heart. I had never actually seen him look so sorrowful. He was almost acting like it was his fault. He walked over and put the tip of his finger on the flower that was pinned on my lapel. I couldn't for the life of me remember how it got there.

Étienne was trying to say something. Maybe he actually was saying something but his words didn't seem to be making it to my ears. His words were like badly constructed paper airplanes that just went straight to the floor instead of having any glide. He didn't have the words to comfort me. Because he would have to have had a lifetime of comforting me in order to be able to comfort me now.

He didn't have any favourite lullabies. He didn't know how I felt about love.

For once, nobody cared that Étienne was in the room. Raphaël had stolen the show. It was a marvel. Death pulled the tablecloth out without upsetting any of the dishes that were on it. Everything was the same even though the world was completely altered.

I turned away from Étienne, still looking for someone. I wanted someone to say that it was okay that I hadn't stayed in the country. I needed to be convinced that there wasn't something that I could have done. I wanted to feel that I hadn't betrayed Raphaël, that I hadn't been the flakiest wife on the whole planet. Someone had to tell me that I had loved him properly.

I didn't think that I could bear having no one to help me with this terrible confusion and sorrow. Everyone in Raphaël's family was feeling their own dreadful emotions. It wasn't for any of them to do anything but deal with their own horrific loss. It would be selfish of me to ask any of them to help me. But I had been desperate, since this happened, for someone to come and let me share my pain with them.

And how could I ask Raphaël to come out of his coffin and whisper to me that I was the most wonderful girl on earth? I thought for a second that I must faint. That was the only way out of this.

Someone asked the people next to me to give him some room. I looked up and saw Misha squeezing through the rows of chairs to come to me. I hadn't seen him in ages. I don't know how he knew about the funeral. I never knew how it was that he was always able to follow what was going on with me. He just knew the way that a parent knew and would show up at your school with your lunch before you even realized that you had forgotten it. And I felt about Misha the way that a child feels about a night light when they are afraid of the dark. For some magical reason, its presence would make the existence of monsters impossible.

It was Misha who came and put his big, fat arms around me.

"You'll be okay, my squishy, tiny sweetheart," he murmured. "There was nothing that anybody could do for that boy. He was very, very lucky to have had you. Everybody, even the butchers and bakers and candlestick makers, wanted to be married to you. He will always be thinking of you in heaven."

This made me smile. I knew that he was an atheist. I knew that he was telling me that it wasn't my fault. There are things that you need other generations to help you with. They knew the tricks of dealing with suffering that have to be given from one person to another. You can't discover them on your own.

Misha had been to funerals before. Misha knew what to do. He knew what to say. He believed that there was a way out. In Moscow there were a hundred different words for sadness, and one of them was *joy*.

I put my head against his enormous heartbeat. Up close like that, it was like the rolling of drums. When you are waiting and waiting and waiting for a parade, you finally feel the drums first, rumbling inside of you, and you know the wonderful spectacle is on its way. Before you can actually see the parade, you feel it inside your belly.

And I suddenly wasn't in shock anymore. I was able to cry and cry and cry.

Sometimes I wondered why we were given all these amazing emotions. How come you got to feel happy while riding the metro with your friends? Why did you feel so awesome getting high? How come you were able to get that rush when someone's dick went in you the first time? Why did you feel so frightened on a roller coaster? And then I realized that these emotions were given to you just so that you could experience the full impact of death.

Étienne moved away from us. I think that Étienne was suddenly humbled at seeing Misha do what he should have done.

One of Raphaël's brothers gave a speech. He stood at the podium in a black suit, shaking and reading from his loose-leaf sheet of paper.

"Raphaël was always a really wonderful big brother to me. He would talk us into going to school in the mornings and come pick us up, even though this must have been really, really uncool to the other kids his age. He would always read to us for hours before we went to bed. We would fall asleep and he would still go on reading. Once I woke up in the middle of the night to go to the bathroom, and Raphaël was still reading out loud to us."

He stopped because his voice was too choked up.

My family would be allowed to get over Raphaël. But his family would never ever be. This was the boy who they had raised. They hadn't been able to look after him properly. They hadn't been able to understand what he had been trying to communicate. This was their tragedy. Nicolas in prison was ours.

*****

When we got into the limousine, Étienne was standing outside on the sidewalk. There was no car for him to go in. He
had been left behind. He didn't belong. Who knew what he
felt about anything? Who knew if he felt at all? Étienne, who
wanted everyone in the whole world to revere him, was the one
who was absolutely alone.

Where does a mythology come from? Who are the myth-
ological figures in Québec culture? They were brand-new.
Whereas the Greeks had Zeus and Athena, we had people who
still lived in Verdun. They had a lot to bear on their shoulders.
They had to invent the whole world themselves. They were
supposed to have supernatural powers and achieve sainthood.
When really they just found themselves peering into the mirror
above the bathroom sink, looking to see how they were aging.
Sitting in the bathtub, smoking a cigarette, terrified of death
like the rest of us.

Raphaël's coffin, piled high with roses, went down the
street. All the wee children came to the edge of the sidewalk as
if it were the edge of the water. And they crossed themselves as
the coffin went by.

So many hearses had passed me on the street since I was a
little kid. I had always wondered who was inside them. Raphaël
had been inside each and every one of them and I hadn't even
known it.

Chapter 64

A Girl from Romania

THE BABY WAS OVERDUE. I WENT INTO A STORE called Babas. There were these miniature jars of feelings on the shelves at the back. They bought them off of poor kids in foreign countries. They had to sell them so that their families could eat. They were so young anyways, they were still going to get to feel that way on their own so many times before they got old.

A pretty Romanian girl in a threadbare black coat and bare knees had filled six jars with that feeling that everything was new and anything was possible. That was the feeling that was the most in demand. I bought three jars of it.

I caught my reflection in a restaurant window on my way home. I was still always surprised when I caught my reflection out of the blue and saw my huge belly. It was ridiculous to be pregnant and to have such a young face. Like wearing high heels and gym shorts. I suddenly expected the world of myself. I expected the world of the baby and I expected the world of myself. I continued home with the jars clinking in the plastic bag hanging from my wrist.

CHAPTER 65

Ne me quitte pas

IT WAS AN INDIAN SUMMER DAY. I KNEW THAT IT was the last one that we were going to have. It was a late Saturday afternoon and the baby still, still, still hadn't been born. I was sitting on a hideous old red couch with burgundy flowers on it, which had been left out on a sidewalk near my building. I had pulled a dress on over my belly and the seams had ripped a bit around the zipper. But I was wearing a green coat that I'd buttoned up, so it didn't matter.

Next to me was a grocery bag with a head of lettuce. I don't know what I intended to do with it. Maybe put it in the refrigerator and just let it rot. I hadn't eaten because, frankly, I had been too lazy to make anything for dinner. I was thinking of ordering a bowl of seafood soup for dinner from the hole-in-the-wall Chinese joint. That was my favourite. But there would be octopus tentacles in it and I had heard somewhere that pregnant women weren't supposed to eat sea creatures. Maybe the baby would turn out blue from the octopus's ink.

I saw people who I knew, but they crossed to the other

side of the street. Maybe they thought that I was going to start talking to them about all my problems and they'd already had enough of them on the news. Or maybe they figured that the Tremblays were such bad luck that they didn't want to be anywhere near me.

I was waiting for someone who I didn't actually believe was going to show up. She had never come to see me in my whole life before. I felt like Linus when he was waiting for the Great Pumpkin to come. I decided to sit there and wait for her and pretend that that wasn't what I was actually doing. There's no way that I wanted her to come over to my apartment. I didn't want to be inside, alone with her. I just felt safer on the street corner with all the strangers around for protection.

There she was.

She got out of a car that she'd parked half a block up from where I was sitting. She was wearing a dark blue suit and was carrying a little box in her hand. She probably knocked a lot of the car salesmen dead while wearing that suit. I couldn't bring myself to stand up; I just stared. She came right over and stood in front of me. She was thirty-five but she looked older. Maybe it was just her style though. Here, no one really dressed like an adult. You might see a sixty-five-year-old wearing a tank top and a pair of Converse sneakers. She smiled and tilted her head in a gentle way that made me feel less self-conscious.

"Do you remember this street?" I asked. "Does it surprise you that we're in the same spot as where you dropped us off?"

"It's colourful here!"

She sat down lightly on the nasty old couch. She sat up straight, more than a touch uncomfortable. She had spent her whole life being told where there were germs, what things were dirty, where to sit and where not to sit. I had never really had those instructions, and yet here I was, as fit as a fiddle. I was impervious to germs. I was a survivor. The cooties on this couch were the least of my worries.

My heart was beating in a funny way the closer she got to me. I felt like one of those alley cats that you put your hand out to pet. You know that they want to come close and let you pet them but you know that they are too terrified. I used to play a Petula Clark record and pretend it was my mother singing. I would imagine her singing in the kitchen as she washed the bits of hardened egg off the utensils.

I was afraid to even move a single inch because I might accidentally touch her. If we did touch, it would mean things that we didn't mean it to mean. I didn't want to give her the wrong idea. I didn't want her to think that I wanted her to be my mother, if she didn't want to be my mother. I was like some absolutely terrified teenager on a first date.

Every time my eyes met hers, they instinctively looked away. Like when you cross glances with someone who is sitting across from you on the bus. She looked across the street. She squinted as if there was someone that she knew on the other side, which of course was impossible. There was no way that anyone she knew would be in the neighbourhood.

"I hear that you're going to be going to university," Noëlle said. "That's a beautiful idea. That's great."

My family never asked me anything about this. They had totally forgotten that I was going to university the next semester. They didn't get that it led to other things. She was proud of the right accomplishments. I paused, still wary of everything I said.

Generally, two people who are that awkward get up and bid adieu. We had to weather the strangeness, hoping that it would eventually pass, like a rainstorm. I needed her. Nicolas and I needed more people in our life. We just weren't enough for each other. What else could I do? Put an ad in the newspaper asking for mothers and siblings and cousins? How many incredibly awkward things were we going to say to each other before we would be able to talk about the latest episode of *La Petite Vie*?

"What are your children like?" I asked.

I really couldn't begin to consider them siblings. I mean, I had no idea whatsoever what a mother was, but I had very grand ideas about what a sibling was. It was somebody who hung out with you in the womb, took baths with you, shared your breakfast, stole your socks, accidentally broke your nose and sometimes had the same dreams as you at night.

"They're very small still. Julie likes dancing. She takes a lot of lessons. I'm not quite sure what Marcel's skill is yet."

My half-brother. My half-sister. Could they possibly add up to even one? They seemed so odd and hapless to me. Poor Fishstick and Dumont! I started laughing a little.

"I don't talk to my parents anymore," Noëlle said shyly. "They wanted to make me feel guilty about my mistakes. I don't want you to feel that way about me. I want to try and be a part of your lives."

I was shocked by how happy her saying that made me feel. I hadn't realized until that moment how much the anxiety of not having a mother had occupied a place in my brain. Because now that the weight of it was gone, I almost felt light-headed.

"I'm sorry that I didn't come to the funeral. I didn't think that it was the right time. After I heard that Nicolas was in prison and that your husband had died, I knew I couldn't stay away any longer. I felt I was responsible somehow. So I told my husband about you two."

"Your husband must have been weirded out by it all."

"Yes."

"Did he, like, shout, even though he's not the type of guy who shouts?"

"Yes. But it was normal for him to be upset, for a while."

I don't know how I had the audacity to ask all these nosy questions. But I sort of liked that her absolutely ordinary family was having all sorts of reactions to us. I liked that they were upset. I always imagined them smiling, the way that they did in the photographs on the fridge. I liked that Nicolas and I were causing them to throw plates around their kitchen and slam doors.

"I'm sorry I pushed you away the last time. I want to be in your lives," Noëlle said.

Almost all the important things in our lives are expressed in such simple and unceremonious terms. Maybe all the best sentiments are tacky. She handed me the box she had with her.

"I picked a little treat up for you on the way. It's silly."

I opened up the box and saw a tiny cake inside that was covered in coconut sprinkles and had a rose made out of frosting on top. It was exactly what I wanted to eat. I took it out greedily and bit into it.

I felt sort of guilty about sitting here and getting along somewhat with Noëlle. It was Nicolas who had instigated all this. He was the one who had sought her out. But now here I was, the one who was getting to have a relationship with her.

"Are you going to see Nicolas?" I asked with my mouth full.

"I'm going to visit tomorrow. I talked to him on the phone already."

She looked for a moment as if she was going to move a lock of hair away from my forehead, but she didn't have the courage.

"It's not your job to worry about him, Nouschka."

She would talk to Nicolas. She would be Nicolas's friend. There was someone else who had offered to take care of Nicolas for me. I just sat for a moment, wiping the icing off my mouth with a little paper napkin that she took out of her pocket. A peaceful feeling was coming over me. That was it. That was how mothers calmed children down. Nicolas and I had always been in a constant state of agitation. Mothers took your problems from you and fretted about them for you, even if there was no reason on earth why they should, even if you had done everything to create your own mess.

A homeless man sat on the other side of the couch. I thought that she might be disgusted with him, but instead she just smiled at him. There was a button missing on my jacket. It had popped off when I had pulled on it too hard, trying to cover up my belly. Noëlle pointed to it.

"You need a new button." As she almost touched the spot where the button should go, a chill went through my body.

"You know," Noëlle continued, "there were times when I put my hands on my belly and I just knew that the two of you were special and that you were miracles. My parents had told me that I shouldn't feel any attachment at all, because I had to give you both away. But I lay in bed and whispered that I loved you and that you would be capable of anything."

The homeless man next to Noëlle gently put his hand on her back, on the beautiful blue jacket.

"I'm so glad to hear you say that," the man said. "Because I have my shit and you have your shit. And everybody has their shit. But that doesn't mean we can't come together at the end."

Noëlle flinched. Then the man stood up and took my hand in both of his and shook it before walking away. I felt no aversion to him; with his plastic bag filled with newspaper clippings, his two scarves, and rubber bands around his wrist, he was one of my people. She was the one who weirded me out. I was over-analyzing her actions and couldn't even begin to think about her touching me. But that was suddenly okay. It was still sort of sweet in its own way.

"Did you used to make up stories about Nicolas and me?" I asked.

A grin spread almost involuntarily on her face and she blushed. She looked impressed and sort of delighted that I knew about this. After all, it was from both her and Étienne that I had inherited the desire to tell stories.

"I used to imagine that I found a suitcase as I was walking home. I opened the suitcase and I saw two babies wrapped up in clothes and underwear and laughing. There was a Montréal address on the label. So then I closed the suitcase and brought it there. I knew that it wasn't possible to keep you. You did not belong to me." She paused. "I was fourteen. I had to invent stories to understand what had happened."

*****

In Québec the church was always on the lookout for storytell-ers. The priests carefully read the essays written by children to choose which ones were right for the cloth. They didn't look for piety or essays about Jesus or Santa Claus or anything like that. They looked for the ones who wrote about strange things, for the ones who questioned religion.

Like a boy who wrote a story about how he looked at his reflection in the mirror and discovered that it was no longer doing what he wanted it to do. It was sticking its tongue out at him and it smiled when the boy frowned.

Or one who wrote about taking a hot bath and then being shrunk. In the tale, he went to live in the walls with the cockroaches. They played dominoes all day long and he discovered that he quite liked being vermin.

A young girl revealed that she drank a bottle of invisibility potion. But nothing changed for her and she realized that she had been invisible all along. She should have just saved the money that she had given to the drugstore clerk.

The church had to get these children on their side. If they didn't, they would end up becoming philosophers and writing existential tracts that would try and kill God. A certain kind of modernist novel was going to make the church irrelevant.

The priests went to collect these children. They had them pack their little suitcases immediately. They would barely have time to say goodbye to their eight or nine brothers and sisters. They shouted adieu to their fat grandfather in his underwear, who waved back with his hand whose pinky was missing from frostbite.

They left behind their tiny houses with all the mice in the walls. They would not be writing about these rooms. They would not be finding any metaphors that would convey what their lives were like. There would be no stories set in these Québécois houses. The children were to give lectures and sermons instead.

It might seem like the easier way to get rid of a poet would be to just take him out to the backyard, have him kneel between the cans with tomato plants in them and put a bullet in his brain. But they knew from history that it doesn't work to kill a writer. Every time you shoot a poet, a dozen new ones are born. It's like plucking a grey hair.

CHAPTER 66

Graduation

I EMPTIED THE MAILBOX WHEN I GOT HOME.
There were about ten advertisements for different barbecued
chicken restaurants. How many barbecued chicken restaurants
could there be in one city? I wondered. There was the Hydro
bill with untold amounts of electricity that we had consumed
over past winters and still hadn't paid for. And then there it was:
my high school diploma. I was the first person in the family to
obtain one. We all had the brains to get high school diplomas.
We just lacked the focus and patience. We lacked a very basic
ability to sit the fuck still and let somebody else tell us something.

Here it was. I don't know why I was so proud. It really
wasn't a big deal. It wasn't the sort of thing that a twenty-year-
old would normally be proud of. But it was so unlike anything
that would normally happen in the Ballad of Little Nicolas and
Nouschka. It was so unnewsworthy that the tabloids would
sneer. It was just a small achievement that belonged to me. It
meant that anything was possible.

I passed a teenage boy singing in the metro. He was singing an Étienne Tremblay song. It was about being noble and being proud no matter what. All you needed in life was your dignity. Just a little dignity and a cup of coffee. I was going to be okay.

I had just stepped into the lobby of the building when my water broke. It spilled all over the tiles. All over the blue and red tiles.

CHAPTER 67

Metamorphosis

I NAMED THE BABY PAPILLON, AFTER THE BOOK that Raphaël had been reading when we started trying to date each other. All babies that are born to twenty-year-olds have ridiculous names.

I shared the hospital room with four other women. There were flowers in vases all over the place. The relatives of the other girls had brought them. I had a vase of white carnations from one of the neighbours in Loulou's building who had visited.

"Poor thing," the neighbour said when I told her the baby's name. "He will be queer."

Véronique came to see the baby too. I liked sharing the baby with Raphaël's family. The baby made them all weepy and happy. They looked and looked for Raphaël's face. But the baby just looked like a tiny stranger with a giant nose who we had never met before.

Loulou gave me a bin of clothes that Nicolas and I had worn as children. There was the tiniest pair of polyester bell-bottoms the world had ever seen and a red shirt with a large butterfly collar. They were such funny outfits. We had run around the neighbourhood in them and now the baby would too. It broke my heart to remember that Nicolas was once so small that he could fit into one of these outfits.

After I got home from the hospital, I came to realize quickly that I was a terrible slob. I was overwhelmed by all the parenting. All my school books from university were covered in Pablum and jam. Noëlle had visited the apartment a few times. She always helped me clean up, and I was getting more and more used to her presence.

The neighbours were always walking right into my apartment and offering to bathe the baby for me. They screamed at me for letting a giant cat doze in the cradle with him. I spilt coffee on his head while drinking as I walked along. I begged him not to tell anyone.

But the funny thing was that I was getting an unbelievable amount of stuff done. I would study like a fiend during the baby's nap time. I put him in daycare even though he was too young to go. I had no time to fool around.

I sort of hated being a mother. But it was a family trait to hate being a mother. I just went about the job every day and it seemed to work. A lot of things in life that suck and are a drag aren't half bad.

Papillon was perfectly healthy. He liked to smack himself on the head with his rattle and then look around furiously to see who had done it. If he could get his hands on one, he would shake the newspaper about wildly. He reminded me of Étienne when he was tearing through the pages frantically in order to get to an article about himself. He actually had Étienne's fantastic nose. Étienne had written a lullaby for Papillon and had sung it on Jean-Pierre Coallier's show. But then he had never actually come over and sung it to the actual baby.

I picked Papillon up out of his crib one morning, and he weighed an extra thirty pounds from all the pee in his diaper. I looked at him, with the bruises on his forehead and his big, giant nose. And then I realized that he was the most extraordinarily beautiful and entrancing human being that I had ever seen. So this was what it felt like to be a mother, I thought.

*****

One chilly spring day, I walked to the laundromat. I had a pile of clothes in the perambulator, on top of the baby. I put all his shitty pyjamas in the washing machine. I put quarters in the slot. And I had that wonderful feeling that things were doable. The baby was sleeping, so I started writing my Guy de Maupassant essay on top of the washer.

When I shut the dryer door, my stomach dropped in a terrible way. Raphaël was standing at the next machine, tossing underwear into it from a basket. He was wearing a brown leather jacket and purple jogging pants. He didn't even acknowledge me.

The strangest thoughts crossed my mind. How had I been so stupid as to think that he was dead? Did I time-travel to the past, or had he time-travelled to the future? Was he going to be upset with me for having thought that he was gone? Did he have a new girlfriend? Had he lied to me about being dead just so that he could see what my reaction would be—and had I completely let him down with my reaction?

Then he turned and I saw that it obviously wasn't Raphaël.

It was just some boy with a mop of black hair and a severe expression.

This kept happening.

I thought I saw Raphaël standing in line at the movie theatre with a girl. I saw Raphaël riding down the street on a bicycle, hands free. I saw him flipping through a box of records. I saw him go into a pet store. I was certain it was him. He was off to get himself a new dog, of course. I pushed the umbrella stroller into the store. All the stupid, clangy bells were banging against the door. The sound broke the spell. When he turned, I saw that he had a thin face and looked nothing like Raphaël.

Raphaël had died, but I hadn't really gone into mourning, had I? Instead I had made a very concerted effort to get on with my life. I had to. As a mother I had to coax the baby down from the ledge of despair every half-hour. When the baby started crying at the laundromat, I looped my thumbs around each other, making my hands into butterflies and flying them wildly around my head until he laughed. And then I realized that through all these gestures, I had distracted not only the baby from anxiety and sorrow but also myself.

On the way back from the laundromat, the baby and I stopped at a park and sat on a bench, waiting for a swan to pass by. There were all these strange things in the universe that you couldn't figure out what on earth they were there for. And then you realized that they were just there to charm little children. They were there for wee babies to marvel at. They were there to make sure that babies weren't so very sad—so that they could stop crying once in a while. To distract them from the fact that they had to sit in their soiled diapers without a penny to their names. I pointed for Papillon to look at the swan, and he stared and stared. A man walking by stopped to say that I was an awfully pretty mama.

I was surprised that men still hit on me with a tiny baby. I was already feeling like dating again. It made me feel guilty. I still had this instinct that I should try and stay faithful somehow to Raphaël. And who cheats on a dead person? I worried that Papillon would be another Tremblay raised by a single parent and haunted by their missing parent. Tremblay children seemed to be doomed to this fate.

I noticed the plastic on the steps was loosening as I pulled the carriage up the stairs. There is nothing like a baby to make you get on with life. No matter what on earth is happening, the baby will just wail at the top of its lungs and get things moving. Without the screaming of babies, we would all stop dead in our tracks; we would all lie in our beds daydreaming for the rest of eternity.

The referendum was no longer on the news. We had to get back to the business of daily life. Most of our life was spent between the revolutions. Most of our lives happen on regular days that are not holidays or saint's days. Days when there's no call for you to put on a mask, stand on a stool and blow kisses to the sound of an accordion. When I got to the second flight of stairs, I saw that Adam was waiting for me.

After all the polemics and all the debates about the two official languages of Canada, here was an English boy sitting in a stairwell, looking to be loved by a French girl.

Adam came down to help grab an end of the baby's carriage. He tilted it up too high and books fell out of the basket beneath the carriage and scattered on the floor around us.

He had a leather satchel slung over his shoulder. He had gone back to law school. His hair was cut short. He wasn't dressed ironically but was wearing a striped sweater and jeans. When we were cast out of heaven, God wished us luck and gave us a watch as a parting gift. We had started thinking of ourselves not in terms of things that we had done, but in terms of what we were going to do.

After we got the baby up the stairs, Adam and I went to pick up the mess, laughing. We were talking about school and life and plans.

When you are born and put into your crib, the whole world sticks their heads over the tops of the bars. They give you a name and they have all sorts of different ideas about you. These are all just strange fairy tales. When they tell you what you could be as an adult, they might as well be telling you stories about knaves and cats that wear boots.

But your task is to become something much more unique and surprising than anyone your parents could ever imagine you to be. You have to know that the life you have is completely yours.

A Note About the Author

Heather O'Neill is a contributor to *This American Life*, and her work has appeared in *The New York Times Magazine*, among other publications. Her novel *Lullabies for Little Criminals*, an international bestseller, won the Paragraphe Hugh MacLennan Prize for Fiction and the Canada Reads competition in 2007, and was shortlisted for seven prizes, including the Orange Prize for Fiction and the Governor General's Literary Award, and long-listed for the international IMPAC Dublin Literary Award. She lives in Montréal, Canada.

Printed in the USA
CPSIA information can be obtained
at www.ICGtesting.com
LVHW040903150724
785511LV00003B/268